Suck It Up and Die

Also by Brian Meehl

Out of Patience

Suck It Up

You Don't Know About Me

Suck It Up and Die

Brian Meehl

Delacorte Press

Text copyright © 2012 by Brian Meehl
Jacket art copyright © 2012 by Brian Sheridan

All rights reserved. Published in the United States by Delacorte Press,
an imprint of Random House Children's Books,
a division of Random House, Inc., New York.

Delacorte Press is a registered trademark and the colophon
is a trademark of Random House, Inc.

Visit us on the Web! randomhouse.com/kids

Educators and librarians, for a variety of teaching tools,
visit us at randomhouse.com/teachers

Library of Congress Cataloging-in-Publication Data
Meehl, Brian.
Suck it up and die / Brian Meehl. — 1st ed.
p. cm.
Sequel to: Suck it up.
Summary: On the first anniversary of the historic day in which the vampires of America began going mainstream, the tension between vampire hero Morning's wish for a simple life out of the spotlight and his mortal girlfriend Portia's obsession with documenting history escalates to the breaking point when a sinister vampire rises from the grave with a powerful thirst for revenge.
ISBN 978-0-385-73911-5 (hc) — ISBN 978-0-385-90772-9 (glb) —
ISBN 978-0-375-89716-0 (ebk)
[1. Vampires—Fiction.] I. Title.
PZ7.M512817Sv 2012
[Fic]—dc23
2011024132

The text of this book is set in 11-point Sabon.
Book design by Trish Parcell

Printed in the United States of America
10 9 8 7 6 5 4 3 2 1
First Edition

Random House Children's Books
supports the First Amendment and celebrates the right to read.

For Gerri and Richard

1

Late Date

Morning McCobb sat at an outside table with a latte to go and a ham and cheese croissant emitting curlicues of steam. Neither was for him. He was drinking his beverage du jour, every jour, 365 jours a year: Blood Lite. The coffee and mortal mouthful were for the love of his immortal life, Portia Dredful. While every sinew of his being tingled with the knowledge that Portia was his *eternal beloved*, he had never uttered the charged words. For good reasons.

One, their "eternal" only had a year on the meter. When it came to the big ride in Cupid's Pedicab of Everlasting Love, that wasn't even around the block.

Two, as a member of the International Vampire League, he was forbidden to turn a mortal into a vampire, even if it meant watching helplessly as the girl of his dreams rode the roller coaster of life through the loop-de-loops of youth, the twists and turns of middle age, into the plunge of cronedom, and finally bump to a rest in her grave.

This inescapable truth brought Morning to the third reason he had never whispered "Be my eternal beloved" in Portia's ear. It was part of the deal they had made a year earlier on the Williamsburg Bridge. Loving each other forever and a day was a done deal, but skipping through life together as boyfriend-girlfriend was a three-legged race. If Morning was fixed at sixteen and Portia wasn't, sooner or later their perfect stride would tumble into a bad game of Twister.

He didn't know when their romantic run would pretzel into a pileup, but sitting in Caffe Reggio, he was beginning to wonder if this glorious fall morning, October 4, would finally bring the dawn of heartbreak. He had a reason for his gnawing dread. Portia was late: seven minutes late. She was never late. "If you're on time, you're late," she always said. For Portia, early was on time.

He took another sip of Blood Lite. The metallic tang of the soy-blood substitute was cold comfort. His mind flooded with a vision of Portia waking that morning and declaring, "What am I doing? I just rocketed past my eighteenth birthday, I've got the mission of my life ahead of me, and I'm dating a sixteen-year-old!"

Morning's head spasmed, shaking away the ghastly thought. He checked his cell phone. She was *eight* minutes late!

He fixed his gaze on the corner of MacDougal and West Third and tried to will Portia around the pizza place. A fat lady appeared, walking two shih tzus that looked like self-propelled bedroom slippers. Morning wished he were one of the vintage vampires who gained extra powers after treading the earth for a century-plus. If he were a Centurion, he could visualize Portia at home, put her in

2

a virtual thrall, and make her zombie-dash to the café. Unfortunately, Morning had been a vampire for less than two years and couldn't thrall a shih tzu to sit.

He couldn't thrall, but he could call. He grabbed his phone and hit the number-one speed dial.

Portia answered. "Hey, Morn."

"Where are you?" he asked, trying to squash the worry in his voice.

"Walking to the subway. Where are you?"

"At our place. Where else—"

"Ohmigod! Are we meeting today?"

He threw up a hand even though his video app wasn't on. "It's Thursday; we always meet today. Why would this Thursday be any different?"

"I thought we were skipping breakfast 'cause we're seeing each other this afternoon at the parade."

He frowned at the reminder of the first Vampire Pride Parade. It was going to celebrate precisely one year since American vampires had flung off their cloaks of secrecy and outed themselves as members of the International Vampire League. Unfortunately, since Morning had been the first nonthreatening vampire to be test-marketed on the mortal world of Lifers, he was expected to be in the parade. Worse, Luther Birnam, president of the IVL and mastermind of the campaign to rebrand vampires as the last minority with special needs, insisted that Morning march at the *front* of the parade. Morning wanted his fading fame as the IVL's first poster boy to be rolled up and tossed. After all, there were Leaguer vampires now more famous than him.

He dropped an elbow on the table too hard and almost toppled Portia's unclaimed coffee. "C'mon, Portia, seeing you at the parade isn't seeing you for breakfast." Hearing needy creep into his voice, he reversed field. "I mean, the only parade I wanna see are the flickers and quirks that march across your face when we talk."

"Ahhh," Portia cooed, "you're so sweet I wanna bite you."

Morning smiled. "But then I'd have to bite you back."

She laughed. "We already tried that and you guzzled all of me but the fumes. No more vein-busting for you, buster; this neck is hickeys only."

"I'm good with that," he said playfully. "Let's see if my phone has a hickey app." He gave his phone a perfunctory look. "Oops. The hickey app hasn't been invented yet. So, do you want your morning nibble over breakfast or at the front of the parade?"

She laughed at his bad joke and gave in. "All right, I'll be there. But it'll have to be quick."

After hanging up, Morning shooed a fly away from Portia's cooling croissant. He opened a paper napkin and covered it. Big mistake.

The sight of the napkin over the croissant resurrected the memory of the night he had almost pulled a sheet over Portia. That terrifying night had been twelve months earlier, but sometimes it felt like the night before. When the horror replayed in his head, he clung to Luther Birnam's advice like a life ring. The night he had plunged his fangs into Portia he had dived into the "forbidden well of bloodlust," and it was not a memory to be repressed, it was to be *embraced*. The horrific memory was the guardrail around the forbidden well, and he was to hold on to it so he wouldn't fall in again. It was the warning Birnam drilled into all Leaguer vampires: "You can take the vampire out of the darkness, but you can't take the darkness out of the vampire."

2

Leech Treats

Morning grabbed a breath and exhaled. The past couldn't be undone, but knowing Portia was coming banished his haunting thoughts. In a few minutes, she would appear around the corner like a second sunrise.

He checked out the street scene. People were in the full-tilt hustle of getting to work. Some carried coffees procured from the West Village's ubiquitous baristas. Others waited in line at the Nosh Cart for their a.m. brew and chew. On the opposite corner was a food cart that wouldn't have been there a year before. It was called Leech Treats and served leeches engorged on animal blood. While grocery stores now stocked animal and synthetic blood drinks for Leaguer vampires, Leech Treats was one of the trendier ways for a vampire to get his daily dose of red stuff.

Since Leaguer vampires had removed humans from the drink pyramid, the term "bloodsucking fiend" was no longer politically correct, and the past year had seen an evolution of what to call Leaguers' dietary habits. "Veinitarian" had had a brief reign but was shot down by vegan vampires, like Morning, who didn't drink humanely milked animal blood. Other than Blood Lite, vegan vamps quaffed vegetable-protein blends like Gourd Gorge, V-Sate, and Suckilicious. After "veinitarian" didn't stick, the term that did came from the prefix for blood: "sang." A "sanguivore" is a creature who survives by consuming only blood.

Whenever Morning observed one of the street carts that catered to sanguivores, he liked to play a guessing game. Was the customer buying a carton of Leech Treats *really* a Leaguer vampire? Or were they one of the vampire wannabes doing everything in their power to pass as a vamp?

A gothy-looking girl with magenta hair stepped up to the cart. Morning noticed she had already conquered the first error goths make when trying to pass as vampires: they can't give up their multiple piercings and jewelry array. Anyone who knows vampire basics knows they don't pierce. What would be the point? The piercing would heal itself in a minute. Even if they made sure the piercing healed *around* a piece of jewelry, the vampire's superconcentrated biochemistry would soon dissolve the metallic invader like a nail in acid.

Morning watched the young woman swap some bills for a small carton of Leech Treats. She passed test number two: she didn't squirm or freak from the hand massage you get from a carton of fat, happy leeches. Her expression remained fixed with the right mix of boredom and gloom, she had learned from watching *The Vampire Diaries,* and by perfecting the look of gaunt vampires obese with melancholy.

As goth girl ambled away Morning concluded she was really a vampire and not a wannabe trying to fool her fellow mortals or hook up with a Leaguer at the leech cart. Then he saw something fall off the front of her leather jacket. Even with his enhanced vision, the thing was too small to identify. He didn't have to guess. A pigeon flapped over and sucked up what had fallen: a bread crumb. The girl had already had breakfast, a *solid* breakfast; she was a wannabe after all.

Morning didn't get Lifers like her, or any goth who wanted to sacrifice their mortality to become a vampire. Sure, mortality was life-shortening, but the alternative was being frozen at the same age forever. Besides vampire wannabes, Morning had heard about "wanna-bleeds": Lifers who hooked up with backsliding Leaguers who popped fangs once in a blue moon and tapped the human keg for a pint. But the Lifers and Leaguers who supposedly practiced this "consensual bloodlust" had to do it in secret because it broke the Leaguers' second commandment: "You shall not drink anything but properly milked animal blood or artificial blood substitutes."

Whether the tales of consensual bloodlust were fact or urban legend didn't matter to some Lifer extremists. They were convinced that Luther Birnam and his Leaguer army were the Trojan horse at America's gate. They trusted Leaguers like they trusted a pack of rabid coyotes. They claimed it was only a matter of time before Leaguers turned all the wannabes into vampires, spawned legions of bloodsucking fiends, and laid siege to the mortal population until red-blooded Americans had been corralled into feedlots for fattening and bleeding by "the vampire empire."

It was these anti-vampire extremists who motivated

Morning to wear a baseball cap and sunglasses or fake glasses in public. He didn't want to be recognized and martyred by some hate-mongering zealot armed with a stake, screaming, "Die, mothersucker!"

Morning took another drink of Blood Lite and glanced up the street. The second sunrise came around the corner.

Portia.

IVLEAGUE

VAMPIRE PRIDE DAY

We greet the first anniversary of American Out Day with great joy. A year ago, on October 4, the world witnessed the first mass outing of vampires. On this historic day, it is only fitting that we recount our triumphs and setbacks in our ongoing march from darkness to the full light of freedom.

TRIUMPH #1: The first outing of a Leaguer vampire, Morning McCobb, led to the announcement of Worldwide Out Day.

SETBACK #1: As we know, this announcement triggered some international riots, mostly in countries possessing dark and long histories with vampires. The riots in Transylvania were the worst. Fortunately, the finer points of vampire slaying have fallen through the cracks of human history, and those who went on staking rampages gave up after their targets kept bouncing back to life. In the aftermath of these riots, I went to the UN and negotiated an interim step: American Out Day. Given America's tradition of welcoming all races, creeds, and colors, it followed that the United States should be the first to embrace a people of different mortality and dietary habits. If vampires can make it here, we can make it anywhere.

SETBACK #2: As much as America is "the land of the free," there are forces that consider some citizens less free than others. These forces went to the U.S. Congress and established the Bureau of Vampire Affairs (BVA). Despite having enjoyed the full rights of citizenship before we outed ourselves, on American Out Day laws were passed limiting our rights as citizens.

- We had to register with the BVA so our identity and whereabouts would be known.
- Our right to vote was suspended. Some fear we will steal drivers licenses, shape-shift into whoever's picture is on the license, and vote multiple times.
- We are forbidden to own businesses. Some believe we will use our shape-shifting skills to gain an unfair advantage over our mortal competitors.
- We are forbidden to join sports teams, break world records, or take part in any competitive gaming in which our hyperacute senses might create an uneven playing field.

Our full freedom has been put on hold until, as the BVA decreed, "Leaguer vampires prove they will not abuse their inalienable rights by doing unholy things." However, even though the door to the American dream has been partially closed to us, Leaguers have much to celebrate!

TRIUMPH #2: For 365 days and nights we have lived openly and peacefully among our mortal brothers and sisters, whom we call Lifers. We have rubbed shoulders without popping fangs. We have vanquished the barbarism of bloodlust!

For this victory, we look forward to our reward. Next week, Congress will vote on the Vampire Rights Act, the passage of which will give us the ultimate prize of freedom and equality.

So, to celebrate this day and our freedom on the horizon, I ask all Leaguer vampires and their Lifer brothers and sisters joining Vampire Pride parades across the country to walk in peace, in pride, and in the hope that we all march toward the ultimate goal: Worldwide Out Day.

Luther Birnam
President of the International Vampire League

3
Neuterhood

Taking in Portia as she came down the sidewalk, Morning pulled off his sunglasses so as not to miss a detail. The long ringlets of her dark hair bounced and glistened in the sunlight. In the past year she had lost most of her gangly-ostrich look. When Morning first met her, he fell in love with the way her long limbs jounced in different directions. But the filling out she had done since then had gathered her limbs, trimmed her flapping sails. Her arms and legs moved in sync now, obeying a torso that was captain of her ship. Morning had no complaints. What she had lost in jouncitude she had gained in curvatude. He only wished he could say something similar about himself, that what he had lost in stickitude he had gained in hunkatude. No such luck. He still looked like Gumby's long-lost twin.

Portia strode into the shade of the awning, dropped her backpack, and swept into the chair opposite him. "Hey."

"Hey," Morning echoed with a grin.

She rubbed her hands over the napkin-covered croissant. "Gee, is it something yummy like a piggy-cheese croissant or a dead rat?" She whipped off the napkin and groaned. "Oh man, a piggy-cheese croissant again?"

"That's your favorite," he protested.

She leaned forward with a crazed look. "Never underestimate a girl's right to change her mind. But, no matter"—she plucked his sunglasses off the table, slipped them on, and lifted the croissant—"I'll just pretend it's dead rat." She chomped off a corner. "Hmm, nice rodent."

Morning shook his head with a chuckle.

"Seriously, Morn," she said, not sounding the least bit serious, "would you still like me if I was a ratavore, or would you dump me?"

Even knowing she was kidding, the word jolted him, especially since she had just mentioned a girl's right to change her mind. "I would never do that. I could never du-du—" His tongue tangled on the word.

She waved the tattered croissant. "Right, forget the d-word. It's a horrible thought." She took a swig of latte. "Notice I didn't say it was 'a dreadful thought.'"

"Yeah, thanks." Morning pulled a pair of fake eyeglasses from his pocket and put them on.

Portia chuffed a laugh. "Thank goodness you're all incognito now. I can get my good-luck rub." She pulled off his cap and rubbed his shaved head.

He submitted with an eye roll. "Feel better?"

She plunked his hat back on. "Much."

Losing his hay-field-hit-by-a-tornado head of hair was the biggest thing that made Morning harder to recognize. It hadn't been voluntary. He had gotten a military-style cut every two weeks since beginning his training at the New

York City Fire Academy. Morning checked his cell phone to make sure he still had time to subway uptown and catch a bus to Randall's Island, where the academy was located.

Portia took the sunglasses off and eyed him. "Do you ever miss your hair?"

"No, it was always a disaster. Do you?"

She answered with another question. "Do you ever regret going to the fire academy a year early and not finishing high school?"

"Hey, I *finished*," he declared. "I got a GED, and now I'm chasing my dream: becoming a firefighter."

"Sometimes I think you blew off senior year for another reason, besides not being in the same high school as me, of course. It was the only way you could be"—she air-quoted with single fingers—"*older* than me. To skip a year."

He grinned. "I hadn't thought of it that way, but I like it. I'll always be your upperclassman."

She tilted her head. "Really, Morn. Do you ever regret missing your senior year?"

"No. I got tired of being looked at like a freak."

"It's not like you're *not* a freak at the fire academy, unless there're other vampires in your class."

"No, I'm the only one, but it's totally different."

"How?"

He finished his Blood Lite. "In high school you're always walking a tightrope over a pit of humiliation. It only takes one slip, one fall, and you're smeared with shame till the day you graduate alongside the other geeks and nerds and losers."

"So there's no humiliation at the academy?"

"No, there's plenty, but it's not the same. For one, the

tightrope stretches over a pit of fire. For two, you're not alone; you're a team, a crew. You're all on the rope together, and if you slip, there's someone beside you who gives a crap. Your crew will reach out and grab you 'cause if they don't you'll be dead, and they'll be the ones smeared with shame for losing you. Instead of the everyone-for-yourself insanity of high school, at the academy you've got a crew that cares. It's a brotherhood."

Portia arched an eyebrow. "I thought there were a few women in your class."

"There are, they're part of the brotherhood too."

"Even though they're sisters."

"You know what I mean."

She waggled her head. "Yeah, yeah, I know. But maybe we should invent a new word for 'brotherhood,' you know, a word that includes guys *and* girls."

"Like what, 'unisexhood'?" Morning suggested.

"No ring to it." She scratched her temple. "What if we cut the gender out of it. What about 'neuterhood'? I mean, think about it, it would be so much more accurate for all those monks and nuns who've taken vows of chastity. Instead of saying 'Sister Mary' and 'Brother Patrick,' it would be much more honest and accurate to say 'Neuter Mary' and 'Neuter Patrick.'" She stoked her monologue with another sip of coffee. "Even better, if priests dropped the whole 'Father' thing and went with 'Neuter,' imagine how it could clean up the church. All those pedophile priests might cool their wicks if they heard boys say things like, 'I'd like to confess now, Neuter O'Conner,' and, 'Okay, I'll give you a neck rub, Neuter Flannigan, but then I have to go home.' One little word change might fix the whole problem."

Morning let out a half laugh.

Portia kept riding her caffeine buzz. "Jeez, Morn, I thought that was pretty good material. Especially for this early." Her eyes suddenly bugged as she slapped a hand over her mouth. "Ohmigod. I'm *so* sorry! I totally forgot about your—" It was her turn to tongue-tangle.

"Yeah, my neuterhood," he said, completing her thought. "My little sterile-as-a-vampire thing." As much as he understood the science of why vampires were sterile—immortals have no need to produce the next generation, so their biology accommodates the lack of necessity with infertility—it was still a major source of embarrassment.

She grabbed his hand and gushed. "I've always said it's never gonna be a problem. I mean, I don't have time to be a baby maker. I've got gobs of films to make. It's who I am; it's what I'm always gonna be: a filmmaker. And that's why we're so perfect together. That's why you're my EB."

Morning blinked. "EB?"

She eye-rolled. "You know what EB stands for, and if I have to spell it out, it might jinx us. You know"—she took his hand—"the love that can't be spoken."

He knew exactly what she meant. His heart thudded with the excitement of another boundary being crossed. *She had said it: EB!* "Right"—he nodded as he heard his voice go scratchy and high—"the love that can't be spoken."

She leaned closer and whispered, "Well, you know, as much *E* as this mortal coil has to offer."

"Please"—he intertwined his hand with hers and put a finger to her lips—"don't say another word."

She looked around, thinking some street crazy was about to pounce. No one was there. Her eyes returned to him as she silently mouthed, *Why?*

After a year of being in love, Morning thought he had memorized every plane and curve of her face. When he looked at people on the bus, he would see the flat space under a woman's jaw, and think, *That's just like the eave under Portia's chin before it corners into her neck.* Or he'd see a portrait in a museum and think, *That lock of hair is exactly like one of Portia's, the way it curls back on itself like a sleeping dog with the tip of its tail over its nose.* But now, over breakfast, he had discovered a new quirk in her face.

He leaned in and gave her a kiss. With every press and parting of lips, with every teasing probe of their tongues, Morning reveled in the feast of firsts that breakfast had served up: how the dimple in her cheek formed a perfect comma, and the letters that had never been uttered.

EB. Eternal beloved.

4

Fire Academy

Morning made it to the academy with time to spare and went to the locker room. He changed into the simple blue uniform that probationary firefighters wear during training. While making sure every button was buttoned and his shirt tucked tight, one of his fellow "probies" came around the corner and opened a locker. Armando was a big Latino who could toss Morning across the room if he wanted. Luckily, Armando was more into tossing trash talk.

"Yo, McCobb," Armando boomed as he pulled a bottle of Rogaine from his locker.

"Hey, Armando, what's up?"

Armando squirted Rogaine foam in his hand. He was convinced it helped his thick, dark hair grow back even though he knew it would be shaved off again. "Did you hear about our first live fire exercise in a couple days?"

Morning had memorized the fire academy's eighteen-week training schedule, but it wasn't something he bragged about. "Yeah, I heard."

"Are you freakin'?" Armando asked, working Rogaine into his scalp.

"Why should I be freakin'?"

"I thought fire ranked ten on the vampire pucker-factor scale."

Morning fought the urge to tell Armando about the time a vampire slayer had reduced him to a pile of ash in the desert outside Las Vegas, and how he had been reconstituted to human form with a few drops of Portia's blood. But he knew Armando would twist it and ask bozo questions, like *When you're running on chick blood do you go all girlie? Do you get PMS?* Morning went with the safe route. "If anyone should be freakin' it's you Lifers. If I get smoke inhalation or get crispified, I'll be the one who heals right up. You're the one who's gonna suffer permanent damage."

Armando laughed as he tossed the Rogaine in his locker. "I'll remember that when I'm screamin' for someone to run through a wall of fire to save my ass."

The morning classes held no surprises until the last one before lunch. It was a one-week course on the history of the FDNY. Morning could have slept through it since he'd already read three history books on firefighting in New York City.

The surprise came when a guest speaker walked through the door to give the probies a special presentation. Captain Prowler was the grizzled firefighter Morning had met a year earlier when he had ducked into Prowler's firehouse. The white-mustachioed fireman had told him about the code firefighters live by, and how the best ones aspire to be "knights of the fire table." More important,

Prowler had helped Morning get into the fire academy. Being stuck at sixteen, Morning was technically too young for admittance, but Prowler got him over the age hurdle by convincing the brass that Morning came to the FDNY with "special skills."

Prowler was carrying a metal bucket. He acknowledged Morning with a wink and put the bucket on the desk at the front of the room. "I'm Captain Prowler," he began with his husky, smoke-eaten voice. "I'm here to talk about a part of fire not many people think about. The spirit of fire."

The probies chuckled at the notion.

"Go ahead, have a laugh," he said. "But if you think fire is nothing but a chemical reaction, I can assure you"—his bushy mustache stretched as he grinned—"you're gonna get burned. The fact is, you don't kill fire till you kill its spirit."

A probie shot up his hand. Joey Sullivan, or "Sully," got away with being a smart-ass because his uncle was second-in-command at the academy. "Sir, if I'd known a firefighter had to get all spiritual, I would've become a cop."

The probies stifled laughs.

Prowler took Sully in. "Son, I knew your dad before he died in nine-eleven. You may have a chip on your shoulder and think this is some woo-woo New Agey crap, but you might wanna take a listen."

Morning was all ears. In the past year, he had hung out a lot with Prowler, listening to his stories, even riding in his fire truck to a few calls, but the spirit of fire was nothing the cagey old firefighter had ever talked about.

Prowler reached into the bucket and pulled out a

candle. "Combustion comes in two varieties: work fire and wild fire." He flipped open a cigarette lighter and lit the candle. The wick ignited to a steady flame. "Work fire is made of two plumes." He passed a finger through the flame. "A plume of burning gases." Then he passed his finger above the flame. "And a plume of radiant heat."

He reached into the bucket again and pulled out a pine bough. "Wild fire is a different animal." He used the candle to light the bough, which ignited with crackling fire. "It's made of *three* plumes: flame, heat, and"—his gray eyes followed the sparks shooting up the swirling column of smoke—"spirit. This is where the wild fire lives: the one that wants to spread and grow and destroy everything in its path. It is a red dragon bent on devouring the world. And when the red dragon wakes, with its crimson terror, it's our job, the knights of the fire table, to slay it."

A second before the licking fire reached Prowler's fingertips, he dropped the burning bough in the bucket. He gazed at the two dozen probies. Then he shrugged and smiled at Sully. "Maybe it's all just a bunch of woo-woo New Agey crap, and maybe there's no such thing as the spirit of fire. But during your first live fire exercise, look into the flames, and maybe you'll see the red dragon."

5

Captain Clancy

After class, Morning gave up trying to get past the probies asking Prowler questions. Figuring he could talk to him at the firehouse later, Morning headed out the door. He turned the wrong way. Captain Clancy was coming toward him. Clancy was the academy's second-in-command, the equivalent of an assistant principal. He looked like a walking steroid storage facility and took particular pleasure in making Morning's life miserable.

Morning spun on his heels, hoping to avoid detection and one of Clancy's pop inspections: one stitch out of place on a probie's uniform could result in a UV, a uniform violation, and the demerit that went with it.

"Hey, McCobb," Clancy barked. "I saw that move! You trainin' to be a ballerina or one of the bravest?"

Morning did a full one-eighty as Clancy closed in on him. "One of the bravest, sir."

"The bravest what?"

"The bravest fire knight, sir."

Clancy's face set in a scowl. "Prowler's been giving your crew that bucket of bullshit about the knights of the fire table, hasn't he?"

"Yes, sir. He told us about the spirit of fire."

"I don't care if he told you about the spirit of upchuck, why you still draggin' your hose in my hallway?"

The question baffled Morning. "Ah, I'm going to my next class, sir."

"You do that, and I'll drop a POOP on your head."

Morning figured it was another one of Clancy's acronyms, but this one he'd never heard before. "A POOP, sir?"

"Probie Out Of Place." Clancy rapped on Morning's forehead. "Hello, McCobb. You've got ED, and I'm not talkin' erectile dysfunction, I'm talkin' early dismissal!"

"Right!" Morning had forgotten about his early dismissal to be in the Vampire Pride Parade. "Totally forgot, sir."

Clancy crossed his arms and shook his head. "Mental screwups, McCobb, they can get you or another firefighter killed." He fixed Morning with hard eyes. "But being immortal, you don't worry about ending up a ten-forty-five, do you? Which makes you a probie with no respect for the dangers of the job." He stuck a finger in Morning's face. "You got ten minutes to get off the Rock, and if I catch you doing some vampire voodoo like shape-shifting into a bird, I'll wash you outta here faster than you can say 'backdraft.'"

Captain Clancy had never approved of Morning's admittance to the academy. It wasn't that he hated vampires, he was just sick and tired of the bar being lowered to make the FDNY an equal opportunity employer. First

23

the Physical Ability Test had been compromised to ease the way for women firefighters, and now the age bar had been lowered to admit some punk vampire. What was next? Letting arsonists be firefighters so the FDNY could keep a closer eye on them?

Before Morning could remind Clancy that he had signed an agreement to never use *any* of his vampire skills while training at the academy, a voice interrupted. "Hello, Clancy." Prowler came out of the classroom carrying the metal bucket. "If you'd like to join the twenty-first century, vampires don't 'shape-shift' anymore, they 'cell differentiate.' That's 'CD' for you acronym freaks."

Clancy chuckled with disdain. "In my book, the only thing CD stands for is controlled descent, which sums up your career move to Department Wizard."

Prowler turned to Morning and put on an Irish accent. "Methinks the Irishman has a hankerin' for me wand." As Clancy flushed with anger, Prowler pulled Morning down the hall. "C'mon, you got a parade to catch."

Morning waited until Clancy was out of earshot. "Why is he so set on washing me out?"

"Don't mind him," Prowler said. "Just keep your nose clean, your head down, and doin' what a probie's gotta do."

"It's not easy when I miss training for stupid things like parades. I mean, I don't see why Birnam still needs me as his poster boy. It's been a year, and not one Leaguer who's gone mainstream has gone human bloodstream."

"Not officially, anyway."

Morning shot Prowler a worried look. He thought only goths and vampire racists believed the stories about back-sliding Leaguers and willing Lifers partaking in consensual bloodlust. But then, Prowler had a way of knowing stuff most people didn't.

"The point is," Prowler continued, "there's all sorts of fires to put out in the world, and your being in the parade will throw water on the friction between Lifers and Leaguers. If that friction ever sparks and burns down the house of peace Luther Birnam has built, Clancy won't need to scrub you on demerits. He'll put a hook through your chest and turn you into a live fire exercise." He stopped at the door of the chief's office. "Morning, you may be a fire knight in training, but you're still a double-hatter."

"What's that?"

"Like it or not, you're still a *Leaguer* knight, which comes with responsibilities."

Morning didn't want to hear any more about the fame that still hung around his neck like a rotting albatross. "Are you driving back downtown?"

"No, got another crew on the other side of the academy waiting for me to introduce 'em to the spirit of fire."

As Morning went into the locker room to grab his backpack he knew Prowler was right. The battle over the Vampire Rights Act was heating up in the run-up to the vote. And if Morning was ever going to get the chance to marry Portia, the VRA had to pass.

It was another right Leaguers had been stripped of: Congress had passed a law defining marriage as the union between a mortal and a mortal. Intermarriage between a Lifer and a Leaguer was a crime punishable by ten years for the Lifer and a hundred for the Leaguer. That way, it guaranteed the star-crossed lovers would never meet again.

6

Zoë Zotz

A bus took Morning over the East River to Manhattan. Getting off at 125th Street, he was surprised by a sign in the Duane Reade on the corner. It advertised cards for American Out Day. He didn't think the day had been around long enough to merit a card. It also messed with his plans. He had hoped to give Portia a funny get-well card urging her to recover from mortality so they could live happily ever after. Now he wondered if her feelings would be hurt if he didn't buy her an official Out Day card on the first anniversary. Normally, he would have trusted his instincts and gone with the get-well card, but Portia's EB bomb echoed in his head. *Eternal beloved.* It was a game changer. And it's not like he had dittoed the letters back. The EB ball was in his court, so she probably expected something more than a goofy card.

Luckily, the choice of Out Day cards was limited. He found one that was sort of funny and would set up what he wanted to say when he gave her the present he'd been saving for more than a year. The front of the card said, *So much has changed between mortals and vampires.* When you opened it, there was a picture of a Lifer and a Leaguer drinking at a table loaded with empty bottles and glasses. The Lifer was drunk and passed out in her chair. The Leaguer was cheerfully consuming a blood drink. The caption read, *But we'll always be able to outdrink you. Happy Out Day!*

After buying the card, Morning headed to the subway that would take him to Delancey Street and the start of the Vampire Pride Parade. A loudspeaker announced that the trains weren't running because of a small fire on the tracks. He went back up to the street and considered his options. Taking the bus all the way downtown would make him late for the parade. He didn't have enough money for a cab. And he couldn't CD into some kind of Flyer because he was a stickler about the rule he had learned at Leaguer Academy: Only CD in the face of a life-threatening emergency. Making the parade in time was hardly life-threatening. His only choice was to take the bus, be late, and join the parade after it started.

As he waited for the bus another option arrived in the form of an urban chariot driven by a two-legged dynamo. Morning recognized Zoë Zotz by her red helmet bobbing up and down as she rode toward him on her pedicab.

For a seventeen-year-old, Zoë was undersized, underdeveloped, but overwhelming. At LaGuardia High School of Music and Art and Performing Arts, where she and Portia were seniors, Zoë had two nicknames: "ZZ" and "MM." MM was a strip down of "mouth 'n' motion machine."

Her pedicab was the same bloodred as her helmet and it sported black gothic letters announcing FANPIRE TOURS. Fanpire Tours was an after-school and weekend business

Zoë had started. For sixty dollars, she wheeled couples around Manhattan to see the real and fictional sites related to vampires: from the stoop on the Lower East Side where Morning McCobb first came out as a vampire by turning into mist to the Broadway theater where Bela Lugosi took his first bite as Count Dracula in 1927. While pedaling between sights she entertained customers with a vampire version of *The Little Mermaid* song "Part of Your World": "I wanna be where the vampires are / I wanna see, wanna see 'em feedin'."

Zoë skidded her pedicab to a stop in front of Morning. She was dressed in her standard-issue tight black jeans and a black tee under a black leather vest she called her "goth padded bra." She sported purple fingernails and her middle fingernails had little skulls on them. Anyone who gave her grief got "flipped the skull." Ever since she'd picked Morning's brain for everything he knew about real vampires, she had jettisoned her pierced jewelry and only wore rings and bracelets. In her words, she was "vintage goth." She also defied cookie-cutter goth with her long blond hair and by not possessing a hint of the mopey ennui goths cultivated. How could she? She careened her pedicab around Manhattan like a Tasmanian taxi driver.

Zoë balanced on her pedals and flashed her sizable grille of teeth. "Hi, A.M.!" "A.M." was the nickname she'd given him to avoid the weirdness of saying "Morning, Morning."

He greeted her with a befuddled look. "What are you doing here?" Not only was Zoë supposed to be in school, but LaGuardia Arts was all the way across Manhattan on the Upper West Side.

"It's my lunch period, I heard the subway was down,

and Portia told me you gotta get to the parade on time," she said. "Besides, I'm more fun than a cab."

"So you're rescuing me."

She nodded, bouncing the blond hair that poured from her helmet. "Yeah, it's payback ahead of time 'cause one of these days you're gonna rescue me from mortality."

That was another thing about Zoë. Her greatest ambition was to become a vampire; she was constantly trying to get Morning to turn her. It's not that she had a crush on him, she just liked the idea of being the blood child of the nicest vampire in the world, and the blood *grandchild* of the evilest vampire in the world, Ikor DeThanatos. DeThanatos was the vampire who had accidently turned Morning two years before. But even if Zoë's dream came true, she would never be able to meet Ikor DeThanatos; Morning and Portia had destroyed him a year before in an epic battle in the Mother Forest. Because he had been slain, and because Morning and Portia didn't want the world to know all the bloody details of that fateful night, only Zoë and a select few knew Morning's fang father by name. The other reason Zoë was convinced she was destined to be a vampire was her name. After all, the diaeresis—the two dots over the *e*— was a sure sign she was destined to be bitten and turned.

Zoë raised her hands in a "no pressure" gesture. "But, hey, you don't have to sip and flip me today. I can wait. Right now, the price for a ride downtown is super simple."

Morning gave her a dubious look. "Which is?"

"You gotta hear my newest blood-obligate trivia." Zoë was a collector of everything there was to know about critters that survived on blood alone. *Blood obligate* was the scientific term for "sanguivore." Zoë was more than a vampire nut, she was a vampire wonk.

Morning climbed into the pedicab's rickshaw seat. "Okay, that's better than having to watch your latest blood-obligate impression and guessing what creature you are."

"Go ahead, make fun." Zoë stood on her pedals and got the pedicab moving. "But when I put my bloodsucker impressions on YouTube and they go viral, I'm gonna be as famous as you."

"Right," Morning scoffed, "then you'll have to always wear a hat and sunglasses and shave your head."

"Are you kidding? I'd do fame the way you're supposed to do fame. I'd flaunt it!"

As Zoë caught the green wave of lights going down Lexington Avenue, Morning steered the conversation. "Okay, I'm ready to pay my fare. What's your new blood trivia?"

She turned and shot him an excited look, like she was about to reveal the secret of time travel. "Remember when I was telling you how most bloodsuckers sink more than fangs? That they also inject their victims with a painkilling anesthetic so the victim doesn't feel the bite, and an anticoagulant that prevents the blood from clotting?"

Morning gave her a behind-the-back eye roll. "Who could forget?"

"Well, I just read about another chemical that bloodsuckers inject into their victims. A vasodilator."

"A vaso-what?"

"Dilator. It means 'to widen.' A vasodilator blows open a victim's veins so they go from sippy cup to super Slurpee. Is that cool, or what?"

"Yeah, you've just given me a new line next time you ask me to turn you."

"What?"

"I don't do vasodilation."

Zoë laughed. "Yeah, well, check this vasodilation out." She pedaled hard to make another green light.

As the pedicab gained speed Morning watched Zoë's boyish butt piston up and down. He realized that the day Zoë finally grew some hips and boobs, her Fanpire Tour business would have to change modes of transportation; she'd get too many customers more interested in Zoë's sights than vampire sights.

7

Rachel Capilarus

With Zoë pedaling hard, they covered twenty blocks before a red light made her hit the brakes. They stopped next to a sprawling studio complex. The studio's huge billboard bragged HOME OF AMERICA'S #1 SHOW: THE SHADOW, and displayed a picture of the show's beautiful host, Rachel Capilarus. Her model-thin arms were thrown wide, and her billion-dollar smile seemed to shout, "C'mon, world! Hug me like a shadow!"

Zoë checked out the billboard and turned back to Morning. "Every guy in the world must look at her and totally vasodilate, right?" As Morning chuckled, Zoë's face set in her least used expression: serious. "Do you ever think you picked the wrong girl?"

She was referring to Rachel Capilarus, the vampire who had graduated in the same class as Morning from Leaguer Academy, the school where vampires learned to overcome their dark desires and mothball their bloodlusting ways.

True, he'd once had a big crush on Rachel, but now the only thing he liked about her was that she was eclipsing his pin spot of fame with the floodlight of her hit TV show.

He answered Zoë, knowing whatever he said would get back to Portia. "No regrets; I picked the right girl." He wasn't lying. He looked up at the towering picture of Rachel and answered her come-to-me gesture with a frown. Yeah, she was still eye candy, but the wrapper had changed.

Back at the Academy, Rachel had been a stunning warrior princess with raven-black hair who even the most hunky prince was intimidated by. After American Out Day she had done an extreme makeover. She changed her wardrobe from tight dresses and curve-flaunting Under Armour to the floaty, multilayered style of bohemian chic: the Olsen twins in pastels. Her posture had gone from head high, shoulders back, to stooped. Morning figured she wanted to look shorter, more demure. She had softened her voice, and while she used to speak in complete sentences, she now flitted from thought to thought like a hummingbird allergic to nectar. Even though Morning didn't trust a girl who changed that much, he had a theory as to why she had.

Rachel had scanned the mortal landscape and seen the fear many Lifers still had of vampires, even though the vast majority had become harmless Leaguers. She observed the disarming effect Morning's wimpy vamp had on Lifers, and took a lesson. She was going to take nonthreatening to a new level. She would kill the last vestiges of vampirophobia with kooky kindness. So she cast off her warrior-princess armor and donned the flowy pastels of fairy queen. She waved a wand and, *poof,* Joan of Arc became Lady Gaga without the glitz. As a free spirit oozing loopy optimism and self-empowerment, she offered a new incarnation of the fangless vampire. By taking harmless to new heights, Rachel was the last vampire anyone could imagine doing something as icky as drinking blood. And if she actually popped fangs, not to worry; she would collapse in a fit of blushing giggles.

Rachel had not performed this makeover alone, or been able to launch *The Shadow* on her own, because of the restrictions facing Leaguers. Her Lifer partner in wild success was Penny Dredful, owner of Diamond Sky PR, which had performed its own transformation to Diamond Sky Productions. While Penny's company's name had changed, her daughter's name had not: *Portia* Dredful.

Morning wasn't the only Leaguer who had watched Rachel's meteoric rise to fame with misgivings. Luther Birnam was concerned for different reasons. When *The Shadow* started to become a runaway hit, he had posted a blog on the IVL website that was For Leaguers Only (FLO).

LURKING IN THE SHADOW

As your president, I am not a dictator. I do not tell Leaguers what they can or cannot do. My role has always been as a guide leading Leaguers out of the dark wood of our past, the *selva obscura*, and into the light of freedom. As your guide, it is my duty to tell you when you have wandered off that path and veered back toward the dark wood.

I have only seen *The Shadow* once. For those of you who have not seen it, here's how it works.

The season began with a group of Leaguer vampires brought together by the host, Rachel Capilarus. In each episode these contestants are given the same category, such as a job title, a workplace, or an industry. Each Leaguer is given three days and followed by a camera crew as he or she gets permission to shadow a worker in the selected category and learns about the worker's goals so the vampire can then CD into something that helps the worker and/or company succeed.

At the end of an episode, Rachel judges the efforts of the various "shadows." The least successful one is presented with a wooden stake and eliminated from the show. During the season, shadows will be eliminated until only one remains. Whoever becomes "top shadow" will win a trophy, fame, and the opportunity to be recruited by a corporation so the company can profit from his or her CDing skills.

While *The Shadow* and these CDing Leaguers have yet to break the letter of the law (using their skills to compete directly against Lifers in business and sports for their own profit), they are breaking the *spirit* of the law. Worse, *The Shadow* is sending a terrible message to Lifers: *We want to exploit our CDing skills and glorify our differences with Lifers; we are vampires first, responsible citizens second.* This is *not* the message we should be sending as we fight for passage of the Vampire Rights Act.

For this reason, I am asking all Leaguers to boycott *The Shadow*. I ask you to not participate in it or watch it, and to tell your Lifer friends that the vast majority of Leaguers obey the third Leaguer commandment: "You shall not frighten Lifers with your powers." That includes not CDing unless in the event of a life-threatening situation to a fellow human being.

Your guide,
Luther Birnam

8
The Shadow

While Morning had read the post when it first came out and had wanted to join the boycott, he couldn't. Watching *The Shadow* was one of his date nights with Portia.

Besides loving the show for its cheesy entertainment value, Portia watched it for "research" on her senior film project, a documentary on Leaguers since American Out Day. While the doc she had made the year before, *Morning McCobb: The Jackie Robinson of the Vampire League,* had won several awards and guaranteed her admission to the film school of her choice, she had to make another doc to graduate from LaGuardia Arts.

The motion of Zoë's pedicab starting up again burst the bubble of Morning's thoughts.

Zoë pumped the pedals and they picked up speed. "You saw the show last week, right?"

"*The Shadow*?"

She scoffed at his spaciness. "No, *Hot Goth Biker Chicks.* Of course *The Shadow*!"

"I missed it."

"What? I thought it was sure-thing TV for you and Portia."

"We had to study."

Zoë summarized the episode Morning had missed with the same energy she pedaled with, and she didn't stop for spoiler alerts. "It was the best one yet! The category was 'boat captain' and the top shadow ended up being Jeremy. He hooked up with a marine salvage company that's been diving for a lost treasure in the Hudson for years. Then Jeremy CDed into a three-foot sea worm, went burrowing in the river bottom, and found the sixteen hundred silver bars treasure hunters have been chasing since 1903. The find was worth twenty-seven million!"

"That's great," Morning said flatly. "I wonder how the other treasure hunters feel about vampires now?"

"Are you kidding? They're probably trying to hire 'em to turn into sea worms for them, too, so they can find other sunken treasures." She shot a frown at her passenger. "You know what you're problem is, A.M.? You look to the future and see doom and gloom. If you ask me, it's totally unfair."

"What's unfair about it?"

"That immortality gets wasted on the shortsighted. I mean, if you'd just turn me, I'd show you what vampires could do!"

"Okay"—Morning flicked a hand at her—"*poof,* you're a vampire. What would you do?"

"For starters, I'd get on *The Shadow* next season, and while I was making my run to the winner's circle I'd turn every vampirophobe into a vampirophile. If the category was 'water department,' I'd become a rat, inspect all the city's water mains and find the ones that were about to break, and no one would ever have their water shut off again. If the assignment was 'nuclear containment,' I'd hook up with the CIA, turn into a camel, and find every secret nuclear processing plant in Iran!"

Morning laughed at Zoë's wild imagination. "I promise if I ever turn anyone, it'll be you."

She hit the brakes and spun around. "You mean that? You'd flip me before you flipped Portia?"

He gave her a stern look. "*That* I will *never* do."

"Never say never."

He shuddered at the thought, which spurred the memory of the night he almost did worse than turn Portia. He hopped out of the pedicab.

"Where are you going?" Zoë protested. "We've got another ten blocks."

He checked his cell to make sure he had enough time. "Thanks for saving my butt, ZZ, but I wanna walk. See you at the parade." He started away.

"I'm not going."

He turned back. "What? The number-one vampire fan is gonna miss the Vampire Pride Parade?"

"Yep. Fanpire Tours has an after-school booking."

"With who?" he asked suspiciously.

She broke into a sly smile. "I'm not sure, but on the phone he sounded like a badass vampire who might tip me with a couple of fangs."

Morning started toward her. "Don't do it, Zoë."

She pushed off with a laugh and leaned into the pedals. "Hey, if you don't wanna be my friend with blood benefits, maybe I'll have to find another." She threw a wave. "Later, vasodilator!"

9

Sister Flora

When Morning reached his narrow street off Delancey, it was jammed with people. His stomach tightened. The only time he had really enjoyed his fame was when he and Birnam were invited to the White House to meet the president. They all shared a beverage in the Rose Garden in what the press had dubbed the "Blood Lite Summit." That was cool.

He scooted down another street, taking the back way into the place he still called home: the St. Giles Group Home for Boys.

He took the stairs up to his room. He wanted to change his wrinkled probie shirt for a newly ironed one. If he had to march at the front of the parade he wanted to send a message: *I'm a cadet at the fire academy first, a vampire second.* He also needed to write his Out Day card for Portia and wrap the gift that went with it.

As he finished wrapping the present, he looked out the

window overlooking the street. It swarmed with people gathering for the start of the parade at the spot where Morning, more than a year before, had first outed himself as a vampire. The throng was the hodgepodge he had expected: a mashup of Leaguers, goths, wannabes, news crews, and vampire fans who liked dressing up as their favorite characters from books and movies. He saw a dozen Edwards and Bellas. The only Edward and Bella he knew were the two pet turtles that lived at St. Giles. They had been named by the Mallozzi twins, who had won the naming contest when they pointed out that turtles were as slow, ponderous, and boring as the "real" Edward and Bella.

As he scanned the VIPs mingling around the stoop, the only surprise was who he *didn't* see. Portia was there, but not her mother. Penny Dredful had been made an honorary Leaguer for her PR work while introducing Morning to the world, as had her daughter, Portia, for her film on Morning. But the most mysterious no-show was the Leaguer of Leaguers: Luther Birnam.

A familiar knock pulled Morning to the door. "Come in."

Sister Flora bustled into the room. She ran St. Giles along with a few other nuns and was the closest thing Morning had ever had to a mother. It was Sister Flora who had discovered the baby, whom she named Morning McCobb, in a shopping basket left on the stoop of St. Giles. It was Sister Flora who felt responsible for Morning being turned into a vampire when she sent him to a host family on Staten Island for a Thanksgiving dinner. Unfortunately, one of the Loner vampires who still practiced the old ways turned the host family into his own Thanksgiving feast and chomped into Morning for dessert. Fortunately, the Loner vampire, Ikor DeThanatos, was so bloated with blood he burped, had a case of backwash, and his saliva, carrying the vampire virus, was injected back into Morning's neck, infecting him and giving him a new lease on life as a vampire.

"What a thrilling day!" Sister Flora proclaimed. "It's put a bee in my wimple!" Morning started to remind her that she no longer wore a nun's hat, but she clapped her hands together. "Are you excited about your parade?"

"It's your parade too," he said, reminding her of her Leaguer status; in fact, she'd been a vampire for more than a hundred years.

"Yes, I know, but this day never would have come to pass if it weren't for you."

"Mr. Birnam had a lot more to do with it than me. By the way, where is he?"

Flora's face dropped, then she jacked it back up. "He wrote a wonderful message on the website." She moved to his desktop computer. "Have you seen it? It's so inspiring!"

"Sister, he's not coming, is he?"

"No, but I'm sure whatever's come up is important."

Morning threw his hands in the air. "What could be more important than the first anniversary of American Out Day? I mean, he's the one who came up with a Vampire Pride Parade, and now he's turning it into the Vampire *Hide* Parade."

Flora chuckled. "Very clever." She took his hand and pulled him to the edge of the bed. "Now, listen to me. I don't know why he's not coming. Maybe he's trying to make a point to Rachel and Penny about that TV show of theirs." Flora was a solid backer of the boycott against *The Shadow.*

"He missed my GED graduation ceremony," Morning said. "And the ceremonial first day at the fire academy. We haven't seen him for almost two months."

Flora's brow knitted. "I'm worried about him too. But it's unwise to question the wisdom of someone who's been taking the world in for nearly eight centuries. Whatever it is, I'm sure he's got his reasons." She reached for something. "Now, what's that doing there?" Off of Morning's bedpost she plucked a leather cord with a wooden pendant hanging on it. "If there's any day you should be wearing your good-luck charm, it's today."

Morning didn't resist her putting the necklace over his head. The cookie of wood was made from bristlecone pine, with a blue Maltese cross painted on it. The points of the stubby cross displayed four red letters: FDNY. It was not just a gift from Birnam when Morning had first been outed; the sight of the pendant with its Maltese cross had pulled Morning from the forbidden well of bloodlust and stopped him from drinking Portia to the last drop. He tucked the wooden disk under his shirt.

Flora patted him on the shoulder. "The parade's going to start without you."

"Would that be the end of the world?"

She gave him a warm smile. "It would be for the beautiful young lady waiting to march with you."

He jumped up. He couldn't believe he'd forgotten about Portia. Of course, that's why he was marching in the parade. That's why he was doing *everything*!

10

Dung Beetles

As Morning and Sister Flora passed through the building's entranceway, she cautioned him not to be surprised by something outside. The night before, the historical plaque on the front of St. Giles that cited Morning's first public CD from human form to mist had been vandalized. Sister Flora told him the mischief had been minor and was being taken care of.

When they moved out onto the elevated stoop, the waiting crowd greeted Morning with a thunderous cheer. Putting on a smile and waving to the crowd, he stole a look at the plaque mounted on the brickwork behind him. It was covered in horse manure. Stranger still, beetles swarmed over the manure.

Flora raised her voice over the noise. "Dung beetles."

Morning spotted a double column of beetles scuttling along a brick ledge. Each beetle leaving the dung-covered plaque rolled away a tiny ball of manure.

Two beetles dropped off the ledge and exploded into the human forms of young Leaguers, one of each gender. They were sheathed in Epidex, the spandexlike material Leaguers had invented to prevent CDing vampires from popping back into human form and being mistaken for streakers. Their appearance was greeted with cheers and applause.

"Hey, Morning," the guy Leaguer said, giving the crowd a fist pump. "We're on a break."

"Don't worry," the girl added, hooking a thumb back at the plaque. "We'll have it cleaned up in no time."

Morning looked puzzled. "Why turn into beetles when a person with a rag could clean it in a minute?"

The girl grinned. "We're making a statement."

"What's that?" Morning asked. "How to turn a one-man job into the bug version of community service?"

The guy jerked his head toward the street. "She can explain it better."

Morning turned to see a cameraman plowing through the mosh, shooting as he came. In his wake were a TV reporter and Rachel Capilarus. The crowd burst into celebration. Morning turned to see why. The two Leaguers had CDed back to dung beetles and now climbed the wall toward the plaque.

"Get the shot?" the reporter asked his cameraman. The cameraman gave a thumbs-up as he pushed in for a close-up of the beetles scurrying up the brick.

The reporter was the blond and smarmy Drake Sanders of Hound TV. Drake was the news-scooper who had shot Morning's coming-out CD on the stoop thirteen months before. There was no way Drake was going to miss the first Vampire Pride Parade. Drake and the cameraman swung around, making room as Rachel Capilarus joined Morning and Sister Flora at the top of the stoop. The throng greeted her with whistles and chants of "Rachel! Rachel!"

Before turning to her fans, Rachel gave Morning a once-over. "Like the uniform, so handsome!" She spun in a corkscrew of silk and taffeta. Her dress, a riot of pastels, looked like several Indian saris had been shredded and reassembled. She wore a matching, tattered headband; her neck was a jewelry rack of a peace sign, a rosary, a Star of David, an Islamic crescent, and the Hindi "Om" symbol. Morning wouldn't have been surprised if a stone from the Temple of Apollo had suddenly popped out of her bejeweled cleavage. Rachel answered the crowd's adulation with a two-armed wave, rattling her dizzying array of bracelets.

Drake Sanders turned on his mike. "So, Ms. Capilarus, what's with the dung beetles?"

She flashed an innocent smile. "Okay, sure, Mr. B says we should only CD when lives are at stake—" She fluttered a hand. "Wait! Pun so *not* intended!" She took a breathy breath as the crowd laughed. "I just think if a little bug magic can make the world a less poopy place, shouldn't we be marines and be all that we can be?"

The crowd bellowed an answer. "Yeah!"

"But Rachel," Drake said, "doesn't this kind of activity alienate people who are still afraid of vampires, whether you're law-abiding Leaguers or not?"

She tossed a hand back at the beetles. "Show me someone who's scared of a few dung beetles and I'll show you someone who's scared of someone stealing their shit."

The crowd broke into laughter and applause. Morning smiled. It was the one hope he still held out for Rachel. As

46

hard as she had worked on her makeover, once in a while, she let loose with a zinger that was straight from the quiver of the old warrior princess.

Rachel pretended not to get the joke. "I mean, if someone's gonna throw a hate crime at us, maybe we should throw something back. Like a CD of a different color."

Drake looked confused. "A CD of a different color?"

"Yeah, instead of 'CD' being 'cell differentiation,' today we're calling it *civil disobediate.*"

After taking a moment to translate "disobediate," the crowd cheered. Then Rachel gestured at the busy beetles. "The point is—and then we really gotta march—is that these little worker bugs aren't *causing* a problem, they're *solving* one. And that's all vampires wanna do for the human race. Hey!" she exclaimed, hopscotching to a new thought. "Why do they call it the 'human race'? 'Cause we're all in the same *race* to do good, to make the world a better place! That's why we're race-marching today!" She waggled her arms like a floppy puppet. "And a race-march waits for no one, not even Mr. B! Let's do it!"

She flowed down the steps as Drake and his cameraman hustled behind her. The mass of cheering paraders, whipped into a frenzy, surged after her like a bursting dam. Morning and Sister Flora hung back on the stoop as Portia squeezed out of the human flood and climbed up to join them.

Portia had changed since breakfast and now wore loose-fitting cargo pants and an untucked button-down. It was one of the things Morning loved about her: the bigger the occasion, the more she dressed down. Right behind her, holding up a camcorder, was a hunky teenager in a pec-hugging tee.

"Hey, Sister Flora," Portia said, gesturing at her friend. "This is Cody, my cinematographer."

Cody's Jake Gyllenhaal eyes rose from behind the camcorder as he flashed a charming smile. "Hiya, Sister."

Morning shot him a scornful look. Besides his ongoing jealousy of Cody's swimmer's body, Morning envied the man-hours Cody got to spend with Portia. Not only did they both attend LaGuardia Arts, they had teamed up on the same senior film project, Portia's next doc. "I thought you were gonna walk with me, not shoot," Morning said to her.

"Don't worry," Portia assured him, "we can do both. I'm gonna march, do a little directing on the side, and Cody's gonna do all the shooting. But here's the problem."

Cody dodged around his camera and finished her thought as he got a shot of himself and Portia. "We don't know what kinda doc we're making yet. Is it about a couple of high school movie geeks and vampire groupies hangin' in the wings of the Leaguer rights struggle, like a vampire version of *Almost Famous*?" He swung back behind the camera and framed Morning and Portia. "Is it a tragic portrait of chronology-crossed lovers—she's aging, he's not!— like *The Curious Case of Benjamin Button* with fangs?" He turned the camcorder on the paraders streaming by. "What we wanna make is a Ken Burns–worthy doc on the vampire rights movement called *Fangs on the Prize*—not easy when you're shooting on a high school budget."

"Cody keeps forgetting we have something more valuable than a megabudget," Portia said as she took Morning's arm. "Inside access." Her eyes darted to Morning's neck, and the leather cord above his T-shirt collar. "Speaking of 'inside' "—she fingered the cord and lifted the wooden pendant from under his shirt—"pride parades are all about not just wearin' it, but flauntin' it."

Morning's only resistance was an eye roll.

She patted the wood disk. "Now you're ready to march."

Cody turned the camera back on himself as he offered his muscled arm to Sister Flora. "What do ya say, Sister? I hate to march alone."

Flora took his arm with a laugh. "Absolutely, but it seems we've missed the front of the parade."

"Don't worry," Morning said. "I know a shortcut."

11

The Parade

Morning led Portia, Sister Flora, and Cody up a side street toward First Avenue, where they could meet the parade. The sound of a roaring lion leaped out of Portia's thigh pocket.

As she dug out her cell, Morning gave her a curious look. "That's a new ringtone."

"Cody found it for me," she explained. "It's the roaring lion that begins every MGM movie."

That was another thing that hit Morning's jealousy button. Cody knew tons about Portia's great love: movies. And when it came to electronics and making stuff, he was as tech-heady as *Iron Man*'s Tony Stark. Morning just hoped Cody didn't know how to write code in Portia's heart.

Portia answered her phone. It was her mother, Penny, reporting that something had come up at work and she would be joining the parade when it passed by her office on First Avenue.

As Portia hung up, the group beat the parade to where Allen Street became First Avenue. Because they were still downtown and it was a weekday, there were no parade watchers yet. Morning looked down the street and watched the phalanx of paraders moving toward them. A crimson banner stretched over their heads, proclaiming VAMPIRE PRIDE PARADE.

As the parade came closer, Morning saw that the letters on the banner were formed with real olive branches, sprayed white. It was a touch Rachel had suggested to counteract the boldness of the banner's lurid red.

Rachel was front and center in her flowing dress. The front row was mostly Leaguers. The signs they carried ranged from prideful statements—BORN & MADE IN THE USA—to political messages: VOTE VRA and NO BITES = RIGHTS!

But Morning was surprised by how many vampire wannabes and wanna-bleeds were also in the front. Their sweatshirts, T-shirts, and costumes announced a different message: THE BITE STUFF, BLOOD DONATION CENTER, and HOW 'BOUT A PIECE OF NECK PIE? A guy in full cowboy regalia had a sign on his ten-gallon hat: SAVE A COW, BITE A COWBOY. Morning muttered under his breath, "Is this a pride parade or a pickup scene for the fanged and the fangless?"

Portia snagged his arm and pulled him into the street. "Don't be a pooper. If the VRA's gonna pass there's gotta be more than just Leaguers under the big red tent. After all, Leaguers can't vote anymore."

Morning resisted the urge to remind her that, being stuck at sixteen, he would *never* be able to vote even if the VRA *did* pass.

The front row of paraders welcomed the foursome with a shout-out. They fell in next to Rachel as Sister Flora moved down the front row to join some friends.

"Thank Godness," Rachel announced, beaming at Morning and Portia, "the first couple of Leaguer-Lifer love is here!" Flipping her long black hair, she shouted to the paraders behind her. "It wouldn't be the first pride parade without the first outie!"

Even though Morning cringed every time he heard Rachel's dorky nickname for him, he focused on a more important matter. "Yeah, but can it be the first parade without the first Leaguer, Mr. Birnam?"

Rachel shrugged. "Truth is, not surprised."

Coming on top of her text-message syntax, her blithe dismissal of the father of Leaguer liberation was more than Morning could take. "You know, Rachel, you don't have to do your goofy-doofy, I-couldn't-grow-fangs-even-if-I-worked-in-a-slaughterhouse act with me. I knew you when you had real chi, not the kind you get from"—he jabbed a finger at the jewelry rack around her neck—"crystals on chains."

Rachel arched a brow and slid a look to Portia. "Ouch, he bites."

"Tell me about it," Portia bounced back.

They shared a laugh, which only stoked Morning's ire. Before he could spin a comeback, Rachel dropped her voice and confided in him.

"I'll tell you why Mr. B's making himself scarce. If you read his parade-day post, you might've noticed what he mostly talked about was the past. I think he knows he's played his part, and he's ready to pass the torch."

"Ha!" Morning blurted. "To who?" He swept a hand, presenting Rachel. "Lady Vava?"

Portia gestured to Cody to get his camera on Rachel and Morning.

Without acknowledging his dig, Rachel gave Morning her positive-energy smile. "No way. *You're* his fav."

He scoffed. "Now I know whatever mind you once had has been sucked out by a brain vampire."

"Too funny," Rachel chirped, giving him a playful punch. Then she shouted down the line to Sister Flora. "Yo, Sister Sis. Morning *is* the chosen one, right?"

Flora pointed heavenward. "Besides *the* chosen one, yes, Morning's *my* chosen one."

"Mine too," Portia piped up, taking Morning's arm. "But my money's on him retiring from the spotlight as soon as he becomes a firefighter."

"Even better," Morning added, "how 'bout I kill the spotlight after this parade?"

"Not gonna happen," Rachel retorted. "When Portia made"—her hands stretched an imaginary marquee— "*Morning McCobb: The Jackie Robinson of the Vampire League,* fame put a lock on you tight as your lock on Portia."

Rachel's flattery cued a question Portia had been waiting to ask. "Rachel, Cody and I are making a new documentary on the Leaguer rights movement, and you're pushing so many hot buttons on *The Shadow* . . . could we interview you sometime?"

"Don't even ask," Rachel answered with a hand flip. "I owe your mom so big-time." She suddenly threw an arm around Morning. "She's almost made me as famous as the superstar, the legend, outie numero uno!"

Morning shrank out of her grip. Rachel was too beautiful to have cooties, but she had something that might be just as contagious: personality shifting disorder.

Portia didn't miss Morning's creep-out as she tried to seal the deal with Rachel. "Cool. When's good?"

"Whenev," Rachel tossed off. "But right now is about gettin' everyone juiced for the media at Fourteenth Street." She raised a hand over her shoulder. "Bullhorn!" A Leaguer plopped a bullhorn into her hand. Rachel keyed it and burst into a rapping chant. "We walk in light, no longer bite, we're in the fight for what is right!"

The paraders answered her call. "VRA! VRA! Pass it now is what we say!"

"Your blood we spurn, we don't turn, we done our provin', now *you* get movin'!"

"VRA! VRA! Pass it now is what we say!"

"Rights and freedom, we all need 'em, we want our sequel of bein' equal!"

"VRA! VRA! Pass it now is what we say!"

12

Wordus Eruptus

At Fourteenth Street, Ally Alfamen sat in a viewing stand having her makeup touched up before beginning her live coverage of the parade. Ally had formerly been the perky host of *Wake Up America* and had become the network's anchorwoman shortly after she covered Morning's second CD. It was a CD seen by billions, and the one that had convinced the world Morning wasn't some vampire poser; he was the real thing, and the real thing could CD into any living form: including an apple tree in full blossom.

Ally faced the camera. "Today, the Big Apple is a little redder. Why? We're about to witness the first Vampire Pride Parade. In addition to being a celebration of our blood-drinking minority, it's a parade reminding us that their integration into society will not be complete until Congress passes the Vampire Rights Act and restores equal rights to our Leaguer citizens."

The big screen behind Ally filled with a shot of the

parade. "So far, the biggest surprise is who's *not* leading the parade. There's the usual 'Leaguerati,' as some call them, such as Morning McCobb and Rachel Capilarus, but the president of the IVL, Luther Birnam, is mysteriously absent. And where is the woman who's the Lifer linchpin behind the Leaguer movement: Penny Dredful? This is her day as much as anyone's." Ally's face warped into a disapproving frown. "It's certainly more Penny's day than some of the other Lifers in the parade."

The screen cut to a group of goth wanna-bleeds at the front of the parade waving VRA signs. The shot panned across the messages on their T-shirts: VAMPIRE RECHARGING STATION, PRICK ME! PRICK ME!, PREY FOR ME, and I WANNA THREESOME: MY NECK, YOUR FANGS.

Down the line, Morning spotted the cameraman shooting the goths. Glancing at a street sign, he realized they were two blocks from the heavy media coverage at Fourteenth Street. "Don't you think we should get the goths off the front line?" he said to Rachel. "I mean, 'Prey for me' isn't exactly the message we wanna send."

Portia directed Cody to get his camera back on Rachel and Morning as Rachel shook her head. " 'Pray for me'? I think it's super we have vampires from all faiths."

Seeing that many Americans might not catch the spelling trick, Morning moved on to a more glaring example. "What about 'Prick me! Prick me!'? Is that—"

"If you ask me," Rachel replied, "it's the most beautiful message in America."

He was momentarily stupefied. "What message is that?"

"The message of free expression, that *all* voices, mortal or immortal, have a right to be heard. And I don't know about you, Outie-One Kenobi," she said, poking Morning in the chest, "but the last time I checked, we can't step into a voting booth, onto a playing field, or even onto Main Street to open a lemonade stand."

Drake and his cameraman emerged from behind them, where they had been getting shots. "Hey, Rachel," he interjected, "if the VRA passes and you *can* open a business, will it be a rent-a-vampire thing? You know, someone has a special problem, so they hire one of your vampires to CD into something that delivers the solution?"

"*The Shadow* already loans CDing vamps to companies for free," she explained. "It's a game show. The companies make the big bucks, not Penny, or me, or anyone else."

"Exactly," Drake said, following up. "But if you *could* turn CDing vamps into a business, you could make millions, right?"

"I don't think God made me a vampire to make millions. He made me a vampire to become an Earth Angel."

"An earth angel? What's that?"

Rachel shot him a wink. "Saving it for a bigger media play, Drako. But for now, I'll land in the money tree of capitalism and sing it to you in ka-ching. Leaguer vampires are like an untapped source of energy. So, if you discovered a giant oil field under your backyard, would you just leave it there?"

Morning answered. "If tapping into it ruined everyone else's backyard, I'd leave it there."

Portia jumped in. "C'mon, Morn, don't be naïve. Someone would drill in sideways and take the oil anyway."

The double shot of her patronizing tone and her taking sides with Rachel made him snap, "Like who, your mom?"

Portia jerked back, stunned.

He desperately wanted to suck the words back.

"Whoa," Rachel said. "Below the belt-us."

"I—I didn't mean it like that," Morning stammered.

Portia glared at him. "I know *exactly* what you mean. You're saying my mom's making tons of money off Leaguers 'cause she's the only one who can own the business. You're saying she's gouging vampires."

Cody lowered his camcorder. "Porsche, maybe I should stop shooting." He gave a head toss toward Drake and his cameraman. "And maybe you should—"

"No, camera up," she ordered. "If our doc ends up being nothing but the story of a couple of chronology-crossed lovers, you might as well get the second the clocks went out of sync." She whipped back to Morning. "Yeah, my mom's made gobs of money repping Leaguers and creating *The Shadow*." She threw a hand at a glistening office building up ahead. "She bought her building with it and the whole place is filled with well-paid Leaguers. She's the biggest donor to vampire causes in the city, and she's gone to Washington countless times to lobby for the VRA. She's totally on your side. She's fighting for Leaguers like Rachel to go into business on their own, and for Leaguers like you to marry who they want!"

Morning was speechless. Not only had he taken a major plunge into humiliation, it was being recorded for the world to see.

Drake pushed his mike at Morning. "Your turn."

Morning's jaw clenched, trapping whatever might pop out.

"C'mon," Drake prodded, "aren't you gonna bite back?"

Rachel jutted her face in front of the cameraman's lens,

blocking the shot of Morning. "This broadcast has been interrupted due to negative vibes."

Drake retreated with a smirk. "No point to a lovers' spat if one side's a no-show." He pulled his cameraman away. "C'mon, let's go see if the goth girl with the T-shirt saying 'Drinks on Me!' has found any takers." As Drake disappeared, Cody stopped shooting also.

Penny Dredful hustled toward them in one of the light green pantsuits she liked to wear to emphasize her flaming red hair. She immediately noticed the tense faces. "I'd ask who died, but that's long odds in this group." She swung into stride next to Rachel. "So who rained on the parade?"

Cody jumped in. "No one, Mrs. Dredful. It's just that someone did die."

As they all turned to him, Penny looked the most surprised. "Really?"

"Yeah," he said sheepishly. "I just gave away who bites the dust in the new *Hunger Games* movie and they're really pissed at me."

Morning wished he had come up with such a good cover. He tried to touch Portia's hand, but she yanked it away.

Penny shook a teasing finger at Cody. "Young man, you need to learn to keep your mouth shut." Then she apologized for being late and explained why. Diamond Sky Productions had been hit with a lawsuit. The salvage companies that had been searching for the sunken treasure in the Hudson River and had come up empty were suing Diamond Sky and *The Shadow* for using a CDing vampire to find the silver bars. They claimed that CDing vampires should be outlawed because they were as unfair in the business world as bribes and kickbacks.

Rachel was taken aback. "When is everyone gonna get it? We're here to help the world, not hurt it."

Morning wanted to tell her that her naïve act was getting scarily believable, but he knew he'd probably just jam his foot in his mouth again. He had cured himself of the fang-popping thing, *dentis eruptus,* but he was still fighting *wordus eruptus.*

13

€arth Angels

The Vampire Pride Parade was approaching Fourteenth Street when two throngs of people poured into the intersection. They filled it, creating a human barricade. The signs they waved bannered messages such as VRA GO AWAY! and AMERICA FOR MORTALS ONLY—IMMORTALS OUT!

The one that bugged Morning the most declared, UNDEAD = UN-AMERICAN. You could argue the un-American part, but the undead part was totally untrue. Vampires were never dead: mortals got sick after being infected with the vampire virus, which turned them into vampires. But there was no arguing with people who believed that vampires—whether harmless Leaguers or not—were the source of all evil in America.

At the front of the human blockade was a sturdy woman with frumpy hair and heavy-rimmed glasses. She looked like the science teacher you didn't want to get locked in a lab with. Becky-Dell Wallace was a U.S. congresswoman from Wyoming, and the head of the Mortals Only Party, or MOP. Their acronym wasn't accidental. Becky-Dell and her MOPers hoped to swab America's deck and wash vampires into the sea. Some of them even wore hats with little mop rags and sponges hanging from the brims.

As the parade came to a halt, Becky-Dell led her MOPers in a ringing chant. "Vampires, vampires, sleazy-sleazy, we're gonna mop ya, easy-easy!"

Rachel raised her bullhorn and led the Leaguer parade in a counterchant. "VRA! VRA! VRA!"

The gap separating the two groups swarmed with camera crews. Drake and Cody were among them.

Rachel waved her arms like a QB trying to quiet the crowd; the paraders hushed. Becky-Dell whipped a boat air horn from her purse and let loose a blast. Her MOPers took their cue and fell silent.

Rachel keyed her bullhorn and politely addressed Becky-Dell and the human logjam in the intersection. "Okay, made your point. Had your little free-speech work-out, but the free-speech gym is open to everyone"—she held up a piece of paper—"and we have a permit to work out today. So, I'm asking you nicely, please step aside and let us free-speech on."

For a moment, Becky-Dell had the blank expression of a TV reporter waiting for a delayed sound feed. She was still unscrambling Rachel's metaphor. Then Becky-Dell reached into her purse, pulled up a pointed wooden stake, and jabbed it in the air. "Free-speech on this!"

In unison, the mass of MOPers behind her thrust their own wooden stakes skyward and echoed, "On this!"

Rachel giggled at the sight of the pulsing Maginot Line of stakes. She answered through her bullhorn. "Let me ask you. When the automobile came along, did you destroy it to protect horses? When the computer came along, did you destroy it to protect typewriters? So now the Leaguer vampires come along and you wanna destroy us? Don't you get it? We're the new technology. We wanna help you! Heck, we're not even 'vampires' anymore. We're *Earth Angels*!"

The parade bellowed its approval, "Earth Angels!"

The MOPers jabbed stakes and screamed, "Vampires, vampires, sleazy-sleazy! We're gonna stake ya, easy-easy!"

Morning grabbed Portia's hand. "This is gonna get ugly. Let's get outta here."

"No way," she countered as her eyes gleamed with excitement. "This is history!"

Rachel waved her parade permit at police officers on both sides of the street. "Men and women in blue, it's time to do the Moses thing and part these troubled waters!"

The men and women in blue backed up, evaporating into the crowd of spectators mesmerized by the confrontation.

As each side pumped up the volume, Rachel walked back to Morning, Portia, and Penny. Cody kept filming. With a put-on expression, Rachel singsonged, "Guess they wanna play by the old rules." She lifted her necklaces over her head and handed them to Penny. "I just hate fighting in a dress."

"Rachel, don't," Morning implored. "It'll make things worse."

"Not what you're thinkin'," she said with a cheerful head wag. "I've been checkin' out my past lives, and in one life, I wore Gandhi."

Portia was the first to ask, "How can you *wear* Gandhi?"

"I was his mistress." Rachel spun, facing the chanting MOPers. She looked left-right down the front of the parade and shouted a command. "Earth Angels, step up!"

Two dozen athletic-looking Leaguers stepped forward. Following Rachel's lead, they all shut their eyes, leaped forward in unison, and imploded. Behind the falling curtain of Rachel's tattered dress and the other Earth Angels' outfits, a phalanx of white doves rose in flight.

As the paraders cheered, the MOPers recoiled, choking on their chant.

The doves wheeled into a flock and swooped across the red banner announcing VAMPIRE PRIDE PARADE. As they swarmed past, each dove plucked an olive branch from the banner. The flock wheeled high, then dived in tight formation toward the stunned throng of MOPers.

"Hold your ground!" Becky-Dell yelled as she lifted her stake against the bird attack.

MOPers jabbed stakes in the air and shrieked. It was unclear what they were more afraid of: their protest being turned into a bad hair day by a flock of birds, or being infected by the avian disease that vampire doves surely carried. Protestors swatted at the diving doves with stakes and signs; the birds slalomed through their flailing attempts and dropped their payload: a dozen olive branches.

Rachel's olive branch stuck on Becky-Dell's outstretched stake. Her peace offering was a bull's-eye. Becky-Dell furiously shook it off as the doves wheeled again and prepared for another dive.

The MOPers, fearing what the birds might drop next, surged out of the intersection in a scattering panic.

———

Across town, in Times Square, a Jumbotron carried a picture of the doves clearing the intersection at Fourteenth and First.

A traffic cop stared up at the screen and nodded in approval. "Dat's right, don't block da box."

Also riveted to the huge screen was Zoë Zotz, frozen on the pedals of her pedicab. In the cab behind her was the "badass vampire" she had picked up after school: a frail old man with a scraggly beard.

The old man crooked a finger at the Jumbotron. "Is that part of the tour?"

14

Paraded Out

From her booth overlooking the intersection, Ally Alfamen gaped at the scene until she remembered "speechless" was not part of her job description. "Ladies and gentlemen," she intoned, "*that's* crowd control."

The doves swooped toward the middle of the cleared intersection and transformed back into human forms. Rachel and her Earth Angels, sheathed in black Epidex, touched down with the grace of ninjas as the jubilant parade celebrated.

Rachel shouted past the only MOPer still in their path: Becky-Dell. "Earth Angels, ho!"

The parade surged forward, streaming around Becky-Dell like a rock in a river. But this rock, red-faced with rage, white-knuckled her stake.

Morning stopped next to her. "Ms. Wallace, are you all right?"

"Go away," she hissed.

He hesitated as he watched Portia being swept along by the parade. He turned back to Becky-Dell. "I apologize for what they did. We're not supposed to frighten people. Leaguers are law-abiding—"

"I know what you are," she growled. "And I won't stop till you're all back in the ground, where the dead belong."

"But, Ms. Wallace, we were never dead."

"You will be when I'm done with you!"

Two MOPers rushed into the flow of paraders and rescued Becky-Dell from the vampire who had started it all.

Morning watched the thinning parade move past him. A ringtone sounded in his pocket. It was John Lennon singing "All we are saying is give peace a chance." Morning pulled out his cell and answered it. "Hey."

"Are you coming or not?" Portia asked.

"I was hoping you'd circle back. Right now, all I want is to give you your Out Day card and a present."

"We can do it tonight," she said. "*Right now,* Cody and I gotta cover whatever else happens."

He sighed. "I'm sorry for what I said about your mom."

"It's okay, Morn. I know you didn't mean it."

His chest collapsed with a sigh of relief. "You know I love you."

"I know. Back atcha. Gotta go."

He hung up. The parade had been a disaster, but he was done with it and Portia still loved him. . . . Okay, it was "back atcha" love, which was better than nothing.

A pedicab raced toward him. Zoë glided to a stop. "I can't believe I missed the fireworks!"

"You'll be able to catch 'em on the news tonight. What happened to your badass vampire?"

"Wasn't badass, wasn't a vampire, so I gave him a refund and promised him a rain check."

Morning looked toward the retreating parade. "You better get going if you wanna catch it. Who knows what fireworks Rachel will set off next."

Zoë studied him. He looked like the parade had marched right over him. "Nah," she said, "I'd rather give the most good-ass vampire in the world a ride home."

On the ride downtown, Morning told Zoë everything that had happened, including his attack of *wordus eruptus* with Portia. When he told her how Rachel's group CD and MOPer terrorization would only turn more Lifers against Leaguers, Zoë disagreed. "I don't think you get it."

"Get what?"

"There's millions of Lifers who still want vampires, even if they're Leaguers, to be a little badass. A lot of us get turned on by the danger of it—from just reading about it to the crazy ones like me who wanna get turned. Then there's the in-betweens who just wanna experience the ecstasy of exsanguination."

"The what?"

"The ecstasy of exsanguination," Zoë repeated. "That's what they call it."

Morning shook his head in dismay and fell silent.

Zoë turned the pedicab onto his street and looked back. "I've always wanted to ask, A.M. When you got turned, was it all bad?"

Shuddering at the memory, he lied. "I don't remember."

She chuckled. "Like I believe that. The point is, from what I saw of the parade on TV, there were a ton of vampire wannabes and wanna-bleeds, right?"

"Yeah, it was gross."

"Gross or not, there's secret underground clubs in the city that cater to consensual bloodlusters."

"That's urban legend."

"What if it isn't?"

"Oh, right, like you've been to one." Zoë silently coasted to a stop in front of St. Giles. "Have you?" he asked.

She flashed a big smile. "Ride's over. Catch ya later, good-ass."

As she rode away, Morning's head was filled with the racket of cross-talking thoughts. He had to clear it. There was one place where he did his best head-clearing: the middle of the Williamsburg Bridge.

15

Williamsburg Bridge

Morning started across the walkway–bike path that arched through the bridge like a spine. He stripped off his blue probie shirt and got down to his white tee to be less conspicuous. Luckily, the walkway was almost empty.

He stopped halfway across and looked through the anti-jumper fence at the Statue of Liberty floating on the distant harbor. His cell phone rang. It wasn't John Lennon; it was the heavy opening chords of Beethoven's Fifth: *dun-dun-dun-duuunn!* He answered it.

Luther Birnam was on the other end and spoke in a husky voice. "I wish you hadn't left the parade."

"I wish you'd been there to stop Rachel from flying off the handle."

"And to stop you from putting your foot in your mouth?" Birnam asked.

Morning huffed. "How do you know about that?"

"I have my sources."

There was no doubting it. Birnam could disappear for two months, but it didn't mean he didn't have eyes and ears everywhere. "Where are you?" Morning asked.

"At Leaguer Academy."

Morning was shocked. "You mean you're just up the Hudson and you couldn't—"

"Not the new academy," Birnam said. "The old one."

Why he was there baffled Morning. The old Leaguer Academy, where Morning and Rachel had become Leaguers, was inside a mountain in California's Sierra Nevadas. The hidden academy had been abandoned when the new one was opened after American Out Day in an old boarding school up the Hudson River. "What are you doing there?"

"That's not important," Birnam replied. "What's important is that we halt Rachel's dangerous behavior."

Morning didn't like the sound of "we." "Why don't you tell her to stop? You're the president of the IVL."

"I'm not king of the vampires. That's not how we play it these days. I'm going to turn my videophone on."

Morning was taken aback; he hadn't seen Birnam's face in two months. The few times they'd Skyped, Birnam had been audio only. He always had an excuse like "computer-idiot" or "technical difficulties." Morning switched his phone to speaker and looked at the screen as it blipped on. Instead of Birnam's face, the screen showed a piece of paper.

Birnam continued. "Since Rachel turned the parade into a showdown between us and them, I want to end the first anniversary of Out Day with a real peace offering, not one delivered by doves with hawks' talons. Read the post I've written for the website."

The writing was so tiny it challenged even Morning's vampire eyes. " 'In celebration of this day, I am requesting that every Leaguer refrain from all CDing whatsoever. In the same way we have proved we no longer draw blood from the human well, we will prove we have no intention of using our powers to our advantage, or to the advantage of Lifers wishing to harness our powers. If even a white dove, the symbol of peace, can frighten a Lifer, then we must stop all CDing. We must show the most skeptical and fearful that the only CD every Leaguer wants to perform is the one that transforms us into citizens endowed with all the rights enjoyed by our mortal brothers and sisters.' "

Morning stared at the screen as it went back to black. "Rachel's never going to go along with this."

"Why not?" Birnam asked.

Morning clicked the speaker button off and re-eared his phone. "If there's no more CDing, it'll destroy her show."

"Our goal isn't the success or failure of a TV show," Birnam said. "It's getting the VRA passed."

Morning frowned. "I'm not sure she gets that."

"That's why I need your help."

Before Birnam could give him an assignment, Morning veered. "Mr. Birnam, you really want to know what I think of your post?"

"Yes."

"It's all good and noble, but a lot of Leaguers are tired of all the compromises."

"What do you mean?"

"You compromised Worldwide Out Day into American Out Day. Then you compromised us to second-class citizens. I'm not sure how much more you can ask Leaguers to swallow before they . . ." He paused, looking for the right word.

"Before they bite back?"

"I wasn't thinking that, but yeah. I mean, if you wanna stop Leaguers from playing loosey-goosey with the rules, why don't you force them to stop?"

"Force them?"

"Yeah, go old school, vamp up, and thrall them into obedience."

Birnam chuckled. "Did I vamp up and thrall you into obedience when you were feeding on Portia?"

Morning cringed. *Why had he brought that up?*

"No," Birnam answered. "I trusted in the self-control you had learned. I let you stop yourself. My vamp-up days are over. I am only here to guide us from the *selva obscura.*"

"I thought we were out of the dark woods."

"We are . . . but they will always be behind us, trying to lure us back in."

The weariness in his voice made Morning wonder: *Does Birnam know more than he's admitting? Does he know about the secret consensual bloodlust clubs Zoë mentioned?*

"The bottom line is this," Birnam explained. "If Leaguers behaving badly, like Rachel, keep stoking the fires of Becky-Dell Wallace and her Lifers behaving badly, it will come to no good. This country has a long history of suppressing the minority it fears. We could be forced onto reservations or put in internment camps. And it's not like we can return underground. We're all registered with the BVA." He paused. "Work with me, Morning. Help me stop

Rachel from waking up the vampire slayer that still lurks in all Lifers."

After hanging up, Morning's eyes traveled back to the harbor. The Statue of Liberty held her torch aloft. He sighed over the irony. All he wanted was to be a firefighter and put *out* fires. Now Birnam wanted him to take up the torch of freedom again, and wave it for the Leaguer cause.

16

𝔐other 𝔣orest

In the White Mountains of California is a forest of bristle-cone pines. The trees are gnarled, bald trunks topped with sparse tufts of green needles. If God were a barber, this would be His worst haircut.

Vampires call it the Mother Forest; it is their cradle and grave. The first vampires, the Old Ones, evolved here from an ancient tribe of cannibals, who, as they ate their way through the neighboring tribes, also began eating the bark and nuts of the bristlecone pines. The trees, being the longest living things on earth, imparted the Old Ones with the gift of immortality. When the Old Ones devoured their last neighbor and faced starvation, the tribe disbanded. That was when the first vampires, the first ambassadors of bloodlust, spread across the globe.

Ever since then, when a vampire is slain and reduced to a pile of ash, it transforms into a seedpod, which rides the wind until it returns to the Mother Forest. There, the seedpod buries itself in the soil and grows into both a vampire's last form and its tombstone: a bristlecone pine.

At the edge of the forest, in the shadow of an older, larger tree, a twisting pine grew. Unlike the bark of the older tree, with its smooth twisting lines like gray taffy, the bark of this young bristlecone pine was different. It was russet red; its lines twisted with a pace and energy that made it appear to be more like fire than wood.

As dusk fell, the tree's green needles rustled. There was no wind; the large tree towering above it was as still as stone. The small tree quivered from crown to root. The twisting creases racing up its trunk vibrated and began to split. One seam in the trunk split wider than the others; a human hand snaked out. Another followed. The hands grasped at the air like fleshy spiders looking for a grip. They found the edges of the widening rift in the trunk, and pushed. With a shattering scream of ripping wood and human lung, the red tree exploded in a cloud of splinters. What remained of the tree's cleaved trunk toppled to the ground in a dusty crash.

Where the tree had once risen, stood the issue of its birth. A man: tall, lean, naked. His skin was copper colored, not unlike the bark of the tree that had birthed him. And even though it was smooth, and streamlined with taut muscles, his flesh bore a pattern of wavy lines. His skin was grained, as if he were partially made of wood.

But this was no Pinocchio. This was a vampire like the world had never seen.

17

Shadow Games

Even though Penny Dredful had become a millionaire by managing talented Leaguers, including her biggest star, Rachel Capilarus, the Dredfuls had stayed in their duplex apartment in the lower half of a West Village town house. The mom in Penny was trying to keep it real for Portia by remaining in their modest home.

In the living room, Morning and Portia lounged on the couch, watching the first airing of the newest *Shadow* episode. Morning had his Out Day card and present for Portia in his backpack, but he wasn't producing them until he had her full attention. At the moment, Portia was like a surge protector feeding energy to various devices. There was the TV, and she was on her iPhone, texting to Cody, who was at home, editing the footage they had gotten that day.

This second distraction irritated Morning. Talking on her cell while on a date was bad enough, but texting was worse because it robbed him of at least one side of the dialogue. He figured this might be intentional on her part if they were texting about the footage of him being a jerk and implying that Penny was gouging vampires.

The third device connected to Portia was Morning. He had a leg draped over hers. It was all he could get, seeing how her hands and eyes were otherwise engaged. If her multitasking hadn't been so vexing, he might have found the situation amusing. He was watching *The Shadow* because it was one of the things they did together, but she was watching her iPhone more than the show, which was turning him into her designated TV watcher. He rehearsed his exit line for later. *Thanks for letting me come over and watch you text.* Like he had the fangs to say as much. No, he was just going to slump on the couch, feign interest in the show, and bide his time until he could blow his EB away with his card and gift.

In California, a carpet of stars stretched over the desert. The only earthly light was the flickering neon of the CA-NE FILLING SALOON. It was the lone sign of life in a cluster of buildings that was three people short of a ghost town. The Ca-Ne Filling Saloon got its name from straddling the California-Nevada border and being both gas station and bar. Its one entrance led on the right to the gas station office and on the left to the garage bay, which had been converted to a saloon.

The man who walked into the Ca-Ne was tall and lean, with a cowboy hat and the dusty duds familiar to the desert rats of these parts. Even the man's coppery skin wasn't that unusual in the desert, but to have coppery skin that was smooth and grained like a greasewood bench *was* unusual.

The bartender held his tongue upon noticing his customer's physical oddity. It wasn't a man's place to talk about another man's looks in this part of the world. And since he was the only customer the barkeep had seen all day, he wasn't going to blow a bar tab by saying something stupid like *Don't worry, Pinocchio, soon as we get a couple cold ones in ya, you'll turn into a real boy.*

Before the bartender could say howdy, the man spied someone by the back wall of the bar. He crouched in a flash and almost sprang at the stranger on the other side of the bar, but seeing the threatening stranger crouch in the exact same motion, he realized the threat was actually his reflection in a mirror.

"Whoa there," the bartender drawled, "you're wound kinda tight."

The man said nothing as he scanned his odd reflection. It was him, but different. His hair was darker, curlier. His face was thinner, his nose more pronounced. Stranger still were the lines streaking his face. He'd never had lines before; he'd become a vampire in his twenties. And his once pale skin was the color of a copper pot.

The bartender tried again. "Everything all right there, pardner?"

The vampire parted company with his reflection and moved down the bar. "Yeah, I just need a drink." He glanced around and shifted the conversation. "Kinda dead in here."

"Yep," the bartender said, then smiled with nostalgia. "But it used to be *undead.*"

The vampire arched an eyebrow as he slid onto a barstool. "What do you mean?"

"Six months ago the Ca-Ne was hoppin'. It was the

waterin' hole for all the vampire fans that visited the Mother Forest. You know, the ol' country for all vampires. But then all the fang-heads—that's what the vampire fans call themselves—started carving up the trees, trashin' the place, 'n' performing crazy rituals. That's when the feds ruined it for me. They declared the Mother Forest sacred ground, made it a Leaguer sanctuary, and closed it up tighter than a missile silo." He looked around his saloon. "Don't look it now, but for a time this place wet some whistles. Yep, when it was still open, the Mother Forest laid me a golden egg or two."

"I just came from there," the vampire offered.

The barkeep cocked his head. "Really? How'd you get in?"

"I flew."

"Chopper?"

The vampire recalled his violent birth from a pine tree. "Yeah, you could say I arrived by"—he air-quoted with single fingers—"chopper." He hadn't finished the gesture before realizing how alien it felt, like some puppeteer was working his strings. Even worse, he detested puns and had murdered people for puns more clever than the one that had shot out of his mouth like unintended spittle.

The bartender clucked. "You must be some kinda VIP."

The vampire's eyes had fallen on his hands, as streaked with russet grain as his face. "Yeah," he said, "but even VIPs get thirsty."

The bartender slapped his forehead with a laugh. "Listen to me, tendin' to talk 'n' forgettin' to tend bar. What's your pleasure, mister?"

The vampire gazed at the skin flushing up on the man's forehead. He tightened his upper lip over his swelling gums and mumbled, "Something with a head on it."

On the way to the two taps, the bartender picked up a remote and flicked the TV on over the bar. "Being into the Mother Forest and all, you must be a *Shadow* fan." The bartender flipped through channels. "It's not on till later out here, but when you get five hundred channels you can grab it early off an East Coast feed."

The vampire didn't know what he was talking about, but he kept watching the strobe of channels until the picture stopped on a beautiful woman with long black hair sitting at a table and talking to several young men and women.

"There she is," the barkeep announced, "Rachel Capilarus, the *Shadow* queen."

18

Leeches at Work

Back in the Dredful apartment, Morning bided his time; *The Shadow* would soon be over. At least Portia had stopped texting Cody and was now only splitting her focus between the TV and the neck rub Morning was giving her.

The episode's theme was health care. Rachel had shown all but one of her contestants' adventures as they shadowed a doctor or hospital worker, then CDed into something to help the medical provider in some way. Rachel gave the last contestant, a young Indian man, an adoring smile. "Prasad, last but not least." She turned to camera. "We won't give away the juicy details how Prasad found a way to make a sucky health care system even suckier. And that's a good thing!"

As the show cut to Prasad's mini-story, Portia broke from Morning's massage. "Did she really say 'suckier'?"

Prasad's segment showed him watching over a difficult surgery. Doctors were reattaching the scalp of a young musician named Skid who had gotten too close to the back-side of a huge wind fan onstage, and the fan had ripped his long hair and scalp off. The scene cut to Skid recovering from the surgery as Prasad explained to viewers that one of the big problems with reattachment surgeries is that healing gets slowed down because the artery side of healing—the side that's delivering oxygen-rich blood to the wound—works faster and more efficiently than the vein side of the healing—the side that disposes of the used "garbage blood" that has been depleted and needs to be moved away from the wound to make room for the next delivery of fresh blood. Because the vein side is slower and less efficient, blood builds up in the wound and can stall the healing process. So all that garbage blood becomes a speed bump to healing, or, as Prasad called it, "a blood bump."

The shot cut to a patient recovering from a hand re-attachment as Prasad explained that the black squirmy things on the patient's wrist were leeches. They had been placed there by medical technicians to suck up the garbage blood, to remove the speed bump to healing.

A grinning Prasad explained, "These aren't plain old leeches you'd find in a pond. They're laboratory-raised 'medical devices' approved by the FDA, and they're very expensive, which really adds up when a scalp reattachment requires hundreds of these little suckers."

As the show cut to a shot of a woman with a hundred leeches attached to her head, Morning recoiled. Not only at the sight, but also at the thought of where this was going.

Prasad announced he was going to save Skid thousands of dollars in medical bills. "But," he claimed, "I'm not going to get all creepy, fang up, and suck on Skid's head. I'm gonna do it the *Shadow* way."

The TV cut to a doctor placing a toaster-sized black leech on Skid's head. As the leech's front end pivoted on Skid's reattached scalp and sucked up small buildups of blood with its mouthparts, Skid pointed at the leech and drawled. "Check out my new pet. I call 'im Prasad."

While the TV cut to the other shadow contestants and Rachel applauding Prasad's solution, Penny came out of her home office on the way to the kitchen.

"Mom," Portia said, "did you know about this?"

"Of course, and I'm ready for the fallout. My lawyers are preparing for the lawsuit that's bound to come from the company that breeds medical leeches." She feigned a freaked-out CEO. " 'You're putting leeches out of work!' " Heading into the kitchen, she added, "They'll probably send a couple of leech goons to suck my kneecaps."

Portia laughed as Morning used the remote to kill the TV. "Don't you wanna see who gets staked?" she asked.

"After Becky-Dell Wallace gets ahold of this," he said with a scowl, "we all do."

In the Ca-Ne Saloon, the vampire sat with his untouched beer and glared at the TV. The shot panned across the *Shadow* contestants as a voice-over pondered who would get staked. The vampire wanted to stake every limp-fanged vampire who had ever turned Leaguer and abandoned the old ways.

His building rage was interrupted by the bartender. "Whoa, that's the first time a Leaguer's tapped human blood. On TV, anyway. What do you think of that?"

The vampire grumbled under the blast of a TV ad. "I'm ashamed of my race."

"What was that?"

The vampire answered with a flip of his hand. On the way to silencing the TV with a thrall, his fingers caught the rim of his glass, knocking it over. The beer shot across the bar like a foamy wave crashing on a beach.

The bartender's eyes darted to the spill, missing the flick of fingers that killed the TV. More distracted by the spill than the sudden silence, the bartender mopped the wet bar with a towel. "Don't worry. I always say, 'If the first hits the bar, the second's on the house.'"

Besides being incensed by *The Shadow*, the vampire was equally perturbed by the betrayals his body kept throwing him. First, he looked like someone else. Second, he did idiotic things like air-quote and make puns, and now he spilled a beer! He had never spilled *anything*, not counting blood, of course. There was only one explanation for his catlike reflexes being dulled, his mannerisms being affected, and his skin looking like cheap wood paneling.

The bartender, feeling the vampire's eyes, glanced up from his beer-soaked towel. "Mister, are you all right?"

"Nothing a stiff drink won't fix."

19

Stake Out

"Don't you get it?" Morning implored Portia and Penny, who had come out of the kitchen with a mug of tea and a cookie. "Prasad crossed the line. He broke the Leaguers' second commandment: 'You shall not drink anything but properly milked *animal* products, or artificial blood substitutes.' "

Penny took a sip of tea. "Our argument's going to be that he didn't do it as a Leaguer. He did it as a leech. And it was for a good cause."

"A good cause?" Morning exclaimed, jumping up from the couch. "Sure, if it's for the good cause of helping Becky-Dell Wallace turn millions of Lifers against us. Of totally destroying the chances of the VRA passing!"

"Perhaps," Penny offered calmly, "Rachel and I decided that Birnam's strategy of compromise, compromise, compromise isn't working. Maybe we decided that going on the offensive would draw out the hatemongering and bigotry of Becky-Dell and her MOPers."

Morning flapped his arms in exasperation. "And having a guy turn into a leech and suck blood out of some rocker's head is gonna do this?"

"It's a start. Now, do you want me to sit down and explain the intricacies of political strategy while I finish my tea and cookie, or do you want to finish your date with Portia on a more pleasurable note?"

Morning flopped down on the couch. From his *wordus eruptus* at the parade to hearing himself spout off like a mini-Birnam for the Leaguer cause, the day kept delivering downers. All he had wanted was a moment with Portia—just the two of them—to give her his card and present.

Portia stroked his back. "Mom, I think he's had enough of politics."

"Haven't we all," Penny said, moving into her office.

Portia pushed Morning's head back on the couch. "Shut your eyes." He obeyed as she stroked his forehead and scalp stubble. "When people get fired up and start seeing the world as black versus white, Leaguer versus Lifer, bloodsucker versus blood-suckee, you know what I think of?"

"What?"

"My favorite page on the IVL website."

"Which one?"

"I'll give you a hint." She lifted his shirt and kissed his belly button.

Her lips tickled his skin and launched a bubble of excitement in his solar plexus. He smiled at the memory of the page. " 'How to see a vampire in three easy steps.' "

"Right. Just go look in a mirror, 'cause that's how we all begin, drinking the blood of our mother through an umbilical cord."

Morning opened his eyes and took her in. That was

why he loved her so much. She could make the whole bad world go away with just a few words and her lips. He sat up, pushed her back, lifted her shirt, and returned her belly button kiss. "Thanks, I needed that."

Portia giggled. "You're welcome."

He reached over the end of the couch and pulled up his backpack. He dug out the card and the wrapped present.

"You got me something?"

"For Out Day, sure."

"But I didn't get you anything," she said.

He handed her the card. "You know me, I don't like to take, I like to give."

She opened it and chuckled at the corny joke about vampires always being able to outdrink mortals. Then she read his note.

Dear Portia,
    The only "out day" that matters is the day you pulled a thorn out of my heart. You've been pulling my heartstrings ever since.

                                            Your EB,
                                            Morning

She mimed plucking his heart strings—"Twang"—then gave him a kiss. Holding up the long box of a present, she had an idea of what it might be. She opened it and laughed with recognition at a croquet stake, painted with multicolored rings. "You kept it?"

"Of course," he said with a warm smile. "It was the first time we held hands."

A year before, the two of them had pulled the stake out of Morning's chest after he had been staked by a clueless vampire slayer that Ikor DeThanatos had hired to destroy him. When Morning had pressed Portia's hand over the wound as it healed, it was the first time she had felt herself dive into the quavering current of true love.

"Yeah," she said with a puckish smile, "when a girl pulls one of these out of your heart, you don't toss it in the sports closet." She leaned in and planted another kiss.

They fell back and made out. Portia was amazed by what a great kisser Morning had become since the disaster of their first kiss, when he had gotten *maximus dentis eruptus* and his teeth had blown up like microwave popcorn.

Throat clearing cut short their makeout session as Penny passed through the living room. They shot upright.

Portia tried to cover being busted by lifting the stake and waving it. "Hey, Mom, it used to be that girls got pinned; now they get staked!"

20

Button Down!

The next morning at the fire academy, Morning's crew gave him a good dose of teasing. "Yo, McCobb, if I lose my head and they reattach it, you gonna turn into a leech and suck my neck?" "Hey, Morning, I hear they're gonna put you on Rescue; with all the road spill they clean up, you could be a one-leech wet vac." Morning took it and gave back as best he could. He didn't mind the trash talk. If his fellow pro-bies *didn't* tease him it would've been worse. Talking trash was part of the brotherhood, part of the glue that bonded a crew. By lunch, the talk had swung to Rachel.

"Hey, Morno, can you get me a date with Earth Angel?" Armando asked. "If that babe wants to turn into a dove and spank me with an olive branch, I am so there!"

"She doesn't have to dove-up for me," another probie added. "I'd have her turn into Siamese twins."

Another urged Morning to take them for a night on the town in which they pretended to be Leaguers so they could meet hot goth girls who wanted to hook up with vampires.

Sully snorted. "Last I checked, you didn't have to be a vampire to get babes. You just had to be a fireman." He leaned across the table to Morning. "Here's what I wanna know. When you were marching in the parade, what was that thing around your neck? A peace sign? I mean, isn't being the first vampire firefighter enough? You also wanna be the first *hippie* vampire firefighter?"

"It's not a peace sign," Morning corrected. "It's a good-luck thing."

"Cool." Sully waggled his fingers. "Let's see it."

"I don't wear it here."

"C'mon," Sully pressed, "if there's anywhere you need good luck, it's here."

"Wearing loose stuff is against the rules, you know that," Morning reminded him.

Sully gave a sneering laugh. "But you're a vampire, McCobb. Bustin' rules is what you do."

Armando cut in, trying to break the tension. "Give it a rest, Sully."

Sully stared at Morning. "After I see it. C'mon"—his hand raised—"give it."

Morning didn't move. "I told you I'm not wearing it."

Sully's hand flew at Morning's collar. Morning yanked back, but Sully's fingers snagged his shirt long enough to rip off a button. The button skidded off the table as a probie uttered a warning. "Clancy."

Every probie in the dining hall jumped to their feet, standing at stiff attention.

"At ease," Clancy ordered. "Everyone but this bunch." He moved around Morning's crew. His eye caught the skewed angle of Morning's collar. "I wasn't planning an inspection, but sometimes I have to surprise myself." He moved in on Morning and fixed on the frayed threads of the missing button. "Your uniform's incomplete, McCobb."

"Yes, sir, I'm missing a button."

Clancy went drill sergeant. "When you're a probie your uniform is the only gear you're a hundred percent responsible for. If you show up to school wearin' faulty gear, you'll show up to a fire wearin' faulty gear! You do that and you'll get a brother killed! You just earned yourself a demerit, McCobb!"

"Sir," Sully said, "it wasn't his fault."

Clancy whipped around to his nephew. "Whose fault was it, Sullivan?"

"Mine. We were roughhousing and—"

"You were *roughhousing*?"

"Yes, sir, and—"

Clancy cut him off. "Is this a mess hall or a romper room for booger eaters?"

Sully answered. "A mess hall, sir."

"The way I see it," Clancy shouted, "if you *were* roughhousing and a probie's button was on the floor, he'd be crawling around lookin' for it!" He got back in Morning's face. "Am I right, hose weenie?"

Morning stared dead ahead. "Yes, sir. There was no roughhousing. I wore a defective shirt to school."

Clancy sneered with satisfaction and lowered his voice to menacing. "That's right. Just a few more screwups, McCobb, and your shirt, along with the pathetic probie inside it, won't be *comin'* to school. You got that?"

Morning nodded. "Yes, sir."

On the way out, Clancy's boot crunched on the button. He never looked back. "At ease!"

The probies sat and stared at their lunch trays.

Sully finally muttered, "Why'd you do that?"

Morning shrugged. "What?"

"Cover my ass."

Morning stood up and grabbed his empty can of Blood Lite. "You don't have to like me, Sully. You just need to know I've got your back. Isn't that what we're here for?"

As Morning walked away, Sully flushed red. From embarrassment or anger, no one could tell.

21

Blood Feud

At LaGuardia Arts, Portia was cramming books in her locker. Nearby, Zoë was on her knees, waving her outstretched arms toward Portia. "Go ahead," Zoë said. "Guess what I am."

"I don't know," Portia huffed. "Toulouse-Lautrec doing a Frankenstein impression."

"No. Hint: I'm a blood obligate."

Portia shut her locker with a bang. "I know you're a bloodsucker. It's the only impressions you do."

"Yeah, but which one?" Zoë stretched her waving arms toward Portia's jeans and monotoned, "Pant leg, pant leg."

"Don't have time for this." Portia moved around Zoë and started down the hall.

Zoë jumped to her feet and followed with outstretched arms. "I'm a questing tick! Pant leg, pant leg!"

Cody sat in the editing room watching TV. Ally Alfamen was finishing a special report when Portia and Zoë came through the door. "You're not gonna believe it," he said. "The Bureau of Vampire Affairs yanked *The Shadow*."

Portia stopped in her tracks. "What?"

"Yeah, show's been canceled," Cody added. "After the big fat leech went Edward Scissorlips on Skid's head, and the clip went pan-viral on YouTube, the network and the BVA got avalanched with protests."

Zoë threw up her hands. "It was just a blood obligate being a blood obligate!" Then she collapsed in a chair. "Do you know what this means?"

"Yeah," Portia said flatly, "my mom's gonna take hormonal rage to uncharted territory."

"That," Zoë lamented, "and I'll never be on *The Shadow*. I'll never be top shadow!"

"Zoë," Portia pointed out, "you're not a vampire."

"I would've been by next season!" Zoë bounced in her chair like she was about to explode. "But that's not the worst part! It's the beginning of the backlash, of shoving vampires back underground, of massive blood shortages!" Her eyes popped wider. "The beginning of blood *prohibition*!"

Cody took her shoulders in both hands. "ZZ, it's only a TV show. You might be overreacting."

Zoë shook him off and leaped up. "Maybe." Her face hardened. "But a year from now I'm not gonna die of thirst!" She started out.

"Where are you going?" Portia called.

Zoë didn't turn back. "To start my blood stash!"

Before Portia and Cody could confer on the mental stability of their friend, the TV grabbed their attention.

It carried a shot of the steps in front of the U.S. Capitol, crowded with members of the Mortals Only Party. Becky-Dell Wallace was beginning a press conference.

She stepped up to the microphones. Light bounced off her glasses. She began soberly. "For those of you who think of me as a stake-rattling, conspiracy-theory nutcase, I respect your right to keep your head firmly buried in the sand. But last night, we saw more than an episode of *The Shadow*: we saw more than a Leaguer turn into a leech and drink human blood. We saw a vampire suck its first blood from the American soul. We saw the true agenda of the International Vampire League." Her voice rose with fervor. "Their cape has been pulled aside and we've seen their one desire: To gorge on our blood! To welter in bloodlust!"

The MOPers shouted and booed.

Becky-Dell cleared a lock of hair from her glasses, and fixed the camera with eyes of steel. "We have seen the red menace of this century. We are going to fight it from the halls of Congress to the streets. We will defeat the Vampire Rights Act! We will not let them turn our country into the new Transylvania! Because we are a nation of the mortals, by the mortals, and for the mortals!"

As the crowd bellowed its support and the picture cut to Ally Alfamen, Cody flipped the TV off. " 'The new Transylvania'? Does she actually think Dracula was real?"

Portia stared ahead, eyes narrowed. "It's rhetoric, Cody, the PR war for hearts and minds." She steepled her fingers and tapped them together. "*The Shadow* getting canceled is bad, but there's a silver lining."

"What?"

Portia turned to her partner in film. "Rachel's schedule suddenly opened up for our interview with her."

IVLEAGUE

AN APOLOGY

The IVL condemns the drinking of human blood, even for medical reasons. It violates the Leaguer commandment of restricting our diet to animal or artificial blood.

The IVL fully supports the canceling of *The Shadow* and offers a profound apology to Lifers for this despicable incident.

To my fellow Leaguers I say this: should we dip into the human well again—for any reason whatsoever—our dream of freedom will drown in it.

Luther Birnam
President

22

Generation BC

In the top-floor office of Diamond Sky Productions, Penny sat at her desk and finished reading Birnam's post. She looked over her desk at Rachel, sprawled in an easy chair. Spread-eagle, with her head thrown back, Rachel resembled a Raggedy Ann doll that had been tossed there.

"Did you hear what I read?" Penny asked.

Rachel heaved a sigh. "Yeah."

"Is that all you have to say?"

Rachel answered in a pitiful voice. "All I wanna do is be an Earth Angel, and what do they do? Crucify me."

Penny's brow knitted. "How 'bout we drop the martyr act and figure out how we're going to respond."

Rachel sprang out of the chair and paced. "I mean, I don't get it. What's the point of freedom? What's the point of the VRA passing or not passing if we can't exercise the ultimate American freedom: making good TV?"

Penny's computer blipped and the Skype menu appeared. She read the name of the caller. "It's Birnam."

Rachel stopped mid-pace.

"Should we talk to him?" Penny asked.

"Damn straight!" Rachel swept around the desk and dropped to her knees so they could both be seen on the Skype screen.

Birnam's video feed was blank, but his voice came through loud and clear. "Hello, my two favorite newsmakers, the Queen of Spin and the Princess of Mayhem. Sorry about playing the Prince of Darkness, but the camera on my computer is on the fritz."

"Is that why you called?" Penny asked. "To see if we can fix it?"

He chuckled. "No, I wanted to talk to Rachel about her dramatic twenty-four hours. Yesterday you soared like bird, today you crashed back to earth."

Rachel eye-rolled. "If you're gonna tell me the Icarus story, flying too close to the sun and all that—"

"I wasn't," he cut in, "but now that I think of it—"

"Now that *I* think of it," she interrupted back, "you might be old enough to have been there when Icarus fell out of the sky, which is my point."

"Sometimes your point evades me, Rachel," Birnam said, sounding bemused. "What point is that?"

"You're from generation BC."

Penny grimaced. "Ooh, harsh."

"I don't wanna hurt your feelings, Mr. Birnam; I don't wanna hurt anyone's feelings. I'm just saying there's a new generation in town."

"And that is?" he asked.

"Generation V."

"Ah, yes." He chortled. "Eternal youth."

Rachel took a breath. "Mr. Birnam, you've done super-amazing things for vampires. If it weren't for you, we'd still be wild-ass punks jumpin' necks for joyrides. But in your long fight for equality, you've gone too far."

"How do you mean?"

"By making us burn our fangs in the public square."

"You lost me."

"Me too," Penny said.

Rachel huffed with impatience. "It's so obvious. The feminists burned their bras back in the seventies, right?"

Penny nodded. "My mother was one of 'em."

"And," Rachel continued, "it turned out bra-burning was a feminist disaster 'cause they weren't listening to all the women who still wanted to wear bras!"

"What on earth," Birnam asked, "does bra-burning have to do with fang-burning?"

"I think I know what she's getting at," Penny said.

"Help me understand," Birnam pleaded.

Penny continued. "Early feminists wanted women to step up to the table of equality and be just like men. It didn't work. Women wanted to be *women*, too. They wanted to be equal and free and *sexy* at the same time. They wanted to step up to the table with their full skill set."

"Right!" Rachel jumped back in. "And just like women, there's lots of vampires who wanna step up to the table with their full skill set. In the seventies when women were fighting for equality, people—*male* people— were freakin' out. They were thinking, *Oh, man, women are gonna cry every time something goes super wrong.* Or, *Damn, women are gonna go hysterical every time they get their period.* Did any of that go down? Don't think so. 'Cause women brought their *best selves* to the table. And now, as vampires are about to step up to equality, mortals are freakin' over the same crap. They're thinkin',

100

Oh, man, every time someone gets a paper cut vampires are gonna pop fangs. And *Oh, damn, every time vampires lose their temper they're gonna turn into a fire-breathing dragon and roast someone.* But we won't do those things, 'cause just like women, we're gonna bring our *best selves* to the table. We're gonna step up to the table and be Earth Angels!"

There was a pause before Birnam spoke. "Very impressive, Ms. Capilarus, very forward-thinking. But I would advise you to head up to Leaguer Academy Two for a refresher course in CD Management and Lifer Awareness. You need to reacquaint yourself with a vampire skill more crucial to our survival than all others."

"What's that?" Penny asked.

"The ability to smell mortal fear. The scent tells us when to pounce, and when to wait. I fear your olfactory powers have been dulled by your naïve belief that the earth *devils* we've been for thousands of years have been completely eradicated, and, with a dash of fairy dust, we have been transformed into 'earth angels.' "

Rachel started to object, but Penny raised a hand, silencing her. "Thank you, Luther, it's all very good advice. Rachel and I will take it to heart."

Early that evening, Portia and Cody were loading Zoë's pedicab with lighting and sound equipment. Penny had told her daughter that Rachel was free to give them an interview that evening at Diamond Sky. Portia was bringing her camera down the front stoop when she almost tripped over Mr. and Mrs. Nesbit, the elderly couple who lived on the top two floors of the town house.

"Goodness, aren't we in a rush," Mrs. Nesbit stated more than asked.

"Sorry, Mrs. Nesbit." Portia squeezed by them. "Great filmmaking stops for no one."

Portia's phone rang. She pulled it out and hit speaker so she could take the call while handling the camera and finding a space for herself in the pedicab not already occupied by Cody or equipment. "Hey, what's up?"

Morning's voice sounded over the speaker. "You got a minute?"

"Not really," she answered, squeezing in next to Cody. "I'm headed to an interview with Rachel for our film."

"C'mon, Harry Potter," Cody urged Zoë as she stood on her pedals to get the pedicab moving. "Get this Firebolt up to speed."

"Is everything okay?" Portia asked Morning.

"Yeah, I'm just a little nervous about our first live fire exercise tomorrow. I wanted to talk to you."

"You'll do fine," she reassured him. "But, Morn, I can't talk now. I gotta work on my interview questions. Call you later, okay?"

"Okay," he said, masking his disappointment. "Later."

23

When in Rome

The extra weight in Zoë's pedicab didn't seem to slow her. On the contrary, delivering her best friend and Cody to an interview with the famous—and now infamous—Rachel Capilarus had Zoë's veins coursing with adrenaline. "You're gonna let me come in and watch, right?" she asked.

Portia didn't look up from the pad she was writing questions on. "If you promise not to say a word or even *think* about entertaining Rachel with one of your blood-obligate impressions."

"Yeah," Cody added, "it's not like we're shootin' the sequel to *Never Been Kissed: Never Been Bitten.*"

"I'll be good, I promise," Zoë declared, then burst into lyrics from her version of "Part of Your World." "I wanna be where the vampires are / I wanna see, I wanna see 'em feedin' / Stalking around with those—what do you call 'em? / Oh, fangs!"

Unbeknownst to Zoë, she was closer to a vampire than she thought. She had just ridden by one in the window of a beauty salon.

The vampire with the coppery complexion sat inside Trixie's Pamper Parlor. He was having his skin exfoliated. While he was an odd combination of flesh, bone, and a touch of bristlecone pine, the beautician, Trixie herself, was a blend of Southern charm and New York moxie.

The vampire was glued to the television in the corner as the evening news covered the story of *The Shadow* being canceled and Becky-Dell's declaration of war against the new "red menace."

Trixie peeled another bacon-sized shaving of dried skin off her customer's face. "I haven't seen skin like this since my Uncle Bodly fell asleep in his fishin' floatie and caught himself a second-degree burn."

The vampire's insides shuddered at the thought of sunlight.

Trixie peeled away another shaving and gave him a flirtatious wink. "But you look more like a lifeguard who fell asleep in his guard chair."

"It's not a sunburn," the vampire declared, wanting to get away from sunny topics. "I suffer from a rare kind of dermatitis: poison birch."

Trixie recoiled. "Is it contagious, like poison ivy?"

"Not at all," he assured her, "that's why it's so rare. It's impossible to catch."

"Then how did you get it?"

"I was born with it. And once a year, I peel like a birch tree."

"Don't that beat all," she said, getting back to her exfoliating. "I just hope your folks didn't name you Woody."

"No, that's my twin brother's name," the vampire deadpanned. "My name is Forest."

Trixie reared back and jammed her hands on her hips. "You're pullin' my leg!"

The vampire's response popped out of his mouth before he could stop it. "And you're pullin' my skin." As Trixie laughed he silently cursed himself. It was the second time in twenty-four hours his mouth had betrayed him with asinine jokes. To change the subject he nodded at the TV. "Does so much always happen in one day around here?"

"Oh, yeah." Trixie nodded. "A day in New York is like six months anywhere else. Did you just get here?"

"I came in on the red-eye last night," the vampire replied. "But I got to sleep all day."

"Well, once you get over your poison birch, you're gonna havta do better than that."

Although the vampire had been visiting Manhattan ever since 1614, when it was a fur-trading post called New Amsterdam, he went with her lead. "What do you mean?"

Trixie leaned back and examined her work. "If you wanna take New York by storm, you gotta go day and night, twenty-four-seven." Her customer's skin was now smooth but still showed a hint of streaking. She squirted a dollop of antiaging cream in her palm.

As Trixie applied the cream to his face, the vampire closed his eyes and pondered her advice. In his long past, working nights had provided more than enough time to exercise his brand of death and devastation. But now, given the heap of revenge, terror, and destruction he had planned for certain mortals and immortals, he wondered if it was time to borrow a page from the Leaguer manual and get over his restricting and irrational fear of sunlight. *Yes,* he told himself, *when in Rome, do as the Romans.*

"All right," Trixie said. "Anything else I can do fer ya? Manicure? Pedicure?" She fluffed his long, curly locks. "Give your hair a little trim and straighten?"

Whatever pleasure lingered from the face massage he had just received evaporated with the reminder that his once straight hair had mysteriously gone curly. "All I need are some directions."

"Where to?" she obliged.

"Leaguer Academy Two."

She stepped back. "Are you tellin' me I just exfoliated a vampire?"

He glanced down at the skin shavings on his spa robe. "Do vampires have problems like this?"

Trixie laughed with relief. "Of course not."

Leaguer Academy II sat on high bluffs rising above the Hudson. The manicured grounds rolled down to the river, sparkling in the light of a full moon.

Inside the academy, an instructor was sleeping soundly in her quarters, when she woke with a gasp. A darting scan of the shadows revealed nothing, but she sensed someone. "Who's there?" she asked breathlessly.

A calm voice came from darkness. "I'm not here to hurt you. My name is Varkos." The figure stepped into the moonlight piercing the window. His copper skin looked black in the dim light. "I'm in need of your expertise."

The Leaguer sat up, her forehead contracted with suspicion. "What kind of expertise?"

106

"I understand you teach vampires how to overcome—how do you Leaguers call it?—solar phobia."

"That's right."

"I need a crash course."

The Leaguer swung out of bed. "Look, Varkos—if that's really your name—you need to do like every Loner who comes in from the dark. You need to enroll in the academy and take all the training that transitions Loners to Leaguers."

He gestured regretfully. "I don't have time for that."

"You're a vampire, you have oodles of time."

Perhaps it was his impatience, or his ears being assaulted by "oodles"—ears that had heard the premiere of *Hamlet* at the Globe—whatever; Varkos had heard enough. He flipped up a hand and put the instructor in a thrall. He had asked nicely, now it was time for his tutor to tute.

Several hours later, Varkos stood on a bluff overlooking the river. His teacher, Beth, stood behind him with a glazed expression. Sometimes teachers just go through the motions of instruction, like they're phoning it in. Beth, still in a deep thrall, had done just that as she had run Varkos through the gauntlet of overcoming solar phobia.

The moment of truth in her crash course was close at hand: the moment the sun peeked over the ridge on the east side of the river. Varkos spread his arms and prepared for his fate: to dance like a worm on a hot griddle, or to become what Leaguers called a day-timer.

For a split second, Varkos tasted the bile of fear. *What if*, his mind fretted, *after more than a thousand years of darkness, the light is too much? What if the demon of my revenge dies in the cradle?* "No matter," he whispered across the river to the blooming sunrise. "I have been destroyed before and rose from the ground anew. Pierce me with light. I am indestructible."

The sun peeked over the ridge; the first ray caught his coppery face. There was no bubbling of flesh, no burst of incineration. His eyes simply squinted against the unaccustomed brightness. Varkos had overcome the vampire's age-old fear of sunlight the same way a fire walker overcomes the pain of fire: mind over matter.

He answered the sun with a beaming smile. "I'll be damned." After his eyes adjusted and he took in an illuminated world he had not seen for eons, he turned and faced Beth. He flicked a hand at her.

She jolted out of her thrall. She was so disoriented she was only capable of one word at a time. "What?"

He thrust an arm toward the river. "Sunrise!" he announced with a boyish grin. "My first in ages."

She blinked at the bluff they were standing on. "How?"

"Night class. You were brilliant."

She gaped at the man silhouetted by the sun. "Who?"

He lifted his arms slowly. "Got an updraft to catch. Thanks for showing me the light."

He suddenly imploded into a peregrine falcon and lifted on the elevator of air rising from the sunlit bluffs.

24

Live Fire

At the fire academy, two trucks—a ladder and a pumper—sirened along the row of cinder-block buildings designed to duplicate the fires New York firefighters faced. The trucks lurched to a halt in front of a four-floor building known as a "taxpayer" because it had a business on the ground floor and apartments above it. Smoke trailed from two top floors. Geared up and ready to fight fire, Morning and his crew leaped from the trucks.

As the crew grabbed their irons, water cans, and various equipment, a bone-chilling cry for help burst from the building's top floor.

"Whoa, that sounded real!" Armando shouted.

Morning wondered if everyone else on the crew was just as jacked with adrenaline as he was. Another terrifying cry for help banged the probies' eyes wider.

Captain Clancy stepped out of an operations command truck. "Those are real flames and real screams," he informed them. "To get you water lilies ready for the real deal, we're throwin' all the reality we can at you."

Another shriek ripped the air.

"So that's *real*?" Armando asked.

"Absolutely, as real as recordings get." Another scream sounded, making Clancy grin. "I love it when they intro a new mix; it even gives *me* the chills." He got back to business. "Okay, tanker piglets, ready to do a victim search and knock down some fire?"

"Yes, sir!" the probies chorused.

Clancy turned to Morning's unit: a half-dozen probies near the ladder truck. "Team A, your job's simple as VES: vent, enter, search." He turned to the group by the pumper. "Team B, you're on fire repression. It's time to see what you hose jockeys are made of."

"Yes, sir!" the probies shouted.

Clancy pointed at Morning. "McCobb, take the point on rescue, call it as it goes, and don't screw up. I got cameras all over the building trackin' every move. After mop-up, we look at game films." Another scream ripped the air. "Now go eat smoke and bring home the bacon!"

Morning assigned two probies to breach the roll-down gate locking up the street-level entrance and two more to search the ground floor. He led the others through the tenant entrance, and they used a "bunny tool" with a hydraulic piston to kick the door open. As he led the team up the stairs toward the screams, he ordered two more probies to reconnoiter the second-floor apartments. He did the same on the third floor as he, Armando, and Sully kept humping up the stairs to the fourth floor.

The top floor was filled with smoke and the flash of flames. They lowered face pieces, connected their SCBA air-tank hoses, and pierced the increasing heat and smoke as Morning sent Armando and Sully to search the front apartments for victims.

Crawling through the smoke toward the rear of the building, Morning could see the grilles and pipes discharging smoke and fire. The emergency was staged, but the smoke and flames were plenty real. Another scream came from the end of the hallway and to his right. He dodged a jet of fire, and the sprays of water now coming through the windows and a hole newly opened in the roof.

Down in the command truck, a technician was trying to figure out why all of the cameras were down and the dozen video screens were black.

"How can I bust my probies' butts," Clancy yelled at the tech, "if I can't see 'em screwin' up?" The tech protested that everything had been working fine the day before, but he got shouted down by Clancy. "Fix it!"

As Morning heard Armando and Sully banging open doors with their Halligans, he made it to the last apartment. Another scream came from inside. He wondered what horror movie the fire academy had gotten the screams from and figured Cody would probably know the answer.

He stood up in the swirling smoke and pulled back his Halligan to ram it into the doorjamb. Then he remembered one of the first rules of firefighting: try before you pry. He turned the knob and pushed the door open against the cushion of heat. He lowered his head into the heat blast, hit the floor, and crawled into what looked and felt like a fiery, smoking oven. That or the mouth of the red dragon.

Crawling and feeling his way around the perimeter, he hit a pile of clothes. His ax got tangled in it and he fell, almost impaling his face piece with the blade. *Great,* he thought, *when everyone sees that, they're gonna have a laugh over the probie who could even screw up a crawl.*

Through the billowing smoke, the shape of a bed appeared as a strangled scream choked to coughing gasps. Morning was startled by the lengths the academy went to re-create the sounds of a smoke-inhalation victim before he or she passed out. He could just make out the silhouette of the dummy on the bed. But it was seated with its back against the bed frame. *Something's not right,* he thought. *Why isn't the mannequin on the floor, where any victim would be as they tried to stay below the heat and smoke?*

The dummy's body slumped forward and the realization hit Morning like backdraft. It was no dummy. It was a young woman with long dark hair. It was *Portia.*

In an instant, the fiery oven of the room became the red dragon. And he was in the grip of the crimson terror. He yelled into his comm device for Armando and Sully, then sucked in a deep breath. He yanked off his face piece and jerked it onto Portia's head. Then he saw why she wasn't on the floor. She was duct-taped to the metal bed frame. He ripped at the tape. Her head lolled into him as she groaned back to consciousness.

He yanked her away from the frame and they rolled to the floor. For a second he saw her terrified eyes through the face piece. He pulled her onto his back and turtle-crawled toward the door.

As soon as they reached the hall, now clearing of smoke and fire, he gulped a lungful of air and rolled Portia off his back. She started to get up, but he pushed her back down, shouting, "On your belly!"

Smoldering lines zebraed the back of her jacket where the metal frame had become so hot it had started to melt and burn the fleece. Morning threw off his gloves, grabbed the jacket's back, and ripped away the smoldering panel.

Armando and Sully ran up. "Holy shit!" Armando hit his comm device and barked into it. "Status change: it's no dummy, it's a live one! Abort the exercise!"

Morning and Sully helped Portia down the stairs and out of the building. Her lungs were too busy trying to purge themselves of smoke for her to answer Morning's frantic questions. When they hit the stoop, the technician ran past them into the tenement, now free of fire but still trailing smoke. Two EMTs rushed up to Portia. Between coughs she waved them off and sat on the steps. "Just give me some air."

Clancy pushed the EMTs aside and stood over Portia. "What the hell were you doing in my building?"

Morning answered. "She wasn't there by choice. She was tied up."

"Tied up?"

Portia coughed, and rasped, "I'm okay."

Clancy thrust out an arm. "Well, I'm not! I need some answers. You could've died in there. Who did this?"

She fought back tears. "I don't know."

"You don't know?" Clancy echoed in disbelief.

She finally sucked in a full breath. "The last thing I remember was going for a run before sunrise. The next thing I knew I was taped to a bed in the middle of a fire." A coughing fit interrupted her. "I don't know how I got here."

The tech came out of the building. "The camera lenses were all spray-painted. This wasn't some prank. Whoever did it wanted her dead."

Hearing that and realizing how close she had come

to dying caught up with Portia. She buried her face in her hands with a sob.

The tech lifted an armful of clothing. "It gets weirder. Whoever it was left these near the bed."

Morning realized that was what he'd gotten tangled in as he crawled toward the bed. His stomach flip-flopped with the knowledge of who might leave clothing behind: a vampire who had CDed into another creature.

Clancy stared down at Portia. "Young lady, were you sexually assaulted?"

Still hiding her face in her hands, Portia shook her head no.

"How do you know if you can't remember anything since before sunrise?"

Her head jerked up; she glared at Clancy through teary eyes. "I would know, okay?"

Clancy took Portia and Morning to his office to record their statements about what had happened. Portia was still in her sweats, minus the smoldering jacket Morning had ripped off her back. Morning had discarded his bunker coat and wore his suspendered turnout pants over a T-shirt.

After hearing Portia's last name, Clancy's eyes darted between the two of them. "Wait a sec. If I remember what I read in the paper a year ago, you two know each other, and you're some kind of item." He said the last word like it was dirty. "Is that right, McCobb? Is she your girlfriend?"

Morning nodded. "Yes, sir."

"Damn." Clancy scowled. "This is getting more bizarre by the minute." He pointed at Portia. "And your mother, isn't she the woman who makes that TV show, *The Shadow*?"

"Yeah," Portia said, without adding the *So?*

He lifted the phone on his desk. "What's her number?"

"Do we have to call her?" Portia asked.

"You were abducted and almost died," he said sternly. "I'm sure as hell gonna call your mother."

"Besides," Morning added, "she's gotta be worried sick since you didn't come back from your run."

"She's traveling," Portia said as she sat up and gave Clancy her poker face. "Look, Captain Clancy, my mother also runs a PR firm. Putting stories in the news is what she does. How do you think the fire academy's gonna look when everyone knows you almost killed an innocent victim in a training exercise that was supposed to be safe? And it was on your watch," she added to make herself crystal clear.

It was hard to tell who was more shocked, Clancy or Morning. As Clancy studied Portia, Morning spoke up. "Portia, we can't pretend it didn't happen."

"I know. But in the end no one got hurt. I'm just suggesting that my mom and the public don't need to know about this until Captain Clancy has completed his investigation."

"What about my crew?" Morning protested. "They all saw what happened."

"I'll handle them, McCobb," Clancy said. "For now we'll keep this investigation internal, except, of course, for having the abductor's clothing scrubbed for DNA by the police." He turned to Portia. "We'll also check the security cameras for the when, how, and who of this unfortunate event. You're lucky to be alive, Ms. Dredful, and I speak for everyone at the academy when I say we appreciate how you're handling this." He pulled a business card from a desk drawer and wrote on it. "The fact that your coughing

115

has abated so quickly is a sign that any smoke-inhalation injury has been very minimal. But if you experience nausea, vomiting, sleepiness, or confusion, don't hesitate to call the doctor's number on my card." He handed the card to Portia. "Whenever we have a damaged set of lungs, he's our go-to doc. Naturally, the bill's on the FDNY." Clancy stood up. "How can I get ahold of you if I have more questions?"

"Morning has my number," she said.

"All right. McCobb, make sure she gets home safe." His mouth twitched toward satisfaction. "And my compliments on your tastes, probie. You picked a smart girl."

25

Involuntary Muscle Contraction

Morning and Portia walked out of the administration building. All he wanted to do was wrap her in his arms. But he could feel dozens of eyes watching from the classroom buildings. By now, word had spread and everyone in the academy probably knew about his rescue—his first "carry," in firefighter lingo. "Walk with me," he said, resisting the urge to take her hand.

They headed out the front gate and into the sports park next to the academy. Morning didn't want to talk, and oddly, Portia didn't fill the silence. He just rejoiced in the brush of her arm against his. Her arm was still there to be brushed. She was still alive. If events had gone down the slightest bit differently, that arm could have been lifeless now. Portia would have been gone.

When they reached a knoll with a bench overlooking the East River, they shared a long hug.

Her smoky sweat suit filled Morning's nose. Not letting

go, he said, "I never thought you'd be the one who smelled like smoke."

She gently snapped the suspenders holding up his big, baggy turnout pants. "And I never thought I'd be rescued by someone dressed like a clown."

He laughed, reassured that she was back to her joking self. They pulled apart and sat on the bench. The silence returned. Something pulled his eyes down to Portia's crossed leg. Her foot twitched a steady rhythm. It wasn't a nervous foot shake, it was something he had never noticed. Then he remembered his basic anatomy. It was the involuntary muscle contraction all humans have in their legs to push the venous blood taking the long journey back to the heart. When you cross your legs, the contraction is so strong it gives your foot the slightest waggle.

He reached down and held her foot, not so much wanting to still it as to feel the life coursing through her. The thrum-thrum of her pulse pushed into his fingers and palm.

"Let me guess," Portia said with a half smile. "You saved my life, so you think you've earned the right to be totally honest, and you're saying, 'Being a vampire isn't my problem, it's this little fetish I have for feet.'"

He let go of her foot. "The only fetish I have is a Portia fetish."

They watched a tugboat pushing a barge up the river.

"Is that really all you remembered?" he asked. "What you told Clancy?"

"For the most part, yeah."

"'For the most part'?" He ignored her beleaguered look. "Portia, it's me. You gotta tell me everything you remember. I'm guessing it was a vampire who did this."

"How do you know?"

"The clothes, your memory loss. He probably thralled you, brought you up here super early, then waited till we started the live fire exercise. As soon as it started, he unthralled you, then CDed into something and took off."

"But how would he know there was a live fire exercise? Are there other vampires in the academy?"

"Nobody but me, that I know of. Whoever this vampire was, he did his homework." Morning realized the vampire had probably done something else—conquered his solar phobia—which he wasn't going to bring up. The last thing Portia needed was to fear for her life night *and* day.

She tossed a hand in exasperation. "But if he wanted me dead why didn't he just kill me?"

"I don't know. But you gotta tell me everything you *do* remember so maybe we can figure out who it is."

She heaved a breath, which made her cough. Then she slipped into the memory. "I left the house and was doing my warm-up walk to the river for my run. I was walking around a corner shop with lots of windows when I thought I saw my reflection. It was my reflection and it wasn't."

"What do you mean?"

"It had my hair, and the face was pretty much mine, but different. The head was higher and looked more like a guy's. For a second, I felt like I was looking at the brother I never had. It was doubly weird; it was a brother and it was one of those I-know-you-from-somewhere moments. Then I saw his arm begin to raise and that was it."

"So he did thrall you."

She pushed a lock of hair from her face. "Why would a vampire want me dead?"

"And why would he set it up so I was going to either save you or be there when you died?"

She stared at the river. "I'm scared, Morning."

"I'm not gonna let anything happen to you," he said, but he heard a hollowness in his voice. All he wanted to do was drown his doubts in a kiss. He leaned in.

She accepted his lips. It pulled her into a river of desire, washing away the fear and the smoky smell.

For Morning, as soon as her tongue sought his, he felt an odd sensation, like her tongue carried two small pills and pressed them against his gums. But there was nothing on her tongue. The sensation was coming from him. He pushed her tongue back, not wanting her to feel the swelling twinge in his gums. He knew the first sign of *dentis eruptus,* a sensation he had hoped to never feel again. He eased out of the kiss, hoping she didn't think it abrupt and hadn't sensed his budding fangs.

Her eyes opened. Her lips quirked with curiosity. "Everything okay?"

"Yeah, fine," he muttered, looking down. His eyes fell on her foot again. It seemed to pulse harder now, like a big heart with toes. "Hmm," he grunted as he yanked his gaze back to her. "Everything's super-fine." He grabbed her hand and pulled her up. "C'mon, I'll take you home."

"I'm not going home," she said as they walked. "I'm late enough for school as it is."

"If you go to school smelling like a smoke machine they'll wanna know why."

"I'll pick up a new outfit at the thrift store near school and catch a shower in the nurse's office." She took his arm and teased, "Is that why you cut our kiss short? I taste like a fireplace?"

"Nooo," he said, stretching the word out as he fished for a lie. "I didn't want anyone to see us and think you were"—he snapped his suspenders—"kissing a clown."

Morning and Portia caught the bus to Manhattan. But not before Morning slipped back into the academy locker room, changed into jeans, and grabbed his cap and sunglasses.

On the bus, he asked her something that had been bugging him about their talk with Clancy. "What's the real reason you don't want Penny knowing about this? I doubt you care that much about the academy's reputation."

"If Mom knew some vampire wanted me dead she'd think it had to do with the movie Cody and I are making. She'd accuse me of looking under too many rocks, and ship me off to boarding school in Switzerland."

They got off the bus and started for the subway, but Portia stopped him. "Morn, you don't have to escort me to school. I'm gonna grab a cab."

He gestured to her empty hands. "And pay with what?"

"A city girl never leaves home without the three Ps." She reached in her sweatpants' hip pocket and pulled out an iPod and her phone. "Pod, phone"—she reached in the other pocket and pulled out a credit card—"plastic."

It didn't stop him from worrying. "But what if—"

She pressed a finger to his lips. "Morning, if the vampire wanted me dead, I'd be dead. I mean, when a vampire tries to kill you and doesn't finish the job, he's got something else in mind. Until we figure out what it is, there's nothing we can do." She took his hands. "I know it's weird to say, but this is the second time you've saved my life and it's not a habit I wanna get into. Not the saving part, of course, the damsel-in-distress part."

He tried to strip the trite from what he wanted to say by tossing it off. "You know me, can't live without ya."

She answered with a warm smile, but there was something in her eyes he had noticed lately. They looked older.

"Someday," she said, "hopefully a long time from now, you're gonna have to." She glanced over his shoulder, gave his cheek a kiss, and hailed a cab. "I'll call and let you know I got to school." She slipped into the taxi.

Morning couldn't remember the last time she had kissed him on the cheek. Watching the cab pull away, a terrible feeling swelled inside him. Sure, he'd saved her life, but he couldn't save her *from* life. The adrenaline fueling him ever since the first scream had shot from the burning building was swept away by a wave of doom. Suddenly, he couldn't face turning around and going back to the academy.

He walked to a vacant lot. He moved into it and disappeared behind a blind of sumac. A few seconds later, a pigeon flew up over the sumac and soared skyward.

Morning knew Birnam had asked Leaguers to stop all CDing, but this was an emergency. He needed to take his tumbling feelings to a place where he could sort them out.

26

Varkos

The pigeon landed on one of the cables sweeping down to the center of the Williamsburg Bridge. The bird scanned the pathway below. A lone cyclist zipped along it.

While it was officially the Williamsburg Bridge, to Morning and Portia it would always be the Williams Bird Bridge. Because that was how Morning had mispronounced it as a little kid, and because the middle of the Williams Bird Bridge was where he and Portia had shared so many big moments. For Morning, it was always rush hour on the bridge, a rush hour of memories and emotions.

The bicyclist cleared the center of the bridge; there was no one in sight for a hundred yards on either side. The pigeon dropped down and reverted to human form just before landing on the walkway. Morning was back in his skin, but that was all he was in. He dropped to his knees, reached down between the railing and the anti-jumper fence, and pulled up a waterproof bag. From the bag he quickly extracted a jumpsuit and jumped into the aptly named outfit. Morning had made this clothes stash in the event he did an unexpected CD and needed to cover up before he got arrested for indecent exposure.

He gripped the rail, looked out on the harbor, and flipped through the bizarre events of the day. Some vampire tried to kill Portia; he saved her; Portia wanted to cover it up; his gums were infested with *dentis eruptus* for the first time in a year; and, out of nowhere, his eternal beloved gave him a passionless cheek peck. "A cheek peck?" he muttered. "What was that about?"

The first answer was a horrific thought. *Maybe she knew.* Maybe when he held her foot so he could feel her coursing blood she caught a whiff of something: the scent of bloodlust. Maybe when they kissed she had felt the hardening buds in his gums before he pulled away. Maybe she was as afraid to kiss him again as she was terrified of some vampire trying to kill her.

But why now? Morning wondered. He looked down at the river. Why would saving her life tempt me to throw myself back into the forbidden well of bloodlust?

The snap of a jacket in the wind pulled him away from the water; he turned toward the sound. At first, it seemed like a vision, a flashback to thirteen months before, when Portia had come to find him on the bridge. As she had loped toward him, her dark curly hair had bounced along with her baggy cargo jacket flapping open. It was the moment he had first thought of her as an ostrich on a bad feather day.

But this was no flashback. It was a tall young man with dark curly hair like Portia's, a flapping jacket, and something between a lope and a long, smooth stride. Morning immediately braced for the worst. It was the "brother" Portia had mistaken for her reflection.

The vampire held up a hand as he drew closer. "I mean no harm." He stopped at the rail, standing a head taller than Morning. His skin was less coppery now, and the lines were gone, as if he had gotten a final exfoliation. His eyes were also less brown and shading toward gray.

"Who are you?" Morning demanded.

"My name is Varkos. I am the brother of Ikor DeThanatos, the vampire you and your girlfriend destroyed in the Mother Forest."

Morning swallowed and wished the walkway was crowded with people. "So you tried to kill Portia in revenge."

"Oh, no." Varkos chuckled. "I knew you would save her. I have faith in you, Morning." He flashed a charming smile. "Faith in your powers of destruction."

"What are you talking about?"

"How do mortals say? That's for me to know and you to find out."

Despite Morning's fear, a thought dawned on him. "You're a Loner, aren't you?"

Varkos answered with a haughty look. "In the end, aren't we all?"

"But"—Morning gestured at the blue sky—"how did you—"

"I took precautions so I could take a lovely afternoon stroll on a bridge and meet new people, like you." Varkos covered a yawn. "But the sleepless days are killing me." He shook off his grogginess. "Now, where was I?"

Morning frowned and took a chance. "Telling me your plans."

"Ah, yes, my agenda. It's really quite simple: to avenge my brother's death." He chuckled with satisfaction. "But not in some swift, boring nighttime raid. Been there, done that. No, I want to enjoy my new day," he declared to the sky. "I plan to extract my revenge in the most leisurely, torturous, and excruciating manner."

"Why don't you leave Portia out of it," Morning said, "and let it be between you and me?"

Varkos touched his chest like his feelings had been hurt. "But Morning, Portia was the one who buried the stake in my brother's heart. And, having the powers of a virgin who had lost her heart to love, she was the one who made my brother's annihilation so swift and final. To let such a vicious vampire slayer roam the earth would be unfair. But I tell you what, I promise to make no more attempts on her life." He gave Morning a wink. "I'll leave that up to you."

"I'll never touch her that way," Morning protested.

Varkos leaned in close.

Morning refused to budge. The price was smelling the vampire's breath. It swirled with scents of mushroom, earth, and iron: the tang of blood. He had recently fed.

Varkos whispered, "You touched her once, you will again. I promise, before it's all over you will raise your fangs in the destruction of your love, and every Leaguer under the sun." His mouth suddenly gaped with another yawn, startling Morning. Then he slid by, giving Morning a pat on the back as he went. "Happy hunting, my boy."

The touch sent a chill through Morning. He watched Varkos stride toward Brooklyn. Then he hurried in the opposite direction. This latest twist wasn't one he could handle by himself. He needed to sound the alarm.

27

The Protection Paradox

Morning fired up his computer, got Birnam on Skype, and told him about Varkos and everything that had happened. As in previous sessions, Birnam's camera was conveniently down.

Birnam responded to all the news with concern, but to Morning's irritation, he never sounded shocked. He even clucked with satisfaction when Morning's report solved one mystery: why a solar-phobia instructor at the academy had been found that morning wandering around in her pajamas. The only surprising thing to Birnam was the vampire's name. He had never heard of a Loner named Varkos and had no idea that DeThanatos had had a brother.

"You're right about one thing," Birnam proffered. "If this Varkos simply wanted Portia dead, he wouldn't have gone to the trouble of forcing you to rescue her. By the way, how did saving Portia make you feel?"

Morning thought the question came out of left field, and he didn't want to answer it. "I'm thrilled she's okay."

"I'm sure you are, but did anything unusual happen afterward?"

Morning hesitated, but he needed to share it with someone; if anyone could help him understand it would be Birnam. "Yeah. For the first time in a year I got a twinge of *dentis eruptus*."

"Don't be shocked," Birnam said. "It's only natural."

"But why? I never want to bite her again."

"Of course you don't, but you also want to protect her from danger, from death itself. So what better way to save her from all danger than to turn her into an immortal."

Morning's head spun at the cruel paradox of it. "That's terrible."

"Yes. What do you think Varkos was up to? He wanted to destroy both of you in a chain reaction. First you save her, then you turn her and destroy who you claim to be. When vampires seek revenge, it's not death they're after; they want to see the dreams of their victims drown in the forbidden well."

"But that could mean the more I want to protect her, the more I'll want to turn her."

"Yes, that's a danger," Birnam concurred. "It's the burden you bear when your eternal beloved isn't eternal."

Morning was shocked by Birnam's use of the term, like he'd been reading his and Portia's minds. *Or worse,* Morning fretted, *being a Centurion, maybe Birnam has one more level of Skype: mind share.* He did the only thing you can do when you think someone's reading your mind: change the subject. "What are we gonna do about Varkos?"

"He's a Loner. They play by their own rules. All we can do is wait for his next move."

128

Morning heard a *crunch* on the other end, like someone biting down on something. "What was that?"

"What?"

"That sound, like a crunching."

"Oh, that's my pet rat," Birnam answered dismissively. "I'm feeding him lunch."

Morning was too worried and distracted to go back to the academy for his afternoon classes, even though his absence might earn him another demerit. He spent the afternoon watching TV and searching the web for any mention of the live fire incident at the fire academy. There was nothing; Clancy really had put a lid on it.

Morning debated how much he should tell Portia. He wanted to call and tell her that Varkos had promised not to hurt her, but he knew he couldn't convince her she was safe unless he got into Varkos's contention that it was Morning who would do the hurting. The last thing he wanted to talk to her about was his flare-up of *dentis eruptus.*

Yet he still needed to call her. Even if Varkos was no longer a direct threat, Morning knew she would be suspicious if he *didn't* act concerned. So he called her to check in. After stepping out of the editing room where she and Cody were working on their Rachel interview, Portia told Morning she was fine and nothing else had happened. Then she told him that she and Cody had seen a flash-mob tweet about a MOP protest that night in front of Diamond Sky Productions. They had to be there. She invited Morning to come, but he declined. He was two days away from an exam in Arson Awareness class and had to study.

After hanging up, Morning had the haunting feeling that Portia was glad he had turned down the invitation.

Early that evening, Varkos stood in Times Square, watching the huge screen on the ABC Studios building. It was broadcasting a news segment on the rise and fall of *The Shadow*. He was highly amused by how the show had started with such noble intentions, like Leaguers flying off to earthquakes and turning into rescue dogs to save people. Varkos resisted rolling on the pavement in laughter as the show progressed from heroics to CDing for profit and finally to a big fat leech sucking on a rock star's surgically replaced scalp. If there was one thing Varkos knew about his kind, it was this: vampires can shape-shift into superheroes, but sooner or later they all shape-shift into bloodsuckers.

On the top floor of Diamond Sky, Penny and Rachel were working on how to continue airing *The Shadow*. They were on a conference call with a honcho from Apple, and Penny had been pitching the idea of turning the rest of *The Shadow* season into an iCast for iPhones and iPads. She had even offered to change the show's name to *iShadow*. The meeting wasn't going well, and Penny had to raise her voice above the roar coming from outside, on the street below.

Surrounding the building were a few thousand demonstrators, all MOPers. They wore MORTALS ONLY T-shirts and were chanting the same slogan at full lung.

The executive told Penny and Rachel he wasn't sure Apple and *The Shadow* were a good fit. As much as he liked the idea of *iShadow*, he kept imagining the jokes Apple would be walking into: iSuck, iBleed, etc. He thanked them for their time and hung up.

Down on the avenue, the crowd chanted "M-O-P! Mortals only! M-O-P! Mortals only!" Portia and Cody moved around the edge of the crowd. Cody was shooting the angry faces, barking mouths, and jabbing stakes.

Varkos saw the twosome coming and slipped into the shadows of a doorway. Even in the darkness, his gray eyes and white teeth caught a glint of light when he smiled at the scene. As he drank in the hatred of the crowd, a master plan began slithering through his devious mind.

28

Meeting Up

The next day, as sunset spilled orange on the Hudson, Zoë was giving a honeymooning couple from Chicago a Fanpire Tour. She had just shown them the old-fashioned barber pole in front of the 3Aces Barbershop on Ninth Avenue and was explaining its deeper meaning. "A long time ago, barbers did more than give haircuts. They applied bandages and did bloodletting, too. That's what the red and white spiral on a barber pole is advertising. And the pole itself represents the stick customers would grip to bulge their veins out so the barber could find them with his lance."

The couple giggled and entertained themselves with jokes about gripping sticks and bulging veins. Zoë closed her ears and pedaled to the next Fanpire attraction in Hell's Kitchen.

She stopped in front of an old granite church with a new congregation. The ex–Catholic church had been converted to a nightclub called Goth 'Em. If you were a goth or a vampire wannabe, it was the hot spot in town.

While Goth 'Em was a thriving business, Zoë had heard rumors that the aboveground club was just the tip of the fang. Supposedly, hidden somewhere on the same block was one of the secret dives for consensual bloodlust. It was where wayward Leaguers hooked up with Lifers who wanted to be nibbled on and feel the ecstasy of exsanguination. But not just anyone got in. It was strictly word-of-mouth; you had to know someone and get a special invitation.

Zoë encouraged the couple to go inside Goth 'Em and check out the scene where Lifers and Leaguers mingled but kept their sipping to cocktails and legal blood drinks. She advised them to hit the bar and have the house specialty, Sang Tang, a mix of alcohols reddened with grenadine. The couple asked Zoë to go in with them, but, despite a few attempts, Zoë had never gotten past the front door. Even with a fake ID she would have a hard time convincing anyone she was twenty-one. She informed the newlyweds that waiting for them was part of the tour, as long as they returned in twenty minutes.

As the couple disappeared into Goth 'Em, Zoë looked longingly through the big window. Her eyes fell on the back of a figure seated at the end of the bar. The person's curly dark hair reminded her of Portia's but shorter. The figure turned, revealing his profile. It gave Zoë a start. There was something in the man's profile that was creepy-strange: a resemblance to Portia.

Zoë flipped open her phone and hit speed dial.

In the Village, Morning and Portia exited the only gelato shop that made flavors for Leaguers. L'Arte del Gelato offered Hemo Gobblin' and Plasmania. Morning held a cone of the former. As they walked, Portia handed him her Banana Cream Pie gelato and dug in her purse. Her phone was sounding off with Zoë's ringtone, a bicycle bell. Portia answered her cell. "Yo, sista, wazzup?"

Zoë explained where she was and dropped her bombshell. "I swear, this guy could be your brother."

Portia's insides fired three different ways: she wanted to scream, call the police, or run off and go stake shopping. "That's wild," she said, trying to squash her fears. "Can you get a picture of him and send it to me?"

"Yeah," Zoë answered. "It'll take some doing, but I'm on it."

Zoë fingered call history on her phone and dialed the newlyweds inside the bar. The husband answered. "Instead of a tip," Zoë said, "could you do me a favor?"

Morning and Portia headed into Washington Square with their gelatos. Portia was so distracted she hadn't touched her cone since Zoë's call. She still teetered between panic and reporter mode. "If it's the same vampire and he's still here, maybe he . . . Should we call the cops?"

Morning led her to a bench and they sat. "His name is Varkos."

"How do you know that?"

He told her about meeting Varkos on the bridge, and how the vampire had promised not to make any more attempts on her life.

Portia chucked her Banana Cream Pie gelato in the bushes. "Why didn't you tell me sooner?"

"I've been meaning to."

"Lame excuse," she snapped. "If it was *your* life on the line, would you like being on a need-to-know basis?" She didn't wait for an answer as she keyed her phone, looking for the picture that hadn't been sent yet.

Morning stared at the ground, his skin prickling from the sting of her words.

Varkos sat at the end of the crowded bar in Goth 'Em and took in the scene with subdued pleasure. This was how the world of outed vampires was supposed to be. There was a profusion of black and red, even a few red-lined capes on the wannabes who revered Dracula as the sultan of sanguivores. The men ranged from a seven-foot Nosferatu with a cadaverous figure to a gnomish man wearing a stovepipe hat announcing SHORT ORDER SUCK. The women covered the spectrum from a curvy amazon in a red wedding gown to a pixie with a tattoo on her neck announcing I BREAK FOR VAMPIRES. And there were the Edwards and Jacobs from *Twilight*. The Edwards sported yellow contacts, anemic skin, and anorexic builds. The Jacobs showed off sculpted chests and twelve-pack Taylor Lautner abs. True, it was a potpourri of clichés from creature-of-the-night pop culture, but it was far more exotic and alluring than the whitewash Leaguers were trying to foist on the world.

What pleased Varkos the most were the snippets of conversation his ears had sampled. Furtive exchanges between Lifers and Leaguers revealed this to be an unusual pickup scene. Several pairs had made arrangements to meet later in the "tasting room." This thrilled Varkos for two reasons. One, backsliding Leaguers craving a sip of their cultural heritage was excellent news. And two, the notion of *consensual* bloodlust, as alien as it was to Varkos, had the potential to be shaped into a devastating weapon.

As he considered how to wield such a weapon against Leaguers, his eyes fell on two of the few people at the bar not dressed in goth or vampire attire. The young couple was happily drinking what the bartender called a Sang Tang. As the young man held up a cell phone to take a picture of his date, Varkos felt the heat of another body and turned. An attractive young woman pushed into his thermo-envelope as she slid onto the barstool next to his. Like Varkos and the young couple down the bar, her attire wasn't vampire-chic. She wore a fashionable business suit.

She greeted Varkos with a friendly smile. "Can I buy you a drink?"

He took in her pretty face, framed by auburn hair. "I thought no one would ever ask."

She laughed at his gender-bending joke. "Does that mean you're a gigolo, or some time ago you figured out you were so gorgeous all you had to do was wait around till some lonely gal came along and bought you a drink?"

He shook his head. "No, it's simply that"—he slipped into his best Bela Lugosi impression—"I don't *buy* drinks."

She laughed again. "Vampire bar, vampire joke. You're good." She got the bartender's attention, ordered a Sang Tang, and asked Varkos what he wanted.

"Make it a deuce," he instructed the bartender.

She leaned back and took him in. "I know why I'm not wearing a costume. What about you?"

"I'm working on my inner vampire."

"Have you found it?"

"It's still emerging. Your turn," he said. "What brings the corporate look to Gothville?"

"I'm at the Javits Center for a trade show. I'm not into inner or outer vampires." She looked around like an eager tourist. "I'm just here rubbernecking."

"I wouldn't bend that pretty neck too far, it might attract the real thing."

She flipped a hand. "Pfff! All those rumors about consensual bloodlust, I think it's a bunch of hooey."

He held her gaze and deadpanned, "I couldn't agree more. 'Consensual' has nothing to do with it."

She snorted a laugh and punched his shoulder. "You are funny!"

The bartender delivered two Sang Tangs. She mouthed her straw and took a good pull. He watched the muscles in her neck contract. "Tell me about your trade show."

"It's the convention for the online dating industry."

"Online dating? What's that?"

She stared at him, unsure if it was another one of his dry jokes or if he was serious. "You really don't have to work at meeting girls, do you?"

29

Discovery

Morning and Portia sat on the bench, staring at the picture on the phone that had e-skipped from the newlyweds' phone to Zoë's to Portia's.

Morning frowned. "It's weird."

"What?"

"It's Varkos, but it's not Varkos."

She slid him a puzzled look. "What does that mean?"

"Maybe it's the quality of the shot or the lighting, but he looks different from when I saw him yesterday."

"I was thinking the same. In the second I saw him the other day, his hair was curlier."

"Yeah, it's just wavy now."

She stared at the picture. "And I swear, the last thing I saw before he thralled me were his eyes. They weren't gray, they were as dark as mine."

Morning looked up. Portia did the same. Seeing her dark brown eyes hit him with a heart-stopping thought. "What if he's not the brother of DeThanatos?"

She sucked in a gasp.

He finished his thought. "What if it *is* DeThanatos?"

"But we staked him," she blurted. "We saw him burst into flames and incinerate into a pile of ash!"

"Yeah, but remember the cut you got on your shoulder during the dust storm, before we left the forest? What if when he took his final form—a seedpod—he rode the wind, stuck you, and collected a drop of blood?"

"That's ridiculous!" she protested. "You can't regenerate from a drop—" A flash of a memory cut her off. She had once revived Morning with a few drops of her own blood. She suddenly felt like a shipwreck survivor clinging to a bit of wreckage and losing her grip.

Morning pressed on, knowing they had to walk to the end of this dark corridor. "If a few drops of your blood can reconstitute me from a pile of ash, maybe DeThanatos could have done it from a seedpod."

"But you never *looked* like me," she protested, clinging to a last hope that might prove Morning wrong. "This Varkos guy ended up looking like me."

Morning nodded. "I know, but I acted like you for a while, until my DNA reasserted itself." He pointed at the phone. "Maybe that's why he's looking less like you and more like DeThanatos: his DNA is reasserting itself. 'Varkos' was a temporary hybrid of you and DeThanatos."

She stared at him in confusion and fear. The bit of wreckage she had clung to was gone. She was being pulled under. "You're saying DeThanatos is indestructible."

"I don't know what I'm saying because they don't teach this at Leaguer Academy. The only one who can explain it is Birnam." He pulled out his cell.

Portia closed his hand over it. "I don't want any more explanations. I wanna go home."

He put his other hand on hers. "DeThanatos isn't going to kill you. That's not his idea of revenge."

She exhaled a bitter laugh. "Yeah, wouldn't be *permanent* enough."

Morning knew what she was implying, but he couldn't go there. Not yet. The moment they voiced what DeThanatos had in store for them would be the beginning of the end.

Varkos listened with fascination as the young woman detailed the world of online dating. He was amused by the money, time, and effort Lifers devoted to connecting, dating, and seeking the holy grail of human relations: a soul mate. But there was something about using the Internet to bring people together to meet instinctual needs that heated Varkos's brain with the fever of possibility.

As the young woman, whose name was Trudi, held forth on trolling the Internet for love, she sucked down three Sang Tangs, while Varkos hadn't touched his drink. Her tipsiness helped her stagger to three conclusions. One, while the handsome man was captivated by her online dating summary, he was equally captivated by the summarizer. Two, the excuse he gave for not touching his drink—that he was allergic to grenadine—was totally viable, because Trudi had once gotten sick after a Christmas party that served red and green shooters made from grenadine and crème de menthe. Her third conclusion was so wild she was uncertain of it. In the hour they had been at the bar, his look had changed. His face had grown leaner, his skin tone was lighter, and his hair, which had started the evening wavy, was less so. Granted, Trudi had been on dates when her carefully coiffed hair had fallen like a soufflé, but she had never had, or even heard of, tan loss or weight loss on a date.

She waved a finger and declared, "You've changed."

Varkos smiled sweetly. "Girls have told me that, but it usually takes a few weeks or months."

"But you *have* changed," she slurred as she reached up to touch his hair.

In a flash, he held her wrist. "You've changed too. You're a bit drunk. Let me walk you back to your hotel."

"All right." She shrugged as she eyed his untouched Sang Tang. "How 'bout we get that in a to-go cup."

"I don't need a to-go cup," he said, offering his arm to help her off the stool. "I have you."

Her eyes wavered into focus and locked on him. "You're gorgeous, you're funny, and you're smooth. But I have one rule. Anyone who walks me home has to have a name."

He smiled. "DeThanatos. Ikor DeThanatos."

Morning and Portia had walked back to her house in silence. They stood on the stoop. He leaned forward to kiss her.

She lowered her head and put a hand on his chest. "If I ask you a question, will you promise to answer?"

"You know I'd promise you anything."

"After you rescued me from the fire, when you kissed me, did you have a feeling you'd had one time before?"

His mind raced, looking for some answer that would both satisfy "one time before" and skirt the truth.

"Morning, did you want to bite me?"

"No, I didn't."

"But I felt something, in your gums. I didn't want to think about what it might be, but now, with DeThanatos back, I feel like we're getting dragged there again, to a dangerous place."

"Okay, there was a moment," he admitted, "but there was a reason for it."

"'A reason'?" She shook her head with a rueful chuckle. "What could possibly be reasonable about popping fangs and wanting to bury them in your girlfriend's neck?"

He let out a sigh. He'd so wanted to avoid this, but—typical Portia—she was too smart and too honest to ignore what had to be said. "I wanted to protect you," he said, even though it felt like he was pushing a stake into his own heart. "To turn you. To protect you with immortality."

She held his eyes for a moment, then touched his cheek. "That's really sweet. But do I look like Zoë? No, I'm me, Portia."

"I know. I know what you want and what you don't."

"Do you?"

He nodded.

She tilted her head in thought. "How can you be so sure, when I'm not sure anymore?"

"What are you unsure of?"

"A lot of things," she said with a muted smile. "I gotta go."

She let him kiss her, but there was no invitation in it. It was the worst kind of kiss. A mercy kiss.

Morning walked uptown to get his bike from in front of L'Arte del Gelato. The only thing that could stop him from being swept away by his torrent of anxious thoughts was to call Birnam. He pulled out his cell, got through to Birnam, and told him about Varkos being DeThanatos, reconstituted from a drop of Portia's blood.

When he finished, Birnam said, "If it weren't so terrible, it might be funny."

"There's nothing funny about it," Morning shot back.

"Oh, but there is. Everyone used to think vampires rise from the grave, out of the coffin, and all that. Now, after being buried in the Mother Forest, finally, one has indeed risen from a grave of wood."

"What are you gonna do about it?" Morning demanded.

"Wait."

"For what?"

"For him to make his next move."

"Isn't trying to kill Portia enough?" Morning blurted. "Please, Mr. Birnam, you gotta come out from wherever you've buried yourself." He waited for a response . . . until he realized he was talking to a dead connection.

30

Vampower.com

The Jacob K. Javits Convention Center is a sprawling glass and steel box overlooking the Hudson River and New Jersey. It looks like it was originally an airline terminal for a city upriver, until a flood washed it downstream and it came to rest on Manhattan's West Side. On this particular morning its big electronic sign announced THE ONLINE DATING TRADE SHOW. Conventioneers poured into the building even though it wasn't yet eight a.m.

In a corner of the largest convention hall, a booth had been hobbled together at the end of a row of far slicker booths. The booth was no more than a table, piled with xeroxed materials, and a banner hanging above it. The banner announced VAMPOWER.COM in large red letters, with another line underneath: BLOODLUST YOU CAN TRUST. The flashiest thing about the booth was the man running it. DeThanatos wore a beautifully tailored suit and had his hair slicked back. He looked as sleek and shiny as a new car.

DeThanatos spent the first hour passing out materials on Vampower.com and answering questions. When the aisles were teaming with conventiongoers, he jumped up on the table and launched into a pitch. "Ladies and gentlemen, mortals of all blood types! Vampower.com may be the newest and smallest online dating service to dive into the pool, but I promise you, we're gonna make the biggest splash!"

His looks and rich voice turned heads. "Some of you have swung by and gotten a taste of Vampower.com, but let me enlighten those of you still in the dark. Vampower .com is the first website to tap into a matchmaking market hiding in plain sight. I'm talking about the secret desire of Lifers and Leaguers to hook up. That's right, I'm talking consensual bloodlust."

The crowd sucked in a collective breath. Some people turned and walked away, but most stayed, wanting to hear this alluring and shocking pitchman.

"There, I've said it!" he proclaimed. "We know the yearning is out there, underground, waiting to surface. Yes, millions of Lifers want to donate blood to a cause, and I'm not talking the Red Cross. These Lifers want to donate blood to the cause of their curiosity, personal exploration, and pleasure. And yes, there are Leaguers who have an urge to tap into the deepest veins of their cultural heritage and nibble on a mortal. Why shouldn't the yearning of some Lifers and Leaguers be answered? That's what Vampower .com offers. A safe and confidential social network for those who want to be sipped and those who want to dip."

A cameraman pushed through the crowd followed by Drake Sanders. He was in the convention hall trolling for a story about some titillating online dating site. From what he'd heard so far, Vampower.com fit the bill. Drake fired a question. "Is Vampower.com only a dating service for bloodlusters, or will it match Lifers who wanna bleed for other reasons than the bang of being fanged?"

"I'm glad you asked that," DeThanatos answered earnestly. "The potential for bleed dating is not limited to Lifers and Leaguers looking for thrills and swills. For instance, on the TV show *The Shadow,* you saw a patient who successfully hooked up with a vampire. Besides Lifers recovering from reattachment surgeries, there are people who suffer from too much iron in the blood, a disease called hemochromatosis, and who need blood drained on a regular basis to remain healthy."

"Wow, sounds like you've done your market research," Drake cajoled before popping his next question. "Are there any blood matches Vampower.com will refuse to do?"

"Absolutely," DeThanatos declared. "While Leaguer-to-Lifer blood sharing has many applications, there are two blood matches we'll never touch. Vampire-assisted suicides and euthanasia."

"Could you elaborate?"

"The suicidal Lifer who registers with Vampower.com because they want to be matched with a Leaguer for a total vein drain will be referred to a suicide hotline. And any fatally ill patient who wants to be euthanized by a vampire will be referred to their local hospice. We don't do death, except in one case."

"What's that?"

"If the government wants to save taxpayer dollars by using a Leaguer to carry out a death sentence by lethal *extraction* rather than lethal *injection,* we will make the match, pro bono. But only if the prisoner and Leaguer agree to a blood match. We don't force death on anyone.

It's all in our motto," he said, pointing to the banner above him. " 'Bloodlust you can trust.' "

"Okay, here's the biggie," Drake asked. "What if a Lifer wanted to be turned, to be changed. Would Vampower.com handle the hookup?"

DeThanatos answered with a stern look. "That, my friend, is against the law. Vampower.com does not break laws. We help those who want to be sipped and those who want to dip, but we don't do flips."

Uptown, in an editing room at LaGuardia Arts, Portia and Zoë gaped at the TV showing Drake's coverage. Portia's mouth hung open enough for all doubt to escape: the vampire who had once resembled her was now running on his own DNA and fully Ikor DeThanatos. Seeing him back from the dead bored a black hole of fear in her guts.

Zoë's insides roiled with something else: high-octane excitement. She punched her laptop on and waved frantically as it booted up. "C'mon, c'mon!"

"What are you doing?" Portia asked.

"Going to Vampower.com before they get bombarded."

"Why?"

Zoë worked her keyboard. "To join, of course."

"But ZZ, he just said they won't turn people."

"Morning got turned because of accidental backwash. Maybe I'll catch the same lightning!"

In a midtown hotel room, an exhausted woman with messy hair and glazed eyes worked a computer in a blur of fingers. It was Trudi, the morning after. Sure, she had a hangover, but she also had something that lasted longer: a fangover. DeThanatos had made Trudi his minion, a sycophant who lived and breathed for his every need. As well as doing a brain suck on her online dating expertise, DeThanatos and his girl Renfield had spent the night designing and launching Vampower.com. She was now handling the thousands of applications flooding in.

"'Zoë Zotz,'" Trudi monotoned, reading the latest application. "'Cute Lifer looking for a dashing vampire with swallow reflex issues or a history of bulimia.'"

After seeing the Vampower.com coverage, Becky-Dell Wallace put her MOP staff on the case. They quickly gathered several facts. They learned the pitchman's name, that he was a Leaguer residing in New York City, and that he was an employee of Vampower.com, which was owned and operated by one Gertrude Blankenship. The only oddity was that the site had existed for less than twelve hours. Confirming that DeThanatos was a registered Leaguer with the Bureau of Vampire Affairs took a little more time because the BVA's computer system had been hacked into the night before and was still down. When it got back online, they found Ikor DeThanatos's Leaguer registration. This was another chore Trudi had helped her master accomplish the night before.

But the seeming legitimacy of Vampower.com, and its pitchman, was not going to stop Becky-Dell from responding to a Lifer-Leaguer dating service. That afternoon she spoke to the media in the halls of Congress. She began by shaking a scolding finger at the American people. "This is what happens when you let a vampire turn into a leech and suck on your head. Give a bloodsucking fiend a drop and they'll want the whole five quarts."

"Isn't that a bit of an exaggeration?" a reporter asked. "The spokesman for Vampower.com only proposed a total vein drain in the case of an execution."

"That's not the point. The point is, Leaguers keep getting thirstier. And in response to them baring their fangs, I've got two points of my own. First, if Leaguers had any restraint, Luther Birnam would do more than fire off web posts. He'd step up and put an end to this escalation of bloodlust. But it seems that Leaguers like Ms. Capilarus, and this matchmaker of bloodlust, Mr. DeThanatos, are out of Birnam's league. Second, if Birnam won't stop them, the American people will. As a congresswoman I'm declaring war on the Leaguer movement and their rising tide of bloodlust. I'm gonna put the 'slay' in 'legislation.' I'm gonna give the BVA the powers and weapons it needs to fight our newest homegrown terrorists: Leaguers!"

31

Sunset Walk

When Morning called Portia and asked her to go for a sunset walk along the river, she surprised him by saying, "Great idea." It wasn't the upbeat answer he expected the day after a bad date that ended with a mercy kiss. Nonetheless, he had a plan to find out what was going on, or not, with his eternal beloved, if that's what she still was.

Small talk about their respective schools carried them to the river. When they turned south on the sliver of park running along the Hudson, Morning got to his plan. "So, Zoë told me about the winter solstice thing coming up at LaGuardia Arts on December twenty-first."

"Yeah, they're calling it the End Is Upon Us Ball," Portia said with a half smile.

"What's an End Is Upon Us Ball?" Even though he had picked Zoë's brain for all the details, he didn't want to sound like he had done too much homework.

"A bunch of doomers are saying the world's gonna end on December twenty-first because it's the end of the Mayans' five-thousand, one-hundred-and-twenty-five-year calendar, so, naturally, the kids at LA are gonna turn it into an event."

He kept feigning ignorance. "Is it like a dance?"

"Yeah, but with an end-of-the-world theme, I'm sure it'll be more than a dance."

"Are you gonna do something for it?"

"Nah, too busy with the film. Besides, you know I'm not into dances."

He wasn't discouraged. He knew Portia wasn't a fan of events that promoted gender stereotypes. "But what if the world is really ending," he mused playfully, "and this is the last dance of all time? Wouldn't you wanna go?"

She gave him an *I'm on to you* look. Surprisingly, she didn't call him on it. "The solstice is a long ways off," she said with a shrug. "Besides, the way the crap's hitting the fan with DeThanatos and Becky-Dell Wallace getting everyone riled up, the world might end before then."

He had figured she would or wouldn't want to go to the dance. He hadn't anticipated indifference or evasion.

She took his arm and led him to a bench overlooking the river. "C'mon, let's sit down."

They did as Morning tried to think of what to say now that his plan to find out if they were still eternal beloveds had been derailed.

"I've been thinking about us," she said. "A lot."

The ominous words churned Morning's stomach. "Me too," he said, knowing what was coming.

"You wanna hear what I think?"

He didn't want to have this conversation; he wanted to

cut to the chase. "Why don't I say it first," he blurted. "It's time for us to break up."

She gave him a tight smile. "That's not what I was gonna say."

He kicked himself for his rush to judgment. "What were you gonna say?"

"I think we just need to take a breather. You know, be friends for a while."

The dreaded F-word twisted his stomach tighter. "Isn't that the same as breaking up?"

"There's so much going on right now," she said, dodging the question. "I'm confused. I'm scared, but I'm also trying to earn my death."

"Earn your death?"

"Yeah, earn my death. It's something Cody told me about."

Morning scowled. "Cody, great."

She ignored his sour expression. "He said that if you're lucky to die old and still be mentally competent enough to look back on your life and not have any major regrets, then you've earned your death."

"Are you saying you already have some major regrets?"

"No, but I know I would if I didn't put my heart and soul into every movie I make."

"You can't do that and be with me at the same time?"

She took his hand. "It's not that, Morn. I'm saying if DeThanatos *thinks* we've broken up, a couple of things might happen. He might stop trying to get to me through you, and you might stop trying to protect me by turning me."

He felt his jaw clench. "I'll never stop trying to protect you."

"Even if I broke your heart?"

"Is that what you're planning? To break my heart?"

Her eyes welled up. "I don't wanna break up. I really don't. But we need to take a break."

"And just be friends."

"It's a cliché, I know, but yeah. And it might just be for a while."

"Till your film is done," he said abruptly.

She wiped her eyes. "No, till all this crap flying around us settles. I can't live with the double fear of some vampire wanting to off me and this wild piece of you that wants to protect me the only way you can. Can't do it anymore. No girl should have to handle that much."

He took a slow breath. He knew she was right; he knew being together had to end sometime. But knowing it didn't prepare him for feeling it. And it felt a hundred times worse than he had ever imagined. He swallowed the thickening lump in his throat. "So, we're just friends."

She nodded.

"On one condition."

"What?"

"We still meet Thursdays for breakfast. . . . That's what friends do, right?"

She managed a kind smile. "Deal."

32

Strange Bedfellows

Becky-Dell lived across the Potomac River in a posh Virginia neighborhood of stately homes and cast iron streetlights.

A peregrine falcon flashed through a pool of light, pierced the lower half of a big oak in a front yard, and landed on a low branch. A second later, the bird dropped down and *whopped* into human form; DeThanatos landed in the grass without a sound, or a stitch on.

Inside the house, Becky-Dell was in her home office, adding an amendment to her bill giving the BVA sweeping new powers and criminalizing such things as "medical vampires" or any form of consensual bloodlust.

The sound of a creaking floorboard turned her head; she gasped at the sight of the man standing in the doorway. It was shocking enough that he was dressed in a hazmat suit—the kind a killer might wear to make sure he kept his DNA to himself while he murdered his victim—but the biggest shock was his face. It was the one she had been seeing all day: the pitchman for Vampower.com.

She started to scream, but DeThanatos flicked his fingers and closed her throat as tight as a vacu-packed sock. "I'm gonna talk fast," he said, "so you can breathe sooner than later. Not going to hurt you, here to help. As you're a worst-case-scenario type I figured you'd have a hazmat suit in the trunk of your car. You did, and I borrowed it so you didn't get the wrong impression. If you promise not to scream, which you can signify by nodding, we can have a little chat."

With her eyes bugged wide with fear or anger or a mixture of both, she nodded. DeThanatos flicked a finger; she sucked air and spit back words. "What do you want?"

"First, may I introduce myself. Ikor DeThanatos." The hazmat suit crinkled as he made a little bow. "Second, I'd like to tell you what we have in common."

She glared at him through her big glasses. "The only thing we have in common is a flair for publicity."

He responded with a gentle smile. "We also want to see Leaguers wiped off the face of the earth."

This took her aback. "How does a dating service that hooks up mortals and vampires for bloodlust bring *that* about? By training the mortals to date-stake?"

He gave her a charity chuckle. "Like so many of your ideas, it's rather tame. It doesn't go for the jugular."

As much as she didn't like being criticized, he had her attention. "What do you mean?"

He pointed at her computer. "It's like the paragraph you just added to your anti-Leaguer legislation. You know, the amendment that strips businesses that hire Leaguers for

155

their special skills from the yellow pages and puts them in a new phone book called the red pages."

Her eyes shifted to her computer, then back to DeThanatos. "You can read that?"

"When you've been watching the world for a thousand years, your eyes get very sharp. My point is, so many of your strategies are all so"—his lips curled like he had tasted bad blood—"democratic. You're tossing splinters at the problem, when you should be plunging a big fat stake in every Leaguer's heart." He raised his hands apologetically. "However, today, you did have one brilliant idea."

As much as she didn't like being lectured, he had her attention. "And that was?"

"Declaring war."

Her brow furrowed with curiosity. "Go on."

He gave her a conspiratorial smile. "What if we were to join forces? Not in public, of course. We need to *appear* to be sworn enemies. But in private, if we could shed our mutual distrust and hatred and the instinct we harbor to slay one another, we could become strange bedfellows. And together, we could achieve what we both desire: the Leaguer apocalypse."

Whatever revulsion "bedfellows" caused in her was swept away by "apocalypse." She took him in with new eyes. "You're not a Leaguer, are you?"

He was pleased she had noticed. "No, but I play one on television."

33

𝔓icking 𝔲p the 𝔓ieces

At dawn, Morning woke feeling awful. His chest felt hollow and heavy, like aliens had kidnapped him, taken him to their spaceship, and filled his lungs with the air of a planet with ten times the gravity of Earth. He didn't want to get up. He didn't want to go to school. Now that Portia had broken his heart, he just wanted to lie there like a pile of abandoned bricks.

But somehow he dragged himself out of bed. He skipped breakfast so he would have time to swing by the one place that might lighten the load of bricks crushing his heart.

By the time he arrived at the firehouse on Great Jones Street, Will Prowler had finished washing his truck. Morning pulled off his cap and sunglasses and they sat in the back corner of the bay. He told the fireman his tale of woe, including the moment of *dentis eruptus* that he'd felt on the park bench. Prowler listened carefully as he ate an egg-and-cheese roll.

When Morning was done, Prowler wiped the crumbs from his mustache. "I'm sorry to hear you broke up."

"We knew it was coming someday," Morning said with a heaving shrug. "I just never thought it would be so soon. What am I gonna do?"

Prowler clasped his hands behind his head. "I've been married twice, divorced twice. I'm not much for advice on the ways of the heart. But along the rocky road of love, I did learn a thing or two about women."

"Since they're totally new to me," Morning said, "whatever you know might help."

The fireman scratched his gray head. "As far as I can tell, women are a force of nature we don't get, and never will. That's the way it is, so don't feel bad that you can't look into Portia's heart like it's a glass-bottom boat. In my experience, women aren't like water, which always takes the easiest path. Women are more like fire."

"Yeah." Morning nodded. "I'm feeling burned."

Prowler ignored his literal thinking and continued. "I'm not talking about *any* fire." His face set in that look he got before he was about to impart one of the secrets of the fire knights. "There's a kind of fire they don't teach you about at the academy. It's a kind of fire you'll never see in a city. I only know about it because I fought a few of 'em when I was a smoke jumper out west. It's called a climax fire."

Morning didn't know what a climax fire had to do with women, but he knew Prowler well enough to know that if he threw out a verbal boomerang, it would eventually circle back and hit you in the head with some revelation about the original topic. "A climax fire?" he echoed.

"Most fires are destructive," Prowler explained. "A climax fire is destructive *and* creative. It's the fire that sweeps through longleaf pine forests. It not only destroys, but the fire's extreme heat opens the pinecones, and the cones release the seeds that go on to resurrect the forest. If there's anything in nature like the mythological phoenix that rises from the flames, it's the longleaf pine."

Morning didn't have a clue as to what pine trees and phoenixes had in common with Portia except they all started with *p*. But he held his tongue and waited for the boomerang to come winging back.

"When smoke jumpers face a climax fire," Prowler went on, "sometimes they fight it and sometimes they don't. They know the fire is Mother Nature doing what she has to do to re-create. And that's how climax fires are like women."

Morning shrugged, still not getting it. "How so?"

Prowler gestured to the two of them. "We're the smoke jumpers, they're the fire. There's a time to douse and a time to burn. Portia put a match to your relationship. She's letting it burn. Maybe your job right now is to *not* fight it. Maybe there's some old trees that need to die before new ones can be born."

And just like that the boomerang whooshed through Morning's head. Maybe his old friend was right. Maybe his relationship with Portia had to take a step backward before it could take two steps forward.

Portia and Zoë walked out of LaGuardia Arts and headed to a deli to pick up a sandwich for lunch. Portia grabbed the chance to tell Zoë about her breakup with Morning. She related how DeThanatos's return had freaked her out and brought up too many old wounds, including the one

Morning had inflicted on her neck the night he almost drained her. Zoë and Penny were the only Lifers who knew about that, and it was the reason Zoë had hopes that Morning might someday backslide and turn her. But Zoë had kept her promise and never breathed a word of it to anyone.

However, Portia did leave out two beats in her breakup story. She didn't tell Zoë about DeThanatos abducting her and putting her in a burning building. And she didn't mention Morning's brush with *dentis eruptus* when they had kissed. It was the last thing Zoë needed to hear. It might finally inspire her to try and turn Morning into the fang ferry that would deliver her to immortality.

But Portia's censored version still shocked Zoë. "I can't believe you broke up with him! How can anyone dump a vampire? I mean, he could knock you up with eternal life."

Portia winced. "Eweee. I don't wanna be knocked up with anything, especially eternal life."

"You say that now, but wait till you're a toothless old goober begging for another day on the planet."

"That," Portia said emphatically, "would be the last moment I'd want to be turned."

Zoë punched her arm. "Exactly! You should get turned in your prime. Like now. I mean, I thought he was your EB."

"He is, in my heart, but—"

"Look," Zoë cut in, "he's your eternal beloved or he's not. You act like your heart's a time-share. Like Morning's gonna have an apartment in it for the rest of your life, but you're breaking up with him 'cause you're looking for another renter. That's not fair to him, and it won't be fair to the next guy you fall in love with and end up telling, 'Hey, amigo, mi heart es su heart, but did I tell you about the vampire in the left ventricle?' "

Portia chuckled. "Okay, can we just agree to disagree on the whole vampire thing?"

"We always have," Zoë answered with a hopeless shrug.

"You just gotta promise me one thing," Portia added. "Don't tell Cody we broke up. It's a secret."

Zoë shot her a suspicious look. "Are you saying you're not sure you did the right thing? Like this is a trial breakup?"

"No, that's not it."

"Then what is it?"

Portia huffed a sigh. "I don't want Cody thinking I'm available."

"You mean, you don't want him asking you out, like to the End Is Upon Us Ball."

"Right."

Zoë frowned. "You've got two awesome guys in your life and you don't want either of 'em asking you out? Are you going lesbo on me?"

"No!"

"What is it, then?"

"All sorts of amazing stuff is happening with our documentary right now. Cody and I have front-row seats at history in the making, and we're a great team with him thinking I'm with Morning. I don't want him thinking otherwise. I need him on the movie, not on me."

"Pfff," Zoë puffed in disbelief. "What makes you think he's hot for you?"

"Believe me, I know."

"Did he do something?"

"No, I just know."

"Well, he's probably gonna find out from Morning anyway."

"No," Portia said. "I think Morning's so upset he's gonna lay low for a while. So come on, ZZ, do you think you can keep your motormouth shut?"

"My lips are sealed," Zoë said, and lip-zipped. Then she squeezed out, "But you owe me."

34

Ramping It Up

Portia and Zoë took their lunch back to the editing room, where Cody was working on a rough cut of their interview with Rachel. As Portia kept one eye on his editing and the other on a TV tuned to CNN, Zoë got on her laptop.

She fired it up and clicked on the Vampower.com icon to see if any hot young Leaguers had responded to her matchup request yet. "What!" she yelped after the Vampower.com home page came up. It was covered by a big red heart pierced by a wooden stake. She tried to click it away like a pop-up; it didn't budge. "My computer crashed!"

Something on the TV caught Portia's eye and she turned up the sound. The shot cut to a press conference about to begin in the White House Rose Garden. The president appeared, leading a group that included Becky-Dell Wallace and several doctors in white coats.

The president stepped to the podium and spoke in his

calm, measured way. "This morning, thanks to the diligence of Congresswoman Wallace and the expertise provided by doctors from the Centers for Disease Control and Prevention, I was alerted to a national health risk. If the exchange of human blood between Lifers and Leaguers is allowed to proceed in the uncontrolled manner in which Vampower.com is proposing, it will present a health risk to the American people. Such blood exchanges could spread viruses like hepatitis C and HIV. For this reason, I have issued an executive order shutting down Vampower.com and banning all unauthorized blood exchange until Congress can write legislation regarding this matter."

"But Mr. President," a reporter asked, "where's the danger of a mortal giving hepatitis C to a vampire when a vampire can't get sick?"

"I'll let Congresswoman Wallace and the CDC doctors handle the technical questions," the president answered before turning and heading back to the White House.

Becky-Dell beat two doctors to the mikes and answered the question. "You're missing the point. We have laws controlling the where, who, and how much of giving blood. By promoting consensual bloodlust, Vampower .com is breaking those laws. And trust me, canceling TV shows and taking down websites is the tip of the stake I plan to bury in the vampire agenda. After the VRA is defeated this week, we will be calling for a new amendment to the Constitution that will prohibit blood-drinking of any kind."

As the doctors exchanged baffled looks, a reporter piped up. "Ms. Wallace, Leaguers can't survive if they don't drink *some* kind of blood."

Becky-Dell fixed the reporter with hard eyes. "If they

can shape-shift into birds and leeches, they can shape-shift into red-blooded Americans who do what all red-blooded Americans do: *chew* their food."

Reporters shouted questions. She paused, then gave their cameras her fiercest gaze. "Here's my message. For two hundred and fifty years American patriots have shed their blood to water the tree of liberty. Our tree will *not* become a meeting place for vampires and mentally deranged citizens who want to shed their blood in debauchery. Our tree will *not* be poisoned by bloodlust. And if I have to pay the ultimate sacrifice defending that tree, I will die with these words on my lips: better dead than bled!"

Before the reporters could react, Becky-Dell marched away.

Portia, Zoë, and Cody stared at the TV. Cody was the first to find words. "Wow, Zoë, you were right. She's talkin' Prohibition Two. Like she's gonna go Carrie Nation and smash up Goth 'Em with an ax."

"Or a stake," Portia added.

Zoë flailed her hands. "And I'll never meet my blood match! Or experience the ecstasy of exsanguination!"

Across town, DeThanatos exited the Javits Center and was surrounded by a media posse. Drake Sanders fired first. "Mr. DeThanatos, do you have a reaction to Vampower .com being turned into Vampower.*gone?*"

DeThanatos shrugged coolly. "Vampires may disappear, but we're never *gone.*"

Another reporter jumped in with a barrage of questions. "What about your boss, Gertrude Blankenship? Where is she? Why have we never seen her? And what about the rumor that she's your pawn, and you're the real mastermind behind Vampower.com?"

DeThanatos replied with a gracious smile. "I will address rumors and respond to Ms. Wallace's hatemongering threats against Leaguers at a press conference tonight."

"Where?"

"Washington Square Park, eight o'clock."

Portia, Cody, and Zoë watched the TV screen as DeThanatos slid into a town car. Portia's face pinched in thought. "Why is the evilest vampire on earth acting like he's the Harvey Milk of the Leaguer world?"

Cody shrugged. "Maybe the leopard has changed his spots."

Zoë feigned a swoon. "You mean the little deuce of spots he likes to lay on necks?"

"It's not funny!" Portia snapped.

Zoë pulled back, hands raised. "Whoa, I bring up a neck nibble and you bite off my head."

Portia knew it wasn't Zoë's flippancy that had upset her; it was seeing DeThanatos in full flesh again, and the terror he stirred up inside her. "Sorry," she said. "It's just that he's a threat to everything Leaguers have worked for. Much more than Rachel and my mom and their puny attempts to push the envelope of Leaguer freedom. DeThanatos wants to rip up the envelope and torch it."

"What can we do about it?" Cody asked.

Portia took a breath. She was on the fence all documentary filmmakers faced sooner or later: *What's more important, personal safety or getting the story?* As much as DeThanatos scared her, she told herself she had to live by her new motto: *Earn your death.* "The only thing we can do," she said to Cody. "Crew up and add him to our doc."

"Cool." Cody grinned. "We're goin' to Washington Square and rampin' this doc up to *The Fangs of War.*"

Zoë squirmed with excitement. "Can I go with you?"

Portia raised a finger. "As long as you remember we're going to get this badass on film, not on your neck."

Zoë clutched her neck. "Are you kidding? I'll be wearing my chastity choker."

35

Bad Day Worse

Prowler's advice on Morning's romantic woes had kept the heartbroken Leaguer propped up through lunch, but after that things began to crumble. For the first time as a probie, he didn't feel like he was living a dream come true; he felt like he was sleepwalking. His mind wandered in class; his body lumbered through roof training; and the thrill of firing up a huge saw and cutting through a roof vanished like dissipating smoke. Morning felt like he'd gone from the first vampire in the academy to the first zombie.

But there was an upside to his numb despair: it would help him meet the goal he had set for the Arson Awareness Chemical Identification test he was taking that afternoon. The test involved opening a dozen different containers, identifying the fire accelerant in the container by smell, and rattling off stats about each one. With a vampire's extra olfactory powers, Morning knew he could easily ace the test. But doing so was a catch-22 for a couple of reasons: (1) Clancy, having spent much of his FDNY career in the Arson Investigation Division, was the instructor, and (2) acing the test would give Clancy the chance to accuse Morning of using his vampire powers and violating his agreement not to do so during his firefighter training. To play it safe, Morning had decided to identify only nine of the accelerants, which was enough to pass the test without rousing Clancy's suspicions and getting slapped with more demerits, or worse.

After lunch, Clancy led Morning's crew to the ventilation shed, known as the stink box, where the test was administered, one probie at a time. As Morning waited with the others outside the shed, his head swirled with doubts. Besides suffering the malaise of heartbreak, and loss of appetite, his senses felt out of whack. The half can of Blood Lite he'd forced down at lunch had tasted thin and flat, and had been *odorless.*

Before going into a panic, Morning took his nose for a test-drive. He sidled over to Armando and sniffed. Armando always used Nivea for Men, which had a distinctive odor. Morning didn't smell a thing. He still refused to panic. "Smart," he said to Armando, "you skipped the Nivea so it wouldn't mess with your nose."

Armando shot him a dubious look. "Are you kidding? I'm wearing a double dose." He lowered his head and inhaled. "It's gonna clear my nose between accelerants."

"Good idea," Morning mumbled as he turned so Armando couldn't see him blanch.

When it was his turn in the stink box, Morning's worst fears came to pass. Even though he knew every fact about the accelerants, from acetone to turpentine, his nose only nailed two of the smells that wafted from the first eleven canisters Clancy opened. Sure, he aced the properties of those two accelerants, but you can't recite a chemical's explosive limits, vapor density, and ignition temperature if you don't know what it is, or guess the wrong one.

When Clancy lifted the last canister, he was wearing an evil grin. It was both from watching Morning blow it and knowing what he was about to unleash. Clancy yanked off the lid; the smell of rotten eggs filled the shed. It was so strong it even wrinkled Morning's dull nose.

"Carbon disulfide," Morning muttered, knowing it was too little too late. "Explosive limits, one-point-three to fifty percent; vapor density, two-point-six; ignition temperature, a very low two hundred and twelve degrees."

"Nice finish," Clancy chortled, "but you just stunk up the stink box."

As Morning tried to think of an excuse Clancy might buy, his mind was invaded by a barely audible voice singing, "All we are saying is give peace a chance." At first, he thought it was his foggy brain making a desperate stab at humor to appease Clancy. But he heard it again: "All we are saying—" He bolted out of the shed.

Running toward a classroom building, Morning followed the "All we are saying" ringtone curling from an open window. He couldn't believe it. His nose had totally crashed, but he could hear his phone ringing from his backpack in the classroom. And it wasn't just anyone's ringtone. It was Portia's.

He whipped into the classroom, snatched up his backpack, and ripped out the singing phone. "Hello!"

"Hello, Morning."

He deflated. It was Birnam.

"I figured you might not answer," he explained, "so I

170

hacked into your cell and borrowed your favorite ringtone. We need to meet."

Morning was stunned. After months of staying out of sight, Birnam suddenly wanted a face-to-face. "What's the big deal?"

"Nothing much," Birnam said, "just the little war between Congresswoman Wallace and DeThanatos that's threatening everything we've worked for."

Birnam's sarcastic tone was another surprise. Morning had never heard the president of the IVL, the great eternal optimist, do caustic.

"Meet me tomorrow after school," Birnam added. "Four p.m., at the Met Museum of Art, in the Medieval Gallery."

"Mr. Birnam," Morning blurted, "I just lost my sense of smell."

Birnam grunted. "Hmm. Another reason we need to meet."

As Morning hung up, Clancy barged into the classroom. He skidded to a stop, wearing a sadistic leer. "Well, look who's rackin' up the screwups. You've just been CPBed, McCobb. That cell phone's busted!" He forked two fingers at Morning. "And that's two more demerits. You know what that means?"

Morning swallowed. "No, sir."

"You've hit tipping-point demerits! You, my pathetic hose weenie, are on *probation*!" He moved closer, with one of the evilest expressions Morning had ever seen on a Lifer. "One more violation and you fly outta here with my boot up your ass. And trust me, McCobb, you *will* screw up."

36

Take Back the Bite

Washington Square was jammed with goths, the curious, and media awaiting the appearance of the spokesman for the first website to have ever been "staked" into silence. Portia, Cody, and Zoë were there too, ready to shoot.

DeThanatos showed up at eight on the dot from an odd direction. He dropped through the haze of light above the square, steering a parachute. As heads and cameras tilted, he worked his chute and landed on top of the rectangular arch in the square. He tossed off the harness and unfurled a long black cape. The goths in the crowd cheered his Dracula-wear.

He spread his arms, revealing the cape's red lining. "Good *eeevening*," he intoned in perfect Bela Lugosi-ese. The goths shouted their approval. He flashed a charming smile as he dropped the cape and the accent. "Forgive my imitation. I'm no Dracula, I'm just the Leaguer spokesman for a website that was shut down faster than a human rights website in Iran." The crowd booed and hissed. "That's right! They can't shut *you* down, and they can't shut *me* down!" He let the following cheer subside. "First, I want to thank you for coming." His eyes found Portia in the throng. "I know, in these busy times"—he gave her a flirtatious wink—"how easy it is to get tied up."

His words sent a chill through Portia, pebbling her skin with goose bumps. But, she reassured herself, she was safe in a crowd.

DeThanatos returned his attention to the throng. "I'm here to tell you that Becky-Dell Wallace is right: vampires *do* have a hidden agenda." A hush fell over the square. "But before I reveal our true agenda, I must expose the falsehoods Luther Birnam has spread in his effort to prove to the world that Leaguers are harmless." The hush was replaced with a murmur of puzzlement. "One, he claims all vampires descended from a 'Mother Forest' in California. False. Do you want the truth?"

"Yeah!" burst from the crowd.

Portia turned to Cody, behind his camera. "Getting this?" Cody nodded vigorously.

"Mortals have had the drop on vampires for hundreds of years," DeThanatos intoned. "We *are* the undead. We *rose* from our graves. And our oldest ancestors didn't come from some California woodland. We came from Transylvania!"

The gathering erupted in a cheer.

Zoë almost peed her pants with excitement. "I knew it!"

DeThanatos raised his arms for quiet. "I reveal these truths in the spirit of full disclosure. But none of them are the greatest falsehood Birnam has spread in his effort to whitewash our race, to turn us into fangless do-gooders with the bloodlust sucked out of us!" His voice rose over the booing and hissing. "Do you want the truth?"

"Yeah!"

"I can't hear you," he appealed, cupping a hand to his ear.

"Yeah!" the crowd boomed.

"A vampire CDing into a leech to wet-vac human blood is more than a medical procedure. Vampower .com is more than a dating service for Lifers who want to bleed Leaguers in need. They answer a *vampire* need!" The throng bellowed its approval as he continued. "It is a need that Birnam refuses to acknowledge. It is a need that belongs to our sacred cultural tradition. If you can give Native Americans the right to hunt an endangered whale in the name of cultural tradition, you can give Leaguers the right to hunt a little human blood in the name of cultural tradition. But we're not asking to kill; we're merely asking to *fulfill*! Our vein-breaking won't be *lawbreaking*. Our vessels won't be victims! They'll be volunteers helping us to reclaim our birthright!"

The crowd roared. Cody kept shooting. Portia's face was a mask of shock and fear. Zoë was enraptured.

DeThanatos spread his cape again. "Let Birnam try to convince the world we have conquered bloodlust! Let him try to be a slayer of our cultural heritage! And let Becky-Dell Wallace scream 'Bloodsucking fiends!' till she's blue enough in the face to drink! But I am here to throw down the cape of our true agenda!" The open cape suddenly dropped to his feet. "I am here to start a movement! I am here to take back the bite!"

The crowd let loose a delirious howl.

DeThanatos spun and snapped into a giant bat,

unfurling a six-foot wingspan. As the bat took flight, something white flashed in its talons. It dive-bombed the crowd. Most screamed with delight, a few shrank in horror.

Watching the bat's shiny black eyes race toward her, Portia was locked in a straitjacket of fear. As the bat's snout opened, she stared into its widening black maw. Cody yanked her down. The bat shot over them with an earsplitting shriek and a flash of white.

Zoë would have turned to watch the bat soar into the haze of light if she hadn't been mesmerized by the white card that had just stuck to her chest. She plucked the card from her vest and read the first line.

"Are you all right?" Cody implored, giving Portia a shake.

Zoë stuffed the card in her back pocket before she could read more or Cody or Portia saw her prize.

Portia found her voice. "I'm okay." She shook off the brain-lock that had gripped her, and turned to Cody. "Did you get that last shot?"

His face scrunched with disbelief. "No, I didn't want a shot of a bat taking your head off. We're not making the next *Final Destination*."

"Never worry about me," Portia fumed. "Always get the shot!" She spun and pushed through the crowd. "I need a director of photography, not a damsel protector!"

Stunned, he watched her go. "Jeez, what's eating her?"

Zoë was so fixated on the card burning in her pocket, the words popped out of her mouth. "She and Morning broke up." She slapped a hand over her mouth. "Oops!"

Cody arched a brow. "Oh, really?"

Zoë swallowed. "Oh, crap."

37

Restless Night

In the St. Giles common room, Sister Flora had just seen the coverage of DeThanatos's appearance. She flicked off the TV in disgust. " 'Take back the bite'? What on earth is he up to?"

Morning sat in a corner chair studying a textbook. "It looks like he's working on a different kind of turning."

"What's that?"

"Turning the majority of Americans for the VRA into a minority."

"Are you going to do something about it?"

Morning hadn't told Flora about his breakup with Portia, or about being one demerit away from being expelled from the academy. It was another reason for him not getting involved. "As long as DeThanatos doesn't mess with Portia," he said, "I'm staying out of it. Besides, it looks like he'll have his hands full fighting Becky-Dell. Portia and I thought we destroyed DeThanatos once, now maybe someone else will get the job done."

His indifference puzzled Flora. "What about Birnam? Why is he letting things get so out of hand?"

"Maybe I'll find out tomorrow. I'm meeting him at the Met."

She gave him a startled look. "Really?"

Morning went back to his book. "Yeah, but he's been such a no-show, I'll believe it when I see it."

Becky-Dell was just pulling back the covers on her four-poster bed when she heard a crinkling in the hall. She turned as DeThanatos, wearing the borrowed hazmat suit again, strode into the room.

She instinctively crossed her arms over her chest even though she was wearing a nightgown. "Do you mind?"

DeThanatos flicked a hand at a robe lying over the back of an armchair. The robe flew across the room, and Becky-Dell, despite her shock, caught it.

"Sorry for busting in so late," he explained, "but I had to fly down from New York, and this is the only safe place we can meet." He took in the luxuriously appointed room with its antique furnishings and brocade curtains. "Believe it or not, I'm not comfortable with this myself."

"Why's that?" she asked, cinching the robe tight.

"I rarely use a bedchamber for a conference room. It's usually my stun-and-kill box."

As he sat in an armchair, Becky-Dell resisted the urge to pluck the revolver from her bedside drawer, especially since she now had two reasons to shoot him: he was an intruder, and his clinical indifference was an insult to her female vanity. But she knew bullets wouldn't hurt him. She fired sarcasm instead. "I suppose I should thank you for making my bedroom the exception."

DeThanatos chortled, not missing the umbrage she had taken of his remark. "No need, it's all part of redefining my notion of prey. But after centuries of vanquishing beautiful women such as yourself," he added with a smoldering look, "stalking a pathetic pack of Leaguers doesn't come with the same thrill of the hunt."

She acknowledged his flirtation with a frown and sat in the armchair facing his. "I'll give you this, Mr. DeThanatos, in the past twenty-four hours we've certainly ratcheted up mortal-vampire tensions. MOP was flooded with callers wanting to join; our website was so overwhelmed it crashed and had to be upgraded to more capacity."

He nodded in approval. "My side did as well. Trudi launched a new website: Takebackthebite.com."

Becky-Dell spread her hands. "What's the point? I'll have the BVA shut that down too."

"Appearances are everything," he answered. "Which reminds me, I need to tell you our next move. It involves a juicy invitation."

She lifted an eyebrow. "A juicy invitation? It better not be from you to me."

He laughed at her paranoia tinged with flirtation. "Please, Ms. Wallace, keep me focused on the mission."

She answered with a self-satisfied smirk. "So, what's this juicy invitation?"

"It's for someone with an itch for exsanguination."

"Drop the vampire-speak," she said, back to her scowling disapproval. "Speak American."

"A need to bleed."

At St. Giles, Morning sat on the edge of his bed and stared at the earth-shattering text on his phone.

M, can't do bfest tmr. 2much 2do on nu vid.
Plz fergiv. Gotta earn my death!
XOXO, P

His eyes scanned the text until the screen became the black mirror of his mind. *Why are all my dreams turning to crap?* he fretted. *I'm one demerit away from being expelled, and now my eternal beloved, who turned into my eternal befriended, can't even meet me for breakfast!*

He tossed the phone on his desk and threw himself on the bed. Even if he could have slept, he was tempted to turn his alarm off. Then he could just get it over with. *I'd be late for school, Clancy would expel me, and I could go back to what I was doing before I met everyone who screwed up my life: Birnam, Portia, Clancy, the whole dream-crushing bunch. I'd spend my pathetic eternity reading every superhero comic book ever written, and seeing every TV show and movie made about 'em.*

Despite his misery, a phrase from Portia's text kept bumping in his mind like a blind bumping against the window on a windy night. *Gotta earn my death!* He wondered if there was a vampire equivalent. *Earn my slaying?* He tried to imagine what it would be like if—with a stake in his heart and facing the fires of annihilation—he had a moment to look back on his vampire life and ask, *Any major regrets?*

The answer came in a flash. *Portia. I'd regret not seeing her every chance I got. But does it count as a regret if you can't control it?* The answer was obvious. *No, Portia has a will of her own.*

He narrowed his regrets to the actions he could control. The first that flashed in his mind was Prowler. He imagined the grizzled firefighter learning that Morning had been expelled from the academy. Why? Because of the lamest screwup of all: he hadn't shown up for class. The disappointment he imagined on Prowler's face was the big regret Morning had been looking for.

He wasn't going to get expelled because of a self-inflicted wound. He was going to get his ass out of bed in the morning and go to school. He was going to go down fighting. He was going to suck it up and *earn his expulsion*!

In another bed, on the Upper East Side, Zoë held the thick white card and read it for the umpteenth time.

THE TASTING ROOM
INVITES YOU TO A BRUSH WITH BLOODLUST
FRIDAY—8 P.M.
YOUR DATE
(MATCHED BY YOUR VAMPOWER.COM PROFILE)
WILL FIND YOU
BYOB (Bring Your Own Blood)

She had fingered the card for so long one edge had begun to fray. As she nervously flicked the splitting edge, it separated further. She peeled away the back of the card. It was another invitation, identical to the top one. And this one also split. Zoë stared at three invitations. Whether the cards had been accidently stuck together or DeThanatos had wanted her to have three, she didn't know. All she knew was that in less than forty-eight hours, she was going to have her first cozy encounter with a vampire. She held the invitation to her chest, closed her eyes, and softly sang a bit of her favorite song. "Bloodlustin' free—wish I could be / Part of that world."

38

Busted

The alarm jarred Morning awake. He was still wearing his clothes from the day before.

He pulled on fresh pants and a new shirt, which he buttoned up and tucked in. He checked himself in the mirror over his dresser. Noticing something sticking from the shirt near the top button and thinking it was a loose thread, he plucked at it. "Ow!" He yelped from the sting on his chest. He undid the button and pulled the shirt apart.

He stared in shock. It was no loose thread. It was a dark, squiggly chest hair. And there wasn't just one, there were three. Sure, he had body hair where a sixteen-year-old should, but this was his first *chest hair*!

The door to his room suddenly opened. He spun around as he fumbled for his top button. "Jeez, Sister—"

Zoë stood in the doorway with a backpack slung over her shoulder. "Oops, sorry, A.M. Sister Flora said you'd be dressed already and it was okay to come up."

"How would she know?" Morning snapped. "Does she have a camera in here?"

"O-kay"—Zoë shrank back in mock fear—"someone woke up on the crappy—" Her mouth froze when her eyes fell on the squigglies escaping from Morning's shirt. She raised a finger, pointing at his chest. "Is that what I think it is?"

Realizing his shirt was still undone, Morning quickly buttoned it, covering his new bodily additions. "It's nothing. What are you doing here?"

Zoë decided to give him a breather before she got back to the mysterious sighting on his chest. She swung the backpack off her shoulder. "One, I've got some daily doses of red stuff, and I was hoping I could start a blood stash here."

"You've already got a stash in Portia's locker and at her house," he protested. "Why do you need one here?"

"If the Take Back the Bite movement dooms the VRA, I'm thinking prohibition of blood products will be next. And if I'm flipped by the time they start yanking blood products off the shelves, I'm gonna be prepared."

Morning eyed her suspiciously. "What makes you think you're gonna get turned anytime soon?"

For a second Zoë was tempted to tell him about her Tasting Room invitation, but she knew he would try to talk her out of it. "Even if I'm still a Lifer," she said, unzipping her backpack, "I'll be able to sell this stuff to blood-starved Leaguers." She turned the pack upside down and a dozen cans and plastic containers of blood products tumbled onto Morning's bed. "Who knows, you might even need it."

"You know I only drink Blood Lite."

"You say that now." She felt the long object still zipped up in her backpack's outside pocket. "The second reason

I came— Wait a minute, it's your turn. Since when do you have *chest hair*?"

Her verbal pirouette caught him off guard, but only for a second. "I always had a little."

"No you didn't. Last summer, at the beach, I checked out your chest—I was amazed that it was as bony as mine," she interjected by way of explanation, "and there wasn't a chest hair in sight."

"Yes there was," Morning claimed. "You just didn't see 'em 'cause they'd been bleached by the sun."

"Nice try, A.M., but I know what I saw, and I know vampires don't do growing." Zoë threw a glance back at the doorframe to see if the markings she'd noticed on a previous visit were still there. She tossed the backpack on the bed, grabbed Morning, and shoved him toward the door.

"Hey!" Morning protested. He resisted, but she was amazingly strong for being so small and bony.

She slapped a hand on top of his head and held it against the frame. He scooted away, but too late. Her fingers touched the doorframe where Sister Flora had marked Morning's height until he had been turned at sixteen. Zoë's fingertips rested a half inch above the last mark.

"You're growing more than chest hair." Her wide eyes moved to his. "What's going on?"

He wished he knew. He wanted to brush off the chest hair as a stress thing: Lifers got hives, maybe vampires got werewolfie and broke out in stress hair. He *had* been under lots of stress. But the height thing was different. Lately, he'd noticed his pant legs did seem shorter. He had dismissed it as laundry shrinkage. Until now.

He shut the door against eavesdroppers. "I don't know what's going on. Maybe I'll find out today from Birnam, but you can't tell *anyone* about this. Especially Portia."

184

"Sure, fine," Zoë conceded as her mind rocketed through the possible repercussions of this development. "But if for some bizarre reason your body's, like, rejecting immortality, and you're growing again, don't you get what that means? You and Portia could—"

He didn't let her finish. "I don't know if I'm rejecting immortality. For all I know I have that disease where people age super fast and I'll be ninety-five next week. You have to promise you won't tell her."

"Okay, okay, but I'm still trying to wrap my brain around this. I mean, whoever heard of a vampire turning mortal? It could be a new species. Right now, you're turning into a *Liger*: half Lifer, half Leag—no, that's taken: half lion, half tiger. I got it! You're a *Leafer*: half Leaguer, half Lifer!" She sprang toward him. "How much do you think you've changed? Can you still grow fangs? C'mon, give it a try."

He waved his hands in exasperation. "You can't grow fangs on cue. You have to be inspired."

Zoë pulled down her collar and thrust her neck at him. "Do anything for you?"

He stepped back. "Zoë, I don't have time for this."

"Not even if you think of Portia?"

He slipped around her. "Put your stash wherever. I gotta get to school." He opened the door and took off.

Taking up her backpack, Zoë unzipped the side pocket and pulled out a croquet stake. It was the other reason she had come. She placed it on Morning's pillow. "Porsche, you're still my best bud, but you're a total wimp for not doing this yourself." She straightened up, lost in thought. "And you have no clue what you're doing, especially now."

39

Crusader

Morning got through the day at the academy without collecting his death demerit, as he had named it. After school, he headed to the Metropolitan Museum of Art.

By late afternoon, the Medieval Gallery was practically empty. Morning wandered through the rooms filled with paintings of Christ and statues of saints. Passing through a special exhibit on the Crusades, he noticed an old man sitting on a bench with his forehead resting on a cane. Morning didn't give him a second glance as he headed for the next room.

The old man muttered, "What's the rush, sonny?"

Morning turned back. Above the man's white beard was a gaunt face, ash white and deeply grooved with wrinkles that ran up his forehead and mingled with his thin white hair. He looked like an albino prune. Morning answered the man as he backed toward the next room. "Just looking for someone."

The man spoke again, his voice stronger. "You found him."

Morning stopped; he recognized the voice, but it didn't match the face. The old man's intense eyes, fixed on him, sparked recognition. "Mr. Birnam?"

The man nodded and gestured. "Come."

In a daze of confusion, Morning moved to the bench. A year before Birnam had been hearty and looked no more than middle-aged. Now he was as wizened as a hundred-year-old. "What happened?"

"It's called aging."

Morning's stomach flopped. "But how?"

Birnam's cracked lips crinkled into a smile. "That answer is more complicated." His eyes shifted to a glass case nearby. "And it begins there. Help me up."

Morning helped him stand and they moved to the case. A medieval manuscript was open inside it. The pages were filled with gothic-looking writing, and one page featured an illustration of a crowned king leading armored knights.

Birnam stared at the colorful illumination for a moment. "In the thirteenth century, what we now call the Middle East was embroiled in the Crusades." His crooked finger lifted to the illumination of the king and knights. "This was the eighth and final crusade, in 1270. When I was still a mortal, I rode with these knights." His finger wavered over the king. "That's Louis the Ninth. He was my king and I was his knight. In August of 1270, Louis and most of his knights died in Egypt from dysentery. Sometimes I wish I had died with them."

Birnam took a labored breath and moved away from the case. "But I didn't. And, as a Knight Templar, I went back to protecting the Christian city-states my fellow crusaders had conquered."

Morning followed until Birnam stopped at a painting. It showed a walled city, filled with knights being attacked by men on horseback wearing broad hats and colorful tunics.

"I don't need eyes to see this one," Birnam said. "I was there. I remember it like it was"—he couldn't stop a smile—"well, maybe not yesterday, more like the day before yesterday. This is the Siege of Tripoli. But I'm getting ahead of myself. By the early 1280s, the Knights Templar cared less about protecting Tripoli from Muslim forces than they did about fighting other Christians for control of Tripoli. When I saw Christian knights siding with our Muslim enemies so they could fight and kill my Christian brothers, God appeared to me in a dream. He told me the Crusades were no longer a holy war; they had become, like all wars, an unholy one over land, wealth, and power. God told me to lay down my sword and become a prophet of peace. So I did. I became, to use the modern term, a pacifist. I campaigned for peace between all the warring parties, whether they were Christian or Muslim. In 1282, when the Knights Templar plotted to attack Tripoli from within, I went with them, without a sword, in hopes of stopping the bloodbath. The Templars—including myself— were betrayed, captured, and condemned to die."

"But you were there as a peacemaker."

"The victorious Count Bohemond didn't think so. The night before my execution I was visited by a vampire disguised as a guard. The vampire didn't believe in taking innocent lives, and survived by feeding on men and women about to be executed or burned at the stake. Having heard of my peacemaking efforts, the vampire gave me a choice: to die as his victim or be turned. I chose the latter."

"That's how you became a vampire?"

"Yes. And my blood sire probably planted in me the seeds of mercy that took so long to grow."

"But Mr. Birnam, what does it have to do with you getting old?"

Birnam turned from the painting and fixed on Morning with rheumy eyes. "Everything. Before I was turned, my mortal dream was to make peace between ancient enemies: Christians and Muslims. Centuries later, in the early twentieth century, I returned to a similar dream: to make peace between vampires and mortals."

"I don't get it. What's the connection?"

"I didn't know until a few months ago when I began to age, rapidly." He reached in his pocket and pulled out a piece of caramel corn and popped it in his mouth.

Morning stared in disbelief. "You're eating, too?"

Birnam crunched with pleasure. "It comes with the territory. When you kick-start mortality, you regain your appetite for all sorts of glorious things." He took Morning's arm. "My legs are tired. Let's sit down and I'll tell you what I know."

40

Invitations

Portia was stuffing books in her locker. She was late joining Cody in the editing room, where he was working on the footage from Washington Square. A figure appeared beside her making her jump. It was Zoë. "God, you scared me."

"Sorry."

"And please"—Portia wedged a last book in the locker—"got no time for your latest blood-obligate impression."

Zoë flashed a smile. "Got something better." She lifted her invitation to the Tasting Room and displayed it like it was a Golden Ticket from Willy Wonka.

Portia's eyes bugged. "Ohmigod! Where'd you get that?"

"Shhh," Zoë shushed as a couple of students walked by. She stuffed the invitation back in her bag and lied. "It came in the mail. They must've sent it before Vampower.com got shut down."

"Is the invite for *this* Friday?"

Zoë jiggled like a bobblehead. "Tomorrow night!"

Portia blanched. "You're not going, are you?"

"Of course I am."

"Zoë, you can't!"

It was Zoë's turn to look shocked. "Why not?"

As another student passed, Portia grabbed Zoë and pulled her across the hall, through a classroom door. The room was empty. She gestured at Zoë's bag holding the invitation. " 'Your date will find you.' For all you know it could be some skeevy Nosferatu with rotten breath, yellow fangs, and flesh peeling off his head."

Zoë frowned dismissively. "You're thinkin' outta-the-grave zombie. I'm thinkin' hot Leaguer looking for a little sip."

" 'A little sip'? How do you know that's all it'll be?" She gripped Zoë by the shoulders. "I'm tellin' you, ZZ, you don't want to do this. I've been there. I know what happens when a guy gets his fangs into you. They go crazy, they can't stop themselves."

Zoë shook her off. "Just 'cause you almost got date-sapped doesn't mean I will. I mean, when Morning almost drained you, he was jealous and pissed off. But this is gonna be with other people around, no enraged boyfriend, just a nice Leaguer who liked my profile and is lookin' for a little meet 'n' greet 'n' neck-nibble."

Portia's heart filled with a black cloud of dread. "Zoë, of all the online hookups with total strangers that you could stumble into, I'm begging you as my best friend, don't fall into this one."

Zoë's lips bent into a smile. "Thanks for caring, but you can't stop me. There's just one thing you can do."

191

"What?" Portia scowled. "Tell your parents, and get you grounded till Saturday?"

Zoë laughed, knowing Portia was incapable of such betrayal. "No, you can come with." She reached into her back pocket and pulled out the two other invitations.

"Holy sh—!" Portia grabbed the cards, her eyes racing over them. "These came in the mail too?"

"Yeah, they were stuck together. And if you and Cody can figure out how to shoot it, you can get my date with destiny on tape. You've been squawking about how your movie has inside access—well, now you've got *underground* access."

With her eyes still riveted on the two invitations, Portia's insides coiled with fear and temptation.

"What's it gonna be?" Zoë asked. "Judgmental best friend, or filmmaker ready for combat?"

41

Pneumabrotus

Morning and Birnam sat on a bench in the gallery.

Birnam took a raspy breath. "I once told you that a vampire craves mortal blood for two reasons. One is nutrition, of course. Do you remember the second reason we lust for human blood?"

"Envy," Morning answered.

"Very good. Envy of what?"

"Human ambition."

Birnam patted Morning's knee. "You were always a good student. Yes, even though vampires harbor ambitions and aspirations, they're not as intense for a reason. We have so much time to achieve them; we have no deadlines. We are clocks without hands. But the mortal clock comes with hands, spinning away, giving each mortal a short time to achieve their dream. This ticking clock embedded in mortal cells infuses the blood of Lifers with what I once called the 'ambrosia of human aspiration.' I've discovered that this ambrosia is more than a bewitching essence we crave in their blood. I don't know the chemistry of it—whether it's a hormone, a peptide, or something else—I'm no scientist. But it's real, and I've given it a name."

"What?"

"*Pneumabrotus*. It's Greek for 'the spirit of death.' This *pneumabrotus* that once coursed through our mortal blood disappears when we get turned. When we are reconfigured into a pillar of regenerating stem cells, our vampire DNA turns off the production of *pneumabrotus* like a faucet. But we haven't lost it entirely. It's still there, dormant, sleeping in our cells, waiting to be woken."

Goose bumps chilled Morning's skin. His attention darted to a sensation prickling his chest; it felt like three tiny darts quivered in his flesh. Is that what's happening to me? Am I aging too? But he swallowed his questions along with a breath. "What retriggers this . . . *pneumabrotus*?"

Birnam shook his head. "I'm not sure, but when I look at what has happened to me, I have a theory."

"What?" Morning asked, trying not to sound impatient with the labored slowness of Birnam's speech.

The old man's brow furrowed, pulling his wrinkles even deeper. "Before I was turned, I had a powerful Lifer ambition: to be a peacemaker. A century ago, I took up a similar dream: to be the peacemaker between vampires and mortals. In the past year, my dream began to bear fruit. If a vampire can return to the essence of what was once his Lifer dream and see it start to bloom, maybe it reawakens the *pneumabrotus* sleeping in his cells. It resurrects the spirit of death and cures his immortality."

Morning blinked with excitement and confusion. "But it took a hundred years for your mortality to kick back in. Why did it take so long?"

"Maybe because only in the past year my dream began to materialize. I don't know for sure. It's all new to me. And maybe vampires like me, who have been immortal for centuries, have some kind of buildup in the DNA, so when *pneumabrotus* does return it breaks like a dam, overwhelming the body with aging."

The bands of tension constricting Morning's chest eased a bit. He had been a vampire for less than two years. Maybe he would be spared the hyper-aging thing.

"If my theory is right," Birnam whispered, "I've stumbled on the cure for vampirism."

Morning was suddenly struck by a hole in his theory. "But Mr. Birnam, over all the centuries, this must have happened before. You couldn't have been the first vampire to start re-aging. Why don't vampires know about this?"

The old man nodded. "A good question, to which I have no answer."

"What if you had to guess?"

He pulled another kernel of caramel corn from his pocket and chewed it pensively. "Knowing Loner vampires, and the depths of their evil, my guess would be that a select few have done everything in their power to keep this a secret. After all, a cure for vampirism is vampire slaying from *within*. Maybe there are vampires, with powers even I don't know about, who have, over the centuries, destroyed anyone who stumbled on this cure."

Morning swallowed hard, feeling like he'd just been given a death sentence. "If that's true, that they destroy those who know about it, why did you tell me?"

Birnam gave him a weak smile. "I think you're smart enough to figure that out. Also, I wanted to tell you before I left."

Morning was taken aback. "Where are you going?"

Birnam jutted his head at the painting on the wall. "Tripoli. If I can make it." He planted his cane and struggled to his feet. "Which reminds me, I have a flight to catch." They started out of the museum as Birnam explained. "It's one of the little surprises that comes with finally growing old. You have this overwhelming urge to return to the last place you were mortal."

Morning wasn't reeling from such a tumble of thoughts and feelings that he wasn't able to add another: *Oh, great. If I'm really aging again and growing old, someday I'm gonna wanna go breathe my last on Staten Island.*

As they crossed the entrance hall, Birnam held Morning's arm. "I only have one last wish, my boy. Like so many last wishes it's selfish, self-centered, and so mortal." He stopped and turned his watery eyes on Morning. "I don't want my dream to die with me. I want you, and Rachel, and Penny, and my Leaguers to keep up the good fight. You've got to stop DeThanatos from pushing us back into a coffin we never rose from."

Morning started to speak, but Birnam stopped him with a hand. "I know what you want to say." He pulled Morning toward the door. "That your days of being the IVL's poster boy are over, that you just want to be a firefighter and go about your quiet heroics."

They moved through the door, and outside. Birnam shielded his eyes against the late-afternoon brightness. Morning scanned the front of the museum for threats, like a bunch of monstered-up Loners coming straight at them with stakes, fire, and leaf blowers.

"What you don't see," Birnam added, "beyond your blindfold of youth, is that if my dream of Leaguers and Lifers living in peace dies, so will yours."

Helping Birnam totter down the steps, Morning knew the old man was right. As he maneuvered him toward a waiting cab, Morning asked, "If you care so much about your dream, why don't you stay and fight for it?"

"It's very simple." Birnam reached into his pocket, pulled out a half-eaten Baby Ruth, and smiled at it like a greedy little boy. "I'm not a vampire anymore. I'm mortal." He bit off a chunk of Baby Ruth, chewed euphorically, and swallowed. He fixed on Morning with dim eyes. "You see, my time is up."

When they reached the cab, Birnam turned to Morning and held up a bony finger. "In the endless relay that is humanity, the baton of time has been passed to you. How and where you run with it is your decision. I hope you choose well."

As the cab pulled away, Morning watched Birnam's wrinkled head, framed in the cab's back window, disappear into the New York chaos.

42

Hair Loss

In Prowler's firehouse, Morning sipped a Blood Lite. He had just finished explaining his predicament to Prowler, including his troubles with Clancy at the fire academy.

Prowler squinted as if the latest flock of wild new developments were still finding a perch in his head. "Let me see if I have this straight. You started to age again because you've been pursuing your Lifer dream of being a firefighter, and you're getting close to achieving it. But before you found this out, Portia broke up with you because, at the time, you were locked at sixteen. But now that you *are* aging, you think you can win her back."

"Yeah, if the major reason she broke up with me was because of the nonaging thing."

"Right, but for all you know it could've been other things as well, trivial things like bad breath."

Morning pulled a long face. "Do I have bad breath?"

"Now that you're half Leaguer, half Lifer, who knows what kind of breath you have?"

"According to Zoë, it's *Leafer* breath."

Prowler gave him a startled look. "Zoë knows and Portia doesn't?"

"It was an accident."

"So be it. But for the future, never, ever let your girlfriend's best friend know something your girlfriend doesn't. If your girlfriend finds out she'll immediately think you've got your fingers in the wrong cookie jar."

Morning eye-rolled. "Do we have to go there?"

"No, back to the facts. So, you have a chance to win Portia back, 'cause you're aging, but you're also one screwup away from being expelled from the academy, and if that happens, your Lifer dream is gonna be aborted and you're gonna stop making some weird body juice called *pneumabrotus*, which means you'll probably go back to being immortal, which means even if you *do* win Portia back, you'll just lose her again." Prowler took a breath and exhaled. "Does that cover the bases?"

Morning nodded. "Yeah."

Prowler waggled his head. "And you thought some of *my* stories were convoluted."

"Yours are always about some myth. This is real."

"Okay, two questions. One, what's more important, getting Portia back or being a firefighter?"

Morning gave him a *duh* look. "Like, both."

"Right, you'll take a pass on that one. Two, what makes you absolutely sure you're aging?"

Morning shot out a leg, showing him the high cuff on his pants. "I'm pretty sure I've grown some."

Prowler shrugged. "Could be laundry shrinkage."

"That's what I thought." He pulled open his shirt, thrust out his chest, and showed off his three hairs. "Didn't have these before."

Prowler's hand shot forward and plucked one.

"Ow!" Morning yipped. "What'd you do that for?"

"Had to see if they were real. Besides, you're a vampire, or half of one. It'll just grow back, right?"

"I hope so!" Morning blurted as he realized what would truly prove he was part mortal. He jumped up, opened the irons box on the fire truck, and pulled out an ax.

"Whoa," Prowler cautioned, "what are you doing?"

"A test." Morning lifted his shirtsleeve, grimaced, and swiped the ax blade across his shoulder muscle.

Prowler jumped up. "What the . . . ?"

Morning stared at the gash on his left. Blood welled in the wound. It didn't heal up. He smiled through the pain. "I think I'm more Lifer than Leaguer."

Using a first-aid kit, Prowler dressed the wound and issued his advice. "For one, no more screwups in front of Clancy, not even the whiff of one. Also, you gotta make sure no one at the academy knows you're going mortal."

"I'm not telling anyone," Morning said. "But why's that important?"

" 'Cause as a mortal sixteen-year-old you really will be too young to be a probie, and Clancy will take the minimum age waiver they granted you as a vampire and shred it."

43

Sire-Spawn Chat

It was late as Morning rode his bike back to St. Giles. He kept feeling the dull ache in his shoulder under the bandage. It was *lingering* pain, something only mortals feel, something he hadn't felt for a long time. Never had pain been so welcome.

He pondered his next move with Portia. First he had to tell her the great news and sweep her off her feet. He had to wrap it like a fantastic gift; then their whole future would stretch before them. They really could be eternal beloveds, as long as mortals can be, and it would begin with him asking her to the End Is Upon Us Ball in December. Sure, she didn't like dances but she did like rites of passage. And if the world was going to expire on December 21, they would miss out on the springtime rite of senior prom. So why not celebrate prom a few months in advance?

Morning's reverie was broken by a man on a bike swerving around a corner and riding behind him. Looking back, Morning's gut clutched with fear as he recognized DeThanatos. "What do you want?"

DeThanatos offered a friendly smile. "I was in the mood for a family reunion."

Morning fought his fear with bravado. "If you're here to recruit me for your ridiculous Take Back the Bite movement, forget it."

"I don't have to recruit *you*," DeThanatos said, oozing lugubrious satisfaction. "You already took back the bite when you gave Portia the ivory deuce." He snapped his jaw shut with a clack of teeth.

Morning thought about racing away, but trying to outpedal a vampire who could turn into a bird and land on your handlebars was pointless.

"I wanted to congratulate you," DeThanatos said.

"For what?"

"For your new lease on life. Or should we call it a lease on death?"

"I don't know what you're talking about."

"Your mouth can feign ignorance but"—he sniffed the air—"your scent gives you away."

Morning wasn't sure if DeThanatos was bluffing. "What scent?"

"I believe Birnam has a term for what we crave in human blood. What did he call it? *Pneumabrotus?* I can smell it coming from your shoulder." He enjoyed a laugh. "You're wondering how I know this. I had a little chat with Birnam at JFK."

Morning's stomach wound tighter. "What did you do to him?"

"Nothing," he said innocently. "I like Birnam; he's been a worthy adversary. And even though it's my duty as a Millennial to destroy him, I spared him."

Morning hesitated, but couldn't stop from asking, "What's a Millennial?"

"Vampires who have stalked the earth for a thousand years are a rare breed. We are the guardians of our cherished traditions, bloodlust and immortality being the most sacred. When we learn of a vampire who has contracted the immortal equivalent of rabies, the lunatic madness of re-aging, we put them out of their misery."

Morning's eyes darted to the vampire's hands, wondering which would deliver the stake to his chest. But the knife of fear dissolved when he remembered DeThanatos couldn't destroy one of his blood children without destroying himself. His fear shifted to curiosity. "What about the treaty all Loners signed after World War V? You agreed not to slay any more Leaguers."

"I didn't sign it, and neither did any Millennial I know of. Even if we did," he added with a beguiling smile, "vampires aren't known for keeping promises."

"Then what stopped you from destroying Birnam?"

"I'm taking a break from my duties."

"What about me?"

DeThanatos let go of his handlebars but kept riding. "As you know, when it comes to you, my hands are tied. That is, until you become a full-fledged re-mort."

"A re-mort?"

"Yes, a re-mortal. It's what we call wishy-washy creatures who get flipped to immortality, then flop back to their formerly mortal selves. When you finish your flop, maybe I'll finish the job I botched that fateful Thanksgiving."

Morning shot him a hateful glare. "We destroyed you once. We can do it again." He turned onto his street.

DeThanatos rested a hand back on his handlebars and followed. "Ah, yes, you and lovely Portia. Hopefully, when we have our little rematch, it'll be just like old times: me against my favorite pair of eternal beloveds."

Morning was glad to finally reach St. Giles. He was tired of listening to the sinister vampire. He carried his bike up the stoop.

"It's been lovely," DeThanatos said from the sidewalk. "Blood father and blood son going for a spin, having a little sire-spawn chat, getting to know each other."

Morning wanted to go inside and shut the door on DeThanatos's unctuous sarcasm, but curiosity got the best of him. "If you mean it, I've got a question."

The vampire spread his arms. "I bleed answers."

"What about you?"

"What *about* me?"

"Do you ever worry about going back to your Lifer dreams and becoming a re-mort?"

DeThanatos's head tossed back with a laugh. "God, no. My Lifer dream is long dead."

"What was it?"

"Do you really want to know?"

Morning nodded. "Yeah."

"Will you use it against me if you can?"

Morning was surprised how easily DeThanatos could read his mind. "Of course."

The Loner wagged a teasing finger. "There's some evil in you yet, a chip off the old block." He chuckled. "It's hard to believe, I know, but I was a Benedictine monk."

Morning scoffed.

"Really." DeThanatos crossed his fingers. "Me and God were like this. I was communing with Him one night in my cell, when a vampire interrupted us. Having taken a vow of silence, I didn't cry out. My faith-filled heart called for God to save me. But God fled the room. I haven't heard from Him since—fine by me. As I pursue my diabolical ways, God is too shamefaced to intervene, and anytime I remember my monk's cell with the slightest whiff of nostalgia, I go out and commit bloody murder." He flashed glistening fangs. "Just talking about it makes me thirsty."

Morning shuddered with disgust, opened the door, and began pushing his bike through it.

The Loner called after him. "I can't guarantee some other Millennial might not come after you."

Morning turned back, swallowing hard. "Like who?"

"We don't communicate much. We simply strike when necessary. As for me, I have my eyes on a bigger prize."

Morning waited, knowing DeThanatos wasn't finished.

"Birnam got one thing right. This Leaguer thing has been a game changer. And yet, it's a Millennial's duty to slay vampires who betray our sacred traditions. I could destroy all Leaguers, one by one, but it would be so tedious. I have a far more satisfying plan." He raised his hands. "Why be a serial killer when genocide beckons?"

Morning shut the door, not wanting to hear any more. What was the point? He knew DeThanatos was too devious to ever reveal more than he wanted to.

44

The High Line

Friday dawned. Morning's alarm sounded. He banged it off. The ceiling swam into focus and the day's first thought dropped into his mind. *Was it all a dream? From Birnam telling me about* pneumabrotus *to DeThanatos calling me a re-mort?*

He pulled down the covers and took in the two hairs jutting from his chest. "Hey, gents. Sorry about the loss of musketeer number three, but if I keep re-mortalizing, re-inforcements are on the way." He rolled out of bed. "Yeow!" He'd forgotten the laceration on his left shoulder.

He grabbed his cell phone and called Portia. She answered, but she was in a hurry to get in the shower. He asked her to take a walk with him later that afternoon on the Williamsburg Bridge so he could tell her some "big news." She explained that she and Cody were prepping for a film thing that night, and they had to finish a hidden camera Cody was working on.

"So let gizmo geek earn his death by doing the camera thing while you give me an hour."

Portia laughed at his cockiness. "Okay, but I don't have time for the bridge. How 'bout we meet for gelato at seven in the Village?"

Morning figured the exact location where he blew her away with his news and asked her to the End Is Upon Us Ball was less important than doing it before someone else did, like Cody. "Okay, seven at L'Arte del Gelato."

"Got it," she confirmed. "Then you're not going to believe what I'm doing after that."

"Try me."

"Zoë got a date with a Leaguer at a secret bloodlust club. Me and Cody are going with her."

"What?" he practically shouted. "I get Zoë, but why are you and Cody going?"

"If his hidden camera works, and Zoë practices what she preaches, we're gonna get a consensual bloodlust hookup on film."

He couldn't believe what he was hearing. "So now you're into blood pornography?"

"It's not pornography," Portia fired back. "It's documenting what people have heard about but never seen."

"Portia, she's your best friend!"

"Believe me, I tried to talk her out of it, but she's got her heart set on it, and best friends let best friends follow their dreams."

Morning got her subtext: his disapproval was slamming *her* dream. He also knew arguing would ruin the news bomb he was about to drop on her. He kept his objection to a sigh and said he would see her at seven.

As he got dressed, he pulled something out of his closet

he had hoped to never wear again: his Epidex. Someone had to be there to make sure Zoë's vampire date didn't pop his deuce, lose control, and overserve himself. Morning knew a thing or two about the dangers of diving into the forbidden well of bloodlust, and he sure as hell wasn't going to let anyone flow all the way with Zoë.

That evening, Morning got to the gelato shop fifteen minutes early, knowing that 7:00 meant 6:55 to Portia. He was feeling light as a feather for several reasons. He was about to win his eternal beloved back, he'd had another demerit-free day at the academy, and his body had produced something nonaging vampires never got: a pimple. However, since the tiny bump on his forehead might telegraph his meganews, he had covered it with makeup.

While his original plan had involved wearing a button-down shirt with the top button open so Portia might discover the new musketeers swashbuckling on his chest, the plan had to be scrapped when his chest had been covered with his Epidex. His new plan was as good, if not better. After getting gelato, they would walk up to the High Line and go to the spot where they had shared an incredible summer night's kiss. The kiss had started when they were standing nose to nose to see who was tallest. At the time, Portia had him by a quarter inch. If Zoë's doorframe measurement was right, and he was now a half inch taller, and Portia had reached her full height, in their next nose-to-nose he would edge her out, and she would realize he was growing and melt in his arms.

Portia showed up right on time. A few minutes later they left L'Arte del Gelato with a Mokaccino for Portia and a Plasmania for Morning. The Plasmania wasn't as delicious as he remembered it, but he wasn't going to tip his hand by bringing it up.

As they climbed the stairs to the High Line, Portia's phone meeped with a text. She handed Morning her cone so she could read it. Morning bottled his irritation as she thumbed a quick text back. He wasn't going to let one text ruin the incredible moment they were about to share: the first moment of the rest of their lives together.

They reached the spot on the High Line where two buildings and a suspended walkway framed the river and the Statue of Liberty.

After Morning made some small talk about how Lady Liberty was holding up her favorite gelato flavor, Torch of Freedom, Portia turned to him. "So this must be some big news you wanna tell me if you brought me to the spot where we gave each other tonsillectomies this summer."

Morning almost snorted his last bite of Plasmania. He was thrilled she remembered. "Yeah," he said, tossing his cone in a nearby trash can. "But I didn't bring you up here to ask for my tonsils back." As she laughed, he pretended to see something on her cheek. "Don't move, found an eyelash." He moved in closer and mimed taking the imaginary lash in his fingers. "You get to make a wish." He didn't retreat, waiting for her to notice his new height advantage. But her eyes didn't fill with the confusion and surprise he had hoped for. Instead, they darted over his shoulder and she stepped back.

"Whoa," she said, "made my wish just in time."

The good news was Morning didn't have to lie about the breeze blowing away the nonexistent eyelash; the bad news sounded behind him.

"Hey, Porsche," someone shouted, "check it out!"

Morning turned to see Cody and Zoë coming toward them. He realized that was who Portia had texted, telling them where she was. He turned back to her, unable to cork his irritation. "What are *they* doing here?"

Her face bunched with contrition. "Sorry. They were clothes shopping for Zoë's date. I thought they'd take longer."

As Cody and Zoë reached them, Zoë spun to show off her date-with-destiny look. She was head-to-toe black leather—jacket, jeans, high-heeled pointy boots—with a ruffly white blouse. She wore dark sunglasses, and her hair was pulled up in a topknot to show off the ruby-colored scarf around her neck. "What do you think, A.M.? Do I look fang-alicious?"

Morning frowned. "To someone, I'm sure."

"It's a fashion mash-up," Cody announced. "It's Cate Blanchett doing Bob Dylan doing a pipette of blood."

Zoë jammed her hands on her hips. "Are you saying I'm built like a pipette?"

"ZZ," Cody retorted, "the guy's not gonna be into your body, he's gonna be into your blood type."

Morning was tempted to tell him vampires were just as interested in girls' bodies as Lifers, especially with all the extra nerve endings vampires had in their fingers, but Portia beat him to it. "Zo, you look totally hot," she said, before turning to Cody. "Why don't you stop talking about things you don't know about and talk about things you do? Show Morning your new camera."

Cody grinned. "I call it the sweat-cam."

Morning feigned interest, hoping that after Cody's show-and-tell, he and Zoë would leave. "A sweat-cam?"

"Yeah," Cody explained, " 'cause it's built into my sweatshirt. I'm shooting you right now." He pointed to the Yankees logo in the middle of his sweatshirt. It featured a baseball and a baseball bat wearing an Uncle Sam hat. "Inside the logo is a tiny digital camera and a mike. It's very *Iron Man,* without the electrical generator. It runs on batteries." Cody flipped up his sweatshirt and showed the battery pack sewn to the inside of it. It also gave him the opportunity to flash his six-pack abs. "Cool, huh?"

"Or totally hot." Zoë giggled.

Portia eye-rolled as she pulled a makeup compact from her pocket. "Drop the hood, Cody, and get back to kickin' the tires."

He dropped his sweatshirt. "The awesome part—it's a hands-free device." He flexed his left pec muscle; it jumped under his sweatshirt. "I just turned the camera off. Flex the right pec"—his right pec jerked—"and I just turned it on."

"Great," Morning said flatly. "Pec on, pec off."

"Yeah." Cody beamed and whacked Morning in the chest. "But you gotta have pecs to work it. Not that it—"

"Hey!" Zoë cut Cody off before he blew his promise not to reveal that he knew about Morning and Portia breaking up. "How 'bout mouth off and pec on to show Morning how the rest of it works?"

Portia shot Zoë a look but sidelined her suspicions; she was in work mode. She opened the compact in her hand and showed it to Morning. "Here's where we view the shot." In place of the mirror was a tiny screen filled with a live shot of Portia showing him the compact. "With this I can tell Cody where to point the sweat-cam, 'cause he'll be shooting blind."

"So what's the plan?" Morning asked. "You're gonna

211

go to some club and shoot Zoë being a recreational blood donor?"

"Go ahead, A.M.," Zoë teased, "try to suck the romance out of it. But you can't 'cause I am dressed and ready for"—she threw her head back, exposing her ruby-scarved neck—"the ecstasy of exsanguination!"

"Yeah," Cody jumped in, "and I'm dressed to get the glory shot, but to be totally safe I gotta pick up some extra batteries."

Portia checked her watch. "Then we're already running late. Let's go."

Morning took her arm and walked her away. "Right, let's go."

As Zoë and Cody followed, Cody protested, "Morning's not part of the plan."

"Oh, don't sweat on your sweat-cam," Portia tossed back. "We've only got three invitations. He won't get past security."

Morning gave her a haughty look. "I have my ways."

"If you sneak in," she warned him, "you gotta promise you won't get in the way or do anything stupid."

Zoë zipped around in front of him. "Yeah, A.M., promise, or"—she poked the middle of his chest—"I might havta—"

"Don't worry!" He jumped in before her threat raised Portia's suspicions. "I'll be good."

45

The Tasting Room

Morning, Portia, Cody, and Zoë piled into a cab, which took them up Tenth Avenue and dropped them in Hell's Kitchen. Cody and Zoë disappeared into a Duane Reade to buy backup batteries. Morning and Portia waited outside.

"So," she said, "what's the big news you're gonna tell me?"

He wanted to tell her, but the moment had been ruined. What could've been a super-romantic moment on the High Line had been knocked to a noisy stretch of Tenth Avenue choked with Lincoln Tunnel traffic. He answered with a shrug. "It can wait."

"Sorry, Morn," she said, sensing his disappointment. "It's still nice to have a moment alone."

He tried to look on the bright side. "Yeah, just like old times." She dipped her head to his shoulder. Morning felt her hair brush across his shirt. He closed his eyes, shutting out the street and the exhaust fumes, and inhaled the green-apple scent of her hair.

When she lifted her head and glanced at him, she spotted the tiny profile of something rising from his forehead. "Ohmigod, is that a pimple?"

"No," he said nonchalantly.

She kept staring. "Then why is there makeup on it?"

"It's embarrassing, okay?"

"Embarrassing? I didn't know vampires got pimples."

"They don't—I mean, they do," he stammered as he groped for a lie. "It's a nerves thing. When we're really stressed over something we can get stress pimples."

Her face rubbered with compassion. "You mean you got a pimple about us breaking up?"

"No, I'm stressing over Zoë's getting a vein popped. It's a sympathy pimple."

Portia smiled. "That's what I've always liked about you. You're the most sensitive guy I've ever met."

He took the compliment like a punch to the gut. In just a few days, love had wilted to "like." *And why stop at "sensitive guy"?* he fretted. *Why didn't she just say what she meant? "I like you because you're like a girl." What's next? Finding out that "EB" means "eternal beliked"!*

Cody and Zoë coming out of the drugstore saved Morning from further torture.

Zoë threw on her game face. "Let's do it!" She grabbed Portia's arm and strode across Tenth. The guys followed in Zoë's train of words. "But this thing I'm about to do, what is it really? I mean, 'ecstasy of exsanguination' is cool, but is it putting too much pressure on me, *and* my date?" She didn't wait for an answer. "'Consensual bloodlust' is way too health class. I could say I'm a 'blood meal on wheels,' but it makes me sound like a carhop. What about this? 'I'm just meeting a friend to have a necktail'? No, sounds like some Chinese takeout: General Tso's necktail. Hey, I got it! Bloodletting used to be called 'breathing a vein.' 'I'm going for a little breather.' 'You wanna go for a breather?' 'Sure, let's take a breather.' 'C'mon, big boy, take my breath away!' Yep, that's it. I'm not going on a date with a vampire. I'm takin' a breather!"

Not even trying to get a word in edgewise, her friends simply listened. They knew Zoë was burning off nervous energy by going motormouth. Actually, they were all apprehensive. There was no telling how this would play out. They stopped across from the old stone church that housed Goth 'Em. Zoë walked across the street and Cody followed.

As Portia started, Morning grabbed her arm. "Portia, I've got a bad feeling about this. Please, call it off."

She had her game face on too. "Morning, you've got a thing for running into burning buildings. I'll never ask you not to. I've got a thing for chasing stories. Don't ask me not to."

He loosened his grip, letting her go.

He watched the trio approach the bouncers at the entrance to Goth 'Em. They flashed their invitations. A bouncer bent forward and whispered something. The threesome walked to the corner of the old church and disappeared into a dark, narrow walkway running beside it.

Adrenaline surged through Morning like an alarm. In a matter of minutes, some Leaguer was going to fang up on Zoë and do a little blood tasting. He had to go in and make sure sipping didn't turn to sapping.

He jogged across the street and into the dark passageway.

A rectangle of light was collapsing, swallowing Cody and the two girls in front of him. A huge bouncer stood in the wash of red light coming from a single bulb over the door he had just closed. Morning moved toward him.

"Got an invite?" the bouncer growled.

Morning glanced past him at the distant sliver of light. "Just taking a shortcut to the next street."

Morning slid by him and continued along the passageway as the bouncer grunted menacingly. "Don't do it again."

Spiraling down a narrow stone staircase, Zoë, Portia, and Cody finally reached the end. It delivered them into a long room with a low vaulted ceiling. In the past, it might have been a mess hall for monks, a wine cellar, or a crypt, but not anymore. It was packed, throbbing with music, and dominated by a long, sharp wedge of a bar.

Zoë tried to defuse her jangled nerves and shouted a joke to Portia and Cody. "I'd say 'Welcome to the Tasting Room, suckers,' but we're *suckees*."

Cody took in the mosh of dancers gyrating under a disco ball that resembled a fiery red mace. The dancers were decked out in goth regalia, vampire capes, or lurid-colored dresses. "It's like *Rocky Horror Picture Show* on 'roids."

A guy walked by with raccoon eyes and the lower half of his face tattooed like the jawbone and bared teeth of a skull. "Or worse," Portia said, "if that's Zoë's date."

Zoë scanned the packed bar. "Like the invite says. My date's gonna find me."

Morning hustled farther down the narrow passageway. Looking back, he saw the bouncer turn toward a couple who had just entered the walkway. Morning ducked behind a thick support abutting the church. He stood for a moment, eyes closed; then his clothes collapsed. His shirt thrashed and a pigeon popped out from its collar. The bird stretched its wings; one extended at an odd angle.

The shadow-consciousness Morning retained as a pigeon caught the weird sensation. His left wing felt stiff and lumpy where it joined his body. Then he remembered the bandage on his shoulder. It had been absorbed into his pigeon body along with the Epidex.

He flapped into clumsy flight. The moment of distraction had ruined his timing. The bouncer was already shutting the door that led down to the Tasting Room.

The pigeon soared over the building, sampling the air for clues. Given his olfactory malfunction during the Arson Awareness test, he was worried his nose would fail him again. But the CD to a pigeon had cured the problem, and his nose holes were sucking up smells like a vacuum.

Hitting a plume of rising heat, Morning picked up a tangle of scents: sweat, booze, the acrid exhaust of human excitement. His head cocked; an eye spotted the open air duct spewing the plume of scents. The bird circled down and flapped into the air duct.

Zoë led the way as the trio squeezed through the throng at the bar. She had seen her share of vampire wannabes and goths but mostly on the street and at parties. The goths in this place had taken body art to new extremes. It ranged from a woman with a target tattooed on her neck, with the bull's-eye being two puncture wounds, to a guy with crossed steak knifes piercing his nostrils.

As they got a half-dozen bodies away from a tall woman with a Mohawk spike of shocking red hair, the woman turned and spotted Zoë. Her eyes, set in spirals of black makeup, widened with recognition. She raised an arm from under a black mini-cape, revealing her body-hugging vermilion tuxedo, and pointed a long purple fingernail as she mouthed *Zoë* over the din.

Zoë answered with a backhand wave so the woman could see they were wearing practically the same nail color.

Cody fingered Zoë in the armpit, making her drop her arm in a ticklish giggle. "Your date's a *she*?"

Zoë turned back to explain. "It's not a lesbian thing, it's an ob-gyn thing."

Cody double-taked. "Huh?"

"Getting my first vein exam from a woman is gonna eliminate the whole skeevy, this-is-too-weird thing."

Portia weighed in. "You're gonna let her suck your blood, isn't that weird enough?"

"No," Zoë answered with dreamy expectation. "I'm thinking of it as a vein-opening, eye-opening, soul-opening experiment in breathing."

46

Bitus Interruptus

The pigeon skidded and flapped down the air duct. While Morning's shadow-consciousness realized a pigeon wasn't the best choice for infiltrating a subterranean club, he nixed CDing into something more functional, like a rat. He didn't want to waste CDing energy he might need later.

The bird slid toward a kaleidoscope of light and banged beak-first into a metal grille. The pigeon shook its feathers and peeked through the grille at the miasma of light and motion. *Good news,* Morning thought, *found the Tasting Room; bad news, I might have to CD to get through this grate.*

Despite the throbbing music, his bird hearing picked up voices in the Tasting Room. Scanning the sea of revelers, he spotted Zoë walking beside a woman with a towering crest of red hair. They were coming toward him. Portia and Cody were following a ways back. Cody had his arm around Portia. Morning had to fight the temptation to CD into a poisonous snake, slither through the grille, and sink his fangs into Cody. But he told himself it was probably part of their cover. To get close enough to Zoë and her date to film them, they had to pretend to be hooking up for a little dip and sip.

Morning watched the Leaguer with the red Mohawk pull Zoë through a section of S-shaped love seats. They sat on a banquette against the wall, directly below him. He pressed his pigeon head against the grille to get a better view. The wall was lined with a long row of scalloped booths, each one big enough for two and curved for privacy.

Portia and Cody slipped into a love seat opposite Zoë and the redhead. Portia sat facing the room, while Cody faced the couple in the booth, giving him a good angle to shoot with his sweat-cam. Cody's sweatshirt spasmed over his right pec. He had started shooting.

Zoë was so jacked with nervous energy she bounced out of the booth and sang a "Part of Your World" chorus that she had written for her date. "Down where they stalk, down where they feed / Down there I go, willing to bleed / Bloodlustin' free—I'm going to be / Part of your world." As Red Mohawk applauded, Zoë slid back into the booth.

To everyone's surprise, Zoë popped out of the booth again. "I'm so excited," she exclaimed, "I gotta pee!"

Red Mohawk laughed. "Go, little bloodmaid," she said in a husky voice. "Absence will make my fangs grow longer."

Morning eye-rolled, which, being a pigeon, turned into a head roll.

Zoë body-crunched like she really had to go. "Where is it?"

Red Mohawk waved toward a far corner. "Over there."

As Zoë scurried away, Morning saw Cody's left pec jump, turning off the sweat-cam. Then he and Portia put their heads together, feigning intimacy to look inconspicuous.

Morning ruffled his feathers, but his protest was short-lived. He was distracted by a young man, a goth, approaching Red Mohawk's booth. He stopped and droned to her, "My date stood me up. Can you spare a fang?"

Cody started to rise to stop the guy from cutting in on Zoë's date, but Portia grabbed his arm and pulled him back down. Morning couldn't hear what she muttered to Cody, but there was no mistaking the twirl of her finger in a "roll 'em" gesture. Cody's right pec jerked.

"Why don't you sit down?" Red Mohawk said seductively to the young man. "And I'll show you my answer."

Goth Guy slid into the booth.

Morning pressed his head into a gap in the grille, but Goth Guy and Red Mohawk had disappeared from view, into the recess of the booth. A second later he heard the *smack* of a mouth sucking blood. Even as a pigeon, he felt his throat jerk with a gag reflex. But there was no getting sick: not with what he had spotted through the grille.

Coming across the room, gliding toward the booth, was a familiar figure. DeThanatos.

Morning's pigeon heart went into hyperspeed. Before he could CD into something that would get him through the grille and stop whatever was about to go down, DeThanatos flicked his hands at Cody and Portia like a gunslinger without a gun. They went comatose.

Reaching them, DeThanatos seized the logo on

Cody's sweatshirt and, without breaking stride, ripped the logo away. Then he threw a flick back, unthralling his victims.

Portia and Cody came to with a jolt. Portia blinked at the gaping hole in Cody's sweatshirt.

The pigeon flew up the air duct and shot out the end like a feathered cannonball. The bird flapped down to the passageway.

The bouncer guarding the entrance turned as the pigeon disappeared behind the stone buttress. The next moment, the Tasting Room door blew open, sending the bouncer sprawling. He did a face-plant on the paving stones.

The door had been thrown open by DeThanatos, who ran down the passageway toward the street at the same moment that Morning, back to human form and in his Epidex, shot around the buttress in pursuit.

Hearing him, DeThanatos looked back and did a quick assessment: he was in no mood for a chase, and the bouncer, struggling to his feet between Morning and himself, hadn't seen him yet. In a flash, DeThanatos shape-shifted into a skinny teenage girl—Zoë—wearing nothing but dark shadows.

Before Morning reached the bouncer getting to his feet, DeThanatos, as Zoë, thrust an arm at Morning and screamed, "He took my blood, my dress, what's next?"

The bouncer turned to see the naked girl running away. He spun back in time to clothesline her "attacker." Morning hit the ground like a flapjack; his head *cracked* on the stones. The bouncer reached down and grabbed

Morning by the front of his Epidex. "A vampire and a *pedophile*! You've crossed the line, punk!"

In the next instance, several things happened simultaneously. The naked "Zoë" shape-shifted into a falcon and flew away with the sweat-cam logo in its talons; the bouncer yanked Morning to his feet to the sound of ripping Epidex; Portia and Cody flew out the door. Seeing the bouncer holding the woozy Morning in his torn Epidex, Portia shouted, "What's going on?"

"Did a guy run outta here"—Cody yelled at the bouncer while pointing to the hole in his sweatshirt—"with a Yankees logo?"

"It was DeThanatos," Morning slurred.

The bouncer, staring at Morning, was fixed on his own question. "Aren't you—" He flipped a Maglite from his pocket and beamed it on. The light zigzagged over Morning's torso before finding his unfocused eyes. "Morning McCobb?"

Zoë exploded through the doorway like a jack-in-the-box with road rage. "I go to the bathroom! You guys ditch me! And my date tells me she has a fang ache! What the hell happened?"

Gaping at Zoë, the bouncer's confusion mounted. "But you were just"—he whipped his Maglite beam to the end of the passageway—"there, naked."

Zoë shot him a contemptuous look. "Have your fantasies, pervert! I'm outta here!" She spun on her boots and clacked down the passageway.

There was a flutter of wings and the bouncer suddenly looked like a magician who turns teenage boys into pigeons. The pigeon flew up, disappearing behind a roofline.

Portia and Cody ran after Zoë, leaving the stupefied bouncer mumbling, "I gotta get a day job."

Perched high above him, Morning's pigeon blinked down at the pile of clothing behind the buttress. His shadow-consciousness cooed, *I gotta get my clothes and cell phone.*

47

Pixel Pandemic

Cody caught up with Zoë first. He tried to explain, as best he could, given the momentary dropout from being thralled, what had happened in the Tasting Room after she had run to the restroom.

Portia trailed behind. Even though her mind swirled with questions like *What the hell was DeThanatos doing there? And why?*, they were blown away by more vexing mysteries. *When the flashlight beam darted across Morning's bare skin and his ripped Epidex, was that a Band-Aid on his shoulder? And what was that on his chest? The hair equivalent of a stress pimple?* But there was no putting Morning in the hot seat until he'd CDed back to human form and collected his cell phone. At the moment, the only person she could interrogate was her best friend.

She caught up with Cody and Zoë and pried the truth out of her. The three invitations to the Tasting Room had come directly from DeThanatos, which meant the whole thing was a setup. As mad as Portia was at Zoë for leading them into a trap, she kept her cool and fired questions. "Why would DeThanatos want footage of you in a blood tryst? Or any blood tryst? And why was your date with the Red Mohawk? Was she in on it too?"

When Cody began to speculate that DeThanatos might be planning to start a website of Leaguer-Lifer bloodlust porn, Portia cut him off and said she was going home. Before heading for the subway, she told Cody to get the still-distraught Zoë home and make sure she didn't do something stupid like throw herself in the river because her vampire date had been a total blood-bust.

As soon as they were out of sight, Portia called Morning. She got his voice mail. She left a message for him to call her ASAP.

When she got home she tried his cell again: no answer. She began to worry. *Maybe he didn't get back to his clothes. Maybe something happened to him.* She called St. Giles. Sister Flora told her that Morning had gotten home, said he didn't want to be disturbed, and gone to his room.

Portia breathed a sigh of relief and tried his cell one more time. Still no answer. She wasn't surprised. He had warned her and he was right; their shoot in the Tasting Room had been a disaster.

Later, as she lay in bed wondering if he would call, she was haunted by mental snapshots: the pimple on his forehead, the Band-Aid on his shoulder, and the hairs on his chest. She thought of them a hundred times before she finally fell asleep.

Portia was woken the next morning by her cell. She fumbled it off the bedside table and answered. "Morning, I was—"

"You can say 'morning,'" the voice on the other end grumbled, "but there's nothing good about it. It *sucks*."

Even though Portia was still pissed at Zoë, she was glad to hear her voice; she had survived the night's humiliation. "I know it sucks."

"No, I mean, *really* sucks," Zoë moaned. "Go turn on any news channel. It's not good, and I'm really sorry."

Before Portia could respond, the line went dead.

Downstairs, Portia was glad to find her mother had already gone to Diamond Sky. She flicked on the TV and surfed news channels until she saw a familiar scene: Red Mohawk moved in and buried her fangs in Goth Guy's neck. He threw back his head with a gasping sigh, and a rivulet of blood ran down his neck as Red Mohawk took a sloppy gulp.

Portia winced as if she were the one being bitten. "Oh, boy."

The television cut to Ally Alfamen at a news desk. On the other side of the desk was Becky-Dell Wallace. Ally didn't have to prompt Becky-Dell. "There it is, my fellow Americans," Becky-Dell intoned, "the Leaguers' hidden agenda, as plain as the blood on that young man's neck and as real as the place it occurred: a secret club called the Tasting Room, operating in the bowels of a building next to and owned by a nightclub called Goth 'Em. Needless to say, the BVA has locked the doors to the Tasting Room and Goth 'Em and thrown away the keys. The participants caught in this monstrous act have been arrested for crimes against humanity." She leaned closer to the camera. "And now, I call on my congressional colleagues to do their duty. To be in the House and Senate this evening, to vote down the Vampire Rights Act, and end the charade of vampires being anything but what they have been, are now, and will always be: bloodsucking fiends!"

Ally finally got a word in, "Ah, Congresswoman, a couple of questions? What about the young girl at the beginning of the clip who was the intended victim but, for lack of a better term, chose to relieve herself of another fluid rather than the one we just witnessed?"

"Unfortunately," Becky-Dell replied, "the young woman, while making bad choices, didn't break any laws that now stand on the books. Because she is a minor, we can't reveal her name, but believe me, her parents will be notified and I pray she will be properly punished."

"Obviously," Ally continued, "this is devastating footage to have acquired on the day of the VRA vote. Where and/or whom did you get it from?"

Becky-Dell raised an eyebrow. "The source of this footage could not have been more fitting."

"Which was?"

"WikiLeaks."

"Liar!" Portia shouted at the TV as Ally couldn't hold back a guffaw.

"It's not funny," Becky-Dell scolded.

Ally dropped back to anchor mode. "I know, it's tragic. Especially for the Leaguers who had hoped this day would bring them freedom and equality. So, did WikiLeaks shoot this footage?"

"No."

"Who did?"

Portia held her breath, waiting for the ax to fall.

"I wish I could say," Becky-Dell explained. "But again, we're talking about minors who need to be punished by the proper authorities. Their parents."

As relieved as Portia was, she yelled at the TV. "I'm not a minor. I'm eighteen! So is Cody!" She jumped to her feet with a revelation. "And you're not saying who gave it to you 'cause it would reveal who you're in bed with: DeThanatos!"

Running upstairs to get dressed, Portia called Cody. He didn't answer; she left an urgent message for him to call her. Before she was dressed she got a text from him.

Blast 2 buds. In *Shawshank* lockdown: fizical, cyber, u namit. Wanna twiddle my thumbs? Gotta ax which way. Nice noin u.

Then she tried Morning again. No answer.

48

Letting Go

When Portia hustled out of the town house, she ran smack into her mother. Penny was accompanied by Rachel, looking pale and uncharacteristically down for an Earth Angel.

"Going somewhere?" Penny asked sternly.

"Ah, y-yeah," Portia stammered, "maybe."

"How 'bout *not* maybe?" Penny steamed. "How 'bout never again, till I drop you at college? I got a call from Becky-Dell Wallace telling me that you and Cody shot the footage that's all over the news."

Portia cocked her head toward Rachel. "Does she have to be here for this?"

"You've mucked up her future worse than mine," Penny snapped. "I'd say she deserves a piece of you."

"Look, I know I screwed up," Portia offered, "but that's not the real news. Becky-Dell didn't get the footage from WikiLeaks, she got it from DeThanatos. He stole it from us last night, and Morning tried to stop him."

The two women stared, trying to connect the dots. "Morning was there?" Rachel asked.

"Yeah, he was worried about us, and he knew something was screwy." Portia's face contorted with frustration. "I don't have time to explain, but I promise, I'll never point a camera at a vampire again. I'll change my senior project to the safest thing in the world."

Penny's eyebrow lifted. "And that would be?"

"I don't know . . . knitting. I really gotta go." Portia tried to sidestep around her mother.

Penny blocked her way. "You're not going anywhere."

"Sorry, Mom." Portia vaulted over the edge of the stoop. "I don't care if this is the last thing I do."

Penny started to shout, but Rachel touched her arm. "Let her go."

"Why?"

"She just gave up her passion: making movies. Let her try to reclaim what's left."

Penny scowled. "You mean Morning?"

"Yeah, love." Rachel offered a hopeful smile. "I hear it makes the world go round."

Penny harrumphed and pushed the door open. "That's probably what they told Romeo and Juliet. How'd that work out for 'em?"

Once inside, Penny put a kettle on the stove to make a cup of tea. "We've brainstormed our way out of a lot of fixes. Got any ideas on this one?"

"Yeah." Rachel pulled her phone from her bag. "Get another brain." She dialed a number. Birnam answered, sounding clearer and more energized than the last time they had talked to him on Skype. "Gee, Mr. Birnam, for someone who's about to see the VRA go down like a cloud with a lead lining, you sound perky. Seen the news?"

"All the juicy details," Birnam answered.

"Well, you called it," Rachel said. "The poo hit the fan. I don't know where you are, but you gotta come to New York and step up to the plate, the saucer, the cup, the works. Mr. B, we need you at the table before Becky-Dell runs us completely off it."

Birnam grunted. "Last time we talked, I was from the BC generation."

"You are, but it's not what you think," Rachel said, tap-dancing away. "When I said 'BC,' I meant brilliant Centurion. Which is what we need right now."

"Perhaps, but this brilliant Centurion's centuries have caught up with him."

"What do you mean?" she asked, perplexed.

"I'll let Morning explain. Right now, as president of the IVL, I only have one official act left in me."

"Right," Rachel jumped in, "to come and tell everyone that one fallen angel, the devil, didn't spoil the barrel of heavenly angels, and one naughty Leaguer falling for a neck peck doesn't capsize the Earth Angel applecart."

Birnam chuckled. "That's what I've always loved about you, Rachel—you're a fruit cocktail of metaphors. And it's exactly your kind of daffy optimism that's going to one day—maybe not today, but someday—convince Lifers that we deserve equal rights. That's why I'm making you the acting president of the IVL, effective immediately."

"What?" Rachel blurted.

"I'll post something on the website to make it official. It'll stay in effect till you can hold a proper election for the next president." Rachel was too stunned to speak, so

Birnam went on. "I've loved my time as captain of the Leaguer ship. But Fate, the mutinous sailor aboard every ship that sets sail from the Port of Human Hope, has put me in a lifeboat and set me adrift."

Rachel's shock gave way to confusion. "*What* are you saying?"

"Nothing," he said with a chortle. "I was giving you a lesson in steering a straight metaphor. Goodbye, Ms. President. The wheel of hope is in your hands."

49

The Secret of Life

Morning stared at his computer. He had scoured the Internet, and so far, "the tempest in the Tasting Room" still revolved around Cody's bloodlust footage and the uproar over it. None of the other participants had been identified, and the bouncer, who had recognized Morning, had not come forward, probably because guarding the door of a bloodlust club was not something he wanted on his résumé.

Morning knew he could only pretend to sleep late on a Saturday for so long. He got up and looked in the mirror over his dresser. He stared at the pimple still growing on his forehead. Whether it had gotten bigger and redder from stress or from *pneumabrotus* and his hormones kicking in, he didn't know. Whatever, it had to be hidden. He covered it with a new smear of makeup.

His computer bleeped with a Skype alert, summoning him back to his desk. He took the call. Birnam's ancient face appeared onscreen. Middle Eastern music played in the background; it looked like he was in a cybercafe. Birnam smiled as his window on Morning opened. "Hello, Morning."

"Hey," Morning said grimly. "Do you get the news in Tripoli?"

"Yes. I've turned the IVL over to Rachel."

Morning blinked, aghast. "You're just giving up?"

"On some things, yes."

"But the IVL, the VRA," Morning protested, "it's all you ever cared about!"

Birnam nodded. "Until now."

"What changed?" Morning demanded, trying not to shout.

"It's hard to explain."

"Try me!"

Birnam answered Morning's frustration with a Buddha-like smile. "It's got to do with what I discovered in Tripoli. Not only is the food utterly magnificent, I also found the secret of life."

"Oh, really." Morning frowned. "What is it?"

Birnam leaned forward to impart his discovery. "Stories. But then, after that, I found the *secret* of the secret of life. I discovered the secret of stories."

"Which is?"

Birnam leaned back with a beaming smile. "The end."

Morning stared blankly. "The end?"

"Yes!" Birnam exclaimed like a scientist discovering the happy gene. "If you don't get to the end of a story, it's not a story; it's an endless parade of events. If you don't get to the end of a life, it's not a life; it's an endless parade of sensations. I don't think of myself as dying, I think of myself as having rediscovered life just before death. Not a bad way to go. Which reminds me, I have a lunch reservation, and I plan to relish each bite like it's my last. It might be." Birnam added a hearty laugh.

Morning shook his head in disbelief. "If you ask me, it sounds like you've still got a few more years left."

"Or not," Birnam retorted. "When you see Death coming around the corner, you get a little adrenaline spike. This is mine."

"But what if it's not an adrenaline spike?" Morning argued. "Maybe your last gasp of health is something else."

"Like what?"

"Maybe because a big chunk of your Lifer dream, passage of the VRA, is about to crash; maybe the fountain of *pneumabrotas* that rebooted your aging has dried up. Maybe you're returning to immortality. And maybe tomorrow, after your Lifer dream is snuffed out, you'll wake up a vampire again."

Birnam contemplated this, then gave Morning a sympathetic smile. "I know why you're saying this. You're scared that's what might happen to you if you get kicked out of the fire academy and your Lifer dream ends. You'll go from re-mort to re-vamp."

"Yeah, it scares me," Morning admitted.

"It's not going to happen," Birnam declared.

"How can you be so sure?"

"Because I've turned so mortal I've acquired a thing called faith. I have faith in you and Rachel. And I can feel in these dying bones that somehow Leaguers, and Lifers, are going to rise above the Becky-Dells and DeThanatoses of the world." He raised a bar of something and began to unwrap it. "Whatever happens, Morning, my last wish is that you get to revel in a long, sweet stumble to an end.

I believe you will because you've always known a simple truth I only learned in the past few months."

Morning didn't have a clue. "What's that?"

Birnam pushed forward the unwrapped bar of candy. "Turkish taffy."

"Not *that*," Morning protested. "What's the simple truth?"

Birnam answered with a beguiling smile. "Life is a gift that requires assemblage. Death provides the instructions." He leaned back; his voice grew distant. "Goodbye, Morning."

Morning refused the finality of his words. "See you later, Mr. Birnam."

The old man's smile widened. "Or not."

As Birnam bit into his taffy, the Skype connection went dead. Whether he had hung up or not, Morning wasn't sure. Whichever, his gut told him it was the last time he would ever see Luther Birnam.

50

Assemblage Required

Morning stared at the blank screen as moisture pooled in his eyes. He heard a tentative knock on the door. It wasn't Sister Flora's. He rose and opened the door.

Portia stood in the hall with a beleaguered look. "I bet you hate me."

He shook his head. "No."

"Can I come in?"

"Sure." He stepped back, waving her in. "I just talked to Birnam. He made Rachel head of the IVL."

Portia entered. "I don't care about that anymore."

"You're making a documentary about Leaguers and you don't care about having access to the IVL's new president?"

She faced him. "I just want access to you."

He let out a nervous chuff. "Portia, I don't wanna be in any more movies."

"I don't wanna *make* any more movies," she replied.

Morning stared for a moment. "Say what?"

"I'm done screwing people's lives up by sticking cameras in their faces," she declared.

He eyed her cautiously. "This isn't like last night, is it? You're not DeThanatos CDed into Portia, are you?"

She smiled for the first time, appreciating his attempt at levity. "No, I'm the new me."

"What's the new you?"

She let down her guard and spewed. "Last night, you were right, okay? We never should've gone in there. We got totally set up. The invites to the Tasting Room came from DeThanatos. We blew it. For Leaguers, the VRA—" She cut herself off and took a breath. "Okay, I came to say I'm very sorry about what's happened—and I am—but there's another reason I'm here. There's something else that banged my eyes wide open last night. The new you."

Morning's insides gripped tight. *If Zoë told Portia about my re-aging,* he thought, *I'm not gonna turn her, I'm gonna kill her.* "Oh, yeah?" he said coolly. "What's the new me?"

She stepped forward and hit him with a full-mouth, curl-your-toes lip-lock. His shock was annihilated by the mouth-probing, heart-ballooning delirium of a kiss he thought he had lost forever.

When he pulled away from their tongue-twisting tumble into the river of desire, the river glistened on in her eyes. He heaved a breath. "Where did *that* come from?"

"The new me," she said. "And something I saw last night."

He was still fuzzy about what exactly had happened during the blurry moments after he had cracked his head on the paving stones, or how his Epidex had gotten ripped. "What did you see last night?"

239

She touched the makeup-covered bump on his forehead. "Looks like that stress pimple is getting bigger?"

"Yeah, after what we've been through—"

"Sure." She tapped him on his shoulder, making him wince. "And the Band-Aid on your arm is covering . . . ?" She spread her hands giving him the chance to fill in the blank. "And the hair on your chest is from . . . ? And the"—she air-quoted—" 'big news' that you never told me was . . . ?"

Morning hesitated.

She stepped back. "After last night, I can understand why you might not want to tell me. But as much as I screwed up, I still think I deserve to know what's going on."

Morning sat Portia on the bed and filled her in on all he had learned about reconnecting with Lifer dreams, re-triggering *pneumabrotus,* and how aging could be rebooted. As he told her, Birnam's last words echoed in his head. He repeated them. " 'Life is a gift that requires assemblage; Death provides the instructions.' " Then he said, "If things keep going right, we can reassemble what we had before. With one difference."

"What's that?" she asked.

"You'll always be two years older than me."

She found his eyes. "I can handle that."

What he didn't tell her, because he was scared to, was that he was one demerit away from being booted from the academy, losing his Lifer dream, and maybe reverting to immortality. But he wouldn't let that happen. He was so sure of it, he popped the question he'd been wanting to for days. "Has anyone asked you to the End Is Upon Us Ball?"

She shook her head. "No."

"Do you wanna go?"

"You know I'm not a dance kinda girl, but since it has such a cool theme, and you're the one asking, yes."

Morning beamed. "Cool. But there's one condition."

"Oh, man," she groaned, "are you gonna make me wear a dress?"

"No, I want you to keep making movies."

Her face quirked with curiosity. "Why?"

"'Cause I don't want some fake you, I want the real you. And it's what you've done ever since I met you."

She nodded slowly, remembering her flippant conversation with her mother. "Okay, but my senior project isn't a doc about the Leaguer movement anymore."

"What's it about?"

"Competitive knitting."

Morning chuckled in disbelief. "There's such a thing?"

"Not sure," she replied, "but if there's no 'competitive' in knitting it's gonna be one boring-ass doc."

Morning laughed from relief. He still had the caustic, funny Portia. He took her hand and felt like he was holding happiness itself. Then his mind tweaked with a guilty thought. "Is it fair to be so happy on such a miserable day for Leaguers?"

"Probably not," she said, before raising a scheming eyebrow, "but the day's not over."

Morning sacrificed his urge to know what she meant for the only thing he wanted to assemble: another tongue-twisting tumble into passion's torrent.

51

Repercussions

As members of Congress flip-flopped and withdrew their support of the VRA, Rachel and Penny swung into damage control. They called a press conference in the lobby of Diamond Sky; the media showed up in full force.

Rachel began the event with her first attempt at an unmixed metaphor. "Now I know what it feels like to be in that race where you drive a dogsled across Alaska."

"The Iditarod?" one of the reporters shouted.

"Right, Iditarod," Rachel echoed, still laser-focused on her metaphor. "Anyway, there we Leaguers were, racing toward the finish line of the VRA, when all of a sudden the huskies pulling our sled turned on us like a pack of wild dogs."

"Ms. Capilarus," a reporter asked, "are you calling the members of Congress who've switched their vote dogs?"

The pride Rachel felt for her purebred metaphor popped in her face like a bubble-gum bubble. She fluttered her hands. "Did I call anyone a dog? And even if I did, why is that an insult? I know dogs who are more respectable than some people."

Penny stepped to the microphones and saved the floundering Rachel. "What my good friend is trying to say is that there are members of Congress who have done a total brain-wipe on the three hundred seventy–plus days that Leaguers have been model citizens simply because of one night in which a few Leaguers behaved badly. We certainly condemn their behavior and any conduct that makes Lifers fear that Leaguers are a bloodlust brotherhood bent on conquering America from within. But we're not here to just talk the talk, we're here to walk the walk."

Rachel jumped back to the mikes. "We're here to put our money where our mouth is! You know the lawsuit the other treasure-hunting companies slapped on Diamond Sky and the company that used a Leaguer from *The Shadow* to find a multimillion-dollar treasure in the Hudson? Well! We settled out of court, and the company is donating the twenty-seven million to clean up the river!"

Some of the reporters were impressed, but Drake Sanders cut in with journalistic cynicism. "So this is the bone you're throwing to the dogs—I mean, members of Congress who turned on you?"

Penny pushed forward. "We think of it as an olive branch."

"Not only that," Rachel bubbled, "we speak softly and carry a big olive branch!"

While the reporters parsed Rachel's latest malaprop, she waved someone to the podium. Portia stepped up as Penny wrapped a motherly arm around her.

"As you all know," Rachel told the room, "this is

Portia, Penny's daughter and an award-winning filmmaker. She's got an announcement to make too." Rachel backed up as Portia stepped to the bristle of mikes.

The room hushed in suspense.

Portia shooed away the butterflies in her stomach and lifted the three-by-five cards in her hand. "Some footage was shot last night in the Tasting Room. It seems everyone has seen it. While there is no disputing what happens in the film—it wasn't staged, faked, or computer generated in any way—there are details the public should know before they pass judgment on every Leaguer in America."

She checked her cards. "Fact number one: Becky-Dell Wallace lied about who shot the film. It wasn't someone whose name she's withholding because they're a minor. It was shot by me and my cameraman; we're not minors, we're both eighteen."

A reporter shouted over the hubbub, "Who's your cameraman?"

"I can only reveal that if I get his permission," she answered. "Right now his parents have put him in lockdown and I can't reach him." She continued her statement. "The reason Congresswoman Wallace lied about us being minors was in the hope we would be too embarrassed to come forward. Ms. Wallace was counting on our humiliation to hide some inconvenient truths about how this footage came to be."

She forged on. "Fact number two: The invitations to the Tasting Room that Zoë Zotz, my cameraman, and I received came from Ikor DeThanatos. He wanted us there for a reason. He hoped we'd try to shoot it, we did, and then he stole our hidden camera and the footage we shot so it could be shown to the world."

"But why didn't he just shoot it himself?" a reporter asked. "Why did he have to trick you into doing it?"

"You don't understand how he thinks. He holds a major grudge against me and Morning for almost destroying him a year ago." She went back to her cards. "Fact number three: Ms. Wallace lied again about receiving the footage from WikiLeaks. She received it directly from DeThanatos."

She waited for the bombshell to reverberate through the room and ignored the flurry of questions. "Fact number four: While Ms. Wallace rails against Leaguers, she's in bed with one. She collaborated with DeThanatos to deliver a major blow to the Leaguer cause."

Portia ignored another salvo of questions. "Fact number five: DeThanatos is not a Leaguer. While he's registered with the BVA, no one ever bothered to check his records at Leaguer Academy. I did. There's no record of him attending the school or becoming a Leaguer. Fact is, he's a Loner. And everything he has done, from creating an online dating service promoting Leaguer-Lifer consensual bloodlust to founding the Take Back the Bite movement, has been a plot to destroy the Leaguer movement. Seeing how Becky-Dell Wallace wants the same thing, it's no surprise they've been working together."

She raised her voice over the growing clamor. "The truth is, the congresswoman has been, and will continue, collaborating with the darkest kind of vampire, a Loner, till the two of them have not only driven a stake in the Leaguer movement, but driven every Leaguer back into the bad old days of human bloodlust."

———

Within the hour, Becky-Dell hit the airways and admitted that it was DeThanatos who had delivered the footage to the offices of the MOP headquarters in New York. "But," she scolded the media, "hell will freeze over before I collaborate with a vampire. If I am guilty of anything," she proclaimed, "it's participating in the American tradition of accepting help from 'the enemy of my enemy' to stop bloodthirsty terrorists from roaming the land."

Only a handful of MOPers were so incensed by her admission that they accused her of being "in league with the devil." After burning their MOP membership cards, they joined a rival anti-vampire organization: IMPALE, short for International Mamas and Papas Against Leaguer Equality.

Morning stayed in his room, glued to his computer, watching the Leaguer and anti-Leaguer forces lob pixel missiles at each other. While he had tried not to get caught up in the suspense of whether Congress would vote the VRA up or down that evening, he now had two additional reasons to follow the story. One, Portia was part of it. Two, his mind was being invaded with strange new thoughts—*misgivings,* actually—about the Vampire Rights Act. *If,* he wondered, *the VRA passes, now or in the future, and if I revert to being mortal, and if Portia and I get married and have kids, would I want one of their teachers to be a vampire? One of their coaches? Would I want my daughter to date a vampire? Especially when I know how easy it is to tumble into bloodlust?* These vexing questions, never entertained before, made him realize that as hatemongering as Becky-Dell

246

was, she was the tip of an iceberg of fear that was real and understandable.

His conflicted thoughts were interrupted by the website he had opened on his computer. It was announcing an address by the president of the United States.

Morning's screen filled with the president seated at his desk in the Oval Office. He looked somber, drawn, as if he had been the one who had visited the Tasting Room and had awoken that next day down a pint.

Despite his strained look, the president spoke in his measured and calm tone. "My fellow Americans, both Lifers and Leaguers, it is my desire and duty to speak to you about the latest twenty-four-hour news cycle, and the film clip that kicked it off. *Where* this clip came from, and *who* delivered it to *whom,* are details for historians to sort out. What's vital is what the film shows us. It is simply this: despite the great strides Leaguers have made in their quest to conquer their darkest urge, it is clear they have not vanquished this inner darkness. For this reason, I am sadly withdrawing my support for the Vampire Rights Act. And I assure you, I will not support full equality for our Leaguer brothers and sisters until the day, and the night, that Leaguer vampires understand one thing above all: the *freedom* Americans have bled and died for for two and a half centuries will never be pronounced 'feed 'em.' "

Without displaying the slightest hint of humor or shame for such a horrendous play on words, the shot faded to black.

Morning gawked at the screen and shuddered.

The president's address was the last nail in the coffin for the VRA. That evening, the bill was crushed by overwhelming majorities in the House and Senate. With a national election less than a month away, no politician wanted to be called a vampire hugger.

Becky-Dell's victory speech on the Capitol steps was brief. "Tonight, we celebrate a great triumph," she announced to her anti-Leaguer constituents. "We have slain the VRA! We have killed what I've always called 'the bill of swill'!"

IVLEAGUE

LAST WORDS

Let me begin by combining two famous phrases. "A plague on both your houses" (*Romeo and Juliet*, act 3, scene 1), and let that plague be "May you live in interesting times" (ancient Chinese curse).

It has been my privilege and honor to help Leaguers and Lifers live in interesting times. It has been my dismay to see the defeat of the Vampire Rights Act. But, like all vampires who are not easily destroyed, our fight against the dark tyranny within us and our fight for equality have not been slain. They live on in a new generation of Leaguer leaders, beginning with Rachel Capilarus and her belief that vampires can be Earth Angels. The torch of freedom has been passed, and my part on the world stage ends with these few lines.

I was midwife to a movement that continues to struggle for survival in the messiness of democracy. Time will tell whether it lives or dies. However, just as the recent discovery of backsliding Leaguers lowering their cups into the forbidden well came as a shock, there will soon be a new revelation about vampires that will deliver a far greater shock: the shock of hope. It is not for me to share this life-enhancing secret, but here's a hint:

Democracy is not our only path to freedom. Another road lies ahead that can deliver vampires to true equality with our Lifer brothers and sisters. As I depart on this road, I leave others to one day lift the barricade of ignorance and reveal this startling path.

Your humble guide,
Luther Birnam

52

Pneumabrotus Patrol

In the week following the VRA's defeat, things returned to normal for all but a few.

Ironically, Zoë was reaping the benefits of having gone pan-viral on YouTube. The clip of her "little bloodmaid" song and putting off consensual bloodlust so she could go pee rocketed her to megastar status with goths and vampire wannabes. She became the It girl for a new concept gripping the goth underground: unrequited bloodlust. Also, due to her celebrity, Fanpire Tours was booked a year in advance.

When Cody finally got out of lockdown, he asked Portia to never reveal his part in the Tasting Room incident. His future as a professional cameraman would be destroyed if he became known as "the cameraboy who couldn't hold on to his camera even when it was sewn on his chest." Portia agreed and told him about her change of plans: to make a doc on competitive knitting. Thinking she was joking, he said, "Oh, you're such a stitch."

"No, really," she insisted, "I did some research and competitive knitting exists." When he asked if he could take over their doc on the Leaguer movement and finish it himself, she told him, "Take it. The only vampire I'm focused on is Morning McCobb."

Rachel and Penny went back to the drawing board and started brainstorming TV shows that Rachel could host without getting canceled by the BVA. They settled on a new show, *Earth Angels,* which would profile Leaguers who did altruistic things for Lifers. Their first episode was going to be about a boy Leaguer who changed into a cat to rescue his Lifer friend's cat, which was stuck in a tree, and save the local fire department for more-important calls.

DeThanatos, having been exposed as a Loner, did what Loners do when everyone starts sharpening their stakes. He took back the night and vanished. So everyone thought.

The person whose life was altered the most was Morning. Despite feeling awful about the defeat of the VRA and how Leaguers would remain second-class citizens for the near, if not distant, future, he was thrilled to be once again focused on the two things that mattered most: Portia and his training at the fire academy.

Whether it was his new happiness, the changes in his newly maturing body, or both, his performance at the academy had gone from screwup-waiting-to-happen to flawless. He was acing his classes and excelling in training drills without the slightest hint of using the vampire powers he still possessed. His fellow probies acknowledged as much when they voted him Probie of the Week. But the changes that excited Morning the most were ones he couldn't brag about. Because his muscles were again firing with growth, he was lifting weights in the gym that had once turned his arms into quivering sticks. For the first time in his life he was getting pecs, and, although he still didn't have six-pack abs, he had a two-pack.

The only downside of all this was the effect it had on Clancy. Morning's run of perfection was robbing the captain of his chance to nail Morning with that one last demerit and expel him. Even though Clancy suspected Morning was violating his agreement to not use any of his vampire powers, he had no proof. All he could do was pull Morning aside and warn him. "Just 'cause you're rackin' up the 'atta boys,' I still got my eye on you."

Needless to say, Morning and Portia were head over heels in love again. She even had more time for him now that she had turned her camera on the quaint world of competitive knitting.

Morning and Portia's favorite activity, besides long makeout sessions at her apartment when Penny was gone, was what they called "going on *pneumabrotus* patrol." These were down-to-his-boxers inspections of Morning's changing body. They included scans for the latest chest hair and peach-fuzz-turned-to-whiskers and measuring sessions of his growing muscles. Not that he was getting as ripped as Cody. He just wasn't built like Gumby anymore. He was like Gumby after two weeks of drinking steroid tea.

Going on *pneumabrotus* patrol was more than playing doctor. Morning had talked Portia into using a measuring tape, charts, and a still camera to keep records of his expanding chest, arms, and legs. It wasn't a vanity thing. He had convinced her that if her knitting documentary didn't pan out, she would have a backup project with a little more bite: the first record of a vampire reverting to mortality.

When she was surprised by his willingness to be the subject of another project, he told her he'd had a revelation about her filmmaking. He saw her passion as another one of her body parts that had to be bowed down to and worshipped like all the others. It was inseparable from her wholeness, her happiness, and everything he loved about her.

During one of these afternoon sessions in Portia's room, which had gotten kind of hot, they were lying on the bed and taking a breather when Portia had an inspiration. "Hey, I just got an idea for a title."

"Let me guess," Morning said. "Take Back the *Knit*."

She laughed and shook her head. "No, not for the knitting doc. For the one on you."

"Right, the backup."

"*The Rise and Fall of Morning McCobb*."

"*The Rise and Fall of Morning McCobb*," he repeated pensively. "I don't get it. What rise and fall?"

She scooched up on an elbow. "Your rise to immortality, and your *fall* back to mortality."

He nodded. "Got it, kind of an Adam and Eve thing. I get kicked out of the garden of immortality."

She squeezed next to him and nibbled his ear. "Yeah, and find your sinful Eve waiting outside the garden with a bushel of apples."

He rolled onto his side and faced her. "So, how sinful does Eve wanna get?"

"I've been thinking about that."

His eyes widened. "And?"

"I think we should make a pact."

He jerked his head in an eager nod. "And?"

She rolled onto her back. "Well, if it looks like the world's gonna end just before midnight, December twenty-first, do you wanna die a virgin?"

"Absolutely not."

"Me neither." She turned to him with a sexy smile. "So, come the End Is Upon Us Ball, I say we go out with a bang."

Morning fell back with a giddy laugh. Then he quickly lifted his head, listening like Penny had come home. "Do you hear that?"

"What?"

"That roar. I think it's the tsunami that's gonna destroy New York ahead of schedule."

She laughed and punched him again. "No, we have to wait till twelve-twenty-one."

He offered his hand. "Deal."

They shook on it.

Then they kissed on it.

53

Petit and Grand Rendezvous

A week after the VRA was defeated, Becky-Dell was still basking in the glow of "putting vampires in their place." She did a few photo ops at BVA raids on consensual blood-lust clubs, where, as Cody had predicted, she went Carrie Nation and broke up the places with a huge wooden stake. But for the most part she had retreated to her home in the Washington suburbs for some well-earned rest.

She was in bed reading when she heard a crinkling sound outside her door.

DeThanatos entered wearing the hazmat suit.

Becky-Dell greeted him with a reproachful look. "When are you going to stop wearing that ridiculous thing and get some real clothes?"

He stopped abruptly, feigning shock. "Does this mean you're not in the mood to celebrate our little victory?"

"It was hardly little," she corrected. "The Leaguer movement has been permanently crippled."

"Ah," he said wistfully, "but crippled is far from an apocalypse. Isn't that the endgame we agreed on?"

She put her book down. "Look, Mr. DeThanatos, I appreciate your help, but it's a giant leap from killing legislation to slaying every Leaguer in America."

He grimaced, putting a hand on his chest. "I don't know what pains me more, your underestimating my capacity for evil, or seeing you underestimate your own."

She tapped her book on the bed. "You're keeping me from a very good book. Why don't you cut to the chase?"

"I thought you'd never ask." He swept into the armchair near the bed so swiftly she flinched. "No need to fear," he said solicitously. "I'm merely here to offer you"— he ran his tongue under his upper lip—"two *choices.*"

"Spare me your morbid sense of humor." She scowled. "Let's hear the options."

"One, you rest on your laurels and leave America infested with Leaguers. Or two, you become the pied piper who rids America of the Leaguer plague."

"And how would this pied piper pipe?"

Before he revealed the next step in his master plan, DeThanatos sensed a tiny tremor coming up through the legs of the chair. He recognized it: the subtactile call for a Rendezvous. But the length of the vibration told him it wasn't just a Rendezvous for the Loners of North America. It was a Grand Rendezvous for all Loners worldwide.

He steepled his fingers. Before he took off, there was another rendezvous he had to finish first: his petit rendezvous with Becky-Dell, the pied piper of the apocalypse.

———

Twenty-four hours later, a falcon soared through the night over the Mother Forest. It wasn't alone. Other birds of prey were silhouetted against the canopy of stars. They were heading for the great tree at the center of the forest, the Matriarch.

The falcon dropped toward the sea of Loner vampires already surrounding the Matriarch. To the sharp eye of the falcon, the sight was revolting. It wasn't the lackadaisical nudity of Loners who came in all shapes, sizes, and ages, it was the sickening paradox of thousands of vampires jammed together who dared call themselves Loners.

Away from the throng, the falcon swooped below the treetops, burst into human form, and landed silently on the dusty ground. DeThanatos stood for a second, bracing himself for the idiot jamboree he was about to walk into. He disdained his fellow Loners for agreeing to the peace that had ended World War V, the conflict that had raged between Lifers and Leaguers for most of the twentieth century. The vast majority of Loners had signed a treaty preventing Loners from slaying any vampire who had become a Leaguer. DeThanatos had refused to sign it, and as far as he was concerned, the war had never ended.

The one thing he couldn't refuse was a call to a Grand Rendezvous—those who did became marked vampires. He strode forward, fairly certain why this one had been called. He wanted to get it over with as quickly as possible. He was supposed to be in New York, ramping up the Leaguer apocalypse.

DeThanatos weaved through the outer ring of the crowd and pushed his way toward the Matriarch. When he reached the great girth of the Matriarch's seven trunk stems, he raised his voice over the clamor and seized the opportunity to sound the traditional invocation. "Who convenes this Rendezvous?"

"We do!" a chorus of voices answered back.

The mass of Loners wheeled toward a rocky slope where several torches bloomed with fire. The torches illuminated seven Loners seated behind the fallen trunk of a tree. Instantly, everyone knew this was more than a Grand Rendezvous: it was going to be a tribunal conducted by the Centurion Council. A wave of excitement passed through the crowd. If they were lucky, the night would end with something that had been the rage during the French Revolution but was now pitifully rare: public execution.

The man seated in the middle of the seven Centurions stood. His square-built torso bristled with hair. His name was Theodore Bosky. "We, the Centurion Council, have called you to the Mother Forest," he declaimed. "For the hearing, trial, and sentencing of Ikor DeThanatos."

Thousands burst into a chant. "Ikor! Ikor! Ikor!" It particularly thrilled the crowd that the name they were chanting was a variant of "ichor," meaning "the blood of the gods." If ichor was going to be spilled, flying halfway around the world would be worth it after all.

Bosky eyed the Loner he had summoned parting the crowd. Bosky raised his hands, asking for quiet. "Now that we've dispensed with the formalities, DeThanatos, you've got some explaining to do."

DeThanatos took a few steps up the slope, turned, and struck a relaxed pose like Michelangelo's *David*. "The truth stands naked before you." The crowd laughed. He threw a glance back at the council. "Are you going to charge me with something, or just stare at my ass?"

As the crowd hooted with laughter, Bosky glowered.

"Besides parading around in daylight like a damn fool, you have broken the third commandment: Thou shalt not leave a mortal with memory of thy darkest powers."

DeThanatos feigned innocence. "I did that?"

"You thralled a young couple in a bloodlust club, and you shape-shifted not once but twice in front of mortals outside the club."

DeThanatos acknowledged the charges with a nod. "You've had someone watching me."

"Ever since you started your absurd masquerade as a Leaguer," Bosky fired back.

DeThanatos was tired of being lectured, especially by a Centurion. "Is that all I'm accused of?"

"On top of conspiring with a Lifer, Becky-Dell Wallace, I'd say that's more than enough."

DeThanatos shrugged apathetically. "Guilty as charged, on all counts."

"So you admit it!" Bosky roared.

DeThanatos did a mocking fist pump. "And proud of it."

Bosky pronounced the sentence. "Then there's nothing left to do but shun you and declare you fair game for any Loner. The one who hunts you down and slays you will join the Centurion Council."

Even though it wasn't the public execution they had hoped for, the Loners let out a raucous cheer.

DeThanatos didn't flinch. He waited for quiet, or for some fool to rush forward and try to dispatch him. No one did. He turned back to Bosky and the council. "You're correct on that part of the law. There's just one problem. I'm a Millennial. Do you know what that means?"

54

Millennials Rule

Bosky's nostrils flared with anger. The rest of the Centurion Council stared at DeThanatos with blank expressions. "Millennial" echoed through the throng. The Loners had no idea what he was talking about.

DeThanatos took in the council with a sneer. "Your ignorance isn't surprising. You're the *Centurion* Council; you don't know about the privileges and powers that come with surviving more than a thousand years."

"You're bluffing!" one of the council members shouted.

Turning to the crowd, DeThanatos asked, "Would another Millennial step forward?" A little girl edged out of the crowd. She looked about seven years old. "Explain the situation to your younger brothers and sisters."

The little girl spoke in a piping voice. "A Millennial is immune to all laws: of man, nature, *and* his fellow vampires."

DeThanatos opened his hands in thanks. "From the mouths of babes."

Bosky flushed with anger. "You mean, from the mouths of little sycophants. We don't know if either of you are one of these 'Millennials.' You're both lying."

"You will know them by three powers," the little girl monotoned.

"Would you like to see 'em?" DeThanatos asked.

One of the council members addressed the little girl with a worried expression. "Do we want to see 'em?"

She broke into a puckish smile. "They're pretty cool."

"All right, prove it," Bosky ordered DeThanatos. "Or, I swear on the Matriarch, I'll annihilate you here and now."

. DeThanatos beckoned to the girl. "Will you assist me?"

Her smile turned devilish. She climbed partway up the slope and faced the crowd. "Beyond a Centurion's powers, Millennials acquire three special powers. One, to replace the Matriarch should she ever be destroyed."

DeThanatos exploded into a giant tree, an exact replica of the Matriarch. His roots bursting through the ground caused a small earthquake. The council's trunk-table started to roll away before they caught it. The crowd jumped back in fear. A second later, the great tree imploded back to DeThanatos.

"Two," the girl announced, "to sustain himself in times of need."

DeThanatos held up his left arm; from the elbow down, it shape-shifted into a bleating lamb.

The crowd gasped at a power they had never witnessed, not even in the crazy things Lifers put in vampire movies.

"And three," the girl continued over the lamb's bleating, "to celebrate his first thousand years with a special set of fangs."

The Millennial bared his fangs: not the customary

long knives of white porcelain, but shimmering gold ones. The throng applauded as if he had been awarded a gold watch at a retirement party. DeThanatos raised the lamb in acknowledgment and buried his golden fangs in its neck.

The Loners roared their approval.

When he was done feeding, he shook the lamb's lifeless body; it imploded back to his forearm. As he spun around, his other hand swept toward the council's trunk-table. The trunk bowed upward and snapped in two with a great *crack* as the seven Centurions went flying to the side. The trunk halves flipped in the air and knifed into the rocky slope, forming a high double pedestal.

DeThanatos shot in the air, landed on top of the pedestal, and glowered down at the stunned Loners. "I've listened to your petty accusations; now it's my turn. Yes, I am conspiring with a Lifer. I am the wolf lying down with the lamb. And yes, the lamb will eventually be devoured. But before then, I plan to gather these American Leaguers in one place and give all Loners the weapons and logistics to exterminate them."

Bosky, unbowed by DeThanatos's display of Millennial prowess, stood on the slope. "And how are you going to accomplish this incredible trick?"

"None of you can be trusted with my plan," DeThanatos answered. "But know this: when I call the next Grand Rendezvous it will be for the Leaguer apocalypse."

The throng bellowed with bloodthirsty glee.

Bosky frowned. "Before he whips you into a Leaguer-slaying mob, remember our treaty. We signed a blood and fire oath with Luther Birnam. Loners will let Leaguers be

Leaguers as long as Leaguers let Loners be Loners. If we break that oath, Leaguers have every right to reveal the exact requirements for slaying a vampire."

"They'll never do it," DeThanatos insisted. "It would be suicide."

The crowd voiced its agreement.

"Would it?" Bosky asked. "Or would Leaguers see it as the ultimate peace offering to Lifers? The Leaguer way of saying, 'See, now we are even more like mortals. We, too, are vulnerable to destruction.' "

The Loners, ceding the point, murmured in confusion.

Bosky turned to DeThanatos. "This plan of yours, if it fails, could backfire. It could not only turn Leaguers back into vampire slayers but also reinforce them with an entire new army of Lifers."

The crowd rumbled in agreement and began to boo DeThanatos.

He answered by raising his arms and thrall-locking the entire mass of them. The Mother Forest went silent except for the rustle of pine needles. "You began by accusing me of breaking the third commandment. But I accuse you of crimes against our *inhumanity*. You've forgotten what it is to be a vampire, and it is this: to shred every rule, to break every oath, to obey no law but the two-pronged law of bloodlust and death!" His fiery eyes blazed down on the sea of traitors. "Who ends this Grand Rendezvous? I do!" He leaped off the pedestal as he flicked his hands.

The mass of Loners snapped into flying forms and rose off the ground like a dust-raising cloud of startled birds.

One flier, a black condor, banked out of the launching flock, circled back, and dropped onto the slope. The condor shape-shifted back to Bosky. He gave his nemesis a tight smile. "These Millennial powers you've displayed tonight—I look forward to acquiring them soon."

DeThanatos nodded knowingly. "You already have. Otherwise, you wouldn't have been able to resist the ultimate thrall: 'Be gone.' "

"Yes," the thickset vampire conceded. "And each being Millennials, we were never to reveal ourselves to lesser vampires. You and the kid blew that one."

DeThanatos answered with cocky disdain. "An educated vampire is a more evil vampire, don't you think?"

Bosky ignored the games and cut to the chase. "As a Millennial, I am required to ask you, why didn't you destroy Birnam and Morning as soon as you knew they had become re-morts?"

"Why didn't you?"

"They're not in my jurisdiction," Bosky retorted. "They're in yours. Do I have to refresh your memory on the protocol for the eradication of re-mortals?"

"Age is destroying Birnam, if it hasn't already. I wanted his death to be long and slow. As for Morning, he's my blood child. I can't destroy him until he's made the complete transition to re-mort."

Bosky stared with wide eyes. "*You* created that pathetic excuse of a vampire?"

DeThanatos scowled. "Regretfully, yes."

"That's rich!" Bosky bellowed with a hardy laugh. "So call me in as your proxy and I'll destroy him."

"No. I made the monster; no one touches him but me."

"Have it your way." Bosky gestured to the Matriarch at the bottom of the slope. "But you must swear on the Sacred Mother, on the cradle and grave of the Old Ones, that you will fulfill the sixth and unspoken commandment."

DeThanatos's gray eyes fell on the great tree. "I did that once; she didn't deliver on her side of the bargain. This time, I do what Loners do best: fly solo." He leaped in the air, snapped into a falcon, and flew over the Matriarch.

As Bosky watched, his night vision picked up a white drop falling from the falcon. It splattered in the top branches of the Matriarch. Bosky felt a subsonic groan snake up from the earth. It was no tremor or call to another Rendezvous, it was the roots of the bristlecone pines in the Mother Forest, filled with the spirits of the Old Ones, shuddering in their graves.

55

Hunger Pangs

Morning and his crew ate lunch in the academy mess hall but paid little attention to their food. Some focused on notebooks; others peppered each other with questions. "What are the elements of the fire tetrahedron?" Armando asked Morning. "Take one away and you put out the fire."

"Oxygen, fuel, heat, chemical reaction," he recited.

Over the next few days the probies would be taking their written finals and field qualification tests. If they passed, they would no longer be probationary firefighters. They would be members of New York's bravest.

"Sully," Armando continued as he hefted a thick sandwich loaded with rare roast beef, "if Clancy throws an acronym test at us, what's BOHICA stand for?"

Sully shot back, "Bend over, here it comes again."

During the laughter, Armando took a megabite of his sandwich. Morning had barely heard the joke. He was

transfixed by the trail of odors coming from the sandwich: a braid of meat, bread, and horseradish. What
Morning had lost in a vampire's hyper sense of smell, he
had gained in the smell of mortal food reawakening his
appetite.

"Yo, McCobb!" Sully yelled, bursting Morning's bubble of olfactory sensation. "If you got such moose eyes for
Armando and his sandwich, why don't you both gnaw on
it till your luscious lips meet?"

As the crew laughed, Morning snapped to. He needed
to answer trash talk with trash talk to cover his sandwich
lusting. "It's not the Tex-Mex gorilla or his sandwich," he
complained, "it's the damn roast beef."

Armando eyeballed his sandwich. "What's wrong with
my roast beef?"

"Look at it," Morning replied. "It's so rare and bloody
it's still pawing the ground." To further banish suspicion,
he picked up his can of Blood Lite and took a big swig.
Then came the hardest part. The taste of Blood Lite began
to make him gag. He repressed the urge but couldn't hide
the grimace as he swallowed. "Oh, man," he said, "I hate
it when it coagulates at the bottom of the can. Anyone got
some blood thinners?"

The laugh he got made him think he'd covered his ass,
but Sully was still staring at him.

In the past weeks, Morning had been careful not to
go too crazy in the weight room or pass people on training runs. He had to uphold his reputation as one of the
most squirrelly guys in the class. He didn't let anyone see
his new muscle definition. When it came to locker room
showers, he had already set a precedent that he wasn't big
on showers. Vampires never were. They were better than

cats when it came to hygiene: they rarely broke a sweat and didn't smell. Morning dealt with the slight body odor he had begun to acquire by taking showers at home. The toughest thing was masking the occasional pimple with makeup. He had a particularly gnarly one starting on his chin. But even if makeup didn't cover it and he was busted by a fellow probie, he had a ready defense: finals can make even a vampire break out in stress pimples.

After school, when Morning hopped off the bus at 125th Street, he got two surprises. Zoë and her pedicab were waiting for him, but Zoë wasn't on the bike seat; Cody was. "What brings you guys over here?" he asked.

"My tour customer canceled this afternoon," Zoë explained. "And I gotta get my daily dose of endorphins, so I thought I'd give you a ride home."

Cody hopped off the bike. "And I'm just lending ZZ a leg before she spins you downtown." He grinned at Zoë. "And giving her a chance to ogle my butt."

"You wish," she quipped.

As Zoë straddled the bike, Cody slapped Morning's arm. "Now it's your turn to ogle hers."

Morning scoffed. "I don't ogle Zoë's butt."

"Oh, right," Cody said. "There's only one backside for you: the rear end of a Porsche." He and Zoë laughed and he hefted his backpack. "I say ogle the one you're with."

As Cody disappeared into the subway, Morning climbed into the pedicab. The scene was being watched by a falcon perched on a flagpole jutting from a building. Zoë started pedaling; the falcon took to the air and followed.

Cruising along, Morning felt like an olfactory

sponge. Each block offered another mouthwatering, brain-expanding cloud of pleasure: hot pretzels, hot dogs, garlic, the pungent smell of sauerkraut, charred beef, falafel, pizza, fresh-baked bread. While the smells were familiar, the urges they triggered were long-lost sensations.

Meanwhile, Zoë kept a running commentary on her latest scheme to get turned. She had been researching companies that employed Leaguers and had discovered the Bureau of Vampire Affairs was hiring a lot more Leaguers to do investigation work into illegal Leaguer activity. She had applied for an internship the next summer at the BVA in Washington. "I mean," she bubbled, "with all those Leaguers coming and going, I'd be eye candy waiting for a nibble. And you know how they treat interns in D.C.: low-hanging fruit ready for picking."

As Morning frowned over Zoë's tireless quest to join the immortal set, she lived up to her reputation for verbally blindsiding friend and foe. "Speaking of low-hanging fruit, has Mrs. Dredful figured out you're a Leafer yet?"

"I don't think so."

"Yeah, you'd probably know if she thought you weren't sterile anymore. She'd totally freak if she thought you could knock up Portia."

He reacted with a mega eye roll and wondered if Portia had told Zoë about their plans for the night of the End Is Upon Us Ball. "Zoë, do we have to talk about this?"

She didn't let up. "Are you? Still sterile, I mean."

He felt his skin get hot. "I don't know! How would I know?"

"I can think of one way: we take you to a sperm bank and have you tested."

"Zoë!"

She ignored his protest. "Nah, there's only one way to test the Morning bullet mystery: real or blanks?" She started a playground chant. "Morning and Portia sittin' in a tree, K-I-S-S-I-N-G."

"Knock it off," Morning growled.

But she was having too much fun. "First comes love, then comes marriage, then comes Portia with a baby—"

"If you don't shut up, I *will* turn you!"

She laughed, tossing over her shoulder, "Big talker." The next light turned yellow, and she braked to a stop.

The trailing falcon pulled up and landed on the streetlight above them.

Zoë turned back to Morning with a wistful expression. "Problem is, I don't think you could turn me anymore. I'm betting you've swapped your vampire-making skills for a set of baby-making skills." She flashed a sweet smile. "But don't worry, A.M., I don't think less of you for it. We're still friends, right?"

The light turned back to green and he waved his hand for her to go. "Yeah, yeah, yeah."

After a block, Zoë asked, "Are you going to Portia's tonight?"

He was glad to get back to a normal subject. "Yeah, she's making me a good-luck dinner before the beginnings of finals at the academy."

"She's making you dinner?" Zoë turned with a shocked look. "If you've turned into a solid-food obligate—"

"No, no." He cut her off. "She's making herself dinner, and pouring me a can of the usual."

"Oh, then maybe I'm bustin' your fangs too soon. Maybe you could still turn me after all."

He realized whether he was Leaguer or Lifer or somewhere in between there was no winning with Zoë. "ZZ,
could you just take me home?"

She shot him a thumbs-up. "You got it, A.M."

Above them, the falcon banked toward the Village.

56

Vampire Up

The falcon swooped into the garden behind the Dredful town house. It landed near the open kitchen window and cocked its head at the smoke wafting out. Inside, Portia was pan-searing a two-fisted, jaw-straining chunk of ground sirloin she called "a comfort-food portion."

She had reason for needing comfort. She had just come back from her first shoot for her knitting doc: an interview with an old lady in Queens who held the world speed record for the stocking stitch. Portia was on the phone to Cody, telling him how much her footage sucked. "I mean, Michael Moore couldn't make this stuff interesting." After that, she didn't want to talk about it anymore because it was so depressing. "How 'bout you?" she asked. "Have you figured out a new angle on the Leaguer doc?"

"Not really," he told her. "Fact is, I'm lost. I mean, who wants to see a doc about the failure of a movement, about how Becky-Dell and DeThanatos win and the VRA goes down in flames? It's such a downer. Bottom line, I'm floundering without you, Porsche. You sure you don't wanna come back and help me figure this out? I mean, c'mon, even a story about loser vampires has gotta be better than any story about competitive knitting."

"No thanks," she said, fighting the temptation. "I promised my mom and Morning. I'd rather stick a knitting needle in my eye than go back to making a doc on vampires."

She got an incoming call and put Cody on hold. Morning was calling to tell her he was running a few minutes late.

She flipped her sizzling burger and got back to Cody. For a second she wanted to tell him that there was actually *one* winner in the vampire story: Morning. She had to bite her tongue not to tell him about Morning's re-aging, and that if she did go back to the vampire doc with Cody she had a potential new title for it: *The Rise and Fall of Morning McCobb*. Instead, she told Cody to hang in there and said goodbye.

By the time she hung up, the falcon had taken off.

The falcon flew across the Hudson and glided over the Jersey side of the river. With its binocular eyes, eight times more powerful than human ones, it spotted what it was looking for: a henbane bush, gone to seed. It landed next to the bush and scooped three henbane seeds into its beak.

By the time Portia finished cooking her burger and went upstairs to change, the falcon was back in the garden. The bird flapped through the open window, landing on the counter. Portia had placed the massive cheeseburger on a paper towel. The falcon dropped the seeds from its beak onto the burger's slather of melted cheese, then tapped the seeds into the cheese.

Having been a monk in another millennium, DeThanatos had never forgotten his skills as an herbalist or the medicinal power of plants. Henbane, or *insana,* as it was called back then, in the right form and dose could rob a person of reason and restraint.

After getting to Portia's, Morning locked his bike to a street sign out front.

A few minutes later, he and Portia sat at the kitchen table over their respective dinners. She gripped the fat cheeseburger, with its multiple overhangs of lettuce, bacon, and caramelized onion, while he popped a can of Blood Lite from the supply she kept for him in the fridge. He had started to drink it chilled to hide some of the tang that his Leaguer taste buds had once craved but his re-mortalizing taste buds were souring on.

After being caught ogling Armando's roast beef, Morning was careful to look away when Portia opened her Jaws of Life mouth, bit down on the burger, and rained reddish blood on her plate. But he couldn't avoid the wonderful waft of charred meat that invaded his nostrils and stirred a growl in his stomach.

"Hmm." Portia swooned as she chewed. "How wong 'fore you're gonna whan onna dese?"

He wanted to say *Let's split it right now,* but he hadn't yet told her about his growing craving for food. Instead, he washed down the mouthwatering aroma of charred meat with a swig of cold Blood Lite.

After Portia wolfed down her burger, she and Morning went into the living room. They sat on the couch. Even though the huge burger in her stomach had turned the three seeds into slow-release henbane, it was already beginning to take effect. The depression over her knitting doc, which had been mild before, was sliding into agitated despair. "You know what the problem with the world is?" she announced.

"Yeah," Morning answered, "that I'm still a few days away from being a firefighter."

She ignored his stab at humor. "No, that people start out wanting to do great things, and what do they end up doing? Knitting. They start out wanting to change the world, and they end up compromising. I mean, that's exactly what happened to the Leaguer movement. Birnam had a vision of vampires being free and equal, and they end up being treated like illegal aliens. Rachel had a vision of vampires doing all this incredible stuff for the human race, of soaring like Earth Angels, but then out of jealousy, or hatred, or fear, the Becky-Dells of the world bitch-slapped Leaguers back to earth so they're nothing but a bunch of knitters."

Morning tried not to smile over one of the reasons he loved her: she was even funny when she was riled up. "Ah, you think maybe you're exaggerating a little?"

"Not at all. It's like all the vampires who wanted to be Earth Angels had their wings clipped, and now they're running around like Boy Scouts doing puny good deeds. They went from Earth Angels to candy stripers like that!" she lamented with a finger snap. "I mean, where are the kickass

276

radicals of the Leaguer movement! Why don't Leaguers grow a set of fangs instead of knitting needles? Why doesn't one of 'em vampire up and just take Becky-Dell out?"

Her diatribe began to concern him. "Portia, you can't change the world overnight. It's still moving in the right direction."

She wheeled on him. "Oh, really? Name one good thing that's happened for Leaguers!"

He raised an arm and made a muscle. "I got biceps."

She didn't laugh. She stared at him for a moment with wild eyes. The henbane had done a number on her reason; now it was working on her restraint. She leaned toward him and spoke in a low voice. "You know, Morning, you're right."

He was intoxicated by her meaty breath.

"And we should celebrate that fact right now."

The scent of charbroiled bliss derailed his brain. "Which fact is that?"

She pushed closer and whispered in his ear. "That we're EBs forever and ever."

Her tantalizing breath covered him in goose bumps. "Yeah, we are," he whispered back. "How do you wanna celebrate?"

"The only way we can," she purred as she turned his face to hers.

They fell into a passionate kiss. Morning was so enthralled by the double ecstasy of kissing her *and* tasting the virtual cheeseburger in her mouth, he didn't realize she was pushing him onto his back. Their makeout sessions were usually slow builds up a yearning curve, but this one was more like a drag race, with Portia taking it from zero to sixty in seconds.

In the middle of their tonguey wet-fest, she raised her head for a breath, gave him a seductive grin, and wiped the kiss-juice shine off his chin. The makeup on his pimple went with it. She stared at the angry little chin mountain. "Is that a pimple, or are you just happy to see me?" She didn't wait for an answer. She let loose with a raucous belly laugh and dived back into his mouth like her first burger had been a slider and Morning was her second.

Her tongue went Christopher Columbus, searching for an unknown passage to the back of his head. Her hands went Magellan and Ponce de León: one circumnavigated his body, the other launched an expedition for the fountain of youth.

As Morning tried to breathe, he felt her hand slip under his belt. He escaped her mouth, grabbed her hand, and exhaled a breathy "Woo!"

She nuzzled his neck. "Is that 'woo' as in 'woo-hoo,' or 'whoa'?"

"A little of both."

She growled softly. "Well, let's turn that 'whoa' into 'woo-hoo.'"

He pulled up her probing hand and kissed it. "Isn't your mom gonna be home soon?"

"Not for hours." She gripped him in an eye lock.

Morning was used to seeing her eyes oozing pleasure, but there was something more about them, something he'd never seen before: total wild abandon.

"C'mon," she cooed, "I know you want to."

He swallowed. "I thought we were gonna wait."

"That's weeks away."

"But I'm kinda in training."

"So am I," she growled, "for love." In one swift move,

she rolled him off the couch, braced their fall onto the carpet with her arm, and rolled him on top of her. She caught him in another kiss as her hand snaked down his stomach.

He escaped and jumped to his feet. "I'm sorry, I wanna do this as bad as you. But tonight's not right. I gotta be totally focused tomorrow. I gotta have my A-game."

She sat up, spreading inviting arms. "That's what I'm giving you. My *A*-game!" She peeled off her blouse and burst into song. "A-more-aaa!"

Morning wavered between laughing, leaping at the luscious opportunity, and leaving.

She reached back to undo her bra.

"Portia, don't!" He knew if he saw any more he'd never leave, and the next few days would be haunted by so many flashbacks of ecstasy that his exams and field tests would have to be rated NC-17. "I—I gotta go," he stammered as he headed through the kitchen to the door.

"You're leaving?" she shouted, jumping to her feet.

He turned but kept going. "Yeah, but I want a rain check."

She followed as he opened the door. The restraint-stripping effects of henbane boosted her shock to fury. "Rain check, my ass! I just offered you everything!"

He backed down the hall as she stalked after him. "And I want it," he blurted. "I really do. But not tonight. I'm sorry."

"Stop saying that!"

Heading outside, he stumbled down the steps to his bike.

She planted herself at the top of the stoop, oblivious to the bra exhibition she was giving the world. "You're such a wimp! Why didn't I get it when I saw that girl throw herself at you, wanting your fangs in her neck, and all you could do was say, 'I don't take, I like to give.' That's your problem, Morn, all you do is give-give-give! When are you gonna show me some take-take-take? I mean, you're still a vampire, right?"

He fumbled with the lock on his bike. He knew the sooner he got away, the better it would be for the both of them. "Portia, you don't know what you're saying."

"Oh, yes, I do!" she stormed back.

He jumped on his bike and started away.

She shouted after him. "I'm saying for once in your wimpy life you need to vampire up and grow a set!"

She spun, marched back inside, and slammed the door.

From the open window overlooking the stoop, Mr. and Mrs. Nesbit stared down with concerned bemusement. "Young love," Mr. Nesbit clucked, "aren't you glad we're over it?"

Mrs. Nesbit gave him a playful punch. "Speak for yourself, buster."

Above them, a falcon lifted off the roof peak and soared into the night.

57

Things That Go
Chomp in the Night

Zoë rode her pedicab up Sixth Avenue. She had just dropped the night's tour clients off at their hotel in SoHo. She spotted a familiar figure walking along the sidewalk. She pulled up beside him. "Hey, A.M., what are you doing out so late? I thought finals started tomorrow."

Morning nodded with exasperation. "They do, but it's been a crazy night. First I had a fight with Portia, then my bike got a flat."

"Do you want a ride home?"

"It's awfully late, and outta your way."

Zoë flapped a hand. "Nah, you're never out of my way. C'mon, get in."

He hesitated. "Really?"

"Really." He climbed in and Zoë got the pedicab going. "Besides, seeing how you're a Leafer and going all mortal on me, I wanna spend as much time as I can with you while you can still grow a set."

Morning let out a caustic chuckle. "Did you talk to Portia already?"

"No. What's so funny?"

"That's what Portia said. She said I was a wimp and I should 'grow a set.'"

Zoë giggled as she turned onto Fifth Avenue. "Which 'set' do you think she's talking about?"

He didn't answer. They rode in silence for a while.

Sitting on her seat and coasting, Zoë turned back to him. "Seriously, which—" Her voice trailed off, her words swallowed by the look in Morning's eyes. They were filled with desire: not just sexual desire, but the locked-on intensity of predator for prey. It sent a wave of fear and exhilaration through her. Trying to ignore it, she turned around and pedaled. But her knees felt weak. She could still feel his eyes on her.

She fumbled for the right words. "You know, Morning, Portia is my best friend. Maybe it's my duty to find out what she meant by 'set.' It would just be an experiment to see what"—she couldn't hold back a nervous giggle—"you know, pops up." She turned back for his answer.

He gave her the slightest smile. "Yeah," he said in a voice filled with invitation. "Let's experiment."

Zoë's legs went so wobbly she wasn't sure she could pedal to the tiny street she spotted up ahead. To give her strength and steel her resolve, she hummed the chorus from "Part of Your World."

The pedicab turned and disappeared into a narrow lane called Washington Mews.

In the city where neon never sleeps, first light had begun to dim neon's wash when the police raided St. Giles. Drake

Sanders had been tipped off and was there to scoop the arrest of Morning McCobb. The raid became a fishing expedition with no fish. Morning was nowhere to be found.

This didn't stop the morning shows and newsstands from buzzing with the shocking news. Besides the predictable headlines—MORNING SUCKS!—the most vivid account was the video captured on a security camera in Washington Mews, where Zoë and her pedicab had been discovered.

It showed the following: Zoë dismounts her pedicab bike, steps back in a zombielike trance, gets into the cab, and sits beside Morning. She falls back and Morning buries his head in her neck. He turns once, as if he has heard a sound, and displays his blood-rimmed mouth. He resumes his feeding. When he's done, he swings out of the cab, sleeve-wipes his mouth, and strides away. In the cab, Zoë remains motionless: unconscious or dead, it's not clear.

The only good news the media had to report was that Morning's midnight feed had not been fatal. Zoë was still alive, and she had gone from one extreme to the other: from the girl who got snubbed in the Tasting Room to the girl who got nearly chugged in Washington Mews. But no one could ascertain her condition, as she had been whisked away to an undisclosed location.

As the shocking day unfolded and the clip of Morning's wet-work on Zoë rolled across the country in a tornado of pixels, several events swiftly followed.

The fire academy delayed the beginning of final exams until Captain Clancy could: (1) triumphantly expel Morning, and (2) train all the probies in stake whittling and stake delivery methods so if Morning dared set foot and fang back on the Rock, they could extinguish him like a fire in a trash can.

Becky-Dell used the tragic event to lambast the nation.

"Do you get it yet? There's no such thing as a harmless vampire! They're hardwired for bloodlust! If this is how the runt of the Leaguer litter acts, imagine what the rest of 'em are capable of. The true vampire agenda has shown its face and it is this: to sink their bloodlusting fangs into the necks of our daughters and sons!"

As Becky-Dell stoked the fires of public fury, hate crimes and vigilante violence against Leaguers spiked. A Leech Treat cart was pushed into the East River. A blood bar was stoned and so smashed up that a reporter proclaimed, "Never have I seen so much loss of blood without loss of life."

Portia had awoken that morning with a splitting headache and a major memory gap from the night before. The last thing she could recall was Morning showing off his bicep. After that, everything was a blank.

She told her mother as much over breakfast, which included Rachel, who had taken refuge at their apartment rather than face the media and the MOPers who had surrounded the Diamond Sky building wanting Leaguer blood.

There was a smaller media contingent camped in front of the Dredful town house. They had not gotten a statement from Penny, but they did get an interview with Mr. and Mrs. Nesbit, who provided them with not only a scoop but also restored some of the data to Portia's crashed memory.

Portia watched on the TV as the Nesbits, thirty feet away on the stoop, spilled to the press. They detailed Portia's near-topless tirade against Morning the night before, right down to her banshee challenge that he should "vampire up and grow a set!"

The Nesbits' account broke the dam on Portia's memory. As her rant against vampire pacifists, her attempted seduction, and raging challenge to Morning came flooding back, she buried her face in her hands.

Rachel and Penny fixed her with disbelieving eyes. Rachel finally asked, "Portia, is that true?"

Still hiding her face, Portia nodded.

"Even being almost topless?" Penny demanded.

Portia raised her face, wet with tears. "Yes, I drove him to it! It's all my fault!"

Rachel put a hand on her knee. "Portia, you're not the real victim here. Zoë is."

"And that's why he chose her!" Portia blurted. "She's been asking for it ever since she met Morning!"

Penny answered her outburst with a severe look. "You need to calm down and tell us exactly what happened."

Portia sucked in a jerky breath, let it out, and collected herself. "Morning left here last night and—idiot boy that he is—jumped on the chance to kill two birds with one stone. He was gonna prove to me he was a taker *and* give Zoë what she's always wanted, to be turned. But I never meant a set of *fangs,* I meant a set of—"

"That's okay," Rachel interrupted, "we know what you meant." She turned to Penny. "The media doesn't know it yet, but that's exactly what happened. Zoë got turned."

"Do you know where she is?" Penny asked.

Rachel nodded.

Portia jumped up. "We have to see her!"

Rachel pulled up her cell and hit speed dial. When someone answered, she said, "Security, we're ready to go."

58

Claiming the Body

After Zoë had been discovered at about one a.m. by a dog walker, she was taken to New York University Hospital and treated for extreme anemia. By the time Mr. and Mrs. Zotz got there, Zoë's body had rejected a blood transfusion, two puncture wounds were found on her neck, and her blood work came back with numbers no doctor had ever seen. She was diagnosed as a vampire in the making. It was the first vampire-in-process doctors had gotten their hands on, and the war over Zoë's ninety-five-pound biomass was launched among the doctors and scientists at NYU. The small group of doctors that won did so by kidnapping. They disguised Zoë as a corpse, smuggled her out of the hospital via the morgue, and moved her to a quickly assembled suite-laboratory in a boarded-up hospital once known as St. Vincent's.

While Rachel had Leaguer spies keeping tabs on this, she also knew that when the Leaguer security detail got them past the media and into the waiting car in front of the Dredful town house, she couldn't stop the press from following them to Zoë's secret location. Rachel wasn't concerned. She had other plans.

After arriving at St. Vincent's, the Leaguer bodyguards kept the trailing media from entering the former hospital, which was in a chaotic state of semi-demolition.

When Rachel, Penny, and Portia entered Zoë's makeshift suite, the attending doctors ordered them out. The doctors claimed they had performed enough tests on Zoë to determine that she was "legally undead," which didn't make her a patient so much as a specimen in their laboratory. The bottom line, they crowed, was that Zoë belonged to them, and to the future of science.

Rachel countered with a barrage of visitors. First, Zoë's parents threw themselves on their daughter's unconscious body. They performed admirably as distraught parents, even though they now knew their daughter was in the process of achieving her lifetime dream: being turned. Then came the team of Leaguer lawyers, who threatened the doctors with malpractice suits for misdiagnosing their patient as "undead," administering mortality-tainted blood to a transitioning vampire, transporting a living and ill patient through the germ swamp of a morgue, and performing medical procedures in an unlicensed building.

Rachel, in a shockingly coherent display, concluded the assault on the doctors. She informed them that, first, Zoë was not ill but in ecdysis, which, if they knew anything about the science of vampirism, or entomology, they would know that Zoë was in the process of slipping out of her mortal body and developing into the instar, or immortal body, of a vampire. And second, since Zoë was not

287

technically ill or in need of medical aid, this was strictly a family matter, and if the doctors didn't give up Zoë peacefully, they would pay with their reputations and their licenses to practice in New York.

The doctors conceded defeat and rushed off to write the papers they could still publish after what they had learned about Zoë's ecdysis.

In one more sly move, Rachel fooled the media circus outside St. Vincent's by announcing that Zoë was going home, and then sending Zoë's parents in a convoy of security cars and an ambulance to the Zotz family apartment on the Upper East Side. Of course, Zoë wasn't in the ambulance. Mr. and Mrs. Zotz had been convinced that Zoë's mortal-to-immortal transition needed to be monitored by her own kind, so, not wanting to impede their daughter's dream, they allowed Zoë to be smuggled to the Dredful apartment, where she would complete her metamorphosis.

The smuggling entailed a couple of Leaguers masquerading as demolition workers, Zoë being hidden in a roll of old carpet, and her three female escorts donning dusty overalls and hard hats, then carrying the carpet-cocooned Zoë to a construction van.

As the van drove to the Dredful town house, Rachel turned to Portia. "We've almost got half the problem home. Do you have any idea where the other half is?"

"Morning?"

"Yeah."

Portia shook her head. "Not a clue."

With the media misdirected from the Dredful apartment, and the Nesbits taking a long nap after their exhausting fifteen minutes of fame, the Zoë transport squad had no problem secreting her into the town house.

When Cody arrived, he and Portia headed upstairs to check on Zoë in the guest room. She was still unconscious but looked comfortable. Cody had done the homework Portia had given him earlier and had brought the most quality-enhanced version of the clip of Morning feeding on Zoë that he had the electronic genius to generate.

In Portia's bedroom, they loaded the DVD into her computer. She fast-forwarded to the part where Morning plunged his fangs into Zoë's neck, and hit play. She waited for when he turned from feeding and stared up at the camera. She froze the frame. "Can we zoom in on that super tight?"

"Sure." Cody took over the keyboard and zoomed onto Morning's face. Despite the image getting grainier, his face was still distinctive enough to see two fangs and the ring of red blood around his mouth.

"Did you see him yesterday?" Portia asked.

"Yep, after I rode Zoë across the park."

"Notice anything different about him?"

Cody threw a hand at the screen. "Yeah, he's feeding on your best friend. If he was feeding on my best friend I'd stake up, find him, and punch him in the heart."

She ignored his machismo. "Look at him closely."

He leaned toward the screen. "I'm looking closely. That's Morning McCobb."

"If it is, there should be red on his chin, too."

Cody's brow furrowed. "Is that some kind of vampire thing? Rusty feeders make sloppy drinkers?"

"I'm not talking blood." She pointed to Morning's grainy but smooth chin. "Last night he had a chin pimple the size of a Jujyfruit. Where did it go?"

Cody shrugged. "Dunno. Maybe he was into poppin' pimples before he popped Zoë."

Portia stood up.

Cody raised his hands in apology. "Okay, okay, I know it's not funny."

"It's not that." She grabbed her jacket.

"Where are you going?"

"To find Morning."

"I'm goin' with."

She plucked a Flip camera off her dresser and handed it to Cody. "No, you're staying here and shooting the first-ever footage of a mortal-to-vampire transformation. It's gonna guarantee you an A on your senior film project and get you into any film school you want."

"If you put it that way." He took the camera. "But who woulda thought it would end with Morning being Zoë's blood daddy."

"*If* Morning's the daddy."

Before he could ask what that meant, Portia was gone.

59

Bridge Talk

On the Williamsburg Bridge, in the middle of the walkway, Morning stood at the rail and gazed toward the Statue of Liberty. Despite the dragnet that had been thrown over the city, he felt safe in his disguise. He was dressed as a Hasidic mom, complete with wig, head scarf, thick glasses, dark dress, gray coat, and a baby carriage. The only thing missing was a baby.

Fixed on the distant statue, he realized that Lady Liberty's words—"Give me your tired, your poor, your huddled masses yearning to breathe free . . ."—would now never include "your vampires yearning to feed without bloodlust." His failure had buried a stake in the heart of Birnam's dream of Lifer and Leaguer living in peace. The Leaguer movement had been slain by footage of the world's most harmless vampire sinking his fangs into every mortal's worst fear: their daughter being skewered by a bloodsucking fiend. Along with the dream of a people,

Morning's dream of becoming a firefighter was as dead as ash.

His gaze drifted to the steely water flowing past the bridge. He didn't know if he still had the vampire strength to leap over the lanes of traffic, make the water, drown, and let the fishy underworld have the last feed. If he didn't make the water, it would confirm he was mortal enough to land in traffic and be slammed around until he was road-kill. After that, he didn't care if they tossed his body in the river or stuck his head on a pike and delivered it to Becky-Dell.

As he gathered the strength to hop on the rail and scale the anti-jumper fence, he saw a figure approaching on the walkway, coming from Manhattan. He recognized the lop-ing gait. Portia. His first thought was she had been sent as a decoy to distract him before they lowered the hammer. His eyes darted high, low, left. There was no sign of a trap. He watched her draw closer. Her face was expression-less. She didn't smirk or raise a brow at seeing him in drag. He wondered what she was thinking. After all, the night before she'd offered him "everything" and he'd run away; now he was wearing a dress. On second thought, he didn't want to know what she was thinking.

She stopped next to him. Catching her breath, she snuck a peek at his chin. She had never been so happy to see a pimple in her life. Not that it made his inno-cence a slam dunk. She had other questions that needed answers. And she had to buy time. "Mind if I join you?" she asked.

"Free country," he said.

She put her left hand on the rail and slipped her right into her jacket pocket. "You just made it a little less free, for Leaguers anyway," she said as she blindly fingered a text into her cell.

Morning nodded. "I know."

She didn't know if that was a confession or not. She only knew she needed to change the subject. Morning didn't like to rush into things, unless it was a burning building. She also knew it from the night before in her living room. She was still trying to figure out what had triggered her episode of bodice-ripping lust combined with no-greater-wrath-than-a-teenage-girl-scorned. But that mystery could wait. The fate of the boy she was pretty darn sure was her eternal beloved couldn't.

Her fingers finished the text and sent it, and she gave Morning a quick once-over. "Nice disguise. I almost didn't recognize you. But Hasidic? I know you've always been into superheroes, but when you went looking for your own superhero alter ego, was a Hasidic mom the only one left?" She slapped her head with a sudden epiphany. "Wait, I get it, this *is* your superhero costume—Super Sadie, right?"

He shook his head in begrudging awe; she could riff even under the worst circumstances. "No, the last nail in my superhero coffin got banged in last night."

"Yeah, looks that way. I'm curious about one thing."

"Just one?" he asked with a scoff.

"Okay, maybe a gazillion, but let's start with one before you"—she feigned shock and touched his arm—"wait, am I stopping you from jumping? I mean, is this a bad time?" She eye-rolled. "Well, of course it's a *bad* time, but is it a bad time, you know, to talk, just before"—she arced a hand over the rail—"wooooo-*kerplosh*! Goodbye, Morning."

He refused to laugh at her ditz routine, but he did

congratulate himself for falling in love with a girl who could even make fun of a suicide in progress. "If I gotta have a last conversation with someone, it might as well be with the only girl who knows my go-to place: the middle of the Williams Bird Bridge."

She squashed the urge to tell him how romantic that was, and got back to detective mode. "How did you know not to be at St. Giles when the cops showed up to grab you?"

"I didn't. When they busted down the front door I was in the basement making a sandwich. When they went to my room I went out the back door."

"How did you know to run?"

"I got a glimpse of 'em as they tore up the stairs. When a SWAT team's packing stake guns and flamethrowers you know who they're looking for."

Portia shook her head in confusion. "Back up a sec, you were making a sandwich? For who?"

"For me?"

"Since when did you start eating solid food?"

"Since early this morning."

Her eyes widened. "But if you've turned mortal enough to eat food, then you couldn't have been vampire enough to pop fangs—"

"I'm not re-mortalizing anymore."

"What?"

"I upchucked the sandwich an hour ago." He answered her confused look with an impatient frown. "Look, Portia, it's complicated, and I'm running out of time."

She bristled at the condescension in his voice. "Well, if you jump and kill yourself I'll never know if the guy I fell in love with was the guy who jumped my best friend's veins

294

and turned her into a vampire, or if it was someone else trying to frame you. So try me, Morning, 'cause ever since we met, I've handled 'complicated.' "

He pulled back, impressed by her bluntness. A thought made him smile. "Is this the part where you get so wound up and passionate you rip off your shirt?"

She chuckled. "Touché. Now, c'mon, Morn, gimme a chance to understand."

He dived in. To the explanation, not the river. "I was re-mortalizing, aging right along as long as I was pursuing my Lifer dream of firefighter. The minute that ended, when I heard on the radio this morning that I'd been expelled from the academy, the re-mortalization process slammed on the brakes. My body stopped producing *pneumabrotus,* and now it's on its way back to being a vampire."

"How do you know for sure?"

He rubbed his fingers across his chin and wasn't surprised when he didn't feel a bump. "Notice anything?"

Portia recoiled in shock. The pimple was gone. "But it was there a minute ago!"

"Exactly. The returning vampire in me healed it, and I have no idea how fast I'm going from re-mort to re-vamp. Which is why I need to jump while I still have enough mortal in me to die."

She studied his jawline. "But the whiskers you've grown—they haven't disappeared."

"Yeah, wow," he said flatly, "if I go back to all vampire I will have matured"—he held up his thumb and index finger mocking the half inch he'd grown—"this much."

He started to boost himself on the rail, but she grabbed his arm and pulled him back. "We can get you out of this! Cody, Zoë, me, we all saw that pimple last night, but it's not on the chin of the 'Morning' on the video who turned Zoë. It was someone else, and you know it because you weren't there. I mean, don't you have an alibi, like Sister Flora or someone else at St. Giles?"

He answered flatly. "No one saw me come home, and the world's not going to believe three kids who happen to be friends of the accused. The world's gonna believe what they saw on the video: me plunging into the forbidden well."

"But *you* know you didn't do it. You know it was DeThanatos after he CDed into you!"

"Yeah." Morning shrugged. "Too bad DeThanatos isn't the confessing type." He looked her in the eye. "Now, please, I gotta go, but I don't want you here to see it."

"But Morn," she pleaded, "if you jump, it's like a confession of guilt. Everyone's gonna think you did it."

"I'm tired of caring what people think. I'm tired of trying to convince people that vampires are just a minority with special needs when some of us aren't." She started to speak but he stopped her. "Portia, you and I had our shot at star-crossed love; for a while our stars lined up, and in the past few weeks we were even growing together. It was the best thing that ever happened to me. But now that's gone again, and I can't explain it, but when you've tasted life for a second time, I mean mortal life, it's that much more"—his eyes scanned her face, looking for the right word—"breathtaking. I can't go back to what I was. I can't suck it up and be a vampire again. I only wanna suck it up and die."

A tear tumbled down Portia's cheek. She batted it away, refusing to break. She had to buy time. "Oh, so now I'm supposed to pour my heart out and tell you how much I love you? Aren't those the last words anyone would wanna hear before they threw their life away? Well, I'm not gonna do that cliché, not gonna do it. If you're so set on jumping, then lemme help, lemme make sure you're miserable to the max." She fought the lump in her throat and plunged on. "Even if you were still changing into a mortal, I wouldn't wanna be with you. Know why? 'Cause when you were a vampire one reason I fell for you was 'cause you never quit. But that's what you've changed into: a quitter. And if you actually happen to survive your little suicide, you and I would be through anyway 'cause I can't love a quitter!" She sucked in a breath.

He stared at her, stone-faced and surprised by how little her words stung. "Are you done?"

She felt the vibration of her phone in her pocket. It was the signal she was waiting for. "No," she answered as she shot a look toward Manhattan and spotted someone approaching on a bike. "I wanna apologize for coming out here and trying to stop you." She gestured to his outfit. "I just wish you'd get out of that dress before you jump, 'cause if you're still wearin' it when they fish you out of the river, it'll be an insult to every Hasidic woman in the world."

Morning yanked off his wig. "Happy?"

She turned without answering and strode toward the approaching bike. It was Cody. As she passed him she whispered, "Stall 'im as long as you can." Then she slipped out her phone and dialed 911.

Cody rode up and jumped off the bike as Morning climbed the anti-jumper fence. Cody climbed after him.

"Do you mind?" Morning snapped.

"It's climb or look up your dress."

Morning wasn't amused. "Since when did suicide go buddy system?"

Undeterred, Cody climbed alongside Morning. "I know you don't like me, but I wish you'd hear me out. I've got two reasons why you shouldn't jump. One, if you do, and you die, I'm gonna steal your girl."

"She's not my girl anymore."

"Okay, scratch that. Here's my second reason. There's a movie you gotta see."

Morning shot him an incredulous look. "You're kidding, right?"

"No, really," Cody implored. "The movie's just like the situation you and Portia are in. It's all about unrequited love. In fact, it's the greatest unrequited love story of all time, and if you'd watch it, you'll understand that you and Portia are just like Rick and Ilsa in *Casablanca,* and you'll see that jumping isn't the only way out of this. I've got the DVD and a DVD player in my jacket. We could climb down—"

Morning clambered up and stood on top of the fence.

Cody followed. "Or we could watch it up here, right now, together."

Morning looked over as Cody stood beside him. "I'm outta here." He sprang away.

"No!" Cody shouted.

Morning cleared the roadway and disappeared below the bridgework.

A shout snapped Cody's head to the right. A heavily armed SWAT team ran up the walkway from Manhattan. His gaze turned to where Morning had disappeared. "Sorry, buddy, I'd jump in after you, but I'm no Jimmy Stewart, you're no angel, and *It's a Wonderful Life* this ain't."

60

After Morning

Portia didn't come out of her room for hours. She was inconsolable; she couldn't silence the "if onlys" plaguing her soul. Even though she was convinced Morning was not the Morning who had fed on Zoë, she knew, too well, that it was her public outburst urging him to "vampire up and grow a set" that had inspired DeThanatos to frame Morning, which had then dominoed into his jumping off the bridge. She was equally devastated that her last words to him were the opposite of what eternal beloveds were supposed to say in final farewells. And the memory of those harsh last words provoked the loudest "if only" wailing inside her: *If only I could see him again!*

The tiny ray of hope penetrating her black grief was the possibility that she and Cody had stalled Morning long enough for his resurgent immortality to make suicide a fool's errand. This hope was reinforced by the fact that, for the short time Portia had stayed on the bridge and watched police helicopters and boats search for him, Morning was nowhere to be found. The search didn't last long because the police, assuming Morning was still one hundred percent vampire, figured he had shape-shifted into some kind of fish and made his escape.

Meanwhile, Becky-Dell stood before a vast crowd in front of the Capitol steps. "Morning McCobb has spoken for his race! He has shown their true colors! Red! Red! Red! No faked suicide will stop us from hunting down Morning and bringing him to justice. Nothing will stop us until we make sure Morning and all bloodsucking fiends are dead! Dead! Dead!" Her voice rose over the forest of wooden stakes stabbing the air. "I am here to tell you our great battle against the vampire conspiracy is far from over! There is still one more fang to yank from the unholy beast! And that glistening and dangerous fang is the outrageous notion that mortals and vampires can live together in peace!"

After midnight, Becky-Dell floated on such a cloud of triumph she made herself a double vodka to guarantee sleep. With drink in hand, she sashayed up to her bedroom.

When she entered her boudoir, DeThanatos was sitting in one of the armchairs. He was dressed in a cherry-red satin dress with a plunging neckline. It was the kind of dress he usually preferred his victims in.

She stopped short. "What are you doing in my dress?"

DeThanatos shot her an innocent smile. "You told me to stop wearing your hazmat suit." He raised a languid hand toward her closet. "This was the only thing in my color."

With a scowl, she banished the thought that he looked better in it than she did. "You look so comfortable, it's probably not your first time in a dress."

"Oh, I don't think of it as a dress, I think of it as one of your skins." He stroked his satin-covered chest. "And I like what I feel under your skin."

She harrumphed. "Is that supposed to warm the cockles of my heart, or send a chill up my spine?"

He took her in with gimlet eyes. "There's only one way to find out."

"Didn't you guzzle a girl last night, or was skinny little Zoë Zotz just an aperitif?"

"Tastes great, less filling."

She threw him a chuckle and concluded they had exchanged enough mortal-vampire banter to confirm there was nothing amorous about their alliance. She sat in the chair opposite him and sipped her drink. "So, what was it like being in Morning McCobb's skin?"

"Very creepy," he said with a shudder. "For a second, I thought I was going to have fang failure."

"Do vampires have a cure for that?"

"We're not so different from mortals. Sometimes we think of someone else."

She laughed. "That's rich! Who were you thinking of?"

He answered with his gimlet gaze again.

She shook her head at his shameless flirtation. "It just proves you can't take the man out of a vampire. Men only want what they can't have."

"Vampires don't do 'can't have.' "

She gave him a dismissive wave. "All right, get your

brain out of your fangs and tell me about our next move. It's been a long day."

"It's so elaborate"—his eyes shifted to her bedside table—"I put it in writing."

She spotted the folder on the table and looked back at him. "Then what are you still doing here?"

He smiled seductively. "Enjoying your company."

"Enjoy it less."

He exhaled the sigh of a spurned lover and started for the door.

"When do I get my dress back?" she demanded.

DeThanatos stopped with his back to her, undid the front of the dress, and let it fall down his slim body. He stepped from the pool of satin and glided out the door.

Becky-Dell stared at the empty doorway, then gave her head a shake. She pressed her cold drink against her chest and scolded her beating heart. "Don't even think about it."

61

Island Getaway

Moonlight tinged the harbor. Tiny waves lapped at a narrow strip of Staten Island sand. A bouillabaisse of human relics littered the shore: tire, broken paddle, tennis shoe, buoys, rope, netting, a garnish of plastic bottles.

The water stirred offshore. A fin broke the surface. It raced shoreward as the top of a large fish emerged. In a clumsy amphibious landing, a five-foot catfish beached itself. With a couple of thrashes, the fish wiggled into Morning McCobb. His hopes for drowning had been dashed several hours earlier at the bottom of the East River.

While Morning had known his vampire survival instinct might overrule his wish to die by CDing into an aquatic creature after his jump, he had hoped his body would have retained enough reemerging mortality that his CD would be incomplete, he would lack gills for breathing, and he would drown anyway. But his transition back to vampire had been so swift his catfish CD had been one hundred percent successful. When his firefighter dream had been dashed on the rocks of fate, its cargo of *pneuma-brotus* had been lost along with it.

That was when he tried plan B. For hours he swam in the murky lower depths of the river, trying to shut down the little bit of human consciousness still nattering away in his brain. If he had eliminated his shadow-consciousness and gone into "CD blackout," he would have gone brain-dead as Morning McCobb, not had the mental skills to CD back to human form, and eventually suffered whatever fate his catfish body met. But when you're swimming in an underwater junkyard with everything from glowing eels to shipwrecks, human curiosity keeps the brain firing, along with the normal plague of thoughts such as: *Could Portia be right? I've not only turned into a catfish but a quitter?*

After failing to achieve death by drowning or CD blackout, Morning went to plan C, which had delivered him to the junk-filled sliver of sand on Staten Island.

He wrapped his body in a makeshift coat of fishnet, buoys, and rope. While he looked like the Ancient Mariner, he wasn't worried about being stopped by a local and told, "Hey, sailor, you look better without the albatross." In the middle of the night, the streets of a neighborhood he had only seen once before were dark, silent, and empty.

After a multiblock voyage, he found the house he was looking for. It was still abandoned, not surprising given its history. Almost two years before, a couple sharing their Thanksgiving with an orphan from St. Giles had been turned into a liquid Thanksgiving for a Loner vampire named Ikor DeThanatos. While the vampire had drained the couple, when it came to feeding on the orphan, DeThanatos mistakenly turned Morning McCobb in a fateful moment of backwash.

Morning slipped into the darkened house, found the living room, and fell exhausted onto a dusty couch. As he lay there trying to quiet his mind, he remembered what Birnam had told him about how, as a re-mortal, Birnam had felt compelled to return to his place of turning, Tripoli, to die there. Morning wondered why he felt compelled to return to the place of his turning, even though the opposite had befallen him: he had returned to being all vampire. *Maybe it's an ominous sign,* he thought, *and even though I'm back to being all vampire, some instinct knows I'm going to be slain anyway by outraged Leaguers or vengeful Lifers.* Of course, there was one more possible cause for his demise. He had returned to his place of turning because he was going to be the first vampire to ever be slain by the invisible stake of a broken heart.

Morning woke as splinters of sunrise stabbed through the curtains. It took a moment to recollect where he was and to realize that the previous day had not been a nightmare. To confirm this beyond a shadow of a doubt, he had to do something.

He went to the kitchen and found a knife in a drawer. Going into the bathroom, he instinctively reached for the switch and flicked it. The bathroom blazed with light. He got halfway to the mirror before he spun back and slammed the light off. *Why was there electricity in a house that had been abandoned for so long?*

Besides being terrified that the neighbors might have seen the light go on, he wondered if the house *wasn't* abandoned. He crept upstairs. The bedrooms were empty. The hallway was lit by a skylight. Glancing up through it, he solved the mystery of why there was electricity. Part of a solar panel was visible above the skylight. Con Edison will cut you off for not paying your electric bill, but the sun doesn't read your meter or send a bill.

Morning went into the upstairs bathroom, lit by the rising sun. He raised the knife, pressed it against his cheek, and sliced. It hurt for a second. The bleeding immediately stopped as the cut knitted itself together and healed quickly. He was one hundred percent vampire.

He went back to the master bedroom. A boxy old TV sat on the dresser at the foot of the bed. After making sure the bedroom curtains were shut, he turned on the TV. It flickered to life, powered by the solar panels. It didn't have cable, but it broadcast snowy versions of the basic channels. Finding a news report, Morning watched in amazement at how badly things had gone south since, as the anchorman put it, "the IVL poster boy had jumped ugly on an innocent Lifer and crushed her sweet arc of mortality into the flatline of immortality."

He learned that the president, acknowledging the vampirophobia gripping the country, had declared martial law. Worse, he had ordered the U.S. Leaguer population to report to Leaguer Mountain in California, where they would be implanted with tracking devices and deported. Becky-Dell Wallace had been appointed the "vampire tsar" and put in charge of the operation.

A clip showed her detailing the plan. "Should any Leaguers fail to report to Leaguer Mountain," she warned, "you will find yourselves in the crosshairs of a new weapon developed by the Pentagon, which you *don't* want to mess with. Leaguers will then be deported to their true homeland, which has been revealed to us by Ikor DeThanatos: Transylvania." Her eyes narrowed as she issued one

306

more threat. "Should any Leaguer be tempted to sneak back into the U.S., their tracking device will trigger the Electronic Vampire Defense Shield soon to be deployed over the nation." Her mouth twisted into an exultant leer. "Yes, vampires had American Out Day; now it's time for Leaguer Outta Here Day!"

Morning banged the TV off. He was stunned by the spiral of events. He stared at the ceiling and wondered what to do. The only thing that came to him was the itch and irritation of the ropes, netting, and buoys of his Ancient Mariner outfit. He even smelled like a bucket of chum.

He got up, took a shower to wash away the fishy smell, and rummaged through the closet and the bureau until he found clothes that almost fit. While looking for a pair of socks, he found a surprise in the bottom drawer of the bureau. It was jammed with old videocassettes, hand-labeled with movie titles. Apparently, the couple that had hosted him for Thanksgiving were movie buffs, and had recorded a ton of them.

One title jumped out at him. *Casablanca.* He pulled it out and shoved it in the TV's VHS slot.

62

Warfarin

While Becky-Dell loathed vampires, she was not numb to the tragedy that had befallen the Zotz family. Having learned—with a little help from the FBI—the location of where Zoë was turning from omnivore to sanguivore, she, and a half-dozen bodyguards, paid a visit to the Dredful town house in the Village. Wanting the world to know she had a heart, she informed the media of her visit. They were waiting in force when her limousine arrived in front of the town house.

Becky-Dell turned the stoop into a soapbox and was giving an I-feel-your-pain speech about how the Zotz family was enduring such a terrible ordeal, when Penny and Portia opened the door behind her.

"If you're finished tooting your horn," Penny said, "would you like to come in?"

"Absolutely," Becky-Dell announced as she gestured to her bodyguards.

"Alone," Penny added.

Becky-Dell hesitated.

"Don't tell me you're afraid of a ninety-five-pound vampire-about-to-be who's still so sick she can't lift a finger, much less a fang?" Portia asked, trying not to sound catty. Although she was still in deep grief over Morning, she wasn't going to reveal a shred of it to the woman she considered one of his killers.

As much as Becky-Dell reviled Penny and Portia for being vampire huggers, she realized this was an opportunity with a double upside. By entering their lair she would show the world her steely resolve and fearlessness against the red menace. And she would be able to take care of a bit of official business regarding Zoë.

Penny and Portia led Becky-Dell to the guest room. Zoë was still unconscious and looked like any other sick teenager, except for the blood products on the bedside table. They were unopened, awaiting her complete turning and the moment when someone would tell her, *Your dream has come true. Would you like to drink to it?*

Rachel was also there, sitting in a chair and watching over Zoë.

Becky-Dell was surprised to see her. "Didn't you hear the president's order?" she demanded. "You and your kind have been ordered to Leaguer Mountain."

Rachel flipped her hand. "Oh, we'll go, all right." She flashed a taunting smile. "The day you figure out how to herd cats."

Becky-Dell answered with a smile of her own. "Perhaps that day has arrived."

Back in the kitchen, Penny and Portia sat Becky-Dell down for a chat.

"So," Portia began, "when Zoë turns total vampire will she be ordered to Leaguer Mountain and deported too?"

Becky-Dell laid a hand on her bosom. "As a human being, my heart goes out to that girl; every vampire was a victim once. But as the president's Vampire Tsar, let me be perfectly clear. Whether someone has been a bloodsucker for a minute or a hundred years doesn't change the threat they pose. America is now a *majority* with special needs, and that special need is to be vampire-free."

In their strategy session for the meeting, Portia, Penny, and Rachel had figured she would say as much. "What if," Portia said, "we could prove that Morning didn't do it? That he's innocent, and that a Loner vampire, probably DeThanatos, CDed into Morning and attacked Zoë."

Becky-Dell laughed at the absurdity of it even though she knew it was true. "If you wanna talk skin-swapping, why stop there? What if DeThanatos isn't even DeThanatos?" She leaned forward and bugged her eyes behind her glasses. "What if he's actually my ex-husband masquerading as DeThanatos just to make my life miserable?"

Undaunted by her sarcasm, Portia launched into the evidence about the pimple on Morning's chin, who had seen it, and how the security video confirmed that Zoë's attacker was pimple-less.

"Ha!" Becky-Dell hooted. "Who's gonna believe a vampire with a zit?"

"What if . . . ," a voice sounded from the kitchen door. It was Rachel. "What if there was a more peaceful way to make America 'vampire-free'?"

Becky-Dell eyed her with haughty contempt. "What if

the sun was green? It's not and never will be. Don't give me 'what if' when 'what if' *isn't.*"

Before their strategy session, Portia had told her mother and Rachel everything she knew about re-morts, *pneuma-brotus,* and the fact that Morning had been re-aging until he had been expelled from the academy.

Rachel was armed with this trump card. She took a seat and played it. She explained to Becky-Dell that Morning had grown a pimple because his growth hormones had kicked back in. She then carefully laid out how Birnam and Morning had discovered the cure for vampirism by return-ing to their Lifer dreams, which retriggered their mortality genes, which began to produce *pneumabrotus.*

Just as Rachel's burst of scientific coherency the day before had stunned the doctors claiming Zoë as theirs, her lucid account of a vampire cure momentarily disarmed Becky-Dell.

Seizing the moment, Portia continued their pitch. "Besides me, my mom, and Zoë—although she's about to not count anymore—and now you, Congresswoman Wallace, we're the only Lifers who know this. You could take this knowledge and become the Madame Curie of vampirism, the Nelson Mandela of America. You could heal the rift between mortals and immortals by giving just about every Leaguer the thing they want most: to be nor-mal again, to be mortal."

"No doubt," Penny added, "there will still be *Loner* vampires lurking in the dark, but they've always lived in the shadows and will never come out."

"The point is," Portia jumped back in, "instead of making America vampire-free by force, you could make it almost vampire-free by *choice.* You'd be up there with

Lincoln, Washington, Jefferson. Heck," she added eagerly, "maybe they'd finally add a woman to Mount Rushmore. You!"

Becky-Dell gave Portia a nodding smile and turned to Penny. "You must be so proud, having trained your daughter so well in the art of BS." Then she gave Portia a condescending pat on the hand. "Nice try, sweetie, but I've got my monument planned: a new Statue of Liberty, me holding a bloody stake." She got up and started to leave.

Portia rushed after her. "But we're not BSing. There *is* a cure for vampires. Morning's suicide proves it!"

Becky-Dell wheeled on her. "I'll believe *that* when I see the body." She stepped to the door and addressed the room. "As for your 'cure,' if there is such a thing, let 'em take it in Transylvania. After that, if they swear their loyalty to a government of the mortals, by the mortals, and for the mortals, then they can bring their newly aging butts back to America."

Out on the stoop, Becky-Dell gave the media a sugar-coated account of her visit to Zoë's bedside and the condolences she had conveyed to Zoë's caregivers. She described the kitchen-table summit with Penny, Portia, and Rachel as "a cordial visit in which we agreed to disagree." She then climbed into her limo with her bodyguards and drove away.

Rachel came outside with Portia and Penny behind her. With the reporters all ears, microphones, and cameras, Rachel launched into a plea to the Leaguers of America. She told them that a compromise with Ms. Wallace had been offered and rejected. She told them that now was the time to stand up for their rights. And, having returned to her linguistic loopiness, she declared, "In the eighteen hundreds, it was wrong when Native Americans were forced onto reservations. In the nineteen hundreds, it was wrong when Japanese Americans were shoved into internment camps. Now, in the twenty hundreds"—she hesitated, wondered if that was a word, then plunged on—"it's just as wrong that we're being sent to Leaguer Mountain to be shipped off to a country that's not our home, never has been, and never will be! So I'm asking all my fellow Leaguers to CD, to *civil disobediate,* and not report to Leaguer—"

A gunshot sounded; as people ducked and screamed, Rachel fell against Portia and Penny. They gaped at the hole in Rachel's shirt and the blood pouring from it. Over the shouting and calls to 911, Rachel pushed against Penny and Portia and stood back up. She raised her arms. "It's okay! It's okay!"

The captivated media watched an act never recorded before: a vampire healing from a wound in a matter of seconds. The blood on Rachel's shirt shrank back into her wound. In a moment, the only evidence she had been shot was a bloodless hole in her shirt.

Rachel spotted the gunman across the street and fired off a question. "Now, who'd be dumb enough to shoot a va—va—" Her face suddenly blanched and winced with pain; she fell back into Penny and Portia. Her eyes went wide with confusion and shock.

"What's wrong?" Penny asked.

Rachel could only manage a groan.

Someone broke through the barricade of reporters and mounted the stoop. It was Becky-Dell. She whipped around and addressed the media again. "Rachel Capilarus is the first field test of the government's newest weapon: a vampire pacification bullet. It's no silver bullet like you'd use on a werewolf, it's a warfarin bullet. Warfarin is a chemical used to kill bats by inducing internal bleeding. Ms. Capilarus won't die, but her internal hemorrhaging will make her so anemic, the only thing she'll want to get her hands on is her next few bottles of blood. And until she does, she'll be as weak as a sick kitten."

Penny and Portia started to help Rachel inside. They knew just where to find what Rachel needed. But two of Becky-Dell's bodyguards, flashing U.S. marshals' badges, grabbed Rachel and dragged her toward the waiting limo. Rachel didn't have the power to resist.

Another marshal pushed Penny and Portia back into the town house, ordering, "We'll come for Zoë Zotz later."

Becky-Dell beamed a mission-accomplished smile and mopped up her cunning operation. "The president of the IVL will be transported to Leaguer Mountain at government expense. As for the rest of you Leaguers, get yourself to the mountain, or you'll be sucking on warfarin bullets faster than you can say 'vampire pacification.' "

63

Morning Message

In the house on Staten Island, Morning was watching *Casablanca* for the third time when the screen went blank. Trying to fix the problem, he hit the eject button on the VHS machine. The video stuck out at a weird angle. He extracted it and a tangle of tape followed. *Casablanca* was casabroka, a victim of age and videotape fatigue.

He lay on the bed and switched the TV back to one of the networks. It showed a news bulletin on a caravan of vehicles heading west, and reported how Leaguers were making a mass migration to Leaguer Mountain by plane, train, bus, and car because of the new fear about being hit by a warfarin bullet. No one wanted to be carted off to Leaguer Mountain like Rachel. As one Leaguer driver in the caravan put it, "If I gotta go live in a foreign country, I don't wanna get there leaking oil."

Morning realized that warfarin was the secret weapon they had talked about the day before. As he thought about

Sister Flora being one of the Leaguers in that exodus west, he wondered if he should join them. Then he reminded himself he was a fugitive; if Lifers caught him they'd just put him in front of a warfarin firing squad. It wasn't the worst thing he could imagine, since he was hardly brimming with reasons to live. But then he also reminded himself that Cody had been right. It had been worth seeing *Casablanca*. It had him thinking.

He channel surfed till the TV settled on a business report. It was on the commodities market in Chicago, which Morning knew about from when he had checked to see if the metals some superheroes used were real, like the vibranium in Black Panther's bodysuit and the adamantium in Wolverine's claws. The business reporter talked about a mysterious buyer who was cornering the market on a type of wood. The wood, hawthorn, was known for its hardness and fine grain and was prized for knife handles and walking sticks. Because this mystery buyer was trying to grab all the hawthorn available, the price was skyrocketing.

It didn't take much mental rummaging before Morning made the connection to what he had learned in Vampire Health back at Leaguer Academy. Hawthorn was also called thorn apple, because of its sharp thorns and apple-like fruit. It was one of two types of wood that, shaped into a stake, could start a successful vampire slaying.

He instantly realized who would (1) know how deadly hawthorn was to vampires, and (2) want to buy it all up. DeThanatos. Morning's thoughts accelerated like a runaway train. *That's why everyone's being ordered to Leaguer Mountain! It isn't to deport Leaguers to Transylvania, it's to dispatch 'em once and for all!*

The next morning at the Dredfuls' apartment, Portia checked in on Cody, who was finishing up the grave-yard shift watching Zoë. During the night, Zoë had re-gained consciousness, sort of. She was in a delirium and half-muttering, half-singing snippets from a song. "Down where they stalk . . . bloodlustin' free . . . I'm gonna be . . . part of your world."

Cody was getting all this on video and was already thinking about renaming his Leaguer doc *The Little Bloodmaid*. He told Portia to go make herself breakfast before starting her shift monitoring Zoë.

After Portia went to the kitchen and got a kettle heat-ing, she noticed an odd arrangement on the kitchen table that hadn't been there the night before: a couple of pigeon feathers and a tightly rolled bit of paper smaller than a cigarette.

She picked up the paper cylinder. On the outside, in a tiny scrawl, was *Only open after Leaguer Outta Here Day*. She recognized the handwriting: Morning's. Her heart raced and her mind leaped to the logical conclusion. Having returned to being all-vampire Morning, at some point during the night or early a.m., had flown in as a pi-geon and left the note. Of course, being take-charge Portia, she disobeyed and opened the tight wrap of paper.

When she unfurled it, she saw more writing inside. *I need a favor,* it said in letters so tiny she almost had to get a magnifying glass. *I'd like you to try to clear my name. Not with the public—I've given up on them—but with my fel-low firefighters at the academy, and Captain Prowler.*

She read on. *Leaguer Outta Here Day is going to turn*

into Leaguer Rubout Day, he wrote. *The inside of Leaguer Mountain is going to get turned into a stake-and-fire pit of genocide.*

He then asked Portia to tell Cody two things: *(1) I watched* Casablanca. *(2) Since my end will probably come before the End Is Upon Us Ball, I hope you'll take Portia and have a great time.*

Portia turned the tiny scroll of paper over. There was more. Much more.

> *And what about us, Portia? Well, to crib from* Casablanca . . . *we'll always have the Williams Bird Bridge. We'd lost it till you found me yesterday. You helped me get it back. Now there's this thing I gotta do. Where I'm going, you can't follow. What I'm doing, you can't be a part of. Portia, I'm crappy at being mortal, and even crappier at being immortal. But you showed me that the problems of a couple of kids don't amount to a bag of Leech Treats in this weird world. Maybe someday I'll understand why you always get it before me. Until then, here's looking at you, kid.*
>
> *Your EB*

The paper went blurry as Portia's eyes welled up. She turned the paper over, and tried to read it again. The note only went blurrier. Then a sound invaded her tunnel vision: the fading whistle of a teakettle.

She looked up as Cody put the kettle on a cold burner. "Why are you crying?" he asked.

Portia sleeved her wet cheeks and sucked in a breath. "I'm not. Get the camera. We're going on location."

"We?" Cody echoed, his eyes popping wide. "You mean you're back on the movie?"

"I'm not back on anything but trying to stop a bloodbath. Now go."

He started out, then turned back. "What about Zoë?"

"When Mom wakes up, she'll take care of her. Go!"

64

Rallying the Troops

It was still early enough for Portia and Cody to sneak out through the back garden and evade the media encampment out front. They also didn't wake the U.S. marshal dozing in the front entrance. He had been posted to whisk Zoë to Leaguer Mountain when she completed her ecdysis to vampire.

Portia and Cody went straight to Prowler's firehouse, where Portia asked a favor. "I know Morning's crew is busy with their last day of testing at the academy, but I need to talk to 'em."

Given everything that had happened, Prowler doubted Clancy would grant the request, until Portia told Prowler about the live fire exercise she had been rescued from. "I've never gotten the chance to thank Morning's crew for saving my life," she explained. "I'd like to, and if Clancy has a problem with it, I'll be happy to tell the world about the time the academy made a fire exercise so authentic they added a live victim to the mix."

Prowler chortled at her moxie, opened the door of his fire engine, and waved Portia and Cody in. "We'll take the express."

On the way to Randall's Island, they filled Prowler in on everything that had gone down in the past few days. The fireman was greatly relieved to hear that his instincts were right and Morning was innocent, that his jump off the bridge was an escape and no suicide, and that Morning was probably headed to Leaguer Mountain to try and stop a vampire genocide. If this last item was true, Prowler suggested they should alert the FBI. But Portia convinced him that the FBI probably wouldn't believe them, and even if they did, by the time they got their bureaucratic butts in gear, it would be too late.

At the academy, Clancy wasn't happy to see Portia again, and was even less happy to hear her request to see Morning's ex-crew. But her threat to blow the whistle on the academy's lack of safety precautions, on his watch, persuaded him to give her a few minutes to talk to them while they were on a break between field tests.

After the exhausted crew finished a grueling 150-pound body carry through an obstacle course, they gathered around Prowler's fire engine, which was parked between the training buildings. As they stripped off turnout coats and chugged water, Portia noticed that they had wooden stakes stowed inside their coats.

Despite the anti-vampire weapons, and the probies' anti-Morning feelings, Portia launched into the details of how Morning had been framed, was innocent, and had been unjustly booted from the academy. "All he wanted was to be here today, with his crew, performing the tests that would've realized his dream: becoming a firefighter. But the world conspired against him, and now he's not only in a fight for his life, he's fighting for all the Leaguers who are being led into a vampire genocide."

Clancy, listening with a skeptical scowl, broke in. "This is America, kid. We don't do genocide."

"Maybe you're right," Portia replied, "but if you're wrong it'll be too late for Leaguers." Then she told them about Leaguer Rubout Day, and how the inside of Leaguer Mountain was going to be turned into "a stake-and-fire pit." When she finished, the probies stared in gawping disbelief.

Sully broke the silence. "Even if all that's true, what can we do about it? We're just a bunch of probies fighting fake fires and trying to earn our badges."

Portia started to answer but Prowler stepped off his rig and asked to respond. Portia nodded.

Prowler took in the two dozen probies. "When you become a firefighter, you don't just earn a badge, you earn the right to wear the emblem of all firefighters"—he tapped the stubby FDNY cross on his T-shirt—"the Maltese Cross. Any firefighter who wears this cross knows the code shared by all fire knights. He lives in courage, a ladder rung from death. He lives knowing he may lay down his life to save others. And he lives knowing that his life is protected by all other fire knights."

Prowler gestured to Portia. "What she's saying is that one of your crew, Morning McCobb, knows too well those first two things: he lives in courage, and he's willing to sacrifice his life to save his people. What he doesn't know is if his crew is willing to go into battle with him and protect him in the ultimate test: to see if every one of you has what it takes to be a knight at the fire table."

Armando stood up. "I'm in. But how are we gonna join Morning in the fight when we're in New York and Leaguer Mountain is in California?"

Prowler gestured to his truck. "They don't call me 'the chauffeur,' for nuthin. Who else is gonna join us in the final test?"

"Armando," Clancy barked, "don't fall for his fire knight bull. If you leave here, you're gonna kiss your badge goodbye. That goes for all of you. It'll be your last probie screwup, and I guarantee you'll never get another shot at being one of the bravest!"

Armando reached under his coat and pulled out a wooden stake. "Captain Clancy, this *is* my shot." Armando tossed the stake on the cement. It skittered toward Clancy's feet. He sidestepped to avoid being hit. By the time Clancy looked back up, Armando stood on Prowler's truck.

One by one the probies tossed their stakes to the ground and climbed on the truck. The last probie stood by himself in the street: Sully. He reached to the back of his helmet and pulled a wooden stake out of his helmet strap.

"Don't do it, Joey," Clancy warned. "Your dad will roll in his grave."

Sully shook his head. "Nah. The last thing my dad did was roll with his crew. I'm gonna roll with mine." As he flipped the stake over his shoulder, his fellow probies cheered.

65

Leaguer Mountain

While the fire truck made its way to New Jersey, Prowler got on his cell and called in the kind of favors you accumulate after forty years on the job. The first was to the district dispatcher, whose job was to know where all his fire vehicles were, and to know when one went missing. The calls the dispatcher received shortly thereafter, from the commander at the Great Jones Street firehouse and from Clancy reporting Prowler's truck along with two dozen probies going AWOL, withered to silence on the dispatcher's desk. The other call Prowler made was to an old smoke jumper buddy in the Air National Guard in Newburgh, New York. His buddy had access to, and the flying skills to commandeer, a C-5 cargo plane.

When they arrived at Newburgh's Stewart Airport, there were two aircraft waiting for them: the C-5 that would fly the fire truck and the probies to Leaguer Mountain, and the Diamond Sky company jet that Penny had sent to whisk Portia and Cody to Leaguer Mountain faster than the lumbering C-5.

After Portia had explained the situation to her mother, Penny had agreed to lend her the jet so she could chase Morning across the country on five conditions: (1) Portia and Cody were going as journalists, not combatants to singlehandedly save Morning and Rachel. (2) They were to get all the footage they could of Becky-Dell's operation so, if it did turn into Leaguer Rubout Day, they could nail the Duchess of Doom. (3) Portia was to never forget that, while Morning and Rachel wore the armor of immortality and would suffer no permanent damage unless they were staked, ashed, and blown away, she and Cody were as vulnerable as balloons in a tornado of tacks. And (5) Portia was to do what all mothers insist their children do on a long trip: "Call home when you get there."

Portia agreed to all of the above with the caveat that Leaguer Mountain might not have cell service since it was in the middle of the Sierra Nevadas. Of course, Penny wanted to go herself, but someone had to stay and be there when Zoë shook off her delirium, realized she was all vampire, and didn't shriek so loud with joy that she alerted the U.S. marshal in the front hallway and got carted away.

While the departure scene at Stewart Airport was orderly and proceeded without a hitch, the scene at Leaguer Mountain was utter chaos.

For two days, Leaguers had been pouring into the cavernous interior of the mountain that had once housed the first Leaguer Academy, where vampires trained to become

Leaguers and take humans off the drink menu. For the majority of Leaguers carpeting the parade ground, the last time they had been there was graduation. But the grounds, surrounded by a horseshoe of buildings jutting from the mountain's interior walls, didn't resemble a festive class reunion. It looked like a concert turned ugly because the band hadn't shown.

The only person on the towering platform once used for graduation ceremonies was an older woman, small and spry. Dolly had once worked the Vegan Veins station in the academy's quaffeteria and had kept Morning supplied with Blood Lite during his school days there. After American Out Day, and the academy's move to its new location, Dolly had stayed on as the old academy's caretaker, and to look after Birnam as he began to age.

Despite having a bullhorn, Dolly was hoarse from trying to persuade the mass of Leaguers to remain calm and to please not trample the flower beds she had carefully tended after she had retooled the streetlights to grow-lights. She was also hoarse from repeatedly answering the same questions. "No, nobody told me you were coming." "No, there's no other Leaguer Mountain, especially one that's hollow!"

Even though Dolly had been in a news blackout since Birnam had left, her uninvited guests had caught her up on the dramatic events that had led to her home being flooded with Leaguers. Most shocking of all was that her blood-intolerant friend Morning McCobb had chucked his bottle of Blood Lite for a mini-keg of Zoë Zotz.

As Dolly was about to yell at a teenage Leaguer Hacky Sacking his way through one of her petunia beds, a pigeon flew toward the platform and landed on the railing next to her. The pigeon flapped its wings and burst into Morning McCobb, sheathed in slightly torn Epidex.

Morning had flown to Leaguer Mountain in record time for a pigeon, but not because he was a super-fast flier. After dropping the miniature paper scroll in Portia's apartment and sneaking back into St. Giles to fetch his Epidex, he had flown to LaGuardia Airport, stowed away in the luggage compartment of a direct flight to Las Vegas, and then bird-winged it from there.

Dolly beamed at the sight of Morning, until she remembered he was to blame for the massive home invasion trampling her flower beds. Her delight pinched to reproach. "Well, if it isn't the boy who couldn't keep his deuce out of the juice."

Morning didn't get the chance to plead his case, since the huge crowd recognized him and began to jeer and throw whatever they had at the vampire who had turned their Leaguer dreams into the nightmare of deportation.

He took the bullhorn from Dolly and tried to be heard. "It was DeThanatos who turned Zoë, but I'm not here to prove my innocence!"

His claim was answered with a volley of blood-drink bottles and key rings.

Out of the corner of his eye, Morning noticed someone scaling the platform. He figured he'd better talk fast before he was pulled off the platform, then drawn and quartered by the first four Leaguers who could CD into horses. "We haven't been ordered here for deportation. We've been sent here for destruction!"

"Yeah, yours!" someone shouted as Morning felt the vibration of the climber hit the platform. He spun around to confront his attacker. He was startled to see Rachel.

"Gimme the horn," she said, joining him at the rail.

"You're okay?"

"Better, but warfarin kicks the crap outta you till you can get enough blood to heal your innards." She took the bullhorn and the crowd settled to a rumble. "It's true, Morning was set up. It was *DeThanatos* who turned Zoë." The rumble dropped to an incredulous drone. "We can prove it later, but for now you gotta give 'im a listen." She handed the bullhorn back to Morning.

The Leaguers quieted.

"The reason there's no Lifers here to receive us or implant us with tracking devices is because this mountain is about to be attacked." The rumble started again. "The most important thing is to not panic. We need to calmly walk or fly out of the mountain and get away from here as fast as possible."

Someone shouted, "Where are we supposed to go?"

"Canada or Mexico," Morning answered. "But we need to leave now."

"Why should we believe you?" another voice shouted, followed by yet another. "If we disobey martial law, they're gonna hunt us down like Loners!"

He waited for the outburst to die down. "If you don't leave, then get ready to fight for your lives. We're not only up against Becky-Dell. We're up against DeThanatos."

"He can't slay us by himself!" someone protested.

"He doesn't have to," Morning countered. "Not when he's bought up all the hawthorn he could get his hands on, and turned it into ammo for Lifers."

It went so silent you could have heard Dolly pick a petunia.

Rachel, looking ashen, stared at him. "Is that true?"

Morning nodded. "I'm pretty sure."

She grabbed the bullhorn. "As president of the IVL, I order you to evacuate—"

An explosion ripped through the side of the mountain. A cascade of rock and dirt showered buildings and spewed out over the parade ground. The multitude screamed as they turned like a giant school of fish and ran for the one small exit at the base of the mountain.

66

Stun, Stake, 'N' Bake

While Rachel beseeched the Leaguers not to panic, Morning and Dolly watched the dust and smoke clear from the ragged hole blown in the mountainside. Ropes unfurled through the hole like the legs of a giant squid. Commandos slid down the ropes, firing automatic weapons as they came. Leaguers fell in the blaze of warfarin bullets.

In the tunnel leading out of the mountain, some were lucky enough to have gotten a jump and not been caught in the crush of Leaguers that clogged the tunnel behind them. Others who had already CDed into flying birds rushed toward the one metal door that sealed the entrance and exit to the mountain. This rush of Leaguers ran out of luck when they reached the phalanx of commandos blocking the door. They were met by a red-hot swarm of warfarin bullets.

Back in the rocky dome, the stream of commandos pouring through the hole had ceased, but they continued disabling hundreds of vampires in a rain of warfarin. The crackling gunfire and the screaming were drowned out by more explosions hitting the breach in the mountain.

Morning, Rachel, and Dolly, now running toward the old administration building, turned to see dust and smoke mushroom around the hole as the first of several Blackhawk attack helicopters shot into the mountain like angry wasps. More ropes uncoiled from the choppers, followed by commandos rappelling down them. They shouldered bulky weapons. One of the soldiers stepped up to a vampire on the ground and fired a stake into his chest. The vampire thrashed like a live bug impaled by a pin.

The Blackhawks wheeled, strafing the parade ground with a hail of bullets.

Outside the mountain, a big command chopper hovered in the darkness. In the glow of the cockpit, Becky-Dell and DeThanatos stood behind the pilots and watched the attack. They both shared the same look of supreme satisfaction. So far, Operation Stun, Stake, 'n' Bake was going flawlessly.

A voice crackled in Becky-Dell's headset. "Fighters in final approach."

She answered into her headset. "Gentlemen, pop a couple more corks."

Within seconds, two more explosions ripped into the mountain, followed by the roar of two fighter jets blasting overhead. When the dust cleared, three gaping holes ringed the mountain. If giants roamed the earth, one of them could have picked the mountain up like a bowling ball.

Becky-Dell got back on her headset. "Stun and stake well under way. Cozy up, bakers, and stand by."

From the starlit darkness, three squadrons of helicopters emerged. Each squadron was led by a V-formation of napalm-armed gunships. Within each V was a Chinook helicopter, laboring under the weight of two giant buckets sloshing with combustible fuel. They were called bambi buckets because they were usually loaded with water or fire retardants to save the Bambis of the forest.

DeThanatos grinned at the sight of so much firepower. He turned to his partner in apocalypse and voiced his pleasure. "Why barbecue when you can incinerate?"

On the ground, under the cover of darkness, an old Jeep with its lights off cut through the desert valley of sagebrush and greasewood. While Cody drove and hit the speed dial on Portia's cell phone to her house, Portia filmed the attack on Leaguer Mountain through the windshield.

"No service," Cody said, braking the Jeep to a stop.

"Hey, Mom, can't say we didn't try." Portia jumped out of the passenger side and kept filming. Sure, it was just a wide master shot in the middle of the night, but between the flashes of explosions and the chopper spotlights hitting the mountain, the assault was more than visible. She handed the camera to Cody, told him to keep shooting, then went to the Jeep and dug out a flashlight.

"What are you doing?" he asked as she started walking through the brush, toward the mountain.

"Morning's in there."

"But you promised your mom not to go into G.I. Jane rescue mode."

She kept walking. "Three and a half outta five ain't bad."

"There's a half?" Cody shouted.

"Yeah," she threw back, "we *tried* to call home."

Portia kept the flashlight off as she moved through the brush. It was for an emergency only. Between the stars and the light-spill from the hovering choppers, she could see well enough to navigate and maybe even spot a startled rattlesnake. She reassured herself that rattlesnakes supposedly gave a warning rattle before they struck.

She was so focused on the ground she didn't see the sign sticking up from the brush until she ran smack into it. Bouncing off it, she cursed, flicked on the flashlight and read the metal sign. Her eyes widened. "Oh, sh——."

67

A Diversion

Morning, Rachel, Dolly, and several hundred Leaguers, including Sister Flora, had taken refuge in the old administration building as the ruthless stunning and staking continued inside the mountain. The only reason the building had not been laid siege to was because of a spur-of-the-moment tactic Rachel had initiated, and the bravery displayed by the ring of vampires protecting the building's perimeter. The outermost ring of Leaguers were CDing into vicious and deadly animals, then fighting tooth and claw with the commandos until the beasts were stunned and staked. Then the next ring of Leaguers CDed and carried on the fight. This beastly defense had stalled the siege enough for Rachel and Morning to consider their shrinking options. They huddled over Dolly, who had been laid on a table after being wounded by two warfarin bullets. Sister Flora held her hand.

Despite her weakness, Dolly spoke up. "There's another

way out . . . the ventilation tunnel that runs underground. The good news: it'll get you out of here undetected."

"How so?" Rachel asked.

"It runs for five miles before it resurfaces."

"What's the bad news?" Morning asked.

"We didn't build it," Dolly replied, and grabbed another breath. "It's filled with nuclear waste. It won't hurt us, but if the Lifers find that rabbit hole and torch it or blow it up, it'll release a cloud of death."

Rachel waved her hands in despair. "And you know who they'll blame for that: us!"

Morning stared at Dolly. "So we need to distract 'em while those who can go down the rabbit hole."

She nodded weakly. "It would help."

Morning jumped on a chair and spoke to the jammed room of Leaguers. "I need a flock of volunteers, and I mean a flock. We'll create a diversion by flying into the fight, and if we can make it out one of the holes in the mountain, we'll draw as many of 'em as we can to the Mother Forest. If we make it, we'll have sanctuary there. In the meantime, whoever sneaks out the tunnel can escape to Canada or Mexico."

As the sound of gunfire and roaring animals drew closer, a dozen Leaguers stepped forward.

Cody's camera still recorded as a beam of light, bouncing through the brush, raced toward him. Portia emerged behind the light, running flat out. She wasn't hurdling the sage and greasewood bushes as much as crashing through them. It seemed her fear of rattlesnakes had been overtaken by something else. The last bush proved too much—she sprawled flat in front of Cody.

After making sure nothing was chasing her, Cody looked down. "Nice impression of Cary Grant in *North by Northwest*. What the hell's going on?"

Portia jumped up. "The mountain's sitting next to an underground nuclear waste site! If they blow up the mountain it could kill millions!"

"Of sheep and snakes, yeah."

"No, you moron, of people! It's called a nuclear *cloud*, and clouds *travel*!"

Cody tried another tack before hitting his own panic button. "Becky-Dell's gotta know it's down there, right?"

"Even if she did," Portia exclaimed, trying to catch her breath, "she'd make America Lifer-free if that's what it took to make it *Leaguer*-free!" She grabbed the camera from him, hit the off button, and started for the Jeep.

Cody followed. "Okay, we're done shooting."

Inside the mountain, a flock of birds sprang from the roof of the administration building. The pigeon in the lead, Morning, snapped a quick look back and noticed how much the building resembled the Alamo. He hoped the outcome for those inside wasn't the same.

The flock didn't get fifty yards before the commandos on the ground saw them and opened fire. Luckily, there wasn't a decent bird shooter in the bunch. A soldier shouted into his shoulder comm device. "Birds outta hole number one!"

Morning heard him but kept beating it for the first hole blown in the mountain. At the last second, he veered hard right and raced toward another hole. His fellow fliers stayed right on his tail.

Outside, the half-dozen gunships that had taken up positions outside hole number one to turn the flock into a ruptured pillow fight veered hard to catch the flock winging it for another hole. But tons of flying steel is no match for hollow-boned birds with millions of years of flight time in their DNA. The flock soared out of the hole and beat wing for the Mother Forest.

Becky-Dell screamed into her headset, "I want that pigeon for breakfast!"

As DeThanatos tracked the flock's escape, he felt the flutter that often rustled inside his ribs like a caged raptor. His inner falcon had a sudden craving for pigeon.

On the ground, Portia was sitting in the Jeep's passenger seat as her Mac Pro fired up. She cabled the camera to it and began sending the footage they'd shot to her iDisk.

Cody hung on the open door. "What are you doing?"

"Our only hope is that the FBI, the CIA, Homeland Security, or *someone* has been hacking my computer, sees what's going on out here, and tells the president."

Cody scoffed. "You don't think he ordered this?"

"No—c'mon, c'mon"—she exhorted her computer— "I don't think the president got to be president by not getting the difference between 'deportation' and 'genocide.'"

A growing sound pulled Cody to the half-dozen gunships racing toward them. "Down!" he screamed as he dived in the dirt and landed on the lit flashlight.

Portia slammed the Mac Pro screen down on her finger, threw her torso over the computer, and prayed she wasn't going to be blown to heaven before the footage uploaded to her iDisk. A second later, she heard the feathery pant of flapping birds. She glanced up as a flock, led by a pigeon, shot over the Jeep. Moments later, the gunships screamed overhead, followed by a fifty-yard dust devil that almost lifted the Jeep and swept Cody under it.

In the command chopper, DeThanatos blinked like the falcon taking shape in his mind. "Call off your warbirds and save them for the mountain," he told Becky-Dell. "I'll deal with McCobb."

She slid him a look. "How do you know it's him?"

"He's my blood child. You can feel when they're being naughty."

"How do you know where he's going?"

"You finish here, I'll finish Morning" was all he said before he snapped into a falcon and banked out the chopper's side door. The raptor glided toward the nearest Chinook hovering above its load: two bambi buckets brimming with industrial-grade lighter fluid.

In the Chinook's cockpit, the startled pilot turned as the falcon landed on the back of the copilot's empty seat. The bird shape-shifted into an exact replica of the pilot with one exception: the new one lacked a uniform.

"Whoa!" the pilot gasped. It wasn't clear if he was more shocked by seeing his exact double, or if this was his first time flying with a naked copilot.

DeThanatos—that is, his incarnation of the pilot—flicked the uniformed pilot into a thrall. "Nothing to fear. Just borrowing your brain for a flying lesson." He grabbed the controls and banked the big Chinook in the direction of the pigeon that had flown the coop.

338

The Chinook and its dangling buckets plowed through the air over the still-darkened Jeep. Portia looked up and watched it pass. She saw the squadron of gunships circle back toward the mountain. The Chinook kept going, tracking the flock of birds into the darkness.

She lifted her Mac Pro screen. "It's sent." Cody popped up next to her. She handed him the computer and the camera and scooted into the driver's seat. "Keep shooting."

She keyed the ignition as he protested. "Where are you going?"

"Back to where all this started."

68

Awakening

In the Dredful guest room, Zoë lay in bed, still as death. Her eyelids twitched, then sprang open. She sat bolt upright, as if a tendril of scent had escaped one of the bottles on the bedside table and grabbed her like a reined horse. Her head snapped to the blood products. She snatched the nearest bottle, ripped off the top, and chugged it like an overheated engine drinking a quart of oil. She was halfway through another bottle of red stuff before her thirst was slaked enough for her gray matter to register what waking up in a strange bed with an overpowering craving for blood meant. She shot a bony fist in the air. "Yes!"

As the blood ballooned through her immortality-charged innards, her brain popped with questions: *Where is everybody? Isn't there supposed to be a vampire greeting committee? Or at least an envelope with a letter telling me I've been accepted to Leaguer Academy?*

She threw off her covers, swung out of bed, and took

her new set of vampire legs for a test-drive. They felt like they could race a pedicab up a pyramid. Hitting the hallway, she enjoyed three first-evers. She could feel the dust on the floor compress between her bare feet and the wood. She heard tiny creaks and groans coming from the boards no mortal could ever hear. She had the sensual radar of a cat; and she had CDing into one to look forward to!

She poked her head into Penny's bedroom. Penny was on the bed, clothed, sleeping. The cell phone on her stomach rose up and down like a boat on a swelling sea of blouse.

Zoë didn't wake her. She wanted to keep riding the flood of sensations that came with being a creature of the night. Along with her catlike senses, she was also imbued with feline curiosity. She wanted an answer: *Okay, after Morning finally grew a set and made this girl's dream come true, why did I end up at Portia's house?*

Zoë padded into Portia's room and found it empty. With no best friend to answer her thousand questions, she sat down at the desk and woke up the portal that just might provide some answers: Portia's iMac.

First she read the date on the dock. She had been out of it for three days, which was in line with what she had pried out of Morning about the time frame for a mortal-to-vampire transition. She checked Portia's email and her Facebook page, but there was nothing of significance. Not surprising, since Portia wasn't big into email, and she'd often said that if she could write computer code she'd write an app called deFacebook, which allowed you to vaporize Facebook accounts that were totally lame.

Zoë moved to the next source that might yield answers. She clicked on the iDisk icon, clicked on Date Modified, and stared at the list of docs and downloads, starting with the most recent. There was a file with no name, from just a few minutes before, and it was huge. She clicked it open.

The screen filled with dark, bumpy footage of some kind of battle. Zoë heard a voice that sounded like Cody's, and then heard Portia say, "Hey, Mom, can't say we didn't try." The shot of the battle went shaky, then resettled as it seemed to move outside of a vehicle.

Zoë turned and called loudly, "Mrs. D."

In the Jeep, Portia sped through the night and checked her cell phone for reception. She finally got one bar. She slowed enough to dial without flying off the road.

The call went through. Prowler answered. "Big Red's an hour out from putting down and comin' round the mountain."

Portia spoke fast before she lost the connection. "Big Red's gonna be squashed like a ladybug if it comes round the mountain. Your fire's at the Mother Forest. I repeat, redirect to the Mother Forest!"

She wasn't sure when the connection went dead. She threw the phone on the seat and kicked the accelerator.

In the Dredful apartment, Penny sat at Portia's desk, waiting for a huge file to download from the iDisk onto a flash drive. "C'mon." The computer *boinged*, she snatched the flash drive and dashed from the room.

Zoë ran out of Penny's downstairs office with a sheet of paper as Penny started down the spiral staircase. "Got it!"

Zoë shouted. "Fastest bird in level flight is a spine-tailed swift, with a max speed of one hundred and six mph."

Penny leaped into the kitchen and yanked a box of Band-Aids out of a drawer. "So, do it."

Zoë held up the paper and focused on the picture of a bird that looked like a bullet with wings. "God, I hope I'm a natural." A moment later, Zoë disappeared; the piece of paper fluttered to the floor along with Zoë's collapsing pajamas. A spine-tailed swift popped from her pajama top and landed on the kitchen island.

Penny jumped with joy. "You're a natural!"

The bird lowered its head and Penny carefully attached the flash drive to the bird's back with a four-pronged Band-Aid. She threw open the kitchen window and the bird shot into the darkness with a shrill *tweet!*

Penny shouted after it. "It's Sixteen Hundred Pennsylvania Avenue. You can't miss it!"

69

Raising the Dead

The bristlecone pines stood with the motionless silence of graveyard sentries. The stillness was broken as a flock of birds swooped down, unfurled into human forms, and tumbled on the dusty ground near the largest tree, the Matriarch. Some stayed on all fours, while others stood as they all gasped for air after their sprint to sanctuary. Their sacred ground was off-limits, to Lifers, anyway.

Catching his breath, Morning looked back at the dark horizon below the star-choked sky. No ominous glow signaled the turning of Leaguer Mountain into a fire-spewing oven. And there was no black plume of nuclear waste poisoning the air. *Maybe,* he thought, *our diversion has given a few hundred Leaguers the chance to escape.*

The recuperating Leaguers heard what sounded like distant thunder. They watched the thunder's source take shape. The Chinook looked like a great armored bee with two wrecking balls dangling underneath it.

DeThanatos, having learned all he needed to know about flying an aerial eighteen-wheeler, had shape-shifted back into his own skin, while the pilot still sat rigidly in his seat. He had been relieved of his duties, and his senses.

The Leaguers watched the Chinook bear down on the Mother Forest. "What happened to sanctuary?" one of them shouted over the growing roar of the chopper.

The Chinook flew straight at them, dropping low. The bambi buckets clipped the top of trees. In the moment before the helicopter thundered overhead, Morning saw who was at the controls. He ducked as the tree-trimming buckets and the double rotor wash whipped the air with sticks and needles. While the chopper rose up and banked, Morning shared his discovery. "It's DeThanatos."

The stunned group watched the Chinook bank in a giant circle with the Matriarch and the cluster of Leaguers in the center. The buckets began releasing a steady stream of liquid. The air filled with the smell of gas.

"He wouldn't," one of them rasped.

Inside the cockpit, DeThanatos worked the stick with one hand as his other pointed at the pilot's pack of cigarettes and the lighter on the center instrument bed. He snapped his fingers and the lighter sprouted a flame. The lighter slid toward the cigarette pack and lit the box. His hand flicked to the side window; the glass shattered. Then he thralled the burning pack out the broken window.

Under the chopper, the tiny ball of fire shot down in the rotor wash and landed in the top of a bristlecone pine. The treetop burst into a crown of flames.

The horrified Leaguers watched as the flames jumped around the circle of gas-soaked pines. Each tree ignited with a percussive *whop* until the twin arcs of racing fire collided, sealing the Leaguers in a ring of fire.

The Chinook hovered outside the fiery circle. In the cockpit, DeThanatos smiled at his handiwork. "Add another shape-shift to your repertoire, bad boy. Vampyromaniac." He shilled his joke with a raucous laugh.

On the ground, Morning yelled over the rumble of the Chinook and the fire's growing roar. "If everybody's got the strength for another CD, we can fly above the—"

A wild sight cut him off. Above the flames, in the plumes of smoke and sparks, eerie phantoms rose like a picket fence of northern lights. As the ribbons of color flickered and danced, they gathered into bodies and heads shrouded in ghostly light.

"What are those?" someone asked.

"Dunno." Morning gaped up at the faces in the veils of light. "Whatever they are, they don't look happy."

A Leaguer announced, "That's it, I'm outta here!"

As the young man snapped into a crow and took flight, Morning yelled, "Don't!"

The crow rose sharply, flying toward the barrier of light wavering above the burning trees. The moment the bird hit the light it burst into flames. The Leaguers watched in wide-eyed terror as the burning crow fell into the inferno.

Morning flashed back on Prowler's demonstration of the burning pine bough and the three parts of wild fire: gas, heat, and *spirit*. He realized they were staring at and surrounded by more than the crimson terror of a wild fire. They were beholding the spirits of the most ancient vampires, risen from their wooden graves.

Inside the cockpit's flickering glass, DeThanatos chuckled. "What do you know? They're on my side."

On the ground, the girl next to Morning blurted, "What's up there?"

"The spirits of the Old Ones," he replied. "And they don't like being disturbed."

"What are we gonna do?"

Morning kicked the ground. Under the dust was nothing but rock. "We can't go up, and even a mole with diamond teeth couldn't tunnel through what's under us."

As the Leaguers murmured toward panic, Morning stared at the wall of flames. Tree by tree, it was pushing closer. The red dragon was stalking, and there was only one way out. Before Morning could even come up with a bad idea of how to bust a hole in a wall of fire, he heard a siren's distant wail.

70

Blowout

Hovering above the forest, DeThanatos spotted the flashing red lights of the fire engine racing toward the scene. "Oh, dear," he said with mocking disdain, "is that a fire truck or a wagon full of marshmallows?"

The truck lurched to a stop as close to the flames as possible. Probies jumped off, buckling up gear and cinching their SCBAs. Prowler dropped out of the cab, taking in the towering conflagration and the luminescent spirits wavering above them. He had never seen anything like it.

Armando and Sully joined him. "Jeez," Armando said to Prowler, "you weren't kiddin' about the red dragon."

"Yeah," Sully added, pointing above the flames, "but you didn't tell us the red dragon ran in packs."

"Didn't wanna spoil all the surprises," Prowler said, masking his concern with a game face.

"You think Morning's in there?" Armando asked.

"There's only way to find out: open a door." Prowler

started shouting orders to pull hose and stretch a line. He eyed the Chinook hovering at a safe distance and wondered whose side it was on.

As the probies laid out a long stretch of hose, a Jeep raced up and fishtailed to a stop. Portia jumped out. She rushed over to Prowler and threw an arm at the fire. "Morning and a dozen Leaguers are trapped in there!"

"You know that for sure?"

She pointed at the hovering Chinook. "Why else would DeThanatos wanna burn down the Mother Forest?"

"That's who's up there?"

"Yeah." She turned to the spirit lights dancing above the flames. "But what the hell's up *there*?"

"Not sure," Prowler answered, "but I got a bad feeling they're not a bunch of looky-loos here to rubberneck."

Armando's voice came over Prowler's walkie-talkie. "We're ready to put the wet stuff on the hot stuff."

Prowler keyed the walkie-talkie. "Then cut me a door."

The probies shot a geyser of water into the fire.

DeThanatos watched the arc of water hit the massive fire and evaporate in clouds of steam. He laughed. "A dog lifting his leg on a house fire could do better!"

Seeing the futility of the effort, Portia nodded at Prowler's walkie-talkie. "You got another one of those?"

"Yeah, in the rig."

Portia grabbed the walkie-talkie from Prowler, ran as close to the wall of fire as possible, wound up, and hurled the walkie-talkie.

On the other side, the walkie-talkie flew through the flames and tumbled to the ground near the Leaguers. Morning jogged over, scooped it up, and keyed it. "Who's out there?"

Portia's voice crackled over. "It's me, Morning."

"What are you doing here?"

"Trying to get us back to the Williams Bird Bridge."

A rueful smile teased Morning's mouth as he took in the impenetrable barrier of flames and wavering spirits. "You got my note."

"Yeah. I'm here with Captain Prowler and your crew. Got any ideas of how we can get you outta there?"

"Lemme talk to Prowler."

Portia handed the walkie-talkie she had retrieved from the truck to Prowler. Morning told the fireman about something he had read in a book on fighting forest fires. Sometimes a wall of fire can be breached using fire against fire. First, a jetty of dry, combustible wood gets built out from the wall of fire, but out of reach of the fire. When the fire is allowed to jump to the jetty, the tinderbox bonfire can be so explosive it creates a backdraft, sucks the oxygen away from a section of the main fire, and momentarily blows a hole in the wall of flames. If it's timed right, someone can escape through this blowout. When he was done, Morning asked, "What do you think?"

Prowler grinned. "Now you're thinking like a fire knight. We're on it."

DeThanatos watched curiously as Prowler, the crew, and Portia collected wood and began building a jetty at almost a ninety-degree angle from the fire. A couple of probies hosed down the end of the jetty closest to the fire to keep the main fire from jumping too soon and igniting it.

A spine-tailed swift raced through the dim light over Washington, D.C. The shadow-consciousness Zoë retained in the swift's bird brain was more than enough. The trip had been the fastest, most vivid flying dream she'd ever had. But it was no dream, it was a dream come true!

She spotted the White House, the lights burning in the Oval Office, and dived toward them. She was so jacked up she realized too late what so many birds realize too late: *Is that a window?* She banged into it with a *thud,* bounced off, and crashed in the bushes.

The president, lying on the rug in front of his paper-strewn desk, was doing a stretch to loosen his back after another stressful day being the most powerful man in the world. He heard the sound and started to sit up, but his . back twinged, sending him back to the carpet. "Ow!"

At the window, which was slightly raised to let in the warm autumn breeze, the swift darted into the Oval Office. Fortunately, the bird was so small it had flown between the motion-sensor laser beams the Secret Service had "barred" the window with as a last line of defense against anyone busting in on the president from the outside.

The swift landed on the paper-cluttered desk as Zoë wondered where she should look for the president next if he wasn't in the Oval Office.

Before she produced an answer, the president's head popped up in front of the desk. The swift shrieked into flight; "Ahh!" jumped out of the president, and he was thrown back to the floor by a back spasm.

The swift darted around the room before Zoë's shadow-consciousness took back the avian controls and landed on the floor behind the desk. She could hear the president moaning on the other side of the desk as he tried to raise himself off the floor with his now seized-up back. Zoë knew it was only a matter of seconds before the president yelled for the Secret Service, or the White House animal-control officer, or whoever rids the Oval Office of unwanted birds. She had to act swiftly. Or, in this case, de-swiftly.

She focused her mind on her human form—like Morning had once told her when she had grilled him about CDing—and was stunned by how quickly she exploded back to herself. Her preening sense of accomplishment was cut short by the breeze coming in the window, which not only goose-pimpled her legs but made her realize that she was—except for an X-shaped Band-Aid on the back of her neck—butt naked.

The president's hand gripped the front of the desk as he started to pull himself up.

Despite being human again, Zoë's nervous system fired with birdlike speed. She grabbed the presidential flag standing next to the window and threw it around herself.

The president's head rose behind his hand gripping the desk. His grimace of pain expanded to stunned disbelief as he spotted the girl wrapped in the blue presidential flag. "Where did you—" His eyes narrowed with recognition. "Wait a minute. You're Zoë Zotz, the girl who got turned by—"

"Yes, yes," Zoë cut in, "by Morning McCobb, but it wasn't Morning McCobb, but I don't have time to explain that now!" Then, remembering who she had just interrupted, added, "Mr. President." While clutching the flag in front of her with her right arm, Zoë reached her left hand up to the back of her neck.

The president, certain she was reaching for a weapon, opened his mouth to shout, but a new back spasm strangled the sound in a painful gasp.

352

Zoë ripped the Band-Aid holding the flash drive off her neck. Still clutching the flag with her right arm, she stepped forward to put the flash drive on the president's desk. "You have to watch this right now. It's footage of—" Having forgotten the flag was attached to a stand and a pole with a sharp finial on top, she pulled the pole over. It toppled toward the desk.

Possessing the hyperacute senses of a vampire, Zoë saw it unfold in slow motion. She flipped the Band-Aid/flash drive on the desk—reached her left hand across her body for the falling pole—realized if she turned and reached far enough to catch the pole she would expose herself to the president—yanked her hand back in time to stop herself from becoming an Oval Office flasher.

The flagpole finial hit the desk like a machete, and stuck.

The president grimaced with a new pain: knowing his legacy would now include a deep gash in the desk that had been used by presidents since John F. Kennedy.

"Sorry!" Zoë yelped as she grabbed her flag-cover with her left hand and yanked the finial out of the desk with her right. "It was the pole or . . ."

"You made the right call," the president sighed. Using the desk, he hauled himself up. "Tell you what, Ms. Zotz. I promise to watch the footage on that flash drive, right now, if you promise to leave the way you came, right now."

"I promise," Zoë blurted. "But do you really promise?"

"I'm not only the president, I'm a father. I never break promises to young ladies."

Before she finished saying "Cool" and flashing him a big smile, Zoë realized how ridiculous she looked. Draped in a flag and holding a spearlike flagpole, she probably resembled a twisted version of Joan of Arc.

She backed up, made sure the flagpole was steady on its stand, and closed her eyes. An instant later the flag collapsed around her and a swift darted out from a fold. She circled the Oval Office once, then darted out the still-open window. This time her wings broke the invisible laser beams barring the window.

A few seconds later, two Secret Service agents burst through the twin doors on the other side of the room. "Mr. President, everything all right?"

The president feigned surprise at their entrance as he walked casually around his desk. "False alarm. A gust of wind must have fluttered the flag in the window. Perhaps it would be best if I shut it."

Back in the Mother Forest, Portia radioed Morning that they were ready. Morning acknowledged they were ready too. Wearing their face masks, Armando and Sully ran in with great bundles of tumbleweed and threw them into the gap between the jetty and the fire. They ran for safety as the fire jumped on the bundles. A second later, the jetty exploded with flames like the lashing tail of a red dragon.

On the other side, the Leaguers heard the *whoosh* of air sucking from the fire. A sooty, fireless tunnel appeared in the flames.

"Go!" Morning shouted. The Leaguers sucked in the breath that would hopefully carry them through the tunnel's heat and gases and sprinted into it one at a time.

From the Chinook, DeThanatos watched the escape. He had seen enough. He banked the chopper toward the blowout.

Morning waited until the last Leaguer had disappeared

into the black hole of swirling ash and smoke, then raced into the darkness himself.

Portia and the probies cheered as the first Leaguer broke through the blowout and ran toward them. Prowler had his eyes on the Chinook dropping closer. He suddenly realized what DeThanatos was up to. "Go! Go! Go!" he yelled as more Leaguers sprinted from the hole.

One of the empty buckets hanging from the Chinook released like a hammer throw and plunged toward the blowout.

Morning ran blindly through the smoke, ash, and blistering heat. Dim shapes began to appear at the end of the tunnel, when a great fiery ball suddenly crushed it, shaking the ground.

Prowler's voice shouted in his walkie-talkie. "Go back! Go back!"

Armando tackled the last Leaguer out, rolling him on the ground to put out the flames licking off his clothes.

Prowler and Portia watched in horror as the chopper's second bucket smashed down through the fire and crushed the inside end of the blowout tunnel. If Morning was trapped in between them, he was toast, ash, and no drop of Portia's blood would ever revive him. His pile of ash would be gone with the firestorm of oxygen that now rushed back into the tunnel, flooding it with fire.

Portia grabbed the walkie-talkie from Prowler. "Morning, you there?"

There was a long silence.

"Morning, come in," she pleaded.

71

Rematch

DeThanatos glared down at the scene with seething rage. The Leaguers had escaped. Worse, Morning had dodged the second bucket and made it back inside the ring of fire and shimmering spirits. Sure, the fiery noose was tightening, but for DeThanatos, it wasn't good enough. The tireless patience that came with immortality had finally been unraveled by his lust for revenge. This colossal mistake of a blood child had once nearly destroyed him in the Mother Forest; now it was the kid's turn.

The Chinook wheeled away from the fire, then banked in a sideways skid toward the wavering veil of spirits. As DeThanatos watched the flickering sheet of light race toward him, he shape-shifted into his falcon.

Everyone on the ground watched the Chinook fly into the spirit shield and explode in a fiery ball. The only shrapnel blasting from the fireball not trailing fire was a falcon. It shot inside the ring of dancing flames, having created its own blowout hole.

Morning saw the falcon flash overhead. He was baffled as to why DeThanatos had risked it. *What's the point?* Morning wondered. *Being blood sire and spawn, it's not like we can slay the other without annihilating ourselves. Unless,* he thought with gut-coiling fear, *after I went re-mort, then back to vampire, the rules have changed.*

There was no point trying to decipher DeThanatos's deranged thinking. Morning had to gather his strength for the battle that was coming. He tried not to think how different this one would be from the fight he'd had with DeThanatos a year before. In that one Morning's veins had been turbocharged with blood tapped from Portia. Now he was running on the fumes of a Blood Lite he'd had forty-eight hours before.

He saw a blur of motion and tried to spin away before it struck. The saberlike claws of a big cat sliced his shoulder as the resounding *clack* of the cat's flesh-ripping jaws exploded in his ears. Morning had barely missed his skull being crushed.

Grabbing his already healing shoulder, he spun to face the next charge of what he saw was a black panther. As the ferocious cat surged forward, Morning locked his mind on an answer before it was too late.

The panther sailed toward him but missed again as Morning dropped and mushroomed into a giant saber-toothed cat from another era: Smilodon.

As the panther whirled and took in Morning's first CD, it wasn't the Smilodon that did all the smiling. Whereas Morning had hoped to be displaying Smilodon's twelve-inch canine sabers and soon sinking them in the panther, something had gone wrong with his CD. The panther yowled with delight as one of its paws pointed at

Morning's head. It was Morning's human head, not the head of Smilodon, that protruded from the cat's huge body.

Morning lifted a paw to his mouth to confirm it. Sure enough, the twelve-inch sabers had remained in the darkness of his imagination; his feline pads felt his human face. His mind raced for an explanation. Maybe he wasn't even fighting on Blood Lite fumes. Or, for some wild reason, he'd begun to re-mortalize again and his CDing powers weren't firing on all cylinders, or on all *body parts*.

No answers charged into his mind. What charged was the panther, looking to take Morning down in the first round and drive a bristlecone stake through his heart.

He dodged the cat's snapping jaws as the partial Smilodon imploded down to a smaller animal: a giant tortoise. But again, the tortoise's head was no wise-looking old reptile; it was the confused head of Morning.

He shuffled and scraped his tortoise body around as fast as he could. The panther was waiting. It lunged forward and swiped a rake of claws. But not before Morning sucked his head into his shell, along with his feet. Sure, it was a totally defensive CD, but Morning desperately needed time to figure out either why his CDs were malfunctioning or how he was going to survive a fight to the death using weapons from only the neck down.

DeThanatos, unable to fully enjoy the moment as a cat, popped back into his naked self and bent double with laughter. Finding his voice, he leaned down to the hidden tortoise. "C'mon, Morning, come out and fight. Or is your head so far up your backside you're tied in a knot?"

The shell remained silent and still.

"Seriously," DeThanatos continued his ridicule, "picking you up, tossing you in the fire, and serving your friends barbecued tortoise ribs is okay as revenge goes, but it's nothing to brag about at the next Rendezvous."

The shell might as well have been a stone.

"All right, if you're not coming out, I'm coming in." DeThanatos dropped to the ground. By the time he landed he had shape-shifted into a six-foot black mamba. With its gray-black skin and sleek body, the snake wasn't terribly scary-looking unless you knew its fangs packed some of the deadliest venom in the animal kingdom. The snake slithered toward the head-hole in Morning's shell.

Morning was fixed on his next CD. His shell disappeared, replaced by a black and white plumed secretary bird with stork-long legs and a bright orange eye mask. Unfortunately, the orange eye mask didn't hide Morning's human face and head. Fortunately, under the head was a four-foot-tall bird with an unusual talent.

The black mamba reared up to strike the bird's white-plumed chest. Before it could shoot forward, one of the bird's legs karate kicked in a blur of motion. The snake recovered, rose up to strike again, and got stomped back down with a left double-kick. The snake hissed violently and slithered in retreat.

Knowing his opponent wasn't going to let himself get pummeled by a snake-stomping bird, Morning flapped his wings and tried to fly. For any bird, getting airborne with a human head would be tough, but Morning managed to lift into clumsy flight and labor toward the treetops. Besides escaping from DeThanatos's next CD, he wanted to check on the fire. What he saw made his wings even heavier.

The fire had spread inward, igniting more trees. Now a double tier of angry spirits billowed and shimmered above the crowning flames. Morning struggled to fly high enough to see if Prowler and the probies had built another jetty to free him from the fire and the fight he would surely lose. But his wings felt like feathered lead. He flapped to the top of the Matriarch and landed clumsily on one of the bald branches.

Outside the fire, Portia, Prowler, the Leaguers, and the probies were working in a frenzy to prepare another jetty for a second blowout. When they saw the second tier of spirits rise above the flames, they realized their efforts were futile. It wasn't their only discovery.

The trees surrounding the fire that weren't burning were filling with the dark silhouettes of birds. Other birds dotted the sky as they descended. The fire in the Mother Forest, and the disturbance of the Old Ones' spirits had reverberated through the Loner world. The first waves of Loners were arriving to witness the cataclysmic event.

Still perched in the top of the Matriarch, Morning looked for whatever creature DeThanatos was going to throw at him next. He noticed something odd. Next to the tree he was in was another huge tree. In fact, it looked like the mirror image of the Matriarch.

Before he could shake away what had to be a vision, the branch under him collapsed. As he fell through the imploding tree, branches transformed into the lines and strands of a massive web. He tried to fly out, but the sticky webbing gathered around him like a net. When he landed on the ground where the tree had been, his secretary bird was trapped in the web like a skydiver under his parachute.

In a flash, he realized what had happened. DeThanatos, CDing into a form known as a Hider, had transformed into the Matriarch to fool him. But transforming into a tree wasn't as shocking as his next CD, a power Morning had never witnessed: the ability to transform into a spider *and* its web. His eyes darted around, looking for the creature that came with the ensnaring web.

A large Darwin's bark spider legged toward him. In its jaws, it carried a sharp wedge of bristlecone pine.

The more Morning struggled against the web, the tighter it bound him. Knowing his next CD would probably fail from the neck up, he CDed into the only animal he could think of that might give him a chance. The secretary bird imploded to a blue crab. Its head was a miniature version of Morning's, but it wasn't the only thing that had miniaturized and failed to CD. The crab had one claw and one tiny human arm. Using its claw, the crab began slashing its way out of the web.

The spider spit out its bristlecone stake. It wasn't clear if DeThanatos was put out by Morning's escape or simply revolted by the sight of a crab with a human head and arm. The spider skittered in the opposite direction.

Morning CDed back into human form. Every muscle and joint ached. He had never felt so bone-weary and wasted after coming out of a CD. The heat of the pressing fire didn't help. It reminded him that the only fight left was over who took him first: the red dragon or DeThanatos.

Not far away, DeThanatos's body popped up from the ground. As the firelight danced on his muscles, it looked like he hadn't broken a sweat. He gave Morning a haughty sneer. "Didn't think I could spin a web, did you?"

"No," Morning admitted. "What other tricks do Millennials have up their sleeves?"

DeThanatos raised his right arm; his forearm and hand snapped into the head of an anteater. "Keep your eyes on the anteater . . . ," he said, raising his left arm.

Knowing this was a trick, Morning locked his eyes on the raising arm, bracing for what was next. But the flash of something red coming from the anteater head grabbed his eyes long enough for him to see that it was only the anteater's bizarrely long tongue.

In the microsecond of distraction, DeThanatos's left arm lashed into a fifteen-foot anaconda. " . . . and something else will getcha!" The huge snake sprang at Morning's neck.

He barely jumped back in time.

DeThanatos had a good laugh as his arms sucked back to human form. Whatever fun he was having disappeared as fast as the anaconda. "Enough show-and-tell," he growled. "Time for the wolf to lie down with the lamb."

Before DeThanatos CDed, a groan coming from the fire pulled their eyes toward a tree consumed in flames. Its fiery crown wavered and fell toward them. They both jumped out of the way as the tree crashed to the ground in an eruption of fire, embers, and shrapnel.

Morning howled in pain. His eyes snapped to a long dagger of wood impaling his shoulder. The pain radiating through his body was overridden by another howl so soul-rending and terrifying it might have come from hell.

He stared up at the yowling face of light above the fallen tree. The visage twisted in pain, shot upward, and vaporized in the vault of stars.

From outside the ring of fire came the keening cry of thousands of birds.

DeThanatos lowered his gaze with a malicious chuckle. "So, when a bristlecone pine falls in the forest, it makes a noise . . . a lot of noise." His eyes turned cold as steel. "Now, my boy, it's time to meet your maker."

72

Last Shape-Shift

Morning raised his hands and offered his last defense. "But if you destroy me, you'll destroy yourself."

DeThanatos shook his head. "Not if you're no longer my blood child."

"What makes you so sure I'm human again?"

"Tell you what. I'll shape-shift into my favorite predator. If you don't have an answer, we'll know what you've become. And I won't even have to use a stake."

DeThanatos's body disappeared, replaced by a ferocious dire wolf. On all fours, the wolf was as tall as Morning. Its slathering jaws were massive enough to decapitate a buffalo, which it used to do ten thousand years ago.

Morning clamped his eyes shut and tried to envision the merest creature, even a moth, to prove he was still a vampire. But all he could sense was the throbbing pain from the dagger in his shoulder. He opened his eyes.

The dire wolf threw back its huge head and howled. His blazing eyes returned to Morning. A strand of saliva rappelled off his bared teeth. Not only was he going to relish the kill, Morning would now supply the blood meal DeThanatos would need to escape the fire. But this time, there would be no backwash, no mistakes.

Leaping out of its tracks, the wolf butted Morning in the chest. He sprawled to the ground, the wind knocked out of him. Morning's lungs heaved for the breath that would be his last.

The wolf landed over him, raising its head to plunge its fangs in Morning's throat. But the beast's ears quirked to a sound. It ducked as a black shape darkened the fiery sky. Something sharp shredded the wolf's ear. The wolf's furious eyes snapped up as the black shape, a condor, wheeled a moment before flying into the fire.

The wolf returned to its kill; its eyes flashed with the sense of something different, something changed. *Where was the wooden dagger that had been impaled in the boy's shoulder?*

The answer came as Morning buried the dagger in the wolf's heart.

The beast's jaws snapped open; its body froze as a tremor of shock passed through it. It began to smolder.

Morning tucked and rolled away as the wolf burst into flames. Within seconds, it was a frame of burning bones; then the skeleton collapsed in a heap of ash.

Morning watched in exhausted wonder as a swirl of wind scattered the ashes until there was nothing left but a bristlecone seedpod. He had seen this before, a year earlier when Portia had used her powers as "a virgin who's lost her heart to love" to slay DeThanatos and bury him in the Mother Forest. This time, Morning was going to ensure that DeThanatos never rose again.

He lifted a heavy rock and dropped it on the seedpod,

then offered the slain vampire a few last words. "I bet you thought I wasn't a virgin who'd lost his heart to love. Still am." His eyes lifted to the roaring fire, adding with a tight smile, "And will die one, too."

He walked to the Matriarch and pressed his back into the seven-stemmed trunk. The fire would soon leap to the great mother tree and consume them both.

The condor sailed to the ground and shape-shifted into the broad and hairy Bosky.

"Who are you?" Morning asked.

"A Loner" was all he answered. "I've been trailing DeThanatos for some time."

"Why did you help me?"

"Because"—Bosky turned to the burning trees—"you helped save the Mother Forest."

Morning chuffed with bitterness. "It doesn't look saved to me."

"It will be soon."

Before Morning could ask what he meant, a sound penetrated the roar of the fire. It sounded like the drone of aircraft. Then he heard the wail of sirens.

Bosky spread a hand on the great trunk and closed his eyes. "I ask you, Mother of the Forest, what will the boy's reward be?" After a moment, he lifted his hand and looked at Morning. "You and your kind, re-mortals, will be spared the wrath of Millennials for one hundred years."

Morning blinked in disbelief. "A hundred years? Really?"

Bosky nodded. "Really."

He didn't have to do the math. "That works for me."

Bosky looked skyward at the birds beginning to rise into the smoky dawn. "It works for Loners, too. It'll clean the gene pool of vampires who, how shall I say, can't handle the long haul of immortality." The vampire's mouth cornered into a smile. "After that, the Matriarch says the world is big enough for Loners *and* Leaguers." He shape-shifted back into his condor and flew up to the treetop.

Through the veil of dancing spirits, Morning and the condor watched flying tankers take their turns as each veered toward the fire, banked, and discharged ribbons of orange fire retardant. Joining the fight from the ground, geysers of water arced through the air, hitting the fire and the great columns of steam now rising from it.

The steam didn't rise high enough to obscure the fluttering shrouds of light above the fire. The luminescent spirit-plumes of the Old Ones began to shrink and retract into the charred yet still-standing trees of their graves. There was nothing joyous about their return to their roots of eternal rest. After all, one of the grave-trees had been destroyed, and the spirit dwelling within it had been cast into the sky of eternal wandering.

With the fire now only steam and billowing smoke, Morning stepped out from under the Matriarch and looked up. The condor soared high and away, racing from the impending sunrise.

When Morning looked down, a different group of apparitions began to emerge from the smoke and blizzarding ash. He grinned as the ghostly shapes transformed into human figures: Portia, Prowler, and his crew of fellow probies. But his joy was cut short as a bolt of fear shot through him. "What happened at Leaguer Mountain?" he shouted.

Portia continued toward him. "Zoë came to, had

her first blood product, and got to the president before Becky-Dell was able to torch the mountain."

Morning started to ask if any Leaguers had been lost, but Portia, closing the gap between them, threw up a finger. "Shhh." She stared at the bloody wound in his shoulder. Then she threw her arms around him and squeezed.

"Owwww!" he yelped.

She pulled back. "Sorry. I had to make sure. You're still my eternal beloved"—she grinned from ear to ear—"but you're not so eternal anymore."

Hearing her utter the words *eternal beloved* for the first time might have drowned him in joy if it weren't for his confusion. "Yeah"—he answered her grin with his own—"but I don't get the no-longer-eternal part. What kick-started my mortality again?"

Prowler answered the mystery with a proud smile. "You don't have to graduate from the academy to become a firefighter. You became one, right here."

The probies seconded him with a huge cheer.

Portia put her hands on Morning's shoulders, being careful not to hit his wound. "I'd give you a big congratulations kiss, but"—she turned to Prowler and the two dozen probies—"you'd never hear the end of it."

The probies shouted in unison, "Kiss him!"

And she did.

73

Fallout

In the next week a smorgasbord of events came to pass.

The president praised the military for its swift reaction to Becky-Dell's deep-cover and illegal "mission leap" from Leaguer deportation to destruction. The attack had been thwarted moments before the Chinooks tossed their buckets of incineration into the mountain. The Leaguers who were shot with warfarin and staked received proper medical attention, and were recovering in the field hospital set up in the old Leaguer Academy.

Portia used the media to give Morning his day in court. She made her case that the "Morning" who turned Zoë was not the Morning the world had grown to know and love. With the help of testimony from witnesses, including herself, she established that the real Morning had a gnarly chin pimple that fateful night. Testimony from video experts confirmed that the vampire on the Washington Mews security video was pimple-free. To prove Morning innocent beyond a shadow of a doubt, she also located footage from another street security camera showing the real Morning walking home with his flat-tire bike at the exact minute DeThanatos was robbing Zoë of her mortality.

Once Morning was exonerated and his heroics out west came to light, he was offered, along with Portia, Zoë, Cody, Rachel, Penny, Dolly, Prowler, the probies, and the Leaguers who flew with Morning, a ticker tape parade down Broadway. At first, Morning politely declined. Now that he was re-mortalizing, he longed to turn off the spotlight of fame for good and bask in the sunshine of normal life. But Penny persuaded him that the parade was the best PR in the world if he wanted back into the fire academy. So it came to pass that Zoë led the parade riding her Fanpire Tours pedicab with Morning and Portia as her passengers.

The FDNY brass did readmit Morning and his crew to the academy for their last day of testing. After passing with flying colors, they attended the fire academy graduation ceremony. Clancy wasn't thrilled, particularly over the age waiver the brass had regranted Morning, but the captain managed to find an upside. Since Morning was now a full-on mortal, the FDNY was still vampire-free.

As for Becky-Dell, the president summed up her villainy in a speech from the Oval Office. "Those of us who were hoodwinked into thinking Leaguer vampires were homegrown terrorists threatening America now realize the real homegrown terrorists were closer to home. In fact, homegrown terrorist number one was right here in the house: the House of Representatives."

Becky-Dell was stripped of her seat in Congress and indicted on numerous charges. Several of her crimes included firsts in American law: from the minor—"altering military weapons to fire wooden projectiles"—to the major—"attempted destruction of a mountain." The biggest surprise was the discovery of her family lineage tracing back to Transylvania, where the original family name was Vallesscu. This inspired Rachel, in a rare moment of Earth Angel cattiness, to suggest, "I say we deport *her* to Transylvania and feed her to the Transylvanian Loners."

The dozens of soldiers and pilots who took part in the attack on Leaguer Mountain were quietly discharged but were allowed to keep their pensions because their lawyers successfully argued (1) that they thought they were following legitimate orders, and (2) the "Van Helsing defense." That is, "The instinct to slay vampires runs so deep in our DNA, to strip the gene from our genome in two years is an unreasonable expectation."

In the following weeks, there was a great thawing between Lifers and Leaguers. Peace and goodwill swept the nation.

The president led the campaign to resubmit the Vampire Rights Act to Congress. Shortly after his reelection in November, Congress passed the VRA, but with a few changes. The Bureau of Vampire Affairs, smeared by Becky-Dell's hijacking of it, was abolished. In its place, Congress created a new agency, the Even Playing Field Agency. The EPFA would establish the rules that would allow Leaguers to compete in the world of business, sports, gaming, etc., without using their superpowers to unfair advantage over their Lifer peers. The president appointed Penny Dredful as the first head of the EPFA. She sold Diamond Sky Productions to a group of Leaguer investors and began spending her workweek in Washington.

While hard-core holdouts from the Mortals Only Party vented about the country turning into a nation of "fang-huggers," most Americans came to believe that, like so many minorities who had joined the great melting pot, Leaguers were here to stay, and despite their liquid diet, sterility, and tediously long lives, Leaguer citizens were endowed with the same inalienable rights to life, liberty, and the pursuit of happiness.

Morning didn't pay much attention to all the hoopla. But he did perform one final act as the retiring poster boy for the Leaguer movement. He posted his "first and last blog" on the IVL webpage.

IVLEAGUE

DEATH NOTICE

Our great leader, Luther Birnam, is no longer with us. He recently passed away in the city where he was turned, Tripoli. Cause of death: old age. How can this be? The fact is, Mr. Birnam not only guided vampires from the dark wood, the *selva obscura,* into the light of Leaguerdom, he discovered the cure for vampirism.

That cure is simple, and one I have taken myself. Return to and pursue your Lifer dream; it will reawaken the gene of mortality that lies dormant within you. In chasing those original dreams, your body will once again begin to produce what Birnam called *pneumabrotus,* the spirit of death.

There's a reason we've never known about this. A secret cult of Loners, known as Millennials, have kept it secret by slaying re-mortals, like myself, as soon as they begin to show signs of re-aging. But I have been promised by the highest authority, the Matriarch, that Leaguers have been granted a 100-year reprieve from the wrath of Millennials.

So, if immortal life hasn't lived up to your expectations, and you've grown tired of age-lock and the bloody diet, you can re-embrace the blessing and curse of the sweet, time-challenged mortal life. It can begin with your last hunt as a vampire: the hunt to recapture your Lifer dream.

Thoreau once said that mortals, haunted by death, "lead lives of quiet desperation." I disagree. I say, lead a life of humming exhilaration. Chase your dream. Take all that life has to offer, good and bad. I say, bring it on. I say, suck it up and do what mortals do: earn your death.

> Your friend, and ex-Leaguer,
> Morning McCobb

LIFE NOTICE

The bristlecone pines of the Mother Forest are making a slow but steady recovery from the fire. Except for one, the grave-trees of the oldest vampires live on, and the spirits of the Old Ones rest peacefully in their roots.

74

More Fallout

Morning's revelation rocked the Leaguer world. Since a vampire cure was seen as the next huge development in what Birnam had once called "the great experiment," the IVL named the cure after him: the Birnam Effect.

About half the Leaguers worldwide decided to re-chase their Lifer dreams, prime the *pneumabrotus* pump, and come full circle to their mortal coils. The other half, led by Rachel Capilarus, chose to remain Leaguers, and set about starting businesses and joining sports teams and gaming tournaments, all in compliance with the new EPFA rules— for example, Leaguer athletes could compete, but there were "term limits" on their pro careers.

Rachel was the ceremonial first Leaguer licensed to do business by Penny and the EPFA. Her company, Earth Angel Productions, produced a hit reality show, *Earth Angels*. Zoë was her first guest, and they re-created, with help from special effects, Zoë's heroic flight from New

York to the White House, dubbed "The midnight flight of Zoë Zotz." At first, the president's advisers were against re-creating this historical footnote because it revealed too much about the president's back problems. But the president overruled them. He wanted the world to know, and see, how the huge gash ended up in the presidential desk.

Special effects were needed to re-create Zoë's flight because, when it came to each vampire choosing to re-mort or not to re-mort, Zoë was a unique case. Her lifetime dream had been to be a vampire. So when the Birnam Effect kicked in and her body realized she'd *achieved* her Lifer dream to become a vampire, she began to re-mortalize. She tried everything—hypnosis, memory-loss drugs—but nothing worked. Within two weeks, she was back to mortally plagued Zoë. She had to accept the tragic irony that if anyone was immune to becoming a vampire, it was her.

Despite this setback, Zoë refused to let mortality get her down. She expanded her Fanpire Tour, adding Washington Mews, where, from a certain perspective, she had been turned by Morning *and* DeThanatos, and became, "the first known case of someone turned in a three-way." She enlisted fellow students and expanded her pedicab fleet. Finally, she began planning to take Fanpire Tours national after she graduated, with the hope of adding a Fanpire Tour to the Leaguer Mountain Battlefield National Park, and, from a respectful distance, the Mother Forest. She also recorded her version of "Part of Your World," which became a mega-hit in the goth scene.

75

Your Pumpkin Is Waiting

Morning's first assignment as a rookie firefighter was in Prowler's engine company. He had settled into the job, and had even seen some action. While his Thursday-morning breakfast with Portia wasn't always possible, he still saw a lot of her when he was off. They happily returned to their *pneumabrotus* patrols, and sometimes got distracted and wandered off trail. But not so far off that they didn't keep their eyes on the prize: December 21, 2012.

The evening of the End Is Upon Us Ball, Morning was in his room putting on his rented tux. The ball wasn't black tie; the invitation simply stated, *Attire: End of the World–Appropriate*. But Portia, Zoë, and Cody had decided, on the outside chance their LaGuardia Arts prom the following spring might be canceled due to worldwide destruction, they should move up their first, and possibly only, black-tie event to the End Is Upon Us Ball.

As Morning fumbled with his first-ever attempt at tying a bow tie, there was a knock on the door. "Who is it?"

Zoë walked in. "Your fairy godmother," she answered. "Your pumpkin is waiting."

He stared at her usual black goth attire. "Are you changing into your dress at Portia's?"

"Nah," she said nonchalantly. "My date bailed on me, said he had to work."

Morning gave up on the bow tie. "What's Cody working for? This could be our last night on earth."

As Zoë answered she began tying Morning's bow tie for him. "He said he's gotta get tonight on film in case the world ends in a radiation blast that destroys all living things, but not thing-things, like his footage of humanity's last gasp. He felt bad about dumping me, but when it got down to choosing between dancing with me all night or getting on YouTube in whatever alien civilization discovers our lifeless planet, he chose YouTube."

"What a jerk."

She shrugged. "Cody being Cody. This way I can pedicab you and Portia to the Waldorf Astoria." She did a last adjustment on his now perfect bow tie. "There."

He stared at her handiwork in the mirror. "Where did you learn to do that?"

"Oh, I've hit a few black-tie events recently. Sometimes I go in a dress, sometimes I go in a tux. C'mon, prince," she ordered as she marched out. "Don't wanna keep Cinderella waiting."

Downstairs in the hallway they were met by Sister Flora. Flora was one of the Leaguers who had no desire to return to her Lifer dreams and reawaken her inner mortal. Before she had been turned she had run a very different kind of house: a house for ladies of the night in Paris. Having been a Sister of Divine Compassion since the 1890s, she had no desire to go back to being a madam of the red-light district.

Flora handed the box she had taken from the fridge to Morning. "Can't forget your corsage." She stepped back and took him in. "I don't know whether to laugh or cry." Something caught in her throat. "You're growing up so fast."

"It's just the tux."

"No," she said wistfully. "It won't be long before you turn eighteen, age out of foster care and out of my life."

"Sister," he said, kissing her on the cheek, "I'll never age out of your life. Besides, now I'm paying rent and making contributions to St. Giles." He gave her a wink. "Maybe you'll let me stay on as the building's super."

Watching Zoë and Morning leave, Sister Flora let a tear tumble down her cheek.

Zoë wasn't speaking metaphorically when she called her pedicab a pumpkin. Her new pedicab, made possible by the initial public offering she had done for stock in Fanpire Tours Unlimited, looked like a pumpkin, albeit bloodred and slightly misshapen. It was a winterized pedicab with the biker and passengers protected by a super-light composite bubble. There was even a battery that provided some extra pedal juice and heat.

As Zoë rode Morning to the Village, he said, "You have a dress, right, ZZ?"

"Yeah, in my closet."

"So, why don't you go home, put it on, and come with me and Portia?"

"Oh, no," Zoë answered with a vigorous head shake. "I

know what you guys are doing tonight, and there's no way I wanna get glommed with virginity-go-bye-bye cooties."

"She told you?" Morning exclaimed loud enough for his voice to bounce around in the shell.

Zoë turned with an evil smile. "She tells me *everything*."

"Oh, great!" He let out a breath. As if he weren't feeling enough pressure, now he had to live with the prospect of Zoë getting a review the next day, if there was one. "How 'bout we change the subject."

"Good by me," Zoë chirped.

"I've been wanting to ask you something for weeks," Morning said. "And if this is our last night on earth, it'd be nice to know."

"Shoot."

"Do you like me less now that I'm not a vampire?"

She shot him a quick smile. "Course I still like you as much. In fact, even though it wasn't really you who turned me, whenever I fantasize about some badass vampire sinking fang and passing me the deuce, the face I always see is yours. You're my one and only fang-stud."

"Okay, okay, TMI," he lamented. "How 'bout we ride the rest of the way in silence?"

Zoë laughed. "Deal."

76

The End Is Upon Us Ball

Zoë delivered Morning to the Dredful town house, but she hung back in the pedicab.

"You comin' in?" he asked.

"Nah." She pulled out her cell. "Got a call to make."

Morning let himself in, having been rewarded with a key to the apartment as part of the "you're just a mortal fireman now" care package Portia had given him for graduation. Besides, she figured he needed a key since he could no longer fly in the window as a pigeon.

He didn't wait long before she came down the stairs off the kitchen. She wore a deep-green gown and looked reluctantly radiant. Halfway down the stairs, she asked, "You still think we're doing the right thing?"

Morning cleared his throat. "You mean going to the ball, or—"

"Going to the ball, of course." She squirmed in her gown. "I feel like I've been vacu-packed."

He stood stiffly. "Me too. But I think we should suck it up and go."

She moved to him. "I'd kiss you, but I had to do my lipstick three times before I got it right. How can my mom do it blind between courses in a restaurant?"

"Speaking of, where is she?"

"She got ordered to stay in D.C."

"Ordered?"

"Yeah, if bad stuff starts coming down tonight, the president and all his cabinet are gonna do a sleepover in some underground bunker."

Morning hid his relief that they now had clear sailing to come back to her place. Provided, of course, the world made it to midnight. He took the longish corsage box from under his arm, opened it, and presented it.

Portia laughed and pulled the corsage out. It was their croquet stake festooned with flowers. "You're such a sentimental fool. Thank God *one* of us has that covered." She jiggered the corsage-stake in front of her. "How am I supposed to wear it?"

He shrugged. "Maybe you're not. Maybe it's a magic wand."

She brandished the stake like a sword. "All for one, and one for all, we must to the End Is Upon Us Ball!"

Zoë dropped Morning and Portia in front of the Waldorf Astoria, all dressed up for the holidays, and they made their way to the Starlight Ballroom.

Before getting into the ball, they had to show their tickets and apply temporary tattoos with the world's expiration date: 12/21/12. They walked past the tables of swag bags:

Yogi Bear and Boo-Boo picnic baskets stuffed with decadent things you just had to have one more time, from Ding Dongs to Sno Balls. Portia explained the Yogi–Boo-Boo connection to Morning, which involved the supervolcano under Yellowstone Park that would be blowing before midnight, destroying everything in a 1,600-mile radius and spewing an ash cloud that would knock half the world into nuclear winter.

Once inside, Morning and Portia were wowed by the amazing doomsday environment the LaGuardia Arts students had created, especially given the prediction that a tsunami was supposed to rise out of the Atlantic before midnight and destroy the original thirteen colonies.

The reason for 12/21/12 being the day to end all days was clearly illustrated by the celestial model suspended from the ceiling of the ballroom. Hanging over half of the room was our solar system, with the planets revolving around the sun. On the other half was a huge cotton and LED light display of the Milky Way—the galaxy, not the candy bar. Laser beams showed how the sun and the Earth were in perfect alignment on 12/21/12 with a certain part of the Milky Way. This dark lane in the Milky Way, known as the Dark Road, and its alignment with the sun and Earth signals the last day, the very end of the 5,125-year Mayan calendar.

If this alignment with the Dark Road wasn't enough to guarantee doom, there was also an alien mini solar system of planets orbiting around their own sun, the Dark Star, which had begun to cut into our solar system's elliptical plane like a circular saw. The sharpest tooth in this saw blade was the fiery red planet Nibiru, which, sure enough, was passing so close to Earth on 12/21/12 that there was going to be hell to pay, because, as every doomer knew, Nibiru had ripped into our celestial neighborhood a few times before. First time, it pocked the moon with craters. Second time, it destroyed Atlantis. Third time, it caused the flood that made Noah a sailor. And now, for its fourth visit, coupled with the end of Mayan time, Nibiru was finally going to put the human race out of its misery.

Under these chandeliers of catastrophe was a festival of end-time fun, which Morning and Portia took full advantage of. They went into the Kiss Your Ass Goodbye photo booth, took pictures of their mooning butts, then took pictures of themselves kissing the pictures of their mooning butts goodbye. They stopped by the Doomsday Vault of All Things Teenage, designed to survive the apocalypse and preserve for alien explorers what life was like for teenage earthlings. They threw in the Silly Bands they had brought for the occasion, along with Portia's first unsuccessful fake ID and Morning's expired IVL membership card. They also signed contracts to participate in Santa's Moving Day, December 22, should they happen to survive all the bad tidings. Santa had to move because Nibiru was going to mess up the Earth's magnetic flux so badly that the magnetic fields were going to be reversed, which meant the North Pole was moving south and the South Pole was moving north. Moving Santa's entire workshop 12,500 miles south three days before Christmas was going to take lots of volunteers.

Morning and Portia were in line to buy a tube of Solar Flare Sunblock: SPF Quintillion, when they got pulled away by one of the endgames that punctuated the evening. The center of the ballroom cleared for a chariot race. One chariot was a model of Earth, pulled by students dressed as the Four Horsemen of the Apocalypse: War, Famine, Pestilence, and Death. The other chariot was a model of Nibiru, pulled by students dressed as the Neo-Horsemen of the Apocalypse: Supervolcano, Quake, Magnetic Flip, and Solar Dragon. After two neck-and-neck laps around the open space, the Nibiru chariot fell behind. Rather than face defeat in the three-lap race, the Magnetic Flip horse forced the Nibiru chariot to reverse direction and raced straight into the Earth chariot. The collision ended in a twisted mass of horse, people, and planet parts, and the race was declared the disaster doomers had predicted.

77

Last Dance

When the band, Cry in the Night, began their second set, Morning and Portia hit the dance floor. In their tux and evening gown, they looked out of place in a sea of doomers. There was a Grim Reaper dancing with his scythe, and dancing coffins. The most annoying couple was a guy in a polar-bear suit clinging to his date, an ice floe. The ice floe kept yelling "I'm melting!" and shooting dancers with a squirt gun.

After a few wild dances, the band put on black hoodies and started the chords of their first slow dance, a funeral dirge written especially for the night, "Globicide."

The only thing Morning knew about slow dancing was that he was supposed to lead, but he couldn't tell who was leading whom. Not that he cared. He and Portia moved in such harmony it was just another sign they were eternally meant for each other, even if eternity was only a few more hours.

His first misstep was when he pulled his nose from Portia's luscious hair and spied a figure dancing toward them. It was Cody. And he wasn't dancing with Zoë.

"Ow," Portia mumbled, taking a shot to the toe.

"Sorry," Morning said as Cody danced his date over. He was wearing an all-white tux and looking more dashing than usual. It only made Morning angrier. "What are you doing here? Zoë said you were working."

"I am," he replied, spinning his date away and opening himself to Morning. "I'm shooting you with my tux-cam."

Morning spied the boutonniere on his lapel and could make out the shiny little lens in the middle of it.

"In fact," Cody continued, "we're thinking you and Portia dancing might be the last shot in *The Rise and Fall of Morning McCobb*. That is, if we're here tomorrow."

Portia gave Morning a sheepish grin. True, Morning had urged her to abandon her doc on competitive knitting and return to working with Cody on the doc about Morning's journey from vampire back to mortal, but he'd thought he would be spared their nosy camera on this special night. "What about Zoë?" he demanded. "Why'd you dump her?"

Cody pulled his date close. "I didn't. She dumped me."

"Don't worry," Portia told Morning as Cody danced his date away. "She'll be here soon."

Morning squinted with confusion. "With who?"

"You'll see." She pushed him into a turn.

"Why am I always the last to know what's going on?"

"Because you're a grown-up now, with a big important job," she said faux-seriously. "And the rest of us are still just kids with kid jobs to do."

"What job is that?"

She gave him a mischievous smile. "To mess with grown-up heads, of course."

Morning was distracted by a red flash between dancers. The whip of long blond hair that followed confirmed his sighting. "There's Zoë." Dancing Portia toward her, he got a quick look at Zoë's tux-clad date. His black hair was even longer than Zoë's. The face behind the hair turned.

"Ow-squared!" Portia yelped as Morning's feet delivered a combination.

"Zoë's with Rachel!" he exclaimed.

"Yeah, I know. Can we get to 'em before you turn my feet into chopped meat?"

Drawing closer, Morning saw that Zoë was wrapped in a bloodred gown. It clung so tight it gave her curves he hadn't realized she had. Rachel was as beautiful as ever, even in a tux. "What's the deal?" he asked Portia.

"They've been an item for weeks. So don't embarrass me." They swerved next to Rachel as she spun Zoë.

Zoë came out of the spin. "Hey, A.M.!" She grabbed Rachel's waist. "Bet you didn't think your fairy godmother was more *fairy* than godmother." A hand flew to her mouth. "Oh, sorry!" she said, feigning shock. "Did I forget to introduce my date? This is Rachel Capilarus."

Rachel played along, extending her hand. "Great to meet you, Morning. I heard you were once a vampire."

Morning frowned. "I heard you were once straight."

As Portia kicked Morning, Rachel shot him a smile. "Oh, I still am. . . ." Her tux seemed to shift and the next second, Morning and Portia were staring at a handsome male version of Rachel. Her-his voice dropped an octave as she-he slid Zoë a seductive look. "If we wanna go that way."

"Isn't that the coolest?" Zoë squealed as he-Rachel CDed back to she-Rachel.

Rachel finished her impressive stunt with a shudder. "Ooh, every time I go guy, I wanna take a shower."

Portia and Zoë laughed. Morning just shook his head.

"The best part," Zoë bubbled, "is if she gets carried away and wants to turn me, she can turn me once, she can turn me twice, she can turn me all she wants, but it'll never stick 'cause I'm the girl who can't be turned!"

Rachel threw an arm around Zoë's shoulders, and they went into an eye-lock. "Which makes her my *unrequited* eternal beloved, which is the sexiest thing in the world." She turned to Morning and Portia. "But that's not why I fell head over stilettos for her."

"Yeah," Zoë cut in. "It was a meeting of the minds. I'm filled with more ideas for Earth Angel Productions than you can shake a stake at. Between the two of us, we're gonna make Steve Jobs and Mark Zuckerberg look like slackers."

Rachel gave Zoë a solemn look. "It's more than that, Zoo-Zoo. It was a meeting of funny bones." She turned back to Morning and Portia. "I mean, have you seen her latest blood-obligate impression? Show 'em, Zoo."

Zoë dropped down and hopped around Rachel's feet like a wounded bird. Her thumbs were jammed in her armpits and she flapped her skinny arms like wings. "Mama Hen, Mama Hen," she squeaked.

"Got it," Morning grumbled. "She's a dying chicken."

"No," Rachel squealed with laughter, "she's a vampire bat! They find a hen with chicks, they flap around like one of the chicks, the hen falls for it, lets the vampire bat under its feathers with the other chicks, and the vampire bat scores some blood."

"Mama Hen!" Zoë squeaked.

Rachel dropped to the floor, flapped her arms, and squeaked along with Zoë. "Mama Hen!"

Morning danced Portia away, leaving Rachel and Zoë rolling on the floor with limbs akimbo, laughing hysterically.

As they danced toward a darkened corner, Morning asked, "Aren't you glad we don't have their problems?"

"You mean of being total whack jobs?"

"No, of the whole Leaguer-Lifer thing."

She took him in with a smile. "Yeah, but in a weird way things haven't changed that much since so long ago on the Williams Bird Bridge."

He stopped dancing. "Really? How so?"

"Well, we still might have only a couple of years together before it falls apart. I mean, I still don't know where I'm going to college, and you're a firefighter."

"Maybe you're right," he said with a nod and a smile. "We'll just have to do what mortals do. Take it day by day, minute by minute, kiss by kiss . . ."

Their mouths pushed closer as she whispered, "And if this is our last night on earth together?"

He whispered back, "We'll just have to suck it up and die happy."

Their lips met . . . and pillowed into perfection.

Glossary

AMERICAN OUT DAY: October 4, the day Leaguer vampires in the U.S. came out, hoping to prove that vampires are just a minority with special needs.

BUREAU OF VAMPIRE AFFAIRS (BVA): The federal agency created to ensure Leaguer vampires don't use their powers to gain unfair advantage over mortals.

CELL DIFFERENTIATION (CD): A vampire's ability to transform into other creatures. Also known as shape-shifting.

CENTURION: A vampire who has been one for one hundred years.

CONSENSUAL BLOODLUST: A hookup between a mortal who wants to be a "blood donor" and a Leaguer seeking a nostalgic nip and sip of human neck.

DENTIS ERUPTUS: The swelling of teeth into fangs.

EPIDEX: The underarmor invented by Leaguer scientists so vampires who CD and lose their clothes, then revert to human form, are not confused with nudists.

EXSANGUINATION: The act of bleeding or being bled.

FORBIDDEN WELL: The human reservoir of blood, five quarts per adult human.

IMPALE: International Mamas and Papas Against Leaguer Equality.

LEAGUER: A vampire who is over bloodlust and has vowed to keep his fangs out of the "forbidden well."

LIFER: A mortal; an age-challenged human being.

LONER: A vampire who remains a "bloodsucking fiend" and considers quaffing humans part of his cultural heritage.

MILLENNIAL: A vampire who has stalked the earth for a thousand years and possesses super-vampire skills.

MORTALS ONLY PARTY (MOP): The organization dedicated to driving a stake through the "vampire agenda."

PASSING THE DEUCE: A specific type of vampire bite that, via infection, turns the one bitten into a vampire.

PNEUMABROTUS: Literally "the spirit of death"; the element in human DNA that controls aging, and, when reexpressed in a vampire's DNA, retriggers mortality.

RE-MORTAL: A vampire who has resumed the aging process.

SANGUIVORE: A creature who survives on blood alone. Also called a "blood obligate."

SELVA OBSCURA: "Dark wood"; the bloodlusting, creature-of-the-night lifestyle Leaguers say they have emerged from.

VAMPIRE RIGHTS ACT (VRA): Legislation that grants Leaguer vampires their full rights as citizens and the chance to tap into the American dream.

Acknowledgments

A writer with a story to tell hurls himself into the sea of words in hopes of returning to shore with a new book in hand. Luckily, this writer did not swim alone. He splashed about with some wonderful mermaids and mermen who helped guide this story to Bookstore Beach.

My mermaids and mermen (and one mermonkey) included Gerri Brioso, Pierre Ford, Monkey, Jen Booth, and the Meehl trio of Holly, Kendall, and Cindy. A splashy thanks to all, plus a resounding conch-blast to the royal mermaids at Delacorte Press: Michelle Poploff, Rebecca Short, and Trish Parcell. Finally, this story would not be in your hands if it weren't for the siren call of my agent, Sara Crowe. She lures me to the depths to be book-borne again.

About the Author

Ex-Muppeteer and three-time Emmy winner for writing for children's television Brian Meehl is thrilled to be immersed in his first great love: books. *Suck It Up and Die* is his fourth novel for youthful readers and the sequel to *Suck It Up*. Meehl has two beautiful daughters and is married to the documentary filmmaker Cindy Meehl. For more on Meehl, visit him at brianmeehl.com.

Find out how it all began. . . .
Turn the page to read the first chapter of

Suck It Up

IVLEAGUE

IVLEAGUE.US

Website under construction.
Launch date to be announced.

1

Commencement

"In the end is beginning." Luther Birnam's deep voice rained down from the high platform, charging the air above a wide semicircle of cadets. "In the beginning is end." Standing in white graduation gowns, the handsome young men and beautiful young women blazed with pride. "Today, you end your life as a Loner, and begin your new life as a Leaguer!"

The cadets erupted in cheering applause.

The last student in the arcing line clapped with just enough enthusiasm not to be noticed. For the ten months Morning McCobb had attended Leaguer Academy, being invisible had been mission number one. It wasn't easy. It never is when you're the class freak.

At sixteen, Morning was younger and skinnier than his cookie-cutter classmates. While their gowns swelled over the bodies of hunks and hotties in their late teens and twenties, Morning's robe hung from his bony shoulders his white gown billowed, and a sleek gray wolf darted from under the falling robe. The wolf trotted toward the tower.

"Our first graduate has chosen the Fifth Form: the Runner," Birnam announced.

The wolf broke into a lope, surged forward, and leaped onto the lowest platform protruding from the spiraling tower. With flawless grace, the animal sprang from platform to platform. When Dieter's wolf landed at the top next to Birnam, the crowd rewarded him with applause.

Birnam held up a long, rolled diploma. The wolf spun and CDed back into human form. Dieter was now sheathed in skintight, black underarmor. The glistening material accented every muscle in his flawless body.

The sight of underarmor gripped Morning in panic. He pulled at his gown, peeked underneath, and sighed with relief. Yes, he'd remembered to put on his black Epidex.

One of the things Morning was thankful for was that he had become a vampire *after* Leaguer scientists invented Epidex. Before Epidex, when a vampire CDed there was no way he, or she, could take their clothes with them. When they CDed back to human form they came back butt naked. Of course, there were still some vampires, known as Loners, who practiced all the old ways, and could care less if they ran around naked. Loner vampires streaked, Leaguers didn't.

In Leaguer Science, Morning had remembered enough about the history of Epidex to manage a C on his final. Epidex was invented when a vampire scientist asked, "If human skin is an external organ, could an artificial skin be invented that became both an external and *internal* organ?" After many failures, a Leaguer egghead invented Epidex. Somehow, Epidex combined a carbon-polymer blend with nanotechnology into a living tissue that fed off the electrical current that flowed through all bodies. And somehow, when vampires CDed, the big electrical surge it created transformed the Epidex into an internal organ. It stayed that way until the vampire switched back to human form and the Epidex re-externalized. While Morning knew his less-than stunning summary of Epidex wouldn't earn him an A, he thought he at least deserved a B because of his clever conclusion: "Epidex is the underwear of underwears."

Birnam called the next name. "Rachel Capilarus." As a raven-haired beauty stepped out from the arc of students, Morning's chest tightened. Birnam had jumped from an A name to a C name. He wasn't going in alphabetical order. Anybody could be next. Morning ignored the knot-tying convention in his stomach and focused on Rachel. She broke into a run. As distractions go, you couldn't do better than Rachel. Of all the gorgeous women at Leaguer Academy, every one of them wished they could CD back to human form, just once, as Rachel Capilarus.

Rachel raced across the parade grounds toward Leaguer Lake. Its still water held a perfect reflection of Birnam's tower. She ripped open the top of her gown, sprang off the ground, and missiled out of her robe in a racing dive.

As Morning's eyes clung to her contours, he remembered the downside of Epidex. While it saved him from streaking, it denied him the ecstasy of seeing dozens of beauties do the same. It wasn't a total loss. Seeing them in Epidex was like a vampire version of the *Sports Illustrated Swimsuit Issue*.

Rachel's body slapped the lake's surface and disappeared. A small wave tracked her position as she torpedoed underwater. The wave swelled, signaling she had CDed into something bigger. A dorsal fin punctured the surface, knifing through the water.

"Ms. Capilarus has chosen the Third Form," Birnam proclaimed. "The Swimmer."

The fin submerged. The water settled to an ominous calm.

Even though Morning thought performing a final CD for graduation was about as bogus as football players dancing in the end zone, he found himself holding his breath.

The water near the base of Birnam's platform bulged upward, then erupted. A great white shark shot toward the top of the tower. Birnam thrust a diploma over the edge. At the peak of the shark's leap, its jaws snapped open and snagged the diploma. The second before gravity planted its gaff and pulled the shark down, the creature CDed back into Rachel. She grabbed a pipe protruding from the platform, spun on it like a high bar, dismounted with a flip, and stuck her landing next to Birnam. Her blinding smile held the diploma.

The grandstand shook with a standing ovation.

Joining the celebration, Morning envied the mastery of her powers, and pitied the cadet who had to follow her.

Rachel descended the staircase spiraling down the middle of the tower as Birnam called the next name. "Morning McCobb."

IVLEAGUE

HOME   ABOUT US   NEWS   COMMUNITY   CONTACT US

HOME

Dear Visitor,

Welcome to IVLeague.us, the website of the International Vampire League.

To learn more about us, please visit our open pages. To log in and access restricted areas you must be a graduate of Leaguer Academy and a member of the IVL.

In the future, we hope to open the site to everyone, including all people of mortality. Our term for those of you who are both handicapped and blessed with aging is "Lifers." (If you wonder how aging can be a blessing, see immortality.)

We hope you will explore IVLeague.us with an open mind. We offer it with an open heart.

Peace and tolerance,
Luther Birnam
President of the International Vampire League